Security Through Absurdity

BOOK FOUR
THE PEANUT BUTTER PIPELINE

Rachael L. McIntosh

EP
EntropyPress

Security Through Absurdity

The Peanut Butter Pipeline

Cover Designer: Kevin Diamond inspired by original series cover art by Catharine M. Matteo

Edited by: Linda Grant DePauw

EntropyPress books may be ordered through booksellers
or by contacting:

EntropyPress

www.entropypress.com
Entropy Press
PO Box 2254
East Greenwich, RI 02818
USA

ISBN: 9798736475575

Also available by Rachael L. McIntosh

Security Through Absurdity Series
Book 1: Little Yellow Stickies
Book 2: Bubbles Will Pop
Book 3: The Big Show

Tres in Unum
All three books under one soft cover

Rachael L. McIntosh remains one of the few authors who can combine expert fiction writing with an insider's understanding of the geopolitical world that is today ensnarling us. *The Peanut Butter Pipeline,* the fourth of her *Security Through Absurdity* novels, takes us into the real world of sinister intel services and technocracy, everything from 9/11 and globalism to nanobots and high-tech weaponry. Yet there is no shortage of the action and villains that underpin any great thriller. As usual, Rachael's writing transports the reader right into the story through her compelling use of vivid imagery. And as with her previous novels, I'd love to see this one made into a movie!

—**James Perloff,** journalist and author of several books, including *The Shadows of Power* and *COVID-19 and the Agendas to Come, Red-Pilled*

Rachael's work is ringing too true and she needs to be very careful…very careful. We are beginning to see clearly that the body count is rising of those who got in the way of "the plan." I can't believe that I'm writing such a sentence, but there it is. It is clear that Rachael has her finger on the pulse. She is intelligent and articulate and a delight to listen to. We need her to continue the work she is doing. Reaching the people with such riveting fiction that rings the bells of truth is a brilliant way to wake up a sleepy society. Great work.

—**Charlotte Traplin**

NOTE FROM THE AUTHOR

This fourth book in the Security Through Absurdity series is only complete because someone didn't want it written.

In early 2017 the nearly finished manuscript for *The Peanut Butter Pipeline* and an associated researchfile unbelievably vanished. There was no way it just disappeared and even if I had accidentally deleted both files (which I knew I hadn't) I knew professionals that could reconstruct everything. I ended up sending my laptop to the best computer forensic specialists in the area. Using a variety of techniques (and fueled by ample amounts of coffee and cash) they poked through the bowels of my computer, my exterior hard drive, and cloud storage only to conclude that there was no evidence of anything that remotely resembled a novel saved or trashed anywhere on my machine or floating around the ether of the vast internet.

Thankfully, I had my handwritten notes to at least "prove" that I had been researching stuff.

After curiously inspecting my pages of chicken scratch, the forensic specialists asked me what the book was about. It was at that very moment we all realized that I must have cut and pasted something I wasn't supposed to during one of my digital fact-finding forays. Whatever snip of text I had scooped up and saved acted like a digital hand grenade and obliterated any file it was unauthorized to be stuck to. I had never heard of such a thing but it made sense considering where my research had been taking me. Apparently this digital hand grenade phenomenon is pretty common when it comes to certain government documentation of particular classifications.

After accepting that all my work was unrecoverable I fell into a serious "woe-is-me" loop. I'm not sure how long that lasted but it concluded after experiencing the standard stages of grief and me getting really angry and reasoning that if someone didn't want this story out in the world, then it was even more important that I write it. So I started over from the beginning and re-wrote the whole thing.

This fourth book is different and darker than the others in this series. I want to make you aware of that right from the start. As with the other Security Through Absurdity books, I have been to andexperienced all the places mentioned. However, unlike books one through three, I did not personally live through the action. The action in *The Peanut Butter Pipeline* was created by the characters themselves as they fought their way out of my hand grenade, fact-filled head and onto the page.

I had no idea until the year 2020 what this book was actually touching upon.

I'd like to thank my family, friends, and most importantly the fans of the Security Through Absurdity series who have been hearing about this book for years now. I'm sorry I've left you in suspense for so long. If it wasn't for me knowing that all of you were out there rooting for this book to get finished I'm not sure I could have completed it. Thank you.

—RLM

"The Old World is dying and the New World struggles to be born: now is the time for monsters."

— *Antonio Gramsci*

FBI MISSING PERSON

ALL POINTS BULLETIN

JOCELYN McLAREN

5′9″, blond / red hair, blue eyes

DOB 03/15/1970

Distinguishing marks: recent surgery on upper torso

Last seen: August 28, 2012

at TAMPA GENERAL HOSPITAL

being loaded onto American Lifeline ambulance

Florida commercial plate: 53742

CHAPTER ONE

The Arrival

JOCELYN WAS JUST BECOMING AWARE that she was wearing red, high-heeled dancing shoes. She was completely captivated by this discovery when a man in a sharply tailored suit emerged from the shadows and made eye contact with her. His eyes, broken Christmas tree lights, scratched as the odd sensation of recognizing an old friend, now shattered and damaged, settled in. The space the two of them occupied was hard to define but Jocelyn knew it was dark. And cold. Mostly it smelled of "after-party," a lingering joy remnant. Yeasty and sweet, like bottles of wine left open overnight scattered between lost stemware.

He didn't say anything. She didn't say anything. A staticky rendition of "Por Una Cabeza" started up as if on a magical phonograph and they accepted each other for the dance.

It would have been a rather monotonous dance had it not been for the fact that Jocelyn mysteriously knew all the steps and could improvise with tricky, hitchy-coo footwork between the crisscrossing of the legwork. She was enjoying herself immensely while floating along, effortlessly spinning around, led by her handsome, but somehow empty, partner. She was elated that she knew the song. She knew the steps. She knew everything and that's when he whispered, "We can create a more perfect union." She was taken aback by the statement. *He's not supposed to talk,* she thought.

Suddenly the whole routine became much more physical and she wanted the broken Christmas tree lights to go away. She found herself uncontrollably lunging forward. She felt like she was being split in two as he manhandled her and she could sense his sweat. She was now breathing hard. Her lungs hurt terribly and her mouth was incredibly dry. She pushed him away with all her might. He was pulling her closer as she resisted. He was hurting her. She kicked him and that's when his yelling woke her up.

"Shit! Jocelyn! I'm trying to help you. Quit kicking me!"

Jocelyn blinked herself into a sketchy consciousness as Ethan Lowe, the father of her children, stepped aside and allowed two men to hoist her off the catering truck and onto the stainless steel table. Another man looked on from a distant doorway.

"So, this is your woman?" echoed across the room as the man entered.

She heard Ethan grumble, "Yup," in his typical American way and it contrasted with the interesting accent the other man had; a sort of Spanish-y inflection mixed with tones of something else. The man sounded old, but not ancient. Jocelyn could hear this man's deliberate footsteps on the concrete floor as he approached.

"Jocelyn McLaren, eh?" the handsome, gray-haired man carefully pronounced as he visually inspected the trembling lump of hospital bedding and the fragile strawberry blond buried underneath. He gently moved the sheet away from Jocelyn's face and studied her features. Jocelyn instinctively held her breath. "Please make yourself comfortable, darling. Me casa es su casa," and then the man walked away with the same metered gait.

Jocelyn exhaled and thought, *That's nice* then took a labored breath. Man, her lungs hurt and she needed water. Better yet, ice. She needed ice to munch on, like the ice in the little blue cups at the hospital. And that's when it all came roaring back—Ethan and some guys had kidnapped her from the hospital! And now here she was, inside a warehouse, on a cold stainless table with a catering truck parked next to her. Even worse was that she was all whacked out on some sort of drug, which she could tell was slowly wearing thin because her chest was beginning to feel...well, it was beginning to feel like death.

Jocelyn's field of view darted around the room. She wasn't even sure what she was looking at. It seemed as if she had been dumped inside a humongous eight-cylinder engine. At least that's what she imagined an engine's cylinders looked like if they were enlarged hundreds of times. There were eight of them, clearly numbered one through eight. They were all constructed exactly the same and they were very tall, made of shiny stainless steel. Each was capped off with a specially designed metal lid that looked like a computer was embedded in it. And she couldn't escape the smell. "Hangover" was the first flash card to pop up in her vocabulary rolodex.

Just then a man with a tribal looking tattoo rolled an IV stand up next to her and proceeded to attach the IV to the tiny port still inserted into the vein on top of her left hand. "You...you...why are you doing this?" she pleaded and an odd déjà vu splashed over her. Instantly the pain in her chest subsided and because of that she decided that she liked this guy. But still... "Why are you doing this?" The guy with the tattoo didn't say anything but motioned with his head over to a tidy arrangement of about forty oak barrels at the far-right side of the warehouse where Ethan was deftly adjusting his tactical leg holster. Jocelyn rubbed her eyes and swallowed hard. She had to think this through. The last thing she remembered Ethan saying right before she had passed out, back in Tampa, Florida was something about it being "kill or be killed time."

"What the heck does he think he's doing?" she asked of no one in particular. The IV guy didn't answer and she watched in silence as Ethan exchanged guns with the other man who had lifted her onto the table. The older man who had welcomed her to his house was nowhere to be seen. Ethan must have felt Jocelyn's eyes on him and he turned to look at her. When their gaze met Jocelyn wasn't sure if she wanted to scream, cry, or simply die. Ethan hastily stashed his gun into the holster before he trotted over to her. Tattooed IV guy headed off toward the large garage door when he saw Ethan approaching. Jocelyn's lip was trembling—heck, her whole body was shaking she was so mad at Ethan.

"You feelin' a little better now?" he asked as he leaned over the side of the table to kiss her forehead. She closed her eyes, pursed her lips and then, with a Herculean effort and somehow possessed with lightning speed because her life depended on it, quickly snatched the gun out of Ethan's leg holster. She jammed the semi-automatic pistol into Ethan's stomach and it was at this very moment the huge garage door loudly rolled opened and a blast of cold air rushed into the room. The catering truck that she had arrived on pulled out and as it drove away rows and rows of some sort of shriveled crop were revealed—dead grape vines?—leading off toward gray snow covered mountains. Now she was completely confused. It was supposed to be summertime. August. At least she knew she had been in Tampa in August. She pushed the gun deeper into Ethan's stomach and in a panic shouted as loudly as she could muster, "Where the hell are we?!"

Ethan sighed, "So that's how it's gonna be, huh? Do you know what I went through to get you here?"

"What you went through? Ethan! I'm half dead! You took me from the hospital. I was on life support last thing I remember." She wanted to cry but was so angry she jammed the gun harder into his stomach and he didn't even flinch. "Where. Are. We?!"

"Argentina," he said like it was no big deal, "on the border of Chile." There was a millisecond of confused silence while the National Geographic wall map unfurled itself in her head.

"Wait. We're in South America?"

Ethan made a weird kind of exasperated snort and almost sang,

"Sí, the water spins down the drain in the opposite direction and the seasons are backwards," and then he growled, "Now, give me the gun."

"No!" she hissed, still white-knuckling the pistol. "What's all this?" she gestured with her chin. "This place. Where are we?"

"What? Those?" He pointed to the huge stainless cylinders. "Those are fermentation tanks. We're at a winery."

"What the…Why?" She jabbed the gun into his belly again as if threatening to pump a bullet into his gut would produce some semblance of clarity. "I'll shoot you Ethan! I mean it!"

"No. No you won't." He didn't try and take the gun, but leaned in closer and whispered, "Seriously, stop embarrassing me. Give me the damn gun."

"No!" she spat back, and he rolled his eyes. "Oh, you don't think I'll do it?" and that's when Jocelyn pulled the trigger.

Click

Nothing happened.

Befuddled because she was expecting to hear a loud bang and see blood all over the place, Jocelyn just looked at the gun and then at Ethan who was obviously pissed. "Give me that friggin' thing," he growled as he snatched the Sig Sauer P226 out of her hands and jammed a magazine into it. "Now this could be dangerous," he huffed.

Jocelyn started tearing up as she watched him secure the now fully functional gun into his holster. She couldn't believe that she had just tried to shoot the father of her children and, almost worse, that she hadn't realized that the darn pistol wasn't even loaded. Suddenly she burst out crying and her tethered-to-the-IV hand shot up to clutch her chest. The sensation that was drilling itself closer to her heart was sheer agony so her wailing was immediately reduced to a whimper. Her fingers sought out, almost as if on a dare, the pathetic reminder of her ordeal back in Tampa, the stiff, black, silk stitches poking out of her, and she wanted to go home. She wanted to go to sleep.

"Just calm down Jocelyn. It's going to be all right. We're with someone who can keep you and the kids safe."

CHAPTER TWO

Family

NEEDLESS TO SAY Margret McLaren was exhausted, but not as exhausted as the kids. She had been hauling her six-year-old, strawberry blond grandkids, Lillian and William, through airports, over aviation-fuel-infused tarmacs; and helping them deal with painful popping ears, not to mention barf bags since the messenger had come and whisked them away to Tampa Executive Airport. It had been abrupt but what else could she do given the circumstances?

At first she hadn't known quite how to respond to the man who had startled her in the hospital parking garage. He was average height. Average weight. Average brownish hair, cut in a very average way. He was wearing loafers and an average THE GAP-type outfit, one that looked like just about everything in all the stores; a white T-shirt with khaki cargo shorts from which he produced the passports.

"Where did you get these?" she had questioned while flipping through the little laminated pages. Her granddaughter, affixed to her leg, and her grandson, holding her purse, were frowning at the man. "This…how'd…" Margret stammered incredulously. "These are fake passports. Where did you get these pictures of us?" She looked at the passports again and turned to the man. "I don't want anything to do with this. I think you'd better—"

"Ethan wants you to come with me. You are in grave danger and he wants you and the children to meet him. I'll get you on your flight. All you have to do is follow the directions of the pilot."

"But, who exactly are—"

"I'm not important. In fact, it's probably better if you don't know who I am. Please, it's critical that you and the children come right away. Ethan will explain everything when you get there. Jocelyn is with him and she needs you. Just—"

"Jocelyn! You know where my daughter is? Where is she?!" Margret screeched. "The police and the FBI and the hospital all told me that they have teams of people looking all over for her and you show up, from out of nowhere, and I'm supposed to just follow you with these passports?"

The messenger was about to say something when KABOOM! KABOOM! KABOOM!! reverberated through the parking garage and car alarms started blaring. Margret and the kids were stunned that the blasts had come from her economy rental as evidenced by the black smoke bellowing out of the little red Kia Rio. Within milliseconds Will and Lilly started crying hysterically. The messenger grabbed Margret's wrist and yelled, "Come with me!" and that's how the whole thing started.

The first leg of their journey had consisted of an enormously noisy one hour and fifteen-minute hop to the Bahamas aboard a tiny four-seater, a Cessna 172 Skyhawk. It was tight, tighter than the interior of a car, and there were bulging, white canvas sacks emblazoned with the US Postal Service logo wedged all around the kids who were sitting very snuggly in the back seat. Margret sat in the co-pilot's seat clutching her pocketbook as if it were the last life vest on the planet. The only time she let her grasp free of the purse was when she had distributed two pieces of Hubba Bubba bubble gum to each of the kids when they started crying and holding their ears. Otherwise, she was chomping her Hubba Bubba vigorously while fighting a lifelong fear of heights.

Finally, but not soon enough for Margret, they bumpily landed on a grass strip on one of the seven hundred islands, or cays, that comprise the Bahamian archipelago. She hoisted the kids out of the plane and onto the grass in much appreciated silence. Only the hum of tropical insects and the calls of exotic birds accompanied the pilot when he had hopped out to scavenge for coconuts which he later hacked with a machete to produce a makeshift snack for them. The kids made themselves comfortable under the wing of the plane to escape the blazing sun and they busied themselves sipping coconut water and eating pieces of coconut meat. Meanwhile Margret tried to extract some sort of conversation from the pilot. The man was friendly enough but not very chatty. Just then a blue-striped, white, turboprop Piper Navajo Chieftain buzzed over and landed on the grass strip right in front of them. That's when Margret found out they were headed to Mexico.

The Navajo Chieftain would have been downright luxurious compared to the Skyhawk had much of its eight-seat passenger capacity not been taken up with four, eighty-gallon fuel tanks. "This is so we don't fall out of the sky," this new pilot had said as he patted the tank nearest to William. That remark did not make Margret feel any safer. About twenty minutes in, Lilly lost it and threw up all over Margret and the past its prime white leather of the plane's interior.

Margret used one of the available snack size club sodas from the built-in refrigerator behind the pilot's seat to deftly clean up the vomit in a way that only a grandmother knows. She apologized to the pilot every chance she got during the next six hours while making sure her grandkids were adequately hydrated with bottled water and soft drinks from the little fridge. This, of course, led to using an old gallon plastic tub, the type used for ice cream, as an emergency potty chair.

As soon as they touched down in Ciudad de Mexico, as instructed, they held hands and crossed the cracked taxiway over to a black Dassault Falcon executive jet for the five hour and forty-five-minute flight to Peru. The kids were able to walk around inside this plane and Margret appreciated the mahogany and supple Corinthian leather interior. They greedily snacked on peanuts, pretzels, candy, and the three little sandwich wraps from the built-in bar and slept very comfortably despite the many cans of Coca-Cola they had consumed. Although Margret was on high alert, she had fallen asleep too. It was only a cushioned bump and the sound of the Falcon's tires leaving black rubber on the runway that roused them.

It almost goes without saying at this point that Margret and the kids were not happy. They were exhausted. As soon as the exit hatch was opened and the stairs rolled out, they disembarked and were corralled into a herd of travelers climbing up the roll-away stairs of a LAN Airlines commercial flight. That four-hour LAN flight from Peru was comfortable enough because it had food. The kids took naps after eating the in-flight meal of omelet, white bread, and fruit salad which they happily gobbled down. The orange juice tasted strange though, so nobody drank that.

Margret was surprised when they arrived in Buenos Aires, Argentina where they breezed through Immigration with their fake passports. No problem. As the man handed back the passports he let them know that their next LAN flight to Mendoza, Argentina would be taking off in fifteen minutes. They ran to the next gate.

When they emerged from the commercial jet in Mendoza no one was there to tell them what to do or where to go, so they fell in line with the other passengers and made their way toward the baggage claim. Margret noticed the local time, 9:57 p.m., was an hour ahead of her watch which was reading 8:57 p.m. She was squinting up at the signage, trying her best to translate everything from Spanish when she realized that the kids had somehow broken away from her. "Oh my God. The kids!" In a panic she slung her pocketbook over her shoulder and started frantically pushing her way through the crowd.

As she was scanning the dark-haired horde for little strawberry blond heads, she mentally recited a prayer to St. Anthony asking for his help in finding her lost grandchildren. It wasn't long after "amen" that she saw William being lifted high above the crowd. She ran toward him as Ethan set him down and started tickling Lilly.

"I'm so happy you guys are here!" Ethan was smiling broadly at his children. "I've been waiting for you!" The kids were clearly happy to see their dad too. Margret, not so much.

"Ethan Lowe! What the hell is going on here?! The kids and I nearly died! A strange man saved us, put us on these flights, and…and…" she started tearing up. Margret was actually very relieved to see Ethan but her anger for being put through everything from the hospital up until now was just too much to handle. She wiped away a tear of frustration and pulling it together asked, "Where's Jocelyn? She's here?"

Ethan nodded. "Yes," and he put his hand on Jocelyn's mother's shoulder. "She'll be happy to see you and the kids." Offering Margret his winter jacket, Ethan led them all through the noisy but amazingly slow-moving crowd to the chauffeured black sedan with black windows that was waiting for them outside. He opened the car door for Margret and the cold, shivering twins scrambled in.

Before Margret stepped foot into the car she asked, "Ethan, seriously, what is going on? Is Jocelyn okay? Is she going to be okay? Why did we have to take such a convoluted journey to get here? And why Argentina? That," she spat while pointing to the gate they had just come from, "certainly wasn't your typical Southwest flight to Disneyland. That was a hell scene! I mean the kids did great, but still, they're just kids and you better believe it wasn't easy for any of us."

Ethan nodded and answered while still holding the door for her. "Let's see Jocelyn before I get into it." Then he scrunched down and shouted into the car, "There's sandwiches and drinks in the big red cooler Lilly, if you're hungry!" With that, Margret hopped into the car without another word.

CHAPTER THREE

Meanwhile
Tampa, Florida

IT WASN'T SO MUCH THE CARDS and flowers that the kids had left behind, or the image of Jocelyn's mother's distraught face that was bothering newly sworn in Special Agent Mark Witherall. It was the fact that now he couldn't find the missing ICU patient, Jocelyn McLaren, or her entire family for that matter, anywhere. It was like the hospital was some sort of Bermuda Triangle for these people. Jocelyn's children, six-year-old twins William and Lillian, and her sixty-five-year-old mother, Margret, all seemingly evaporated—disappeared without a trace. And the kids' dad, Ethan Lowe, former navy SEAL turned defense contractor, was MIA too.

During his initial investigation of last week's shootout in front of Tampa Police Headquarters, Mark had discovered that Jocelyn McLaren, although having had children with Ethan Lowe, had never married this man who had bailed her out of jail thirty-seven minutes before bullets struck both of them. Lowe had been conveniently wearing Swiss-made body armor under his clothes and obviously fared much better than his female companion during one of the certifiably most bizarre shootings to ever take place in Tampa. Someone had filmed the whole disastrous event with their cell phone, posted it to YouTube, and the clip instantly became an internet sensation. The curious, almost comedic haphazard blasts from a flamethrower, culminating with a bush and a bench bursting into flames as the confusion of the shooting commenced, really did make for interesting viewing. However, regardless of its extremely short-lived internet notoriety, the original footage and the phone were now officially in FBI custody.

Mark had watched that footage more than enough times because it captured the exact moment Jocelyn had been shot. Now he was sick of looking at film in general. He had pored over the hospital's security reels and gotten some decent screenshots of the tattoo on the guy wheeling Jocelyn over to the ambulance bay. These images were the only pieces of hard evidence he had regarding her kidnapping. He was still waiting to find out if the tattoo matched anything in the national registry. A search of the Florida prison system had not yielded any positive results.

The ID of the ambulance Jocelyn had been rolled onto wasn't going well either. It appeared that there had been two of the exact same ambulance driving around that night. They had the same license plate and markings but had been clearly traveling on very different yet overlapping courses. Although Mark was having the Interstate tollbooth video being analyzed again, the ambulance thing was turning into a wild goose chase. He had to give credit to whoever it was that planned this. They had certainly put a lot of effort and money into Ms. McLaren's abduction.

Add all this to the fact that since Mark had been the last "official" to speak with Jocelyn at the hospital about the document dump before her disappearance, people from all sorts of agencies from all over the world were breathing down his neck. The last inquiry from the Vatican had totally thrown him for a loop and he hadn't slept in two days. Stacks of manila folders were haphazardly piled up next to his two computer monitors. He cringed because his desk at the Tampa Field Office was an uncomfortable mess, almost as messed up as his wrinkly Gentlemen's Warehouse suit. He hadn't felt this discombobulated since sophomore year final exams at Wentworth Institute of Technology when his long-time girlfriend, Britney, had broken up with him.

*You'd think I'd be getting more backup on something like this."*He sighed as he rubbed his eyes and, taking another gulp of tepid, black coffee, he checked his watch. "*Damn. 8:57. Almost nine o'clock. I seriously cannot believe someone thought I could handle all this.* He reached into his jacket pocket and pulled out a folded piece of paper that he had been carrying around since The Dump. That's what the FBI was calling it now.

The Dump was when Jocelyn's laptop had distributed over sixteen thousand pieces of paper to each and every FBI office via a network hack the day before she was shot. If Mark had been tasked with figuring out how the photocopy machines had been exploited to litter paper copies of all the bitter details of a child pornography ring, a complete catalogue of bejeweled butterfly inspired brooches, and the particulars of an intellectual property lawsuit in Italy involving Formula One race cars, he would have been fine. Just fine. But instead, he had been assigned a full-blown international investigation and he knew that he wasn't equipped to handle the whole thing.

"I'm in the Cyber Crime Unit for Christ's sake. This is way above my pay grade," he complained, overwhelmed. He was determined that he was going to tell his boss again that they really should get someone else, no, make that a team of someone elses, to take over.

This was more than a just messing around with code. This was a missing person/international conspiracy case.

"And somehow, someone thought I would be the best person for this?" Mark was skeptical. Especially when his boss, Associate Deputy Director Fitzgerald S. Crowley, had told him to just focus on the missing woman and not worry about the other stuff.

Mark smoothed the paper taken from his pocket and beheld, between creases, the short message, which when translated from Wingdings 3 font, said: "I am the ghost in the machine and I love you." Even though Jocelyn McLaren had been locked up at Tampa P.D. when The Dump occurred, Mark instinctively knew that his missing female "person of interest" had not written this even though it had come from her laptop. He also very much suspected that the last page transmitted during The Dump was a geeky love note, one delivered with such an epic, sweeping gesture that it would make any Dungeons and Dragons-playing IT guy proud. This hunch led him directly to Jerry Apario, the person wielding the flamethrower during last week's shootout. Apario was the former IT guy where both of the shooting victims, Jocelyn McLaren and Ethan Lowe, had worked, and it only made sense that he go see him.

As Mark was searching the monumental stack of paper files on his desk for the current whereabouts of Apario his phone rang and he snatched up the receiver. "This is Witherall."

"We have a match. The tattoo. We've been looking in the wrong place. The guy was never in jail. He's former Special Forces."

"Seriously, Dan?" Mark made himself comfortable in the desk chair. He was eager to hear what Dan, who was working on the Next-Generation Identification program for the FBI, had to say. Mark knew that Dan was under the gun too. The iris scan function of NGI was due for a rollout in a few months, and Dan's face search function was expected to be fully operational by summer 2014, along with tools for matching scars and tattoos.

"So whatcha got on this guy?"

"His name is Akecheta Whitebloom…"

"Excuse me?"

"Ack-uh-chet-ah Whitebloom. It's Sioux," Dan explained. "Aka 'Ache' or 'The Medicine Man.' He was honorably discharged from the 10th Special Forces Group in 1992 because of an injury to his left arm."

"Wait." Mark leaned across his desk and dug out a color print of a screenshot of Ache from the huge pile of files. "Wasn't the tattoo on his left arm?"

"Yeah. Probably to cover up the scar," Dan offered.

"Where was he when he got the injury?"

"Uh, let me see. Oh, okay. Bosnia." Mark scribbled that info down on a yellow legal pad as Dan continued. "So it looks like this guy was able to hammer out a respectable career for himself as a private contractor despite the injury. He's had US gigs at Triple Canopy, 3-D, MPRI, MVM, and Blackwater right after it changed its name to Xe Services."

"Wait. I thought Blackwater was called Academi," Mark interrupted.

"Yeah, it's gone through a lot of name changes. Xe became the company's legal name for like a year in 2009 when its founder, Erik Prince, picked up and moved to Abu Dhabi, United Arab Emirates. That's when Blackwater was facing all sorts of legal problems here in the United States for the thing in Iraq. Despite the legal quagmire here, Mr. Prince was immediately hired by the crown prince of Abu Dhabi to put together an eight hundred-member battalion of foreign troops for the U.A.E."

"Wow. Who's better than Erik Prince?"

"I know, right? Especially since he got $529 million for that contract and the recruiting for that project happened in more-bang-for-your-buck Columbia where everyone is dirt poor."

"Jeez," Mark sighed.

"So yeah, you're right. It's not Xe anymore. It's Academi but I bet they'll change their name again someday. Anyhow, Ache fell off the radar after a stint at Serco in the UK, doing some sort of tech security. I'm really not sure what he was doing. I don't think he was marching around with an AK, but who knows? Then he was spotted in Israel at Black Cube, a company founded by retired Mossad intelligence agents aaaaand," Dan dramatically dragged out, "of course, there's been no record of him since."

"Any arrests?"

"No. He's got, or at least had, clearance."

"Really?"

"Secret."

Mark's eyebrow twitched. "Jesus. Why would he put his clearance in jeopardy by getting involved with this hospital kidnapping?"

"Maybe he got paid a shitload of money or maybe he's motivated by something more personal. I'll send you over his history that we've pieced together. Hold on." Mark could hear Dan typing and almost instantly saw the email show up in his inbox.

"Got it," Mark said as he clicked to open the message.

"Notice anything about Ache's dad, Lenard?"

"Hold on, I'm not there yet."

"I'll cut to the chase. Daddy Whitebloom had been active in the American Indian Movement advocacy group, AIM, during the 1970s when Ache was a kid and was arrested multiple times while protesting. It looks like dad was pretty passionate about everything from civil rights with the Black Panthers to protesting government-sanctioned commercial uranium mining operations on tribal land."

"Good Lord! I'll say so. The guy's rap sheet is as long as my arm," Mark remarked when he got to that part of the file.

Dan continued, "Interestingly, Ache's mother, Claire, was a Caucasian woman with no history of arrest, just three semesters at the Minneapolis College of Art and a smattering of jobs at laundromats, grocery stores, and a few stints as a waitress. Looks like her parents disowned her and stopped paying for art school when they found out about the impending grandchild."

Mark scanned through the photos included in Ache's history as Dan spoke. He noted that Ache had grown up in a Minneapolis "red ghetto," a neighborhood established by the US Housing Authority in an attempt to integrate Native Americans into urban settings. These "red ghettos," as the report highlighted, were plagued by unusually high unemployment, overt and covert racism, police harassment, epidemic drug abuse (mainly alcoholism), crushing poverty, domestic violence, and ironically, substandard housing.

"Both Ache's parents are dead—dad of liver disease, mom of lung cancer. And that's all I've got for you. No siblings."

"Okay. Thanks Dan. Seriously, thanks." They chitchatted a bit about how it was going with Dan's FACE (Facial Analysis, Comparison and Evaluation Services) Unit now they were supporting investigations with external databases of states' drivers licenses and mugshots. The program had really been in existence since 2008 but only since 2011 was NGI-IPS (Next Generation Identification Interstate Photo System) officially "a thing" and it wouldn't be authorized by the Department of Justice as NGI-IPS PIA until 2015. Even then, it would still be glitchy, you know, like not recognizing people of Asian descent. The computer couldn't do a positive ID because of the way Asian eyes are set and would ultimately conclude that the unknown person was asleep. The computer tagging dark-skinned African American people as gorillas certainly didn't help either. All this was bogged down with paperwork problems since the FBI hadn't really let the states know they were using the images and even if they did, the states hadn't really told the people that's where their images were being used.

Anyhow, after Mark and Dan commiserated they said their good-byes and Mark was really confused. He spent about twenty minutes with his eyes glued to the computer screen trying to get his head around this Ache guy. He knew it was J.V., but he was at a loss, so he did a Google search for "Akecheta." Immediately the screen filled with blue hyperlinks and the Native American meaning of Ache's name provided additional illumination.

Akecheta translates to Fighter. You stand up for what you believe in, nobody can stop you once you've found your passion. One of your best qualities is that not much can bring you down, so people can always count on you to help them out.

Mark nodded his head at the computer screen and mumbled, "Well, it looks like I've got to find out who your friends are Mr. Ache." Mark felt rejuvenated. He was in his element. Having access to the FBI's social media monitoring tools didn't help one bit though. Ache had left no digital footprint online. "Naturally."

Mark was getting together the list of contracts Ache had worked on for the military security contractors when his phone rang again. He glanced at his desktop clock, 10:03 p.m. Chuckling while picking up the phone, Mark chided, "Pretty late night for you, eh Dan? What did you forget to tell me?" His smile quickly faded when he realized that he wasn't talking to Dan. The phone made some clicking noises and for a short burst sounded like a fax machine.

Just as Mark winced at the high-pitched tone it stopped and a man's voice excitedly asked, "Special Agent Mark A. Witherall?"

Mark was silent because if he didn't know better he would swear someone just did a 1972 Captain Crunch-style phone phreaking thing and broke into the FBI phone system. He could hear the man on the other end of the line despondently utter, "Shit. I really did think this was gonna work."

With that Mark responded, "This is Witherall. To whom am I speaking?"

"Yeeees! Okay, great! Mr. Witherall, sorry, Special Agent Witherall. I really need to talk to you, but not on the phone."

"Well, you're the one who called me."

"I know but I was just gonna leave a message. I didn't think you'd actually be in your office at this hour."

"What's your name?" Mark demanded. "Or I'm hanging up."

There was a moment of silence and Mark could hear the man sigh. "Darn it. This connection is gonna end in like thirty seconds."

"Yes it is if you don't tell me your name."

"Right. Sorry. I'm Jerry. Jerry Apario." Stunned, Mark leaned back in his chair with the phone still to his ear and peeked out his office door, scanning the empty beige workstations. "Where are you Jerry?"

"I can't tell you that, but we can meet in Disneyland. I'll be there tomorrow morning wearing—" and the phone went dead.

CHAPTER FOUR

Meanwhile
Uco Valley, Argentina

JOCELYN'S ROOM HAD ONE HUGE WINDOW from which she could see the moonlit snow-covered mountains. The room also featured a bullet hole in the wall opposite the door. Other than that unpleasant reminder of her injury, the room was very comfortable—a scaled-down version of something you might see in a home decorating magazine but more gritty. The walls, papered with a faded, pinkish flesh tone 1950's era "race-to-space" starburst pattern, were adorned with two unframed pieces of artwork. The floor was well worn hardwood and a little hooked rug was nestled next to her bed. The Egyptian cotton sheets smelled of lavender and the caramel-colored blankets were the softest cashmere. At first Jocelyn was mildly disgusted, but the Scandinavian blue fox fur throw soon became a comfort and she snuggled with it when the Spanish-speaking doctor wasn't there. It kept her warm and smelled of friendship.

Peeling through layers of cognition Jocelyn realized that she hadn't seen many people since they rolled her out of the fermentation area on that stainless steel wheeled table. Ethan had unceremoniously left her when the doctor arrived. The doctor and the guy that Ethan had gotten the unloaded gun from pushed her and the IV stand out of the warehouse. They had gone through a deserted office outfitted with filing cabinets and a long desk with three flat-screen monitors on it. Then they slipped out an exit and made their way over a bumpy and cold cobblestone path through an expansive, wintered-over, classically designed garden to the main house.

As Jocelyn remembered it, the house looked like it was some sort of attempt to replicate Frank Lloyd Wright's seminal work of architectural genius "Fallingwater" back in Pennsylvania, USA. Most of the structure was anchored to a dense, four-story stone wall. Long rectangles of reinforced concrete terraces, opened by broad bands of windows, seemed to be hovering in space. But unlike Fallingwater there was no waterfall, just a wide cement gully with a stream of icy water flowing from the mountains. The water cut under one of the cantilevered balconies and out toward the vineyard.

Jocelyn had wondered, as she braced herself while bouncing along, if the house was designed to feature this water or if the gully was built after construction of the house. These thoughts were kind of funny to her when she realized how stoned she was. Whatever they were pumping into her via that IV was serious. There she was, hanging on for dear life to a catering table, on a bumpy path in Argentina, accompanied by two men she didn't know, contemplating a cement ditch and if form followed function. She burst out laughing, "Good thing I have that art degree!" The men had stopped, thinking something was wrong, but then continued and brought her to this room.

She didn't know how long she had been here. Time had been doing something funny. Had she been here for hours or days? She couldn't be sure and quite frankly didn't care. But she did know one thing, it was nighttime.

Jocelyn reached over, turned on the nightstand lamp, and shot a glance at the bullet hole. She looked at that for a while and decided to look at the artwork. The smaller piece, which Jocelyn didn't care for, looked as if it had been inspired by Picasso's Blue Period. The other, a portrait of a woman, seemed like it was painted by someone inspired by Mary Cassatt. Jocelyn spent a lot of time studying the artwork. It was dead quiet and the brushstrokes of the oil painting spoke to her.

She was lost in thought when she realized someone was coming down the hall. Lots of feet were moving toward her room and she braced herself. Suddenly the door burst open and in tumbled both her kids! And her mother! Ethan wandered in last. Everyone was shouting and laughing and crying, trying to hug and kiss her. Ethan, positioning himself next to the bullet hole, stood and looked very pleased with his arms crossed over his chest, watching the reunion.

"Lilly! Will! Oh, my God! Mom!" Jocelyn wept as the kids scrambled to climb into bed with her and her mother swooped in and hugged all of them. "Oh. Oh. Be careful everyone. I've got a serious boo-boo." Lilly backed away but Jocelyn grabbed both her kids and hugged and kissed them anyway.

Tears were streaming down Margret's face as she beheld her clearly messed up daughter with her grandchildren. Placing a trembling hand over her mouth, shaking her head Margret sighed, "Oh, Jocelyn, honey, I'm…I'm so…" she clasped her hands as if in prayer, and looking up at the ceiling quietly uttered, "Dear God, thank you."

"Mom, did you know we're in Argentina?" Jocelyn asked Margret while still cuddling her kids. "How'd you guys get here?"

"We took lots of planes," Lilly answered.

"We even got to go on a Cessna. A little plane! That was cool,"

William explained excitedly.

"It was a long journey," Margret cut in, "but damn it, we made it. Nothing, and I mean nothing, was going to stop me from being with my daughter." She sniffed, wiped another tear away and then gently held Jocelyn's hand. "The question is how did you get here?"

All the excitement in the room stood still in anticipation of the answer. Jocelyn thought about it, tilted her head to face Ethan, and then responded simply, "I don't know."

Now Margret spun around. "Okay, Ethan what is going on? How'd Jocelyn get here?"

Ethan uncrossed his arms and took a step away from the wall. "She followed a path very similar to yours Margret."

"What!? You mean to tell me that my daughter," her arm shot out and pointed to Jocelyn, "a woman who was last seen on life support in Florida, survived that sort of journey? Ethan, I'm a registered nurse...wha...what were you thinking? What the hell?" Margret looked incredulously at Jocelyn and back to Ethan. Her brows furrowed and she angrily spat out, "How? No. Why? Ethan, she could have died!"

"She was a sitting duck in that hospital Margret. I had to get her out of there," Ethan responded.

Margret stood in silence as she processed that statement and Jocelyn dreamily asked Ethan, "You mean because it's kill or be killed time?"

"Okay. What did you do to her Ethan? What is she talking about?"

"I didn't do anything to her Margret. I saved her. I saved you and the kids. It was a lot of work but I pulled it together and got it done. They don't know what they're dealing with. There are a lot of people on my side." Ethan put his hands in his pockets and continued, "Well maybe not a lot, but enough."

Margret and Jocelyn were staring at Ethan wondering if he had gone crazy or something. What he was saying didn't make sense to either of them. Margret was trying to remember anything of relevance from her clinical psych experience and Jocelyn was amazed by how blue Ethan's eyes looked next to the little Picasso-inspired painting. Just then Lillian jumped off the bed and ran to her father proclaiming proudly, "Yay! Daddy saved us!"

Beaming, Ethan snatched up his little girl and kissed her on the cheek. Holding his daughter on his hip he looked at Jocelyn and said, "Look, Joss. It wasn't fair what I did to you and the kids but I had to do what I had to do. I know I've hurt a lot of people, you especially," Jocelyn rolled her eyes and frowned, "and for that I am very sorry."

"Daddy, I have to go to the bathroom," Lilly interrupted.

"Oh, sure Lil. Here. You can go in there." He plopped her down and opened a skinny door, not far from the bullet hole in the wall, to a tiny outdated half bath no bigger than a closet that held a toilet. "But while you were in Tampa I made it right. I'm not going to be working for those people anymore."

"Oh, you quit your job?" Jocelyn blinked and asked, "Are you going to be able to pay child support?"

Margret was still doing the rundown on the psychiatric nursing stuff.

"Don't worry about that Joss. That's like the last thing we have to worry about. You just get better," Ethan said.

Margret, doing her best impression of a psychiatrist, asked, "Then, what should we be worried about Ethan?"

"Right now the best thing to do is lay low. Stay off the radar." Lilly poked out of the bathroom, smiled at her dad, and joined her brother on their mom's bed. She and Will started whispering to each other as Ethan continued. "I've thoroughly insulted the organization I was working for and it's not beyond them to seek you guys out to get to me."

"What do you mean?" Jocelyn's mother wanted to know. "Like you just walked off the job and didn't give them two weeks' notice? Something like that?"

Ethan rubbed the stubble coming in under his chin and answered, "Not quite like that Margret. Just know it wasn't an amicable parting of ways."

Jocelyn lazily observed the interaction between her mother and Ethan but found herself more interested in what the kids were quietly doing, scrunching their noses and making fish faces, so she joined in

"That's not a very responsible thing to do Ethan," Margret reprimanded.

"Well, I think bringing you guys down here was the most responsible thing I could do, especially if I wanted to stay alive and not have you guys tortured, or killed, or worse."

Jocelyn, pressing her fingers into her cheeks to create a more realistic fish face, blurted out, "Mom, ask him what could be worse than being tortured or killed. Ethan, your eyes look so darn blue..."

Both Ethan and Margret turned to look at Jocelyn.

"First things first Ethan. My daughter needs medical attention.

What's in this IV?" Margret asked while inspecting the plastic IV bags. "Hydromorphone? Why, that's the same thing as Dilaudid. How much are you giving her?"

"I don't know. See, that's kinda one of the other reasons I wanted you here. You're a nurse and I figured you'd be able to follow what's going on. So, you know this drug?"

"Oh, yes, it's been around since the 1920s or '30s. I'm pretty sure the Germans invented it during one of the world wars. I'm not sure which one. It's several times stronger than morphine. Does she have a chart or anything like that?" Margret asked while scanning the contents of the bedside table's drawer. "Who's been administering this?"

"A former Special Forces guy I met in Bosnia years ago gave her the morphine. He helped set her up. Right now, some doctor that B.B. knows was the last one to see her."

"Who's B.B.?" Margret asked just as the kids both stopped making funny faces and seemed to snap to attention.

"Aaaah, I see everyone has arrived. Welcome." It was the same Spanish-y but mixed with something else voice that had greeted Jocelyn when she first rolled onto the scene in the fermentation room. She twisted around to see the graying senior saunter into the bedroom. He was wearing a deep burgundy smoking jacket and an ascot. Naturally, given the state Jocelyn was in, she immediately thought of Christopher Walken doing his famous comedy skit, The Continental, on *Saturday Night Live* and she burst out laughing. Mortified, Ethan glared at Jocelyn then closed his eyes and shook his head.

"I'm sorry. She's not normally like this. I'm her mother..." Margret apologized.

Opening his eyes Ethan stepped forward and said, "No. I'm sorry, allow me. Margret McClaren please meet Brunhold Bertram Keller Wolf."

"Oh, you must be B.B.," Margret remarked and Ethan cringed, now thoroughly embarrassed. Margret extended her arm to shake the gentleman's hand.

"I prefer Brunhold, but you may call me B.B. madam." The smoking jacket/ascot man bowed slightly as he sensually took Margret's hand and kissed it. Margret looked completely taken by this gesture and Jocelyn couldn't stop thinking about The Continental. She tried to stifle her laughter but it was only making things worse so she jammed her face into a pillow. The kids were completely confused by what was going on and remained silent.

"I know my daughter would like to make your acquaintance too

Brunhold but as you can see she's having a reaction to the meds." They both looked at Jocelyn as she spasmed with laughter under the pillow. "I'd like to speak with the attending doctor. I'm a registered nurse and might be able to assist."

"By all means señora. I will summon him immediately," and he bowed slightly. Backing his way out of the room, he gave a nod to Ethan.

"Thank you Mr. Wolf," Ethan said.

When Mr. Wolf was gone Ethan carefully shut the door then spun around to address Margret, Jocelyn, and the kids. He was clearly agitated. "Look," he took a deep breath through his nose, "Mr. Wolf is the guy funding this little get-together. Mister Wolf," he glared at Margret, "not B.B. or Brunhold. Mister Wolf. Joss, I know you couldn't help it, but shit! That was ridiculous!...Kids," the twins sat completely still, "you did great. Just be as polite as you can to that man." He repeated for emphasis, "His name is Mister Wolf. He owns this vineyard. His family immigrated here because of World War II. Treat him with the utmost respect. Got it?" The kids and Margret nodded and Jocelyn, covering her face with her hands, started to cry. "Good." Everyone else was staring at the floor in silence. Ethan was still glaring at them when a gentle knock at the door broke the awkward stillness.

"Perdón. Lo siento. May I enter?" Jocelyn noticed that Ethan put one hand in his pocket before opening the door with his other hand. "Buenos. I am asked to check on the patient."

"Oh, that was quick." Margret seemed genuinely surprised.

"Sí," the man smiled. He was blazingly handsome with perfectly styled dark hair. "I am resident physician." Jocelyn wasn't quite sure if she recognized this thirty-something-year-old GQ cover model. He sort of looked like the guy who had rolled her into her room; he had on the white lab coat, but right now she couldn't be sure.

"Well, thank you for coming so promptly Doctor. I think my daughter isn't handling this medication very well. Maybe we should change it up or reduce the dosage?" Margret suggested.

The dark-haired doctor came over and touched the IV bags.

"Okay, sí." He then fiddled with a little plastic mechanism on the tube coming from the bag to the IV port on Jocelyn's hand. The drips sliding down the plastic tubing slowed. "Eso es mejor. That's better. Is there anything else I may help you with?"

Margret was about to ask a question when Ethan said, "No. We're all set now. We just didn't know how to deal with that morphine." He shot a devastating look at Margret which obviously meant “don’t open your mouth” and he walked the man to the door. “Morphine can be tricky and we didn’t want to mess it up. That’s morphine in that bag, right?”

The man, still smiling, replied, “Sí, por supuesto. Of course.”

“Gracias señor,” Ethan said calmly as he whipped out the P226 and shot the man in the back. Margret screamed and the kids literally dove for their mom. Jocelyn winced as her trembling kids flopped onto her for safety and she closed her eyes. When she opened them she looked directly at Ethan, who was rummaging through the doctor’s pockets. A red stain was slowly spreading across the man’s white lab coat.

Jocelyn noticed the blood but that wasn’t what was freaking her out. Over a looping soundtrack of her children crying she whispered, “Ethan, your eyes…they look like broken Christmas tree lights.”

CHAPTER FIVE

The next morning
9:00 a.m.
Orlando, Florida, USA
Disney's Magic Kingdom

AFTER MARK PAID FOR HIS ADMISSION with his AmEx card and passed through the turnstile with its fingerprint scanner, he headed directly up the gentle rise of Main Street, USA to the castle. He was among the very first to be admitted to the park and as he walked he kept a very sharp eye on the growing crowd. Families with strollers and a larger-than-life Mickey Mouse were happily wandering around amongst colorful banners, exquisitely manicured flower beds, and bouquets of festive balloons. It was still early but somehow excitement and song were sneakily permeating the scene.

Being grateful that he had chosen to wear Bermuda shorts, Mark reached into his pocket, fished out his phone, and tapped on the mug shot of Jerry Apario. He wanted Apario's image fresh in his mind. He knew this whole thing was sketchy but what else could he do? He wasn't even sure he was in the right place considering Disneyland, which Apario had said they could meet at, was in California. This was Disney World, specifically Disney's Magic Kingdom. He had debated calling Anaheim and asking them to surveil Disneyland, but then had thought better of it.

"Apario must be here," Mark figured while making his way up Main Street. "I mean the guy knew I was in Tampa." Finally arriving in the shade inside the arched passageway cutting through Disney's iconic Cinderella's Castle, Mark decided to just stay put and watch the passersby. "He contacted me. He'll be here." These thoughts, along with overpriced bottled water, sustained him as he leaned against the classically inspired Italian glass mural of Prince Charming placing a shoe on Cinderella's foot.

Eventually, Mark noticed a man sitting on a bench facing away from the castle, just outside the north entrance to the passageway. It wasn't the red Adidas sun visor so much as the red Adidas interval wristbands—one on each wrist—that made Mark look twice. Just as he was wondering what kind of person would wear sport wristbands to a theme park, the man turned his way. The guy looked at least fifteen years older than Mark and was instantly recognizable. Mark checked his cell phone just to compare. Yup. It was Apario. He popped the phone back into his pocket and casually headed over to meet the man.

"Jerry Apario?" Mark asked.

Jerry furtively glanced around before he looked Mark in the eye and replied with a false type of bravado, "Maybe. Who wants to know?"

"I'm Special Agent Mark Witherall," Mark said as he extended his hand for a shake. "I believe you wanted to meet." With the visor bobbing up and down like a spastic duck quacking, Jerry excitedly jumped up and shook Mark's hand.

"Oh, yes! I was starting to worry. I didn't know if you were coming, what with the way we got cut off." Jerry smiled but then looked over Mark's shoulder and under his breath said, "Let's go somewhere else to talk. Don't turn around, but that person over there is making me nervous."

"Sure thing Jerry. Let's walk and talk," Mark said as they started moving, but he did nonchalantly look back at the person who was making Jerry nervous—just some kid, about twelve years old, wearing a Minecraft T-shirt.

They were quiet as they walked, then Jerry finally said, "Look, I know about McLaren. I want to help."

Mark nodded, unsure of what exactly Jerry knew about McLaren. Jocelyn's disappearance had not been publicized. "That's very generous of you Jerry but aren't you in the witness protection program right now?"

"Yeah, well, it's not what I thought it was going to be."

"Really? We were all wondering why you volunteered. You were only looking at community service and a fine for the fire damage, but you were pretty adamant about the witness protection program. So it's not living up to expectations, eh?" Mark asked as the two followed the path to It's A Small World.

"No. It isn't. In fact, I'm not even sure it is the witness protection program they have me in."

"And why do you say that?"

"Well, first off, they gave me a lame new name, John Smith. I mean, give me a break. Like that doesn't scream, 'Oh hi! I'm in the witness protection program!'" He frowned. "They set me up in a trailer park and told me that my new 'John Smith job' was flower delivery."

"Uh-huh. That seems like a decent, under-the-radar-type job

Jerry," Mark remarked as he kept a watchful eye on their surroundings.

"I guess, if I was actually delivering flowers. But I'm not. I'm driving around toys. Specifically, toy guns."

Mark stopped walking so Jerry stopped. "What do you mean toy guns?"

"I'll show you." He waved his arm for Mark to follow him. "I had to deliver them here. Today. That's why I wanted to meet you. I figured if I hooked up with someone from the FBI, I'd be safe. I don't think what they have me doing is kosher and I want out. If you help me, I'll help you. Like I said, I know a lot about the McLaren thing. I made it my life's work to really study it for a while there."

Furrowing his brow Mark asked, "Thing? It? What are you referring to?" Mark was concerned that Jerry was, for some psychotic reason, dehumanizing Jocelyn McLaren.

"The McLaren Racing lawsuit. Intellectual property," Jerry said like it was obvious.

Mark was grateful that he wasn't dealing with an "it puts lotion on itself" *Silence of the Lambs*-type situation but he was confused and shook his head. "I'm not following you," he said as they continued to walk past flower beds that were almost vibrating because they were so colorful.

Jerry elaborated, "That thing in Italy about the Formula One race cars? There was a whole bunch of stuff about it in the documents that were dumped…I mean the documents your FBI guys showed me during interrogation…"

Mark almost snickered. Jerry really was a bad liar but they couldn't bust him for the dump. There was no hard evidence. That's why they gave him the witness protection he requested. The FBI figured it would only be a matter of time before the guy slipped up. "Oh, I thought you were talking about Jocelyn McLaren," Mark said.

At the mention of Jocelyn's name a softness spread over Jerry's face. He kind of shrugged and said, "Yeah, I know, right? Her last name. Some sort of miscommunication or something. Probably why she ended up getting shot. I'm so glad she's okay. I mean, well, not okay but still alive and is going to be okay…"

He paused, took a deep breath, and continued. "Whatever happened in Italy with that intellectual property settlement, I swear, that's the key to all this. I mean, that money, millions and millions of dollars, is deposited at the IOR. Now, if that doesn't tell you something, right there…"

Mark, still confused, asked, "What's the IOR?"

Jerry's pace slowed down and he sighed. "That's alright, I didn't know about it until I looked it up. IOR is the Italian abbreviation for Institute of the Works of Religion. It's one of the," he made little quote marks with his fingers, "untouchable banks at the Vatican. There's like eight banks there. Who knew? Eight different banks and the Vatican is literally the size of this place." He expansively waved his arm around, showcasing Disney's one hundred and seven acres of Magic Kingdom enchantment.

A little light bulb snapped on in Mark's mind. *The Vatican? So that's why they were calling the other day. Shit. Follow the money, stupid.*

Jerry stopped acting like a tour guide and asked, "You okay?"

"Yeah."

Jerry then took the red terrycloth wristband off his left wrist and handed it to Mark. "Here. I've got one for you."

Mark didn't know if he should accept it—he was still processing the toy guns and the Vatican revelation—but he took it anyway and said, "Gee…thanks Jerry. I think."

"Oh, you're welcome. Put it on. Which is your favorite ride by the way?" he asked while looking around the park. "Have you ever been to Disneyland before?"

Still holding the floppy red terrycloth with his fingers Mark answered, "No, actually, I haven't."

"You're kidding me! Not even as a kid?" Jerry was suddenly excited and Mark felt the nauseating weight of his childhood years bearing down. Not-so-happy memories when his parents would take him to St. Maarten's to go scuba diving or Telluride to go skiing during school breaks. It was supposed to be a "family vacation" but really it was for his parents to firm up contracts and drink…a lot. He would end up with a nanny at the hotel pool or he'd be left alone in their suite flipping through cable news and staticky pornography until his parents rolled in bickering and stinking of booze.

"You aren't an American!" Jerry chided. "Seriously, put that thing on. If you haven't been here before, hummm…well, do you like rollercoasters?"

"Not really. Inner ear problem," Mark replied, still holding the wristband like an old piece of bologna as Jerry started walking away.

"Jerry, stop!" Mark called out. Jerry stopped and turned around. "I didn't drive three hours from Tampa just to go on rides with you. You said you wanted to help me. Then you told me that you were going to show me a truck full of toy guns. Well, guess what? This," he shook the red wristband, "isn't helping. I've got real work to do and I don't appreciate this at all. If this is it, if this is all you've got for me, I'm leaving."

Jerry nodded, then his gaze shifted to something over Mark's shoulder. Squinting his eyes he hissed, "Oh, shit," and that's when Jerry bolted.

Mark looked behind him and saw the kid in the Minecraft shirt and four other boys of about the same age.

"That's him!" Mark heard one of the kids yell.

Another screamed, "Let's get him!" and the chase was on.

Mark slipped the red wristband onto his wrist as he ran after his person of interest. He was ahead of the kids as they screamed and ran to catch up to Jerry. Meanwhile, the red Adidas sun visor flew off Jerry's head as he jumped over a flower bed. The gang of kids, resembling something out of *Lord of the Flies*, plowed through the flower bed. Mark stayed on the path but kicked his speed up a notch. He was really running now and sweating profusely. The path twisted and turned and suddenly Jerry was gone. All the kids were confusedly wandering around an ornate fountain featuring a Disney stylized cast bronze of Cinderella perched on a rock talking to some little birds.

"Where the heck did he just go?" one kid asked.

"Man, that guy is like a superhero," enthused another.

Mark stopped running and wiped his brow with the wristband. Breathing heavy, he walked up to join the kids. "Hey guys!" He waved. A couple of them waved back. "Why were you chasing that man?"

The Minecraft T-shirt kid said, "That's the Flame Thrower Guy!"

Another kid jogged up and added, "Yeah! We saw him on YouTube. I can't believe he's here at Disney World! How cool is that?!"

The other kids agreed and Mark, still recovering his breath, shook his head. Some other kids huddled around to listen in. Two started talking about the time they watched the clip during health class and how funny it was when the teacher busted them.

"Oh man, have you seen it?" Minecraft kid asked Mark. "I've watched that video like a million times. It's freakin' hilarious."

"I'm afraid I have," Mark answered. Then, in his best middle school principal/Officer Friendly voice, "I think you've all really freaked that poor guy out. You can't be chasing people around like that. You should be ashamed." He looked each kid in the eye. "Didn't they teach you about bullying in school?" The kids all looked at each other and some were staring at their shoes when, just to drive the whole act home, Mark asked, "Where are your parents?" The kids sort of mumbled in unison and instantly dispersed.

With the kids now gone, Mark found himself wandering around, searching for any signs of Jerry Apario. Nothing. Where the heck could he have gone?

CHAPTER SIX

Meanwhile
Casa de Wolf
Uco Valley, Argentina

"OW! OOOOOOOOOOHHHHH OWWW…" Jocelyn growled. Her hair was all matted down from sweat and every tense and contoured facial muscle was basted with salty tears. "Mom, make him turn it back on. I can't take this. Please, Mom… "

Margret, steely-faced and sitting on the edge of the bed, gently stroked her daughter's hand. William and Lilly were huddled together on the far edge of the bed near Jocelyn's feet. The kids had stopped crying hours ago when the blood turned brown and were just staring mutely at the shiny brown leather shoes peeking out from beneath the cashmere blanket. "Honey, we don't know what's in that IV It could be any—"

"I don't care! Turn it back on!" Jocelyn demanded just as the door opened. Ethan and a man wearing a puffy blue Patagonia winter coat and hauling a backpack came in. The man stopped when he saw the covered remains on the floor. With everyone watching, he silently took off his backpack and carefully lifted the blanket to reveal a colorless man in a blood saturated white lab coat. He replaced the blanket and quickly tapped out the sign of the cross before heading directly to Jocelyn.

"This is the real doctor," Ethan announced as he handed Jocelyn a crystal brandy snifter full of ice. Jocelyn eagerly took the stemware and scowled at Ethan as he kissed each of the kids on the top of their weary heads. She was angrily chomping ice when Margret stood up and moved aside so that the doctor could get to her.

"Buenos señoras," the doctor said, nodding to Margret and Jocelyn as he sanitized his hands.

"Thank God you're here," Margret greeted the doctor. Then, glaring at Ethan, she made her way to the end of the bed and stood next to the kids, trying to avoid looking at the obvious dead elephant in the room.

"What the heck took so long?" she whispered to Ethan. Then motioning with her chin, "That person is going to really start smelling soon, you know. It's been eight hours since you shot him and just about seven hours since he actually died."

Ethan responded, "Margret, you don't have to whisper, okay?"

"Okay, fine," Margret huffed. "Then what the hell took so long?" she asked more forcefully.

"We're on South American time," Ethan said matter-of-factly. "It was the middle of the night. Things move slower down here. And it's Sunday. The place grinds to a halt on Sunday." Ethan pointed to the corpse. "I'm just glad we identified that joker. We're good. Relax."

Margret screamed, "We're good?! This is what you call 'good'?!" Her anger became animated and her arms quickly flew up in Jocelyn's general direction to help illustrate her point. "Jocelyn's dying over here!" she screeched. "That guy's locked up in full rigor mortis!" She emphatically pointed to the man in the crusty, blood saturated lab coat whose right arm was frozen in a very unnatural position. "The kids are suffering from some sort of post traumatic shock after seeing their dad shoot someone right in front of their faces!" Lilly started crying and Will, with his eyes stuck wide open in a panic, was sucking his thumb. "And what was worse, if this can even be quantified, was when you had to break the dying man's arm. God damn it Ethan! Look at your kids. This is years of therapy! Years!"

"Calm down! I mean it Margret! You aren't helping!" Ethan snapped back. Then turning to the kids he pleaded, "Everyone, stop freaking out. Please. It's going to be okay." That threw Margret into a serious tizzy. Meanwhile, Jocelyn, if she was able to make herself heard over all the commotion wanted to ask the doctor to put her out her misery and just shoot her.

The doctor, seemingly unfazed by Margret's and Ethan's outburst and Lilly's sobs, touched Jocelyn's forehead to check her temperature and then grabbed her wrist to check her pulse, all the while studying the IV bag on the stand. "¿Cuántas horas sin medicamentos?" he asked Jocelyn who was swearing under her breath and clenching her fists. "How much hours without medicine?" he asked in English.

"Too many," she snarled. "I have no clue…Mom!" At the sound of Jocelyn's pained call, Margret and Ethan stopped fighting. "Ask them!" Jocelyn angrily instructed the doctor. "They're the ones who shut me off."

"We didn't know for sure what was in that bag," Margret responded sheepishly, and added while glancing at Ethan, "He's the one who persuaded me to shut it off." As the doctor asked Margret again how long Jocelyn had been without the medicine, he opened his backpack and removed a new IV bag.

"Solamente water. Saline. To keep hydrated," the doctor

explained unsmilingly to Jocelyn as he removed the old bag on the IV stand and replaced it with the saline solution. "There is no trouble breathing, yes?"

"Well, it freakin' hurts, but I can breathe," Jocelyn grumbled. With that he reconnected the IV port on the back of her hand and made sure that everything was dripping properly. He produced a syringe and a little vial out of his backpack. He popped the needle into the vial and loaded up.

"What's that?" Ethan and Margret asked at almost the same moment.

"Morphine," the doctor said simply as he tapped the syringe. "Just enough to kill the—" and that's when William, removing the thumb from his mouth and as quick as lightning, hurled himself onto the doctor who stumbled backward and dropped the needle. Margret gasped and Ethan jumped to untangle the doctor from his son's tackle. Lilly, of course, was screaming and Jocelyn, with eyes closed, had tears pouring down her face.

"William!" Ethan yelled as he restrained his kid. "Relax buddy."

"He was going to kill Mommy!" William sobbed.

"Just enough to kill the pain," the doctor clarified. "The pain. You did not let me finish, did you little man?" the doctor attempted to soothe Will as he brushed himself off and gathered up the now unsanitary needle from the floor. "I was not to kill your mother. I would give to her just enough to kill the pain. That is how you say it, yes?"

Ethan nodded, letting the doctor know that he had used the right term. "This is the good doctor, William. Dr. Fernandez. He's good Will. I promise," Ethan explained, hugging William tightly and rocking the weeping child in his arms.

Meanwhile, Margret was sitting on the bed hugging and rocking inconsolable Lilly. Between the gentle cooing of, "It's alright sweetie. Daddy has Willy now and Mommy's gonna be okay," Margret shot a look like a laser beam of disgust at Ethan and hissed, "Years of therapy. Years."

The doctor, who had regained his composure, disposed of the soiled needle and began preparing a new shot of morphine. Jocelyn's tears were still flowing when the doctor administered the dose. Within moments she began to calm down and a small smile crept across her face.

The doctor watched her intently and asked, "Es bueno, no? It's good?"

Jocelyn nodded and sighed, "Sí. Muy buen, gracias," and closed her eyes. But she quickly opened them again when the door flew open and three men wearing hooded winter coats burst in, followed by Mr. Wolf who was outfitted in a gray Ralph Lauren turtleneck and a tweed sports coat. Two of the winter coat guys made the sign of the cross before unfurling a white PVC body bag. The other guy, who had a thin small mustache, looked like he was going to puke as he watched the men struggle with the stiff corpse, then he made the sign of the cross and helped them.

Ethan, with weepy William still stuck to his hip, walked up to Mr. Wolf, who was intently watching the removal of the body, and flatly asked, "You mean to tell me that you had no idea?"

Wolf didn't answer but shook his head as he watched the men gather up the stiff and broken remains of the vineyard's office manager. "Tito has been with us for…"

"Five years," Ethan finished the sentence.

Wolf nodded and then, as if noticing the cast of characters in the room for the very first time said, "Dios míos, Ethan. How long have these beautiful children and their lovely grandmother been in the room?"

"Eight hours, twenty-three minutes," Margret rattled off, consulting her wristwatch.

Shocked, Wolf exclaimed, "Ethan! What kind of monster are you?! You kept them captive while all this was going on? Did they see—"

"Yes," Margret answered abruptly before Ethan could. "We hid in the bathroom for most of it." She pointed to the minuscule half bath that just barely fit a toilet. "We heard everything."

Wolf scratched his forehead. "This is not good for the children Ethan." Margret smirked and William continued to sob quietly in Ethan's arms as the body bag was zipped up.

"Mr. Wolf, this man who attempted to kill Jocelyn, he's a known agent and—"

"We do not know if he was trying to kill her," Dr. Fernandez cut in. Ethan and Mr. Wolf turned to look at the good doctor. "I will have this tested," he said as he cradled the IV bag of hydromorphone that he had taken off the IV stand. "The question is: where did this come from?" He held the bag of clear fluid up. "She was on morphine from Los Estados Unidos when she arrived, yes?"

Ethan, rubbing William's back answered, "Yes. As far as I know, yes." William was still clutching Ethan's neck like a baby koala bear, but he had pulled himself together and had calmed down, unlike his sister who was still whimpering in Margret's arms. Jocelyn, meanwhile, was enjoying the morphine.

"Brilliant idea Doctor!" Mr. Wolf exclaimed. "Yes, get that tested immediately. We'll get to the bottom of this." Wolf directed that statement primarily to Margret. "Do everything necessary to make our guest comfortable while she is with us Dr. Fernandez." He then turned his attention to the three men and the body bag making their way out the door. "José!" the men stopped in their tracks. "Te quedas y limpias este desastre."

Ethan and Margret watched in bewildered silence as the man with the little mustache broke away from the body bag group and opened the door for the two carrying the bulky load. Mr. Wolf faced the non-Spanish speaking crowd as the men exited the scene. "I have instructed José to return and clean this mess." He made an arbitrary flourish with his hand toward the bloodstained floor. "Poor Jocelyn should have clean and calm as she recuperates."

"Thank you Mr. Wolf," Margret said with sincere appreciation. "Can we move her to another room to get her away from all this?"

Upon hearing that she was going to get moved and before Mr. Wolf could respond, Jocelyn burst out, "Mom, Mom! I'm fine here. I just want to sleep. I don't want to be moved," Jocelyn said with finality and closed her eyes.

Margret sighed and said, "Thank you anyway…"

"You are more than welcome my dear lady. It is the least I can do in this circumstance. Come. Bring the children." He gestured with his arm for them to follow him. "You must all be exhausted. Let me show you to a room where you can get cleaned up and I will have the kitchen prepare a nice breakfast for you," and leaning over to speak directly to young William, "then you can explore, if you wish, or rest."

Margret, still holding Lillian, glanced at Ethan who nodded at her. "It's all right Margret."

"I don't know. I think I'd rather stay here with Jocelyn," Margret said, squeezing Lilly tightly.

"Me too," William chimed in.

"I'm staying with Nana and Mommy," Lilly bravely blurted out.

Mr. Wolf bowed slightly to Margret. "As you wish, madam. Dr. Fernandez, please advise the kitchen regarding Miss Jocelyn's diet." The doctor, adjusting his backpack on his shoulder, nodded. "And Ethan, meet me in my office. We have important matters to discuss." Ethan nodded and Mr. Wolf and the doctor made their exit as José, outfitted with yellow rubber gloves, a plastic apron, and pushing a cart full of industrial cleaning supplies entered.

After acknowledging José, Ethan, still holding William in his arms, shut the door and sidestepped the pool of stale blood. He put William on the bed, at drowsy Jocelyn's feet, next to Margret and Lilly who were both eyeing José skeptically. "Ethan, is it safe here?" Margret wanted to know.

"As safe as is it's gonna get. That guy they just hauled out of here was CIA." They all watched as José sloshed a wet mop around on what was now, essentially, a giant, dark scab caked on the hardwood floor.

"Just like the Cozy Inn...," Jocelyn remarked from a far-away place, "only different." Ethan blinked and the rest of her family, puzzled, turned to look at her as she shut her eyes and slid into a painless sleep.

CHAPTER SEVEN

Meanwhile
Orlando, Florida, USA
Disney's Magic Kingdom

"BOO!"

Mark flinched and exclaimed, "Damn it, Apario! Where were you? I've been searching everywhere for you."

"Well, not everywhere." Jerry grinned and wiggled his eyebrows. "Come on. I'll show you." They walked not fifteen feet away from the water fountain that Mark had circled back around to, the one with a cast bronze Cinderella talking to some birds, and Jerry led Mark under a columned portico. This portico was visually overwhelmed by the eye-catching dominance of Cinderella's Castle and there, in the darkest faraway corner, was a door. The door looked like it was probably fake because the rest of the area under the portico was classic set design, decorated with fake store windows and signage.

"Pretty cool, huh?" Jerry was grinning wildly as he slid up next to the door, opened it easily, and waved Mark inside. Mark cautiously looked around then entered. "You're officially backstage now," Jerry said as he shut the door.

They were in what looked like a giant closet with a couple of random baby strollers and wheelchairs strewn about. "They don't keep this thing locked?"

"Nope."

Mark was skeptical. Looking past Jerry, Mark noticed a stairway. "What's down there?" he asked, pointing at the stairs.

"Oh, that's where the magic really happens! I haven't been all the way through, but I have a map. Hold on." Jerry pulled a piece of paper out of his pocket and unfolded it as they both headed down.

"Is that ASCII art?" Mark asked when he saw that the text on the paper lined up to reveal what looked like a poorly rendered smiley face composed of plus signs, asterisks, and back slashes.

"Correction. An ASCII map!"

Mark nodded and remembered that this was the same guy who plea bargained his way out of the flamethrower incident with a circa 1995 neon pink beeper. "Oh, makes sense," he said with a hint of sarcasm. Mark knew about ASCII art from a "History of Personal Computing" class he had to take.

"Yup! I got it off an old BBS. I know the sysop."

"Uh-huh. Of course. An old bulletin board system and you know the system operator…" Mark muttered while trying to assess if Apario actually was a crazy person.

"They built all this first," Jerry explained when they got to the bottom of the stairs, "and the Magic Kingdom was built on top of it. Tons of earthmoving for this project. This is actually ground level. The park is fifteen feet above us."

Mark was fascinated with the construction of the place. It was basically an enormous hallway, very much like a subway system but missing trains and rails. And it was very sterile. Poured concrete with lots of huge cooling ductwork. Water and wiring, pipes cluttering and junking up the ceiling. Mark's initial reaction was that it was like an underground military base with all the people walking around beneath industrial strength florescent lights. The branded Disney golf carts zipping around and the Mickey Mouse vibe helped tone it down though. Some of the people walking by were in full Disney character costumes with the oversized head of the character tucked under one arm. Others were dressed as chefs or waitstaff. A lot of the foot traffic just looked like office workers changing shift. Jerry and Mark fit right in and no one gave them a second look. Purple banners hung from the wall.

"You can tell which area of the park you are under by the color of the banners," Jerry excitedly explained as they walked along. "Purple is Fantasy Land."

"Uh-huh," Mark sputtered.

"Need to go to the restroom or anything? Looks like there's one right by the Mouseketeeria." Still consulting his map, Jerry said, "I'm sorta hungry. I bet the food down here is cheaper than the food up there." He looked up from the map toward the Mouseketeeria. "You know if we go the other way down this hall we'll end up at Revenue and Currency Control, the heart of the place really. And right under Main Street is the digital animation control system for the entire park. Total Wizard-of-Oz stuff."

"Jerry. This is amazing. It truly is," Mark said with all sincerity. "However, I'm in the middle of a very complex case right now…"

"Oh, right. The truck. You still got your wristband?" Jerry wanted to know. Mark held up a fist, displaying the red band snuggly around his wrist. "Good. Let's go." As they walked toward the Mouseketeeria Jerry said, "My buddy that I used to work with at Hertz Rent-a-Car when I was setting up their nationwide computer network…"

"Wait. I thought you worked at the Conglomerate, that big defense contractor that Jocelyn McLaren and Ethan Lowe worked at."

Jerry sighed and scratched his nose. "Yeah, well, Hertz was the job I had before that. Anyway, my buddy has been working on the RFID system that Disney is going to be rolling out soon. It's pretty slick. Everyone will get a colorful, personalized bracelet and when you get to a ride, the greeter will actually welcome you by name."

"That's nice," Mark halfheartedly commented while still absorbing the new environment.

"You can even buy stuff with your bracelet and charge stuff to your hotel room just by waving the thing in front of a scanner. I'm not sure if it's going to be US dollars or some sort of Mickey Mouse money, but it will be linked in with GPS so that Disney knows how long you stay in one place or roam around. The marketing department here is all about it. Serious analytical data to work with. It will be great for finding lost kids too, of course. I think the launch is supposed to be next year, but you know how this stuff goes." Mark nodded. "Anyway, my friend sent me the hardware for these a while ago," he held up his wristband, "because he knew I was interested in this sort of stuff and figured I might want to check it out."

Mark looked at his red Adidas wristband. "You mean you jerry-rigged this thing to be like one of the Disney bracelets?" To say the least, he was amazed and asked, "Will it work?"

"I tried it out at 'It's a Small World' right before you showed up and naah. The system isn't hooked up yet."

"Oh." Mark looked at the red wristband with new appreciation. "Do you think people would willfully walk around with a tracking device, like a home confinement ankle bracelet, linked to their bank account like that?"

"Well, you've got a cell phone, right?" Mark blinked in response and Jerry continued, "That's where this is all going. I mean, they have to make you want the thing, like it adds value to your daily life or somethin'. That way they can make their money back. If they make it a fashionable accessory that needs upgrading like every other day it's worth it. Good return on investment. Not like the implantable chip they tried out at the nightclubs in Sweden and in the Netherlands."

Mark had heard of the nightclub implants. He had figured that it was some sort of painful hand stamp that got you VIP access at the bar and had smirked about it at the time. It was a real thing, so he listened as Jerry went on. "They found out, even though they advertised it as wicked trendy, finger-on-the-pulse, the implants were way too easy to hack into. How funny is that? Plus the implants caused cancer, which isn't funny. So it's cell phones, bracelets, clothes…whatever."

As Mark was thinking about the implantable chip thing he realized that, of course, Jerry was right. People would happily sign on; especially if they made it some sort of cool looking status symbol. "Don't worry, the thing you've got isn't hooked up to any real database…yet," Jerry added as a comfort, motioning to Mark's red wristband as they walked toward the exit.

Upon emerging from the climate-controlled industrial tunnel, the natural light and oppressive, humid heat momentarily stunned their senses as if they had run into an invisible brick wall. To their left was a multiple bay loading dock. Straight ahead, an enormous, packed, employee parking lot emitting visible heat waves welcomed them to the outside world. Jarringly gone were any indications of anything whimsical. The towers and attractions of the amusement park weren't visible from this vantage point. Jerry motioned for Mark to follow him as he made his way across the scalding hot pavement to a white, 2012 GMC, sixteen-foot box truck. It looked like a U-Haul rental but without the U-Haul logo.

"This is what you're supposed to be delivering flowers in?"

"I know, right? I'm pretty sure 'flowers' is a code name at this point." Jerry unhitched the lock at the back of the truck and threw up the noisy, rolling, garage-style door. The only cargo: about a dozen lonely, medium-sized, long cardboard boxes, haphazardly just sitting there in the dark heat.

Jerry hoisted himself up into the truck. "Hold on," and he scurried to get one of the boxes. Mark was studying his red wristband when he heard the grating noise of a heavy box being slid across the floor of the truck. Jerry, pushing it with his foot toward him, stopped in front of him and opened it. "See! Toy guns."

Mark leaned over to take a look at the contents and his brow furrowed. "Wow. These rifles look pretty realistic Jerry."

"Huh? What do you mean? They're made of plastic." Jerry squatted down to really study the guns and then started bumbling, "I…I…these aren't the guns that were in here before. I swear. I… " Mark searched his pockets for a handkerchief as Jerry rambled on about how someone must have come, broken into the truck, stolen the toy guns and replaced them with real ones.

"Don't touch them," Marked warned as Jerry was about to pick one up.

"This is crazy. I'm tellin' ya, these were toy guns this morning. They were made of weird plastic. It looked like someone had melted leftover broken crayons to make them." He ran back to the other boxes and flipped off the lids. "Shit."

Not having found anything to keep his fingerprints off the rifle, Mark took out his cell phone and started snapping pictures. As Mark was documenting the guns, Jerry mumbled, "I don't even know what to say here."

"Neither do I Jerry. I'm not sure if I'm supposed to arrest you, or what. I'll have to call back to headquarters and—"

"That won't be necessary," a deep voice barked. Startled, both Jerry and Mark spun to see a well-built, bald, black man, wearing a Hawaiian shirt and aviator sunglasses. "I'll take it from here." Mark was about to reach for his FBI credentials when Hawaiian shirt guy shouted, "Hands where I can see them!" and whipped out a standard issue Glock 27.

Mark slowly put his arms out to his sides with his palms facing the man. Jerry's arms, naturally, shot up over his head as he flopped to his knees pleading, "Don't shoot. Please don't shoot. Please."

"What's with him?" Hawaiian shirt guy asked Mark while using the gun to point at Jerry, which only caused Jerry to burst out crying.

Mark sort of shook his head.

Turning his attention and the gun back to Jerry the man yelled, "Man up motherfucker! What's your problem?" Jerry sucked in his sobs but tears were still running down his face. "Stand up."

"Oh, God…please…"

"Shut up for Christ's sake! Which one of you morons has the keys?"

"To the truck?" Mark asked as Jerry slowly stood up.

Hawaiian shirt guy looked incredulous and sighed, "Yes. To the truck." His gun was again fixed on Mark.

"He does." Mark motioned with his head to Jerry who was blinking a lot and biting his bottom lip.

"Of course," the man said, smirking. And turning the gun back on Jerry the man said, "Let's have 'em," making a "give me" motion with his hand. Jerry instantly complied and handed over the keys. "Great. Thanks fellas." Jerry and Mark just stood there, frozen. "You guys waiting for a tip or something?" Jerry and Mark looked at each other. "Scram! Beat it!" the guy yelled.

Jerry jumped off the truck and Mark asked the man, "Who sent you?"

"Same folks that sent you," Hawaiian shirt guy said, more than pissed off as he pulled down the noisy garage-style door and secured the lock. "Get out of here." He waved the gun as if shooing them away. "Take a motherfuckin' hike already. Seriously. Beat it!" Then he turned and jogged up to the cab of the truck, hopped in, and started the engine.

The truck was making a loud pitched *BEEP BEEP BEEP* sound as it slowly rolled, in reverse, past Mark and Jerry. Mark quickly fished out his cell phone and took a picture of the license plate as the truck drove away.

"See! See that?! I told you. I want out! This is messed up!" Jerry wailed as Mark sent the images of the guns and the license plate to the FBI's Tampa field office. "Those were toy guns this morning. Chunky plastic, swirly-colored toy guns. I swear to God! You gotta believe me—"

"But now they're not toys and, to be honest with you, I'm not sure I believe you at all. You were the one who lured me out to witness all this. For all I know, you were trying to distract me from the case I'm supposed to be working on," Mark grumbled as his thumbs twitched out as much information as he could remember in text form. Still cradling the phone, he squinted his eyes and veritably hissed at Jerry, "Do you know how much paperwork what we just witnessed is going to generate? Do you?"

"Oh, like this is my fault?!" Jerry retorted. "How come you didn't just whip out your badge and arrest him?!" That statement made Mark stop what he was doing. "You froze up. I was counting on you to protect me. This whole thing is a complete farce. I'm obviously not delivering flowers like the witness protection guy told me. I'm not even delivering freakin' toy guns at this point. For all I know, it was you who set me up."

Still holding the phone, Mark stopped what he was doing and studied Jerry for a long moment. "Who exactly is this witness protection guy you keep talking about?"

"His name started with an F." Jerry rubbed his temples. "Something like F. Bauerly...hold on." Jerry reached around to his back pocket for his wallet. "I actually have his card right here." He tore open the velcro and quickly produced a business card. "Oh, I was kinda close. Fitzgerald Crowley."

"What?" Mark's shoulders fell. "You're kidding me."

"No. It says so right here," Jerry said, passing the card to Mark.

"This is a joke, right?" Mark sputtered, scanning the card.

"Where did you get this?" He was completely flabbergasted to be holding what appeared to be Assistant Director Fitzgerald S. Crowley's FBI business card.

Confused, Jerry said, "No. I'm not playing a joke on you. Why? What's wrong?"

"This guy. He's my boss…in Tampa. How'd you get this?"

"He gave it to me."

"When?"

"The day they moved me into the trailer."

Mark, still holding the card asked, "The assistant director moved you into your trailer?"

"Well, he didn't actually move any boxes or anything. He was just there. He told me this was my 'get out of jail free card'."

"Uh-huh." Mark was shaking his head in disbelief as he began poking around on his phone. "Do you think you could identify him again?" and he turned the phone toward Jerry showing an image with two different men in business suits. Jerry leaned in close and instantly pointed to one of the men. "Are you sure?" Mark, more irritated than incredulous, questioned again.

"Yup. That was him."

Perspiring even heavier now with the realization that his boss had something to do with Jerry, the toy guns, and "black *Hawaii Five-O*," Mark put the phone back in his pocket and wiped his brow with the red wristband as Jerry continued.

"But I didn't believe him. That's why I came with my own insurance policy," he said, pointing to Mark's wristband. "Notice I don't have mine on anymore?" He waved both his naked wrists around. "I slipped it over the barrel of one of the guns when I fell to my knees begging for my life." Jerry grinned. "I made a big scene to divert the guy so that maybe you could do the same. You don't really think I'm that much of a wuss? Do you?"

"Yes. Yes I do," Mark promptly answered. He wanted to punch Jerry he was so fed up, but when Jerry explained that the red wristband contained a live GPS transponder he decided against it.

CHAPTER EIGHT

Meanwhile
Casa de Wolf - vineyard office
Uco Valley, Argentina

BRUNHOLD BERTRAM KELLER WOLF was awkwardly crouched, rifling through one of the tall filing cabinets that lined the dark, wood paneled office when Ethan barged in and slammed the door. "Okay. What the hell is going on? For a company guy he was way too easy to break." Ethan thumbed over his shoulder back to Jocelyn's room in the main house. "My question is, why has he been here for five years like it's cool?" Ethan stood, arms crossed, facing the owner of the vineyard.

Mr. Wolf, still bent over, looked at Ethan and drearily responded as he slowly stood up, gripping his lower back, "My question to you Ethan is, why did you allow your children see all that?" Mr. Wolf slid the drawer shut with his foot and let out a huge sigh. "And why did you keep poor Tito right there in front of them as he died? This is a horrible thing. It makes me question your judgment."

"Don't change the subject Wolf, but yeah this is a horrible thing. Like I really wanted to put the brakes on the guy in front of my kids. Right now I'm more concerned about response time. I was calling you all night to get you over there and you never picked up the God damn phone. That's why he was just bleeding out in front of the kids. Wouldn't have happened if you had picked up the phone."

Mr. Wolf tapped his ear. "I take these hearing aids out for my sleep." A manly onyx and gold pinky ring punctuated this comment. "But you raise an important point..."

"Damn straight I do. Look, I don't speak Spanish. I know literally no one here but you. What was I supposed to do? You weren't responding. Finally, against my better judgment, I left everyone and got your doctor. Thank God the word 'doctor' translates well. I'm just glad the stateside team walked me through everything. I really wasn't expecting to run into the friggin' CIA. Not this early at least."

Mr. Wolf nodded thoughtfully. "It seems as if the CIA has been with me, in one form or another, ever since I was born."

"Oh. So you did know. And you didn't feel compelled to tell me this before?" Mr. Wolf blinked and rubbed his eye. He didn't say anything as he shuffled over to the large plateglass window that looked out into the fermentation room. “So, you’ve been letting the CIA use this place as a front? And you’re okay with that?” Ethan waited in silence for an answer as Wolf absently surveyed the numbered, shiny, stainless tanks. When Wolf didn’t answer Ethan continued, “And you let me and my family walk right into this? How am I supposed to trust you? We’re all going to get friggin’ killed!”

Wolf moseyed to the desk with the three large, flat-screen monitors positioned on it. Carefully plopping his aged body down in the circa 1980s burgundy, upholstered, wheeled office chair, he looked up at Ethan. “You make it sound so…so dirty.” He made a quick, dismissive gesture with his hand and continued, “This is how business is done. Has always been done.”

He paused while considering his next words. “Americans, you live in an empire but have sanitized fantasies about how your wealth is generated.” Smirking he continued, “As if the whole planet had not been completely shaped by commerce and its armies.” He shook his head. “Because of war I came to inherit this place.” He made a sweeping motion with his arm as if showcasing the vast expanse of the vineyard. “I have no love for business. I have no mind for it. But I have common sense and I took what was given to me and made of it what I could. It has been a struggle. And now look at me. I am getting too old for all of this.”

Ethan, with his arms still crossed over his chest, was studying Mr. Wolf intently as he spoke. “Tito kept this place alive.” Pinching his fingers together as if describing a perfect spaghetti sauce, “He was the vitality.” Then resting both hands on his stomach he continued despondently, “I liked Tito. He ran the office better than I ever could have.”

He nodded at the three computer screens. “I cannot do this. Computers? Accounting? Tito had a mind for it,” and then giving it some thought added, “They say people who are good at math are good at music. Tito was a good musician. A very talented percussionist. Timbales. We all teased that he must have chosen timbales because of his name. He played just like the great Tito Puente. Well,” he paused as if recalling an awkward memory, “maybe not just like Tito Puente, but he was passionate when he played and we all enjoyed it. The customers too, they love when we play,” Mr. Wolf said proudly.

“Why do you think they come here? Not because of the wine. The wine produced here is terrible but people will buy what they are repeatedly told is wonderful. Have you tasted it?” Ethan shook his head. “Wine aficionado awarded to us Best Malbec two years ago because of Tito and his connections. Prestigious international awards do not go to just anyone. Money must be moving in the right direction."

"Look," Ethan responded, "I don't give a shit about the wine. I just dragged tons of people into this plot. People who risked everything to do this. Now, for all I know, you and Ledergerber are best friggin' buddies! The CIA agents answer to someone. Someone concerned with finance and I'm certain they know that I stabbed Ledergerber and he's someone pretty high up on the economic food chain. I'm a marked man," Ethan said, jamming his thumb into his chest. "I honestly have nothing left to lose. My family on the other hand…," he shook his head and continued, "I can't believe you had all of us dive into this shark tank."

Mr. Wolf smirked and shook his head again. "You are mistaken. Tito held no command of—"

"No!" Ethan cut him off. "I'm not talking about Tito. I'm talking about Jonas Ledergerber, the guy I used to work for. That's why I ended up here with you. You and I and our shared vision of what the world could be without people like Ledergerber and his snooty cartel. I'm committed to that vision and I thought you were too. We both know what passes for money today is a crime." Full of purpose Ethan started walking menacingly toward Mr. Wolf, "But then after I get Jocelyn and the kids here the next thing you know I've got the CIA in my face! What the hell, Wolf?" He smacked his palms down on the desk and Mr. Wolf involuntarily twitched at the sound. "I should kill you too! Right now. You set me up!"

Leaning back in his chair Mr. Wolf tapped his belly. "I have only set you up for your ultimate success Ethan. The CIA agents in my experience are far more interested in having parties. That is why they are here."

"And it has nothing to do with the fact that you are moving mountains of money around for them? Yeah, like someone's not gonna notice their man's missing?!"

Continuing on as if Ethan hadn't uttered a word Mr. Wolf said, "I've learned to live with them. Adapted my lifestyle around them. They are part of the landscape here in South America as they are the business intelligence unit of the United States empire. I am not afraid of them. I have been nothing but gracious. You on the other hand, you have acted very rashly. The children did not deserve that either. They are now scarred by your hand though you did not touch them."

"Oh, please! They'll be fine. We just have to figure out how to do this." Ethan sat down opposite Mr. Wolf. It was at times like this that he just wanted to call the man "B.B.," to treat the guy like an equal. Ethan felt equal to him, but Brunhold Bertram Keller Wolf was much older, not to mention much richer. Mr. Wolf had been born into his fortune and if the guy wanted people to call him Mr. Wolf, fine, so be it. It was fair considering the vast investment the man was making into the project. "Mr. Wolf, you knew about me and Ledergerber. You applauded my action. Now, I'm not convinced of your intentions at all."

Wolf held up his hand. "Un momentito, my intentions have not changed. I hold the same opinion of the money changers and their system of enslavement as my father and millions of other people. Their system must end and when it does the world will spontaneously erupt into peace. However, Ethan, I did not realize you would be instantly killing people upon arrival. I think you are—how do you say?—jumpy?"

"Careful," Ethan corrected. "I'm careful. But now we have a situation. Someone is going to start missing Tito very soon. We have to hatch a plan. Where's the body?" Rubbing his nose, Mr. Wolf was silent, avoiding the question. "I watched your guys carry him away. How did you get rid of him? We have to create some sort of plausible cover and start bracing ourselves. It would be better to have this go down diplomatically but I'll get my guys organized and ready."

Mr. Wolf just sat, staring out the window into the fermentation room. "Hello? Can you hear me? We need to start making plans." Leaning across the desk, Ethan asked more forcefully, "Are the hearing aids on? Where's the body?"

Still staring out over his fermentation tanks, Mr. Wolf responded, "What's left of Tito is well hidden."

"And where would that be exactly?"

"He's in three."

"Three? You cut him up into three pieces?"

"No but that's not a bad idea."

"Well, where's the body?"

"In number three." He motioned with his chin to the fermentation tanks. Ethan quickly stood up and walked to the window to get a look at tank number three. "It was a bad batch anyway. We did something wrong with the sulfur dioxide and ascorbic acid. It was ruined almost from the beginning."

Ethan raised his eyebrows and nodded. "Okay, but what about the guys who put him in there? I'll need to take them out too to cover all tracks."

"No es necesario. I did it myself. The boys hardly touched him. Don't bother with the boys. They need the job."

"They need the job. That means they can be bought. Where are they?"

"No Ethan." Mr. Wolf stood up in protest and instantly grabbed his lower back. "You are meant to take down a financial system, not my winery. You are too eager to kill."

"And you don't think this whole thing isn't gonna get stupid messy?"

"Ethan, please. I have lived through La Guerra Sucia, the Dirty Wars here in Argentina and over those mountains in Chile." He pointed to the window overlooking the fermentation room. "Right over that mountain out there, from 1974 to 1983. We do not want to go back. Military, security forces and right-wing death squads calling themselves the Argentine Anticommunist Alliance, the Triple A, hunted down and murdered political dissidents. Anyone believed to be associated with socialism was hunted down. The worst repression occurred in 1977, when the church, labor unions, artists, intellectuals, university students, and professors were targeted."

Talking faster and with much more emotion Mr. Wolf continued, "I had several classmates, friends, who just disappeared after an exam one day. I never saw them again. Our professor, he too just disappeared. Everyone knows of someone who was taken and never returned. The junta justified this mass terror by exaggerating the guerrilla threat and even staged attacks to be blamed on the guerrillas. They used frozen dead bodies of guerrilla fighters that had been kept in storage for this purpose."

"Clever," Ethan quipped while turning his full attention to Mr. Wolf. "I was just a kid and I vaguely remember hearing the word 'junta' on the news back in the US."

"Not clever. Evil. Over thirty thousand people disappeared or were eliminated during this time. When government goes through the trouble of staging an attack on its own people in order to gain support of its policies, that government needs to be abolished and—how do you say?—reset."

"Tell me about it," Ethan grumbled under his breath.

"They did an amazing job of the reset in Chile," Mr. Wolf said matter-of-factly. "Chile is now the most modern and fastest growing economy in South America. They took the time to study the elements of a successful nation and sent their young economists to M.I.T. in Massachusetts, USA to learn the teachings of Milton Friedman."

Wolf sighed and continued almost apologetically, "This is unlike Argentina. The IMF collaborated with Argentine President Carlos Menem in liberalizing the economy, deregulating financial markets and privatizing over a thousand enterprises. The crises which ensued led to the worst depression in Argentine history, with over twenty thousand bankruptcies, twenty-five percent unemployment, and poverty rates exceeding fifty percent in working class districts. Menem was never arrested. Argentina had been proud of overthrowing the military dictatorship and restoring a republic; however, because of an infantile understanding of economics, which even I could comprehend, namely: you do not borrow more money than you can pay back," Mr. Wolf made a show of banging his knuckles together and wiggling his fingers, fluttering them down as if illustrating snow falling, "the currency collapsed and that was no mistake.

"Now instead of people disappearing all the time Argentina is a poor country where thousands of people are literally starving to death among architectural artifacts to the contrary. People do not understand the deadly consequences of financial warfare and I am not sure you do either Ethan. That is why your CIA is here. Financial war and war of all sorts creates enormous opportunity."

Ethan rolled his eyes but bit his tongue. Mr. Wolf added, "You will soon learn. Remember Ethan, if you are the hired gun," and pointing at Ethan with a flash of black onyx and gold, "then I am the trigger. If I find any more of my staff dead, you and your family will not be far behind. "

CHAPTER NINE

Somewhere on Florida I-4
Between Orlando and Tampa, USA

"DUDE, YOU STINK," Jerry said casually while slurping down the very last molecules of his supersized, cherry flavored Slushie.

To be fair, after walking almost the entire outer circumference of the Magic Kingdom in ninety-eight degree, glaring, midday heat to get back to the parking lot where Mark had left his car, both men were pretty ripe. Unlike Jerry who had taken off his shirt, put it over his head, and had used his Adidas headband to hold the shirt into position, Mark had yellow sweat rings permanently stained to his polo shirt.

"I'm tellin' you, you should have gotten one of these at the gas station." Jerry held up the jumbo plastic cup. "They really do cool you off." He angled his straw and sucked loudly one last time before wedging the plastic cup under the front passenger seat.

Meanwhile, Mark was just finishing his second liter of natural spring water. Seeing Mark's empty bottle in the cup holder Jerry picked it up and studied the label. "They call this natural spring water? It's full of salt and potassium and, quote, unquote, 'natural flavoring.'"

Irritated, and with one hand on the wheel, Mark kept his eyes on the road and took another gulp of his water.

"I bet that wasn't originally in there," Jerry continued. "They put that salt in there to make you more thirsty so you'll buy more. I swear to God every time some product proclaims that it's natural, look at the darn label. I heard they were using aborted fetal cells to enhance the flavor of some bottled water…"

"Oh! For heaven's sake!" Mark burst out, spitting water out of his mouth. "That's it. Stop talking. Just stop talking. I don't want to hear another peep out of you until we get to your place. Like I want to hear a critique of my water from a guy who just drank a certifiable chemical dump complete with red food coloring." Mark shook his head. "Just shut up Jerry. Seriously. Take a nap or something."

Dejected, Jerry silently placed the empty water bottle back into the cup holder. "I'll just let you know when we're coming up to the exit."

"Perfect," Mark snapped back. "And this better be worth it Jerry.

I swear to God, if you don't have that wristband hooked up to GPS tracking I'm going to take you directly to jail and I'll leave you there."

"Uhm…can you stop talking?" Jerry asked.

"Oh, so now you're telling me to stop talking? You're too much." Mark took a long deliberate breath through his nose and took another gulp of water, but this time before he finished swallowing, he briefly looked at the label.

"Well, this car is a new Buick Regal GS, right?"

"Yeah. So? Rides pretty good."

"This model has OnStar installed and might be listening or recording everything we say. It can also blow up."

"What?!"

"It's been known to happen."

"Jerry, where the hell are you getting all these fun facts?"

"Originally I saw it on the internet but then I checked it out. It's true."

"Great." Mark grumbled as he flicked the blinker on and slid the Buick into the high-speed lane, sarcastically adding, "Let's just pray that we defy all the odds and make it safely back to Tampa."

They rode in silence for the next forty minutes as they traversed the wide, smooth lanes of the Florida highway system. The cars they were sweeping past were all bright and shiny and new, not like the muted palette of older models dulled with grime and rust commonly seen in New England, where Jerry was from. The sun reflecting off these sparkly new cars was creating a dazzling effect when mixed with the heat waves emanating from the hot pavement. Even though it was a comfortable sixty-eight degrees in the car, Jerry leaned over and set the air conditioning a few degrees lower and readjusted the vent so that it blasted him directly in the face.

With an icy coolness blowing his dark hair, Jerry noticed a big digital billboard hanging over the highway announcing a SILVER ALERT. The Silver Alert contained the license plate number of a confused or missing elderly driver. Jerry was keeping his eyes peeled for the Silver Alert license plate when, from out of nowhere, Mark said, "You know, I'm curious. How'd you hack into the FBI's phone system?"

Jerry gasped and glared at Mark. "Did I, or did I not, just tell you this car could hear everything?" Mark shrugged and they drove in silence for another ten miles until Jerry pointed and said, "There's a rest stop up there. I need to use the john."

"I could use a break myself," Mark said while considering the traffic before swooping the Buick over to the exit.

Once there, Mark turned off the car and began collecting his empty water bottles. "Grab that thing under your seat and throw it out," he instructed Jerry. "And don't you think of running off. You stay with me." Jerry stuck his head back in and grabbed the super-sized Slurpie cup.

Tossing their empties into the garbage can as they entered the public restroom both Jerry and Mark surveyed the place and headed directly to the urinals. "So you want to know about the call?" Jerry said as he relieved himself.

Mark, taking care of his business, sort of shrugged and said, "Yeah, sure."

"Okay. Well, I latched on with NASA's disruption-tolerant networking proto—" Just then the door squeaked and a bearded, scruffy man wearing a vintage Rolling Stones T-shirt ambled in and unzipped his fly. The man parked himself right next to the two of them even though there were five other urinals available.

Jerry nodded at the guy, finished up, and headed to the exit. "I'll meet you outside," he called over his shoulder to Mark, who was left awkwardly staring at the wall.

Swinging the door open Jerry headed to the vending machine. He was digging around in his pockets for change when the Rolling Stones guy and Mark came out. "You want a Snickers or something?" Jerry asked Mark.

"Huh?" Mark muttered. He was watching the man in the Rolling Stones shirt.

"A Snickers," Mark said as he pushed the button and a Snickers bar tumbled down. "They've got Reese's Peanut Butter Cups in here too, and…"

"No thanks."

"You're a better man than I," Jerry said as he unwrapped the candy and hungrily took a gigantic bite. They began walking. Mark was still watching the man in the Rolling Stones shirt when they exited the building. "Do you still want to hear how I did it?"

"What?" Mark said, still captivated by the Rolling Stones guy, who disappeared walking between some tractor trailers.

"Want me to go over how I called you?"

"Why not?" Mark turned his attention to Jerry. "How'd you do that?"

"Well, I wasn't sure it was gonna work, but it was pretty neat." Jerry proudly puffed up his chest. "I latched on with NASA's DTN protocol. That's why we got cut off. Telemetry and all that." Mark was curious about this and listened with great interest as Jerry continued. "But I was a little disturbed by how I was able to get on to that. They've got to sure that thing up. I mean, well, it's not super easy, but still…" He shook his head.

"I had to get into the European Space Operations Centre in Darmstadt, Germany. That was probably the trickiest part. They're getting ready to do some LEGO robot test on board the space station. You know, you heard about that, right? Someone in Germany is gonna remotely control the little toy robot up in space. It's supposed to be a big deal." Raising his eyebrows Mark nodded.

"Anyhow, I had to weasel in over there. The core of the DTN suite is the bundle protocol or BP, which is roughly equivalent to internet protocol and that's what we use here on Earth for the internet—you know, IP addresses. Well, DTN is part of NASA's Space Communication and Navigation, SCaN, program. So I logged in with a password from SCaN and long story short, once I was up there," Jerry pointed to the sky, "I called back to Earth and just did a basic phone phreak inspired hop with Voice Over IP from there."

Mark slowed down and grinned. "I thought you were phreaking when I got that call." Then restraining his admiration with skepticism he put forth the obvious question, "But why did you have to do all that? You couldn't just pick up a regular phone and call me?"

"Well, in retrospect I guess I could have…"

"In retrospect?!" Mark gasped. "Jerry, there are serious consequences for what you just did. You know that. You also know I'm with the FBI and that I have to document all this."

"Oh, pee-shaw. No you don't. Plus, no one is up there. I mean, look, it's 2012. The network is set up for almost all of the planets in our solar system now. I'm pretty sure me showing up there," he continued, pointing to the sky, "as if anyone even noticed, would probably make someone jump for joy."

"Huh?"

"Yeah. They'd be psyched. E.T. phoning home and all that. I called you from dotMars." Jerry grinned and Mark frowned. "Don't worry. They aren't moving anything of value through that network…yet."

"Well, they're communicating and more importantly, it's not your network."

"Nothing's going on up there. I'm not even convinced we went to the moon. I mean look at those shadows on the first lunar landing photo."

Oh brother, Mark thought, *this guy is in tinfoil hat land.*

Jerry continued, "Look, they're not banking or dealing with financials through that network. There is no commerce yet. That's when people will start to get hyper. Until then, I'm really not worried about it. Everyone involved with space is pro this network. No one wants to take it down. Myself included. I didn't wreck anybody's stuff. Anyhow, it wouldn't be you or the FBI dealing with it anyway. The Air Force has dominion over the internet and anything in space is governed under maritime law. I'm still sketchy on how the NSA fits into this but Americans better get used to that maritime law stuff. I mean we already have the gold fringe flags in our courthouses so maybe people will just..."

Jerry trailed off and Mark studied him as they walked back to the car. Mark was trying to figure this guy out. *Is he one of those sovereign citizen types?* Mark had recently learned about that during a breakout session he was forced to endure before the Republican National Convention.

All sorts of documents had been covered at that meeting in order to get Tampa staff up to speed. *Rage on the Right: The Year in Hate in Extremism*, in which groups opposing issues such as the president's health care plan and illegal immigration were lumped in with white supremacist groups like the National Socialist Movement and skinheads. And the exhaustive *Domestic Extremism Lexicon* which profiled people as possible threats if they were actively upset or preoccupied with any of the following: the economy and the Federal Reserve; loss of jobs; foreclosures; critical of free trade programs; stockpiling food; opposing illegal immigration; opposing a "New World Order"; opposing the UN; opposing global governance; fear of communist regimes; opposing the loss of US manufacturing to overseas nations; opposing gay marriage; or were anti-abortion. If these people used the internet or alternative media to express themselves and their ideas, these people might be suspected terrorists according to Mark's pre-convention training.

Inside the same binder of documents, Mark had also received a color photocopy of the *MAIC Report.* That's where he learned about the obsession with gold fringe flags by sovereign citizens. He'd never really thought about gold fringed American flags as being a signal that maritime law, also called admiralty law, was being followed by a court. But sovereigns, who considered themselves not bound by the legal system, were apparently highly attuned to this and knew that maritime law was established during ancient times and flourished during European colonial expansion. That it has to do with how countries conduct commerce over the world's waterways as opposed to inside national boundaries. Justice is meted out quite differently in that case. Mark had thought the gold fringe was just to make the American flag look fancy and he honestly hadn't thought twice about those "Don't Tread on Me" bumper stickers which were also an indicator of a possible domestic terrorist threat according to the FBI.

Jerry continued as they stepped up to the car, "I mean you could turn me in, I guess, but why would you want to? Especially since I'm trying to help you." Mark unlocked the car and Jerry called out before hopping in, "Now remember what I told you about OnStar," and placed a finger over his lips. "Shhhh."

They were driving for about twenty silent minutes when both Mark and Jerry noticed the police lights. Jerry quickly pivoted in his seat to look behind them. Mark casually slid the Buick out of the high speed lane to let the police car pass. But the police car and lights, and now sirens, didn't pass; they stayed right next to the Buick. The officer driving the police car motioned for them to pull over. So Mark put on his blinker and started easing his way through the shiny foreign-made traffic to the breakdown lane. Jerry was visibly nervous but wasn't saying anything which Mark appreciated.

Once both the Buick and the police car were safely tucked to the side of the highway, Jerry made sure his seatbelt was buckled and stared straight ahead. The state trooper came up and knocked on Mark's window. Mark slid the window down and the trooper leaned in.

"What seems to be the problem officer?" Mark asked.

"You're lookin' pretty good there, Dr. Polofsky. Would you step out of the car, please?"

"Uh...I'm not Dr. Polofsky," Mark said as he opened his wallet to show his credentials.

"I can see that. Dr. Polofsky is eighty-two years old. I'll need your license and registration. Would you step out of the car, please?"

Mark was unlatching his seatbelt when Jerry grabbed his wrist, leaned over and whispered, "I wouldn't get out of the car. Who's this guy with this Dr. Polofsky crap?"

Mark sighed. "It's okay Jerry. I'm with the FBI."

"Oh, and look how great that worked with the last guy and the truck," Jerry snapped just as Mark opened his door. Upon hearing that comment, the officer instructed Jerry to get out of the car too.

Jerry hesitated and, swinging his door open, begrudgingly got out of the car. With the sound of the traffic swooshing by he heard, "No, this isn't my father's car." And then the officer forcefully grabbed Mark and spun him around to face the Buick and Jerry.

"Hands on the car! Feet apart!"

Mark did as he was told but Jerry started screaming as the officer began patting Mark down, "It *is* his car! What are you doing?!"

"Jerry, please shut up," Mark said over the hood of the car.

"Just whip out your badge and tell him to take a hike!" Jerry yelled back. That's when the second police car arrived, skidding to a stop with all its lights and sirens blaring. A policeman jumped out and hurled himself toward Jerry, knocking him to the ground.

As Jerry struggled Mark angrily shouted over his shoulder, "Would you mind telling me what's going on?!" Ignoring Mark, the officer continued with the pat down. "Look, I'm with the FBI and I need to get that suspect back to Tampa."

"You don't say. And you have absolutely no clue why I pulled you over," the policeman said as he fastened the handcuffs onto Mark's wrists. Meanwhile Jerry, now bound in handcuffs too, was being helped to his feet.

"That's right. You saw my ID."

"I did see your ID and I also saw this…" The officer sort of smirked and pointed down the highway to the large digital billboard about seventy-five yards away which read: WHITE 2012 BUICK REGAL FL ZN9875.

"But…but…that's got to be a mistake," Mark sputtered.

"Is this the car that sign is talking about?" the officer asked while patting the roof.

"That's my car, but I'm not eighty-two-year-old Dr. Polofsky. It's just a typographical error. "

"Look, for all I know you stole the old man's car. His family called this in about twenty minutes ago. They're worried sick about him."

"Look, you have my license, you have my registration, you also have my FBI credentials. What else do you need? I'm not Dr. Polofsky!" Mark yelled as he was hustled into the back seat of the squad car where Jerry had also been deposited. The two of them, with their wrists locked up behind their backs, were forced to uncomfortably lean forward in the seat as they listened to the officers outside the car say goodbye to each other.

"Dude. This sucks," Jerry grumbled.

Mark, with jaw clenched, shook his head. He didn't even look at Jerry. The police radio was really loud and the two of them sat in silence and listened.

static "We have no record of that. Over." Long pause…*static* "FBI cannot confirm." *static* "Roger that. Bring 'em in." *beep*

Jerry looked at Mark with horror.

"Wait! What?!" Mark called out from the back seat.

The officer hopped in the car and slammed the door. "You guys are in a shitload of trouble. Stealing a car and impersonating an FBI agent…"

"Look, I'm in the middle of a very important case right now!"

"Whatever you say buddy."

"No, he really is!" Jerry added.

"Get FBI Tampa on the radio," Mark pleaded. "Tell them you've got the lead investigator in the abduction of Jocelyn McLaren. It's a huge international missing persons case right now." Jerry almost broke his neck snapping his head to look at Mark in disbelief. Mark continued, "Seriously, call them. And if they don't believe you, get INTERPOL on the line."

Jerry, with his disheveled hair, gasped. Leaning over, and in a low, hushed whisper asked, "What are you talking about? Jocelyn's missing?"

Ignoring Jerry, Mark continued making his case as the officer, seemingly unmoved by this information, jumped on the gas and joined the highway traffic. "Seriously, just call the Tampa office! Hell, highway patrol must know about his case. We were searching for ambulances. There were two that looked exactly the same." Jerry's squirreled eyebrows only got untangled when the radio announced a car fire in their proximity. Mark was still going on, now talking about the Vatican, which had absolutely no effect whatsoever on the policeman driving the car when Jerry twisted around to watch the fire engines rushing by in the other direction down I-4.

"Uh, Mark," Jerry interrupted.

"I'm telling you I've been working on this case since she disappeared. Just call them. You'll see."

"Mark."

"Not now Jerry,"

"Mark!" Using his head to butt into Mark's shoulder Jerry shouted, "Look at your car!" If his hands weren't cuffed behind his back he would have pointed.

Twisting around and looking through the rear window Mark saw it. WHITE 2012 BUICK REGAL FL ZN9875 was now fully engulfed in flames.

CHAPTER TEN

Everywhere and Nowhere

RE:futbol

The Internet combined with 4GW the nation state cannot move fast enough and has no chance in the long game unless they decentralize. That won't work in the US because US leadership is pushing for increased scale, more top-down, command and control systems from the all-knowing know-nothing idiots at the top. Even with the smartest people in that position they would fail. Decentralized systems at the speed of social media = too fast for them to react. The choice becomes decentralize and de-optimize the system which would take away most of their power or carry on. Carrying on will spell their doom but so will the alternative. Pick your poison. I have chosen mine. I am waiting nearest point of entry: Santiago, Chile cleanest point of entry: Buenos Aries, Argentina

1HDubS4aZHviwdhCf4wYzk6NZ5ZL98PRr3

After pressing send, Ethan scratched under his arm where the bulletproof vest he hadn't taken off in days was chafing him and watched as funds began trickling into the bitcoin account. He was running his messaging system off a completely insecure server in Dublin, Ireland owned by a startup company called Four Square Solutions. People from around the world flocked to this server, investing hours of their lives playing a browser based, massive multiplayer strategy game called "Utopia." Burrowing himself into the middle of pathologically addicted gamers to evade detection was the easy part. Now came the hard part. Akecheta Whitebloom and the guns would arrive soon.

CHAPTER ELEVEN

Casa de Wolf
Uco Valley, Argentina

"WILLIAM AND LILLY LEARNED SOME SPANISH today," the singsong-y voice said.

Jocelyn awoke to find her mother sitting next to her on the bed and, doing a quick self-appraisal, concluded that she didn't really hurt. She was mostly sore, really stiff, and groggy. Absently rubbing her eye she became aware of the IV and stupidly tried to manage the tubing running from the port on her hand to the stand. "Oh honey, let me get that for you," Margret said, making sure that the tubes were still connected. "Are you hungry? You want some jello?"

Instantly and from out of nowhere, a little dessert dish of green jello appeared. The gelatinous cubes trembled as Mom held the dish in front of Jocelyn's face. "This will feel really good on your throat." Jocelyn attempted a smile. "And it's got protein in it."

The jello wiggled some more and Mom cheerily produced a spoon. Jocelyn obediently took the jello and noticed her kids sitting at the foot of her bed. Both had dirty faces but their hair was perfectly coifed. William's hair was parted to the side and his cowlick was somehow missing. Lilly's hair was in two cute little braids. They were staring at Jocelyn with tired eyes.

Whispering to her grandmother but fixated on her mom Lilly asked, "Is it okay to talk now?"

"I think it's all right. Why don't you tell her what you and Willy just finished eating?"

Squirming around Lilly said very deliberately, "El helado."

Appearing as if she might physically burst with pride, Margret exclaimed, "See! The kids are learning Spanish! Isn't that great?!"

Nodding, Jocelyn put the jello down on the bedside stand and waved for the kids to come and sit closer to her. "I want to squeeze you. Both of you. Come here." The kids tumbling over the bed to their mom's side were afraid to get too close. "So that must be helado on your chin, huh?" Jocelyn grabbed Lilly and kissed her all over her helado smeared face. "Did Nana do your braids?" Lilly nodded yes.

Will smoothed his hair and said proudly, "She did mine too."

"Oh! Muy guapo," Jocelyn cooed. "Very handsome," and reaching out she pulled him in for hugs and kisses too. "Mom, how long have I been sleeping?" she asked while still snuggling with the kids.

Margret consulted her wristwatch. "About a day."

"Seriously?" Jocelyn blurted. Everyone nodded yes. "Were you here in this room the whole time?" Everyone nodded yes again and Jocelyn looked at each of them and began crying.

The kids shrank back and Margret stepped closer. "It's okay honey. We wouldn't want to be anywhere else but here with you."

"But where did you sleep?"

Margret pointed to a neatly folded pile of blankets with pillows stacked on top. "We slept on the floor."

"Nana slept by the bloodstain," Lilly said matter-of-factly.

Jocelyn spotted the stain. The blood had discolored the wood floor despite the clean-up effort and her stomach sank. Confused and teary she asked, "Mom, what's going on? I don't understand what's happening."

Margret sighed. "I don't know Joss. Ethan's gotten himself involved in something very, very sketchy. At first I thought he was insane but now I'm pretty sure there are other people involved." Margret shook her head. "I can tell he thinks he's doing the right thing and I can tell he's ferociously defending you and the kids but other than that I'm clueless."

Leaning back Jocelyn took in what her mother said. Smiling weakly at the kids she turned to look at the bloodstain again. "He shot someone."

Margret nodded.

"Who was it?"

"Apparently it was someone from the CIA."

"What?!"

"We were worried about the meds someone had given you. Do you remember that?" Jocelyn nodded yes. "What you were hooked up to, we didn't think it was morphine. So Ethan shot the guy who was pretending to be a doctor."

Jocelyn looked even more confused. "Pretending to be a doctor? But how does this work into the CIA?"

"I heard Ethan mention something about his friend. I think his name is 'Ache'? Have you ever met this person?" Jocelyn shook her head no. "Well, Ethan says that he's coming to join us. I guess this Ache person is who identified the man as a CIA agent…or something." Everyone was silent.

"Where's Ethan now?"

"Not here. I sent him away. I didn't want you waking up and him making you upset."

"Mom! Now you're making me upset. He's got some serious explaining to do. Can we get him back here?" Looking around the room, at the tidy pile of blankets and pillows next to the IV stand, the faded wallpaper, the artwork, and the bloodstain, Jocelyn began crying again. "This is too messed up."

The kids slowly migrated back to the foot of the bed and were watching her intently. "Mommy, please don't cry Mommy," William begged.

The tiny voice injected Jocelyn with new resolve. Wiping her tears, she said, "You know, you're right Willy. I'll stop crying." And looking directly at Margret, she said, "I'm going to get mad. Get Ethan in here now!"

There was a knock on the door. They were all stunned and Jocelyn whispered, "If that's Ethan that's just uncanny."

Margret yelled out, "Who is it?!" and they all braced themselves. The kids slid off the bed and hid under it.

"Dr. Fernandez."

From under the bed came a muffled, "That's the good doctor."

"Please come in," Margret shouted back. Entering, he seemed to notice the bloodstain, but walked directly to Jocelyn while nodding to Margret.

"How do you feel?" Dr. Fernandez asked Jocelyn. "Sleep is good, no?"

"I'm stiff and sore but not in a lot of pain."

"I see gelatin," he said, referencing the green jello. "Are you hungry? Hunger is a good sign."

Jocelyn saw her mother leering in over the doctor's shoulder and despite not feeling hungry at all answered, "A little." Smiling, Margret slowly pulled herself away.

"Very good," he replied, taking her pulse and temperature. Then he began checking and refreshing the bags on the IV stand.

Seeing an opportunity Margret asked, "Did the test results come back yet? You know, from that IV bag we were all wondering about?"

"No," Dr. Fernandez answered simply. "I, as well, am waiting on important deliveries. We must be patient." Margret looked disappointed and the doctor changed the subject. "I will have the kitchen deliver a meal."

"Thank you Doctor," Margret said.

Jocelyn followed up with, "Gracias," quickly adding, "If you see Ethan, would you please send him to us. I'd like to talk with him."

"I will." Nodding to both women the doctor exited the room, closing the door behind him.

When the coast was clear the kids got out from under the bed and hopped back up near Jocelyn's feet. They all sat in silence for a long while. Looking at her fearful children Jocelyn lamented, "Mom, what are we gonna do? We have to get out of here. We're trapped. I mean, look at me." She held up her hand, showcasing the IV port. "How much longer do you think it's gonna take to get me well enough to go home? For all of us to go home?"

Sadly shaking her head Margret said, "I don't know sweetie. It all depends. The thing I'm worried about is passports. We used fake passports to get here."

"Seriously? Why?"

"Ethan had sent someone to get us and this man gave them to us. That's how we got here. I don't know how we'll get back. You didn't have a passport coming here. Did you?"

"No. Some guys stole me from the hospital, put me in an ambulance, drugged me, and I ended up here. I remember Ethan was driving the ambulance. That's all I remember."

"My God!" Margret gasped. Rubbing her temples and then fighting back tears she said, "Oh, honey, you've been through so much." Tenderly touching Jocelyn's cheek she continued, "Everyone back home is looking for you. I'm just thankful we're with you."

At that point the door squeaked open a hair, just enough for someone to peek in. They all heard it and Margret called out, "Who's there?" The kids scrambled back under the bed. "Who is it?!"

A muffled, "B.B." came through the door. Margret and Jocelyn looked at each other in disbelief and heard someone clearing their throat. "Brunhold Bertram Keller Wolf. May I enter? I come bearing gifts."

Margret took a deep breath and swung the door open. A well-dressed Mr. Wolf was standing behind a white linen-covered room service cart. The cart contained an array of covered dishes, bottles of water, a basket of sliced bread and croissants, a coffee carafe and cups. The bottles rattled as he slowly pushed the cart into the room. He then made a grand display of removing the lids from the plates. An assortment of sliced meats and cheese; a bowl of some sort of soupy yogurt; fruit salad; another plate of meat; little ramekins full of jelly, butter, mixed nuts, sunflower seeds, and raisins. "And the 'pièce de résistance,' a delicious, chilled gazpacho infused with healing herbs and garlic accompanied by an assortment of different oils for

Miss Jocelyn to dip her bread in. Mas importante. Dr. Fernandez says this is very good for your health," Mr. Wolf said proudly.

"Oh, why this is wonderful. Thank you," Margret enthused. "Kids get out here and see what Mr. Wolf brought us."

"Where are the children?" Mr. Wolf asked.

"Hiding," Jocelyn answered. "They've been traumatized."

Hanging his head Mr. Wolf said, "Sí. I understand," and then more loudly for the benefit of hidden ears, "but we must push on. We cannot ruminate on the trouble. I can assure you that Casa de Wolf, this place has, for decades, been always full of laughter. Friends sharing their passion..." He paused, looking meaningfully at Margret before continuing, "Their passion for wine and music. I have made it my life's work to create a respectable sanctuary in honor of my family."

"Oh..." Margret sighed, "That's so...so special."

Clearing her throat and rolling her eyes, Jocelyn took a sip of ice water. Margret noticed but pretended not to.

"Keller means 'wine maker' in German," Mr. Wolf offered. "My father wanted to reinvent himself after the war so he picked Wolf as a name. Keller was chosen because of the acquisition of this vineyard."

"Fascinating. Kids, get out from under that bed and say hello to Mr. Wolf."

"No. It is quite alright. The children will come out when they will be ready. We are holding la fiesta soon. Perhaps you can bring the children and they can experience Casa de Wolf as pleasant?"

"That sounds lovely," Margret said, taking a spoonful of the yogurt. "Oh, this is just like my mother would make! I haven't had this in years. Jocelyn, you have to try this." Digging around with her spoon she continued, "My family came from Czechoslovakia to the United States because of World War II." Mr. Wolf nodded solemnly as he placed the bowl of chilled cucumber and tomato soup next to Jocelyn on the bedside stand. Jocelyn smiled in appreciation.

"Yes. Yes. The war. Very disruptive," Mr. Wolf said, slowly shaking his head. "Many people died." Meanwhile, Jocelyn was mentally giving her mother the "for-the-love-of-God-change-the-damn-subject" vibe.

"Tell us about the fiesta," Jocelyn cut in before her mother could continue rambling about World War II.

"Oh, it will be wonderful!" Mr. Wolf proclaimed. "All of Tito's friends will be there and we will be playing some of Tito's favorite numbers."

From under the bed someone asked, "Who's Tito?" Margret and Jocelyn were curious too.

Mr. Wolf sadly smiled. "A dear, dear friend of mine." And then kind of grimacing, "I will not be seeing him anymore. So I am having for him a goodbye party." Mr. Wolf pointed at the bloodstain for the benefit of Margret and Jocelyn, who were both horrified upon realizing that Tito was the name of the man Ethan had shot. Margret put her hand over her heart.

Then came, from what was clearly Lilly, "And el helado?"

"Sí. We can have ice cream." Smiling, Mr. Wolf turned his full attention to Margret and said, "Then it is settled, yes? You bring the children and I will inform the staff to prepare and see to your needs before the party. Please do me the honor of accepting my invitation."

Margret looked to Jocelyn for approval and when her daughter gave the same "it's your call" gesture she had seen earlier, Margret answered, "I'd be happy to attend the party. Thank you."

Giving a slight bow and then turning to Jocelyn, Mr. Wolf asked, "Might you be in need of anything else?"

"No. So long as I have this morphine," she grabbed the IV stand and gave it a little shake. "Gracias señor."

"Muy bien." Then with a little more volume he announced, "Okay children, I am leaving. I will see you at la fiesta." Mr. Wolf made another little bow to the ladies and exited.

As soon as he was out the door, from out in the hallway, Jocelyn and Margret could hear, "Oh good, you're up here. Ache will be here soon."

Within moments Ethan swung through the door and said, "Hey, Joss. You woke up. Dr. Fernandez told me you wanted to see me." Grabbing a croissant from the room service cart and planting a kiss on her forehead before taking a bite he asked with his mouth full, "How ya feelin'?"

At that moment Jocelyn appreciated why her mother had sent Ethan away. "Mom, can you get the kids out of here? I need to talk with Ethan."

CHAPTER TWELVE

Polk Correctional Institution
Polk City, Florida, USA
Cell Block 3

"ABERCROMBIE SAYS HE'S IN FOR attempted murder!" Leaning against his cell door with his arms poking out between the bars, Jerry yelled across the ridiculously noisy hallway to Mark. "He says we're lucky we're here! They have all sorts of classes! They even have an aerobics class!"

Mark didn't answer. He was in own his cell, directly across from Jerry's, pacing back and forth, wearing a bright orange prison outfit that proudly advertised POLK COUNTY JAIL in big black letters. Of course, Jerry had the same outfit on too and he was beginning to appreciate how the whole place was like some sort of hornet's nest with all the angry buzzing and tight movement within the confined spaces. The orange and black somehow made sense. Anyhow, Jerry was getting concerned about Mark and the pacing, considering he had been doing that back and forth thing for a couple hours now and it couldn't be good. The two of them had been locked up for over twenty-four hours and the whole scene had been a certifiable disaster, starting off when they found out that the guy who arrested them was named Officer Kuntz and Jerry asked the man if he had ever thought about legally changing his name considering his occupation. Naturally, things went downhill from there.

At that point, they had been driven directly to jail and immediately processed for intake. That's where the wallets, watches, phones, and eventually clothes were collected. Mark had been out of his mind the whole time, protesting that this wasn't how things were done, that they were supposed to get a phone call and wanting to talk to superiors, which quickly moved them to first in line for the full body check and showers. While Mark was freaking out, Jerry let the corrections officer know that he was allergic to latex and asked if they had any alternatives available. The CO didn't know the answer but promised to go easy on him. They ended up in their cells shortly after a meal had been served to the inmates and the nauseating smell of institutional food and incarcerated bodies hit them hard as they were escorted to their cells in block three. And although they had been ravenously hungry, by then they were fine with not eating. Mark, who was not acknowledging Jerry during this time, had mostly been lying on his cot with his hands on his head while Jerry took the time to acquaint himself with his cellmate Abercrombie.

Everything was relatively fine until lights out. That's when Mark, unfortunately, was forced to interact with his cellmate Emilio, who preferred to go by the name Emily. Emilio started sharing intimate stories of his awakening to the fact that he really was a woman deep down inside and had attempted to snuggle in next to Mark on his cot. Mark, having been thoroughly trained in self-defense, had sprung into action and broke not only Emilio/Emily's nose but also fractured the pubis area of his cellmate's hipbone. There had been other moaning and groaning going on in cell block three while all that was going on, so medical attention didn't reach Mark's cellmate until breakfast was served a few hours ago. That's about the time Mark started pacing like a caged animal.

"Mark! Dude!! At least we can see each other!! How messed up would it be if we couldn't?!" Mark kept pacing. Jerry sighed and picked at the black ink that was still staining his fingertips. He sniffed his fingers, taking in the ink smell that wouldn't go away. Through the bars, he waved his hands and shouted, "Mark! Look! Look at me! Quit walking back and forth like that! You look like a crazy person!" No response. Jerry pulled his arms in from the bars and asked Abercrombie what he was reading while climbing up to his cot.

"The Holy Quran," Abercrombie answered simply from the bottom cot.

"Oh," Jerry said as he flopped onto his bed. "I would have thought you'd be going for the Bible. No offense."

"Been there, done that. Just widening my horizons. You know how it goes."

"I guess. Speaking of widening horizons, you said they have lots of classes here. Do they have classes where you can learn how to use computers?"

Abercrombie put the book down and, looking up at the cot above him said, "Are you kidding me? This place is like a full on voc/tech school. You can take courses to get certified in IT and there's even job placement."

Jerry, lying on his back with his hands behind his head said, "Cool. How do I get myself into one of those classes?"

"I bet you can slip into one. Here," Abercrombie sat up, "I'll get the CO over here and we'll hook you up."

Jerry smiled.

CHAPTER THIRTEEN

Meanwhile
Buquebus Fast Ferry
Colonia, Uruguay to Buenos Aires, Argentina

AKECHETA WHITEBLOOM, holding a soccer ball under one arm, pulled back the hood of his black Mountain Hardwear ZeroGrand trench coat as he grounded his combat boot firmly aboard the modern ferry. His dark ponytail was well hidden behind the folds of his jacket as he made note of all the emergency exits. Slowly moving through the crowd, Ache surveyed the situation. People with shopping bags and small pieces of carry-on luggage were babbling and laughing and organizing themselves into the rows of seats. The setup reminded him of a 747 but much wider. All the seats were facing a cafeteria style snack bar and two big flat-screen TVs.

Ache inched his way through the tourists, businessmen, and families filtering into place and flipped down a cushioned seat next to the sweeping, tinted starboard window. Ache was impressed. He had been anticipating a jalopy of a ferry, but this was a sleek, high-powered boat that the residents of both Uruguay and Argentina were very proud of. Formerly it would have taken him three hours to get to Buenos Aires. Now the journey took only sixty minutes.

This hour was the worst part. Fifty kilometers, on the water, trapped, unarmed, on a crowded fast-moving boat, and changing time zones. Ache glanced out over the gray massiveness of the Rio de la Plata estuary. This body of water between Uruguay and Argentina seemed like a sea unto itself and it might as well be if he didn't make contact or had to abort the mission. Somewhere, parked beneath him with the other cars and motorcycles, was a truck. Someone who he didn't want to know was going to give him keys to that truck. The soccer ball was the signal that he was ready to roll.

Ache deliberately positioned himself so that he could watch the people moving through the line at the snack bar while making sure to appear as if he was watching the soccer game on the flat-screen TVs. None of the multitude seated in the rows and rows of passenger seats looked out of place. No one seemed to take notice of him as they sat, staring straight ahead, fixated on the soccer game. He looked at his watch and figured he might as well set it to Argentina time—one hour earlier.

"Ah, last of the Charrúan peoples, eh?" a young British man in his late twenties or early thirties wearing a 2012 FIFA World Cup beanie hat commented casually as he stopped in front of Ache.

Ache looked up from his watch to find the man obviously inspecting his facial features. "Excuse me?" Ache asked.

"You. You look as if you have Charrúan blood." Ache looked blankly at the man so the man continued, "The Charrúans were the native people of this area, but they were annihilated mostly because of wars with the immigrants who were better equipped." The man obnoxiously leaned in for a closer look. "Later, state organized repression took its toll and eradicated the language and the memory of the race," the man said without emotion, studying Ache's face but not making eye contact. "Fascinating."

Ache grunted and started setting his watch again.

"Oh, I'm sorry, please excuse me. Allow me to introduce myself." The man patted around on his pockets and produced a business card. "I'm Leighton Evans." Ache glanced at the card and nodded. The man held it out a little longer waiting for Ache to accept it, but seeing as he had no takers the man put the card back in his pocket.

Leighton Evans pointed to the seat next to Ache, the one with the soccer ball just sitting in it. "Mind if I join you?" Ache picked up the soccer ball and put it under his seat, holding it between his feet so it wouldn't roll away as the ferry boat sliced through the gray waves. "Ah, thank you," the man sighed as he sat down and unfastened the meal tray from the seat in front of him, effectively blocking Ache from leaving his seat. "So, are you of Charrúan descent?" he asked as he began unpacking a waxed paper-wrapped sandwich. Ache shook his head no. "I think the last person who actually spoke that language died in 1980. I'm very interested in languages…"

And it went on and on like that with Ache not responding and Leighton trying to make conversation. Eventually the ferry pulled up to the port in Buenos Aires. Throngs of people hauling everything from, shopping bags, fishing poles, luggage, and laptops smushed themselves together over by the exit in anticipation of the door being opened.

"Well, I guess we're here," Leighton said closing up the meal tray and standing up. "It was a pleasure to make your acquaintance," he finished, holding out his hand for a shake. Ache shook Leighton's hand fully expecting some keys to be slipped to him. But there was nothing. Leighton gave a courteous smile and moved off to join the others waiting to disembark.

Taking a deep breath through his nose Ache sat absolutely still. He knew eyes were on him. There had to be. The crowd by the door was getting antsy and the boat was rocking more now that they weren't speeding through the waves. Ache, still waiting, watched as the ferry's human cargo lost balance and collectively cried out, grabbing for the nearest support as the ferry docked. A huge hatch was opened and everyone in the herd wedged themselves and their luggage off the boat and quickly fled up the gangplank.

Finally, only Ache remained on board. No one had approached him and he was wondering if he had taken the correct ferry given the time difference. He reached down under his seat to get the soccer ball. Upon pulling it up from between his feet, he was honestly surprised to find a car key taped to the thing. He quickly stood up and looked at the empty row of seats behind him. Then peeling away the masking tape, he snagged the key and tossed the soccer ball back onto the seat Leighton had been sitting in.

Ache dodged around the rows of seats to the stairs that led down to the lower deck where all the cars were parked. As he descended the echoey clanging of his footsteps competed with the sounds of cars starting up. The boat's idling engine became louder and louder too. When he hit the noisy, exhaust-filled parking area Ache looked at the key. It was a copy of a key. There were no identifying marks to let him know which vehicle was his. He waited.

Eventually Ache spotted it. The only car that wasn't moving or pumping out exhaust was a black, antique El Camino SS circa 1968. He walked over and inspected it. Long and sleek. The paint job was aged but clearly this chariot had been cared for. It certainly was not what he had been expecting. Especially since there was no cargo in the bed of the vehicle.

He slipped the key into the door lock and it fit. He paused and quickly pulled the door open while turning his head and shielding his face in anticipation of an explosion. Nothing. The other cars were slowly and noisily filing onto the ramp and out onto Argentinian soil. Ache reached under the driver's seat. Nothing. He hopped in and opened the glove box. It contained the original Chevrolet El Camino User's Manual. Surprisingly, at least to Ache, this car had been made in Argentina. There was also an Argentinian passport sitting there bearing the name Emanuel Martinez, a registration for the car, and some stamped paperwork. The person who had this car before him definitely smoked cigars. He could smell it. The cigarette tray was full of Honduran cigar ash.

Ache pulled out the cigarette lighter and studied it, then ran his fingers over the radio with its bulky buttons. He popped the hood of the car and hopped out to behold the V-8 engine. Nothing. There were no apparent signs that it had been tampered with. The only thing left to check was under the car. So he flopped to the ground and shimmied under the El Camino as the last car drove off the ferry.

"¿Cuál es el problema? ¿Necesitas ayuda?" Ache heard an Argentinian ask.

"No. No problema!" Ache shouted back while quickly inspecting the undercarriage. "Es solo viejo. It's just old," he said as he slipped out from under the car, satisfied that there was no bomb planted there. "Gracias."

"Muy bien, pero tienes que ir." The workman pointed to the ramp as he urged Ache to leave.

Ache nodded. He smashed the hood down and then settled back into the driver's seat. Slipping the key into the ignition and, holding his breath while depressing the clutch with his left foot, he turned the key. Nothing but the sound of U. S. of A. designed classic muscle car badassery. The man who had been concerned about him getting off the boat smiled and waved him toward the ramp.

With the car's mechanical purr echoing through the empty garage, Ache slipped the four-speed into first and drove the car over the ramp into Puerto Madero's northern dock passenger terminal lot. He followed the other cars up to what looked like a tollbooth and the man inside asked him for his passport and ticket receipt. Ache reached into the glove box and produced both. The man stamped his passport and pointed him to his left, over to what looked like a fishing boat. But before the uniformed man gave Ache the passport he rubbed his fingers together, making the international sign for "give me money." Ache complied and gave him a US one hundred dollar bill. The passport was back in Ache's hands and the man motioned again toward the boat. Ache nodded and drove over to it.

As he sat sizing up the situation the V8 rumbled. What he had imagined to be rigging on the boat started to move. It wasn't rigging after all. It was a type of crane and he watched as the crane hauled a large wooden box out of the boat's hold and deposited it onto the bed of the El Camino. Ache felt the rear of the El Camino sink with the weight and, with the engine still running, he got out of the car. Two men in work overalls came up and made the same international signal for money with their fingers while offering to unhook the crane from the wooden crate. This time before Ache doled out the cash he asked for a crowbar, which one of the men quickly handed over.

Ache hopped up onto the bed of the El Camino with the crowbar and wedged the cover off the crate. He carefully removed the heavy piece and laid it to the side. Brushing away the packing material he found that the crate was divided down the middle with a big, thick piece of plywood. What he found inside the two halves of the shipping crate puzzled him.

"¿Que es esto?!" he shouted over to the man who had given him the crowbar. "What is this?!" The El Camino's engine was keeping steady time as he shouted again with confusion, "Mantequilla de maní?!" Half the shipping crate appeared to be filled with cases and cases of jars of peanut butter and the other half was chock full of an assortment of colorful toy guns.

CHAPTER FOURTEEN

Casa de Wolf
Uco Valley, Argentina

"THEY OWN THE MEDIA."

"Yes. I know that. You know I know that," Jocelyn said while critically analyzing Ethan's clothing, trying to figure out if he was concealing a gun.

"They own the banks."

"Again. I sorta figured that out. Why do you think I've been paying everyone with money orders from the credit union for the past two years?" Jocelyn nonchalantly remarked as she moved the spoon around in the gazpacho, but inside she was shaking. Sure she had wanted to literally kill him before she sent the kids and her mother away but she also knew that he was her ticket out of here. She had to be calm. She had to listen. She had to not let emotions get in the way and just let him talk if she wanted to understand what brought her here and glean some sort of clue as to how to escape.

Studying Ethan carefully she identified, at his ankle, a lump in his jeans as he paced in a controlled panic around the breakfast cart that Mr. Wolf had rolled in earlier. "They own and manage every major religion. They govern every financial trust. They own all the bits and pieces of the entire friggin' carnival Jocelyn." He threw his arm out as if tossing confetti. "They will manufacture consent endlessly while making sure that the people who are aware that things are messed up are occupied chasing rabbits—no make that *shadows* of rabbits—down endless rabbit holes. They have everyone else completely brainwashed to ensure there is nothing but success for their co-intel slavery operations."

"Whoa, whoa, whoa, whoa." Jocelyn put the bowl of cucumber soup back on the nightstand next to the lamp. "Hold on a second there Ethan. You're losin' it. Seriously. Stop talking like that. Brainwashed? Co-intel slavery?"

Ethan bit his lip and, shaking his head, walked over to the wall with the bullet hole in it. He put his index finger on the hole and tapped it. "You don't know Jocelyn. These people are maniacal. I'm not even sure they're human. You don't know how lucky you are."

"How lucky I am? Are you kidding me!?" Jocelyn's plan of staying even keel just evaporated.

"No. No I'm not," Ethan responded. "I saved you. I saved the kids. Heck, I even saved your mother for God's sake. And, well, that right there…"

"Oh. Okay. So basically, we should all bow down and be grateful that you had me put in a medically induced coma, kidnapped me, dragged the rest of my family halfway around the world to witness someone getting shot and bleeding to death. Is that what I hear you saying?" Ethan rolled his eyes. "Because if that's what's coming out of your mouth, I do not agree!" Jocelyn, gripping her chest yelled, "I'm friggin' pissed! What the hell is going on?! Seriously?" Tears began welling up. "Especially with shutting me off. What the hell was that all about Ethan? You wanted to physically hurt me. I know you did," she accused. Ethan shook his head no. "You're an asshole!" she screamed and threw the soup spoon at him. It bounced at his feet. He stepped over it and walked back to her, avoiding the stack of neatly folded blankets Jocelyn's mother and kids had used as bedding.

"Jocelyn you don't understand. There's much more at play here. I've seen it. These assholes don't mess around. They simply don't care about people like us…like you. But I do."

"What?" Jocelyn was taken aback and she stared at him before she blurted out, "Ethan you are so freakin' full of it! You're a selfish prick! Someone else obviously cares about me. They wanted me dead for Christ's sake! I will never ever trust you. Never! You murdered someone right in front of us. You showed us what you're made of. Why would I trust anyone like that?!"

"Well, you're gonna have to trust me now."

The urge to scream "fuck you!" as Ethan's statement hung in the air was put in check by her achy body and scratchy throat. She hung her head and focused on the tube pumping morphine into her. That feeling, or lack thereof, that was dripping through her veins was her one saving grace. She focused on that and tried to be grateful. She knew from the beginning of this conversation that Ethan was a critical piece of the puzzle to them all getting home. She had to be smarter, or at least act smarter, than throwing a spoon at a man with a gun strapped on his ankle.

She looked out the window to the gray angles of the snow covered mountains and felt very small while wiping away a tear of frustration. *Calm,* she repeated to herself as she took a deep breath and pulled the blue fox fur throw up over her shoulder. The fur made her feel almost regal despite the IV tubes and messy bedding. "Okay, fine," she mumbled and then pulling herself together, more forcefully proclaimed, "but you have to answer some serious questions Ethan. I mean it. I don't even know why I'm here. At this…this place." She glanced at the paintings on the walls, the sparse 1960s furnishings of the room, and then deliberately made it painfully obvious that she was staring at the bloodstained floor before looking him in the eye. "Why Argentina?"

Ethan sighed as he sat on the edge of her bed. "Because they already had their collapse and Wolf's here. He's the one who paid for your escape."

"Well, that was nice of him. But what collapse? What the hell are you talking about?"

"Their currency got wiped out. Argentina's money is worth like nothing now, meaning American dollars will give you a lot more bang for the buck."

"Huh?"

"Inflation hit them really hard. Stupid hard. Almost seventy percent of the country fell into poverty when the rug got pulled out from beneath their government issued money. This place was really rich once Joss. Honestly. Wait till you see it. But they borrowed a lot of money that was pegged to the US dollar and they couldn't pay back their loans. So they sold off their infrastructure and natural resources and now one in four children here are officially documented as starving, not just hungry like "let's give the kids reduced school lunches"—starving like those kids you hear about in Africa. People of all ages are suffering. Most of the country is still living at poverty level since the collapse."

"Oh, that's really terrible Ethan, but more on point, why are all of us here in the middle of it?"

"They already had their monetary collapse and their revolt. The thing is, they didn't have guns for that. Think about it Joss. When this all goes down in the US it will be a totally different story. That's why I wanted you and the kids out of there. It's gonna get bloody soon. Plus you were gonna get finished off at that hospital."

"By whom Ethan? Who was going to finish me off?"

"The bankers."

Jocelyn looked at him with furrowed brows and then fought off the urge to laugh, "Oh, just some random bankers, huh? Like some guy from Citizen's Bank was just gonna wander into the intensive care unit and shoot me?"

"Pretty much," Ethan answered simply and Jocelyn looked at him in disbelief. "But it wouldn't be some random bank teller from

Citizen's. It would definitely be one of Ledergerber's people. He's got the best network of assassins in the—"

"Wait," Jocelyn cut in, "you think you know who would try and kill me?"

"Oh, I don't think I know. I *know* I know who would kill you. Ledergerber. He'd have no problem with that."

Jocelyn's mind was reeling. "Who's this Ledergerber?"

"I had a contract with him. He's pretty high up, connected with the IMF and World Bank. For all I know, he's even higher up than that. He's probably with the Bank of International Settlements. I don't really know Joss. He's connected to real wealth. I stabbed him."

"What?!"

"Yeah. In the throat." Jocelyn just looked at Ethan, realizing it was kind of pointless to wonder if he had the capacity to do such a thing seeing as the whole family witnessed him shooting someone in the back. "I'm not sure if he actually died or not, but it gave me time to get to you when I heard he had put Heartbreaker on a job."

With the mention of the name Heartbreaker it was as if a very specific frequency had been blasted directly at Jocelyn's torso and something essential at her core shattered and fell away. The sharp gasp of breath she was pulling in through her mouth chased away part of her spirit, and had she not been lying down with pillows propping her up she would have collapsed. This name Heartbreaker, it was the name of a Serbian woman she had met back in Tampa. The woman had long black hair and a size seven foot. It was the name of the woman who had come to visit her in jail. The thing that was profoundly disturbing to Jocelyn was the realization that she had always known that Ethan knew this woman and that she had chosen to ignore her intuition.

Within this brief moment of clarity Jocelyn was transformed. Although she was horribly injured, both physically and psychologically, she purposefully adjusted the fur throw on her shoulder and in a cold, detached state experienced, in silence, all emotion leaving with her spirit. It was at this very moment that she took on the persona of a lawyer or, more correctly, a queen and asked, "And Heartbreaker was important why?"

"Oh, she was the one who shot us," Ethan responded matter-of-factly and Jocelyn didn't even flinch.

Unmoved by this information Jocelyn asked, "Why would she do that?"

"I told her to."

Now, it goes without saying that Jocelyn would have been emotionally reduced to amoeba-like status with this news not two minutes ago; however, she remained solid in her questioning. "Why?"

Ethan, likely sensing that he was entering "the danger zone" quickly stood up and moved toward the little Picasso Blue Period painting. Stopping in his tracks at the bloodstain, his shoulders slouched and he turned to face her. "How else was I gonna get you safely out of the country?" There was a long pause while Jocelyn studied him. Shaking his head he whispered, "I'm so sorry Joss."

Still staring at him, Jocelyn slowly reached for the cup of ice on the nightstand and proceeded to chomp on a cube. The tiny sound of her jaws crushing ice might as well have been thunder as the two stared at each other. Finally, when the ice was melted, she spoke. "You told this woman to kill me?"

"No!"

"But—"

"Believe me, if she wanted to kill you she would have. The woman is a machine. She is undoubtedly the best sniper I have ever met." Looking at his shoes he hesitated and confessed, "I trained her."

"You trained her to shoot me?"

"No. I trained her to shoot in general." He sighed and scratched the back of his neck. "I've known her since she was a little girl."

Jocelyn was processing it all like a computer at this point. She had absolutely no emotion left to expend. The bits of information being fed to her were burned into her long-term memory for later review as Ethan continued, "She's talented. I knew when Ledergerber mentioned her, in the context that he had mentioned her, that he had hired her to kill you. I immediately contacted her and offered her more money not to wipe you out. She's a mercenary after all. She doesn't give a shit."

"But she still shot me."

"Yeah, but she didn't kill you. She shot me too. She had to or else she'd get whacked herself."

"Why would this Ledergerber want to kill me?"

"Probably because he was getting pissed with me." Jocelyn's eyebrow twitched and she could have sworn she heard Carly Simon singing "You're So Vain" off in the distance as Ethan continued. "But I'm pretty sure he was just done with whatever chapter you represented. I think what ticked him off had something to do with human trafficking." Carly Simon stopped singing.

"Human trafficking? What do I have to do with human

trafficking?"

"Nothing. But you were in direct contact with lots of people who were deep into it."

"I was?"

"Jesus Joss. Yes. You were in the belly of the God damn beast and because you had never been exposed to any of that sort of stuff, you couldn't recognize it. You were probably so nonchalant about it as it rolled by that they thought you were down with the sickness too." Jocelyn took a very deep sigh. The morphine was working and she felt no pain as her heart broke some more and Ethan rambled on. "Sex and slaves. It's all very profitable. Hell, even respected nonprofit organizations working with the spooks recognize this income stream."

"Like which ones?"

"Oh, I don't know. Try any foundation with an ex-US president's name attached, or one of those 'do it for the children' associations. Dig deep into any of these organizations and you'll find connections to dirty money. Rich people's money all mixed in with the proceeds of prostitution, drugs, diamonds, gold, radioactive material, not to mention human organs and guns. These are all serious sources of income for covert operations and, because of that, that money needs to get laundered and inevitably ends up on the balance sheets of these nonprofits and important banks. Heck, the logo for HBC bank was originally a poppy flower because they were making so much damn money off the opium trade. The money's got to get laundered somewhere. Think about it. Banks always have the tallest building in any city. It's not just car loans and home equity lines that build those skyscrapers."

"That sounds more like mafia Ethan. Organized crime. Why do you keep saying bankers?"

"Okay, I'll call them 'banksters.' Banks are legitimate businesses. The moving around of dark money stuff is not. They launder their money through connected organizations and banks. Currently they have arranged themselves, like the mafia has, into legit businesses. Burrowing themselves into government and corporations and creating straw men. This has been going on since the US was created.

"The biggest triumph of all for these assholes was the incorporation of the United States of America in 1871. The US government is a corporation Joss, and at this point it's a complete and total sham. These criminals have planted themselves deep within the company. Why do you think they're hell bent on nationalizing education? No Child Left Behind? Bullshit! They are indoctrinating everyone to believe that the normal person has some sort of working power within the bullshit system of governance. Seriously, what the fuck is the Electoral College all about?"

"It's so that New York and California don't—"

"Yeah, yeah, whatever. It's a big fucking game Joss. Elections for things like president—it's all a big show that keeps everyone captivated while the money moves where this other group has already predetermined it was going to go in the first place. Do you think they really care about *anything* critical for life on a mass scale?" Jocelyn was about to respond but Ethan keep talking. "No. No they don't. These people actually believe in *slavery*. 'Popular vote' is a subterfuge argument that only exists in the minds of the uninformed. While everyone's going nuts about the Democrats and the Republicans they are setting up funding for going off planet. Off. Fucking. Planet. Joss! This is not for the benefit of humankind. This is a business opportunity available for exploitation by a very select few."

"Alright. That's it," Jocelyn interrupted. "You've got to calm down Ethan. You're spiraling way out of control with this. Now we're talking about outer space. Who cares if someone wants to spend money to go to the moon—"

"Not the frickin' moon, Joss. Mars and beyond."

"Okay, fine. Who cares if someone wants to go to Mars and beyond? Let them do it. Seriously, good for them. Who cares if they want to spend their money doing that?"

"That's the point Joss. It's not their money!"

"Well then, whose is it?"

"It's ours! They stole it from us! It's a Ponzi scheme, get it? The average American worker is used as a time based debt slave for a very small percentage of the population. Modern day serfdom is an understatement. I'm takin' it all down Joss. All of it."

"I'm not following you."

"It's straw men buried in the wording of the pork—in the bills Congress signs. Next thing you know Congress will be worried about the weather in space or some bullshit thing and the Intelligence Committee will need to get their fingers on the bill and after that, suddenly it's black budget central. Alphabet agencies will be piling in to get their share of the money funneled into their projects which they will promptly lose into a pit of undocumented adjustments. There is no possible oversight at that point Joss. It's a parallel financial universe. These off-the-books, black budget initiatives are generating almost as much money as the entire US gross domestic product now."

"They are?"

"Yes and that's a fact. Naturally this lost money doesn't pay into Social Security or anything like that. And Joss, that's just the stuff the legit spooks are doing. Remember the billions missing from the Pentagon right before 9/11? Remember that?" Ethan waited as Jocelyn scrolled through her memory banks. "Conveniently, the Pentagon's accounting department got blown to bits the day after the Secretary of Defense, Donald Rumsfeld, testified that he had no clue where the money was."

"Oh, I remember that."

"Then that shit with the ninety-fifth floor of the North Tower." Jocelyn looked blankly up at him. "Remember that?" She shook her head no.

"You don't? Well, it's pretty funny how a commercial jet heads directly there, the fucking epicenter of a huge electronic money moving machine—the first of its type in the world—that linked AIG and Marsh & McLennan. It was just moving money back and forth and back and forth between the North and South Towers. Eventually the programmers and staff who suspected something was up reported what they were doing was probably illegal to their boss, who, upon finally acknowledging their concern, scheduled every single one of them in for a morning meeting on September Eleventh. They all got killed, of course, while that manager who scheduled the damn meeting was listening from the comfort of his upper west side luxury apartment. The only guy who lived to tell about this whole fucked up scheme was luckily stuck in a traffic jam and missed the meeting. I bet he's looking over his shoulder every day."

Ethan made a disgusted face and shook his head. Jocelyn noticed he was sweating. "And look, I'm not even getting into the friggin' gold stolen out from under the World Trade Center. Fuck. This money, Joss, all this wealth, it doesn't just disappear. It still exists. It's out there somewhere. It was stolen. Someone, or a bunch of people, made off with a lot of money and thought it would be okay to simply murder two thousand people and obliterate a good chunk of Manhattan to cover their tracks. These people are fucked. And it didn't just start with 9/11. Hell, look at Oklahoma City. It's been probably going on even longer than that. They simply don't care! So you getting shot and getting the bullets removed almost immediately at a nice cushy hospital and..." He chewed the inside of his cheek. "You've got your morphine. Just suck it up, okay? We've got real issues to deal with here."

Jocelyn scratched her forehead and grabbed for the ice cubes again. "Since when have you been into 9/11 and black budgets? And where'd you get all this information? The internet? You sound like a professional conspiracy theorist." She popped a cube in her mouth and started chomping on the ice as she waited for his answer.

"Ledergerber told me about the black budget stuff before I stabbed him and Ache got me up to speed with the intelligence community and how they operate."

"Okay," she raised her index finger. "Who's this Ache guy?"

"I've known him since my time in the Balkans."

"Is he Serbian?" Jocelyn asked.

Ethan shook his head no. "He's American. Half white, half Native American Indian. He doesn't talk much but he's wicked reliable and super stealthy. I'm glad to have him on the team."

"Oh, so there's a team involved?"

"Well, yeah. But it's more like a network than a team. There's no team captain."

"I'm not sure if that's a good sign Ethan."

"It's the only way this will work. This is a leaderless global revolution."

"Oh, Jesus…" Jocelyn shut her eyes and shook her head.

"Don't worry Joss. This bullshit will end. It's just a matter of when and how. History shows that it usually takes a big plague to kill off all the workers to starve them out because they can't do anything themselves, but we're approaching peak complexity. Entropy is bleeding out the system. They know this too, of course. We are in devolution and unfortunately, most people can't raise a tomato, let alone shoot a squirrel. The majority have absolutely no skillset whatsoever to take them to the level of a hunter gatherer or subsistence farmer. What will bring humanity back in line is collapse of the system and, realistically, the end of billions. We have to prepare for that."

"Billions? Of people? Or dollars?" Jocelyn asked.

"Both."

"Great." Jocelyn popped another ice cube in her mouth and stared at him long and hard. "Ethan, I don't know what happened to you, or what is currently happening to you, but I'm letting you know right now that what you're talking about is freakin' creepy and I think you should stop—"

"This is reality Joss. It's not pretty. It's not Hollywood-ized. But this is what is happening. The money powers have no home, no allegiance to any nation and they have taken over. They know this is the scene. There isn't much of the pie left. That's why some of them are looking at their options out in space. The others are earthbound and will beat the piss out of each other for a slice of the terrestrial pie—which means war for the rest of us. The more of us they kill off, the more for them. The most crafty, and possibly the most deadly of the bunch, will use their financial magic and slide into wherever with 'new products and services' to move digits around in incestuous, codependent, data streams. It's all going digital Joss. In fact, everything is moving very quickly into make believe land. And that's exactly how they want it. Hell, everybody likes it that way." He threw his hands up. "Fantasyland and a brand-new car!" Stopping only momentarily for dramatic effect he continued. "Governments want to skip the whole printing of money thing because it costs more money to actually print and distribute the currency than the currency is worth. So long as people can get food and water and keep moving that money around with all the service charges tacked on, it keeps working—*for them.*" He stressed that last part. "Joss, it doesn't even matter what the money is. It could be water, wampum, whatever! Heck, it could just be a cartoon, an untouchable, computer animated, twirling gold coin with a cool logo. They need to inject a new type of exchange unit because what they have going on is gonna completely implode and they know it."

"Look. I don't know how—"

"I know what you're gonna say." Ethan cut her off as he walked directly over to her and leaned on the bed. With their faces about eight inches apart he continued, "They've already got everyone's permission to do whatever the fuck they'd like to do. They'll fuck the kids, murder anyone they choose, create extinction events, and run their banana republic corporate empires any way they see fit. What everyone is dealing with, but they don't know it yet, is completely outside the popular concept of government. There actually *is* a parallel society that rules the world. It's us versus them."

At that, the door squeaked open a crack and a tiny voice said, "Mommy can I come in now? I need to use the bathroom." Jocelyn and Ethan, still locked in the drama of impending doom, blinked, and Ethan stepped back from the bed and opened the door for his daughter. William and Margret, who were jammed up against the door, basically tumbled into the room behind Lillian as she ran to the toilet.

Ethan rustled William's hair and Margret, looking more freaked out than ever, sought eye contact with Jocelyn.

"Where'd you guys go?" Jocelyn asked William.

"Nowhere. We just sat by the door."

"Oh." Jocelyn looked at Margret while addressing Will. "Did you hear Daddy and I talking?"

"Not really," Margret quickly offered.

"I liked the part about the spinning gold coin," William answered.

Ethan, Jocelyn, and Margret just looked at each other and Ethan said, "You'd think a house like this would be more soundproof."

"You'd think," Jocelyn commented as Lillian emerged from the bathroom, heading to Jocelyn's bed, and crawled up to assume her spot by her mother's feet.

"Can I get on the bed with you too?" Will asked.

"Sure, honey." Jocelyn patted the bed. "Get on up here." With that, Jocelyn felt her spirit rush back into her and her heart beat with pure love for her children.

As she relished the moment of humanity's return, Ethan's phone rang. She didn't hear what he said because she wasn't listening to him anymore, but she was surprised to hear him say, "Are you kidding me? Toy guns?"

CHAPTER FIFTEEN

Polk Correctional Institution
Polk City, Florida, USA
Cell Block 3

IF ALL OF THIS WAS just some bizarre misunderstanding and things were normal, Mark would have called work and told them to spring him from this prison cell immediately, but things weren't normal. He didn't even get a phone call before they locked him up, and even if he had, he wouldn't have known who to call anyway.

Things were obviously screwed up. *Why did Jerry have Crowley's business card?* kept circling around in his brain. What was clear in Mark's mind was that this numb nut, Jerry, who was connected to the missing person, Jocelyn McLaren, had something to do with his boss, Associate Deputy Director Fitzgerald S. Crowley—the guy that had flat out told him to focus on the missing woman and not worry about all the other stuff The Dump had brought to light.

"Crowley's in on this," Mark grumbled as he sat alone in his cell, festooned in a Day-Glo orange jumpsuit. He tried to remember the other Dump stuff and if any of it fit together: some sort of race car lawsuit, some jewelry, and an FBI in-house child pornography ring, and figured he might as well start there. *Someone on the inside must have got busted and maybe Crowley's providing cover or something.*

Mark slowly rocked back and forth on his cot with fists clenched as he riffled through every single thing Jerry had told him, or implied, since their initial late night contact and the scene at the Magic Kingdom. Mark was convinced that what he was experiencing, namely his car exploding and being inexplicably incarcerated, was about keeping him away from The Dump.

Is Jocelyn a distraction from the action? he asked himself, *or is she the key to this whole thing?* The troublesome thing about The Dump was that it was literally everywhere within the FBI. *What am I so close to that's making this as messed up as this? Why would anyone go through all this? Someone's buying time; otherwise they would have just killed me.* But then it occurred to Mark that if he hadn't been arrested, someone may very well have killed him when his car exploded. Maybe someone was trying to keep him alive. As Mark ruminated about that he ran his fingers through his hair and itched his scalp. *Those files. I gotta start there. But how do I do that if I'm locked in here?*

Mark was absently examining the remnants of dandruff in his fingernails when above the usual cacophony of jail sounds he heard the buzzing and clanging of one of the cells being opened. He looked up and saw Jerry being removed from the cell across from him. Jumping up, and almost in a panic, Mark yelled through the prison bars, "Jerry! Jerry!"

Jerry smiled at Mark and was about to walk over to him when the corrections officer redirected him by grabbing his elbow.

"Where are they taking you?!" Mark, clutching the bars, wanted to know.

"I'm going to learn how to use computers!" Jerry yelled over his shoulder as the corrections officer led him down the hall. "You should sign up too! It's free!"

Mark was going to yell back but instead swallowed his words when a loud buzzer sounded and a corrections officer and an enormous black man, who was built like a steamroller dressed in standard issue bight orange, appeared before him. "Say hello to Devaun," the corrections officer said. The cell door made a loud clunking sound and the CO ushered the man into Mark's cell. "Since things didn't work out between you and Emily maybe you and Devaun are better suited cellmates."

Devaun didn't acknowledge Mark. He headed directly to Mark's bunk and flopped down. On his back, he let his legs, which were supporting huge feet, cantilever over the end of the bed.

Mark was aghast but then got angry as the lock to the cell noisily clunked shut and the corrections officer walked away down the hall. "CO!" he shouted, "I don't belong here! Call the FBI field office!" It was at that moment Mark started crying.

CHAPTER SIXTEEN

Later
On the road to Mendoza
Argentina

ACHE DIDN'T HAVE TIME to screw around in Buenos Aires. He had wasted too much daylight waiting for confirmation that the peanut butter and plastic toy guns were actually the stuff he was supposed to be hauling around. Being surprised when the text "YES GO TO GLORY" came in, he had thrown everyone some cash and drove the El Camino, laden with the weight of the shipping crate, out of Puerto Madero. With both hands on the wheel he looked at the streets laid out in front of him and made a guess as to which path led to El Obelisco. Once he located that, he knew he'd be able to find his way.

Everything was very gray because of the winter weather, and he noticed that the colorful, striking angles and curves of the modern architecture associated with cruise ships and the fast ferry soon transformed into an 1800s European styled city. Gorgeous, yet tattered and obviously neglected, the densely populated capital of Argentina, Buenos Aires, featured the world's largest and widest tree-lined avenue with a centrally located, two hundred thirty-five-foot tall, white obelisk that unabashedly signaled, like only a gigantic alabaster phallus can, that Buenos Aires was an important global hub along with the city of London, Washington DC, and Vatican City. But unlike the city of London and Vatican City, this obelisk was not a pillaged artifact from ancient Egypt. This monument had been erected in 1936 in honor of the four hundredth anniversary of the founding of the city. A German company had completed the obelisk in a record time of thirty-one days, with one hundred and fifty-seven workers.

Ache only knew all this because B.B. regularly felt the need to ramble on about the construction of El Obelisco to showcase how awesome the Germans were at pulling off big technical projects. If Ache possessed any sense of humor at all he might have snickered at the dark irony of a German Argentinian, clearly a descendent of relocated Nazis, completely blowing off other German accomplishments during World War II, but Akecheta Whitebloom figured this omission was a symptom of a deep-seated sense of guilt and he found nothing to laugh at.

As Ache snaked the El Camino deeper into the bowels of the old city, he thought about B.B. He had known of the man and, more importantly, of his money for years now. It had been around the time that Ache had made the decision to slip off the radar that he had offered his services to CdW Enterprises. It had been Ache who had brought Ethan and B.B. together with lightning speed after the situation with Ledergerber.

The three of them were a good match. B.B. had the means at his disposal. Ethan had proven himself as serious and Ache, now inspired by the official motto of the Israeli Mossad "by way of deception thou shalt do war," was quick with the plan. Ache had handled not only the dosing of Jocelyn, but the surveillance camera situation in Tampa.

There had been only one ambulance, but through the miracle of modern digital filmmaking software, a network of satellites, and the internet, he had been able to completely obfuscate the particulars of Ethan and Jocelyn's escape from the US. It was simple cut and paste actually. Take the image of the ambulance from one tollbooth and overlay it on another image of another vehicle going through a different tollbooth somewhere else and press save. Sure, a decent analyst could probably figure it all out, but how long would that take? This was the beauty of Florida's abundant selection of highway tollbooths being digitally monitored at all times by a system created by a defense contractor with all files living on relatively low priority servers.

Meanwhile, Ache was grateful that Buenos Aires was so financially broke that they didn't have cameras mounted all over the place, not even in the thriving gold and jewelry district that he found himself in. Finally, he spotted the obelisk, and driving around it in the Batmobile-reminiscent black El Camino he noted how similar it was to the Washington Monument. Now knowing exactly where he was on his mental map, he pointed himself toward Route 7.

After almost forty minutes of stop-and-go inner city traffic, the city shadows finally spilled away behind him and he hit the open road. The engine was humming along perfectly and he twisted the big knob on the radio. He was surprised. The songs on the preset stations were mostly current US pop hits interspersed with Argentinian, hyper-masculine, superfast commentary on par with Univision's hit TV show *Sábado Gigante*.

He turned down the volume and looked at the fuel gauge. He would be driving through the night and he knew this car couldn't be good on gas. His first priority was to find a gas station and stock up. He'd find one.

The highway was very modern, four lanes, all well-kept

compared to the city itself. He remembered that B.B had told him that during the throws of the economic death spiral, Argentina had nationalized and sold off just about everything that had potential for income in order to pay back its enormous national debt. Major national companies, like utilities and roads, were sold at well below market value to foreign corporations. The country then had no means of creating its own income to maintain itself other than taxing its people even more. When all the income producing elements had been sold, the country began printing ridiculous amounts of money to cover its bills, which unleashed cataclysmic inflation on the poor Argentinians. Meanwhile, the proceeds of the privatizations were diverted into the pockets of corrupt officials. Hence the revolt in 2001.

It was only recently, in 2006, that Argentina got the International Monetary Fund off its back by using the very last of the national bank's reserves, which rendered its money pretty close to useless. Ache was happy for Argentina and hoped that they would never again be indebted to the IMF.

Ache shook his head as he thought about it. The whole mess in Argentina was because of $9.8 billion US dollars. He wondered if the people of the United States knew what their country owed to its creditors, or if they even knew enough to care. He watched as the sun started to set and he stepped on the gas, driving faster and faster into the twilight. It would all be over soon enough. He just didn't know what these cheap plastic guns and peanut butter had to do with it.

After another thirty kilometers Ache spotted a gas station with a convenience store and pulled in. He shut off the engine and as he was getting out of the car, two young men wearing winter parkas approached, obviously admiring the El Camino. "Bastante agradable," one of the guys said as he sauntered up and made a low whistle.

Ache nodded and headed into the store. He wanted to find a bunch of those 5 Gal./20 L. gasoline storage tanks, the type with a spout. Luckily for him they had a few on a shelf. He grabbed them all, but after doing the currency conversion in his head on the way to the counter, he was completely surprised by how much the things cost: forty dollars each. Sure Argentinians were used to bargaining, but in a gas station? For something like this? He plopped them down on the counter and did the obligatory haggling with the guy as a dramatic crash and breathless commentary of the Formula 1 Pirelli Belgian Grand Prix rambled in the background from the little TV behind the counter.

Ache ended up getting all four fuel tanks for thirty US dollars and the gas, of course, was extra. He paid, grabbed the gas cans, and headed out to fuel up. As soon as he stepped foot outside, one of the young El Camino aficionados, whom Ache immediately noticed had a tattoo of a stylized snake eating its own tail on his neck, slid up next to him and said in broken English, "You know you tienes something I need." This statement was immediately followed by the unmistakable sound of a jackknife being expertly swung open.

Mildly surprised and still holding all the gas cans, Ache kept walking and replied, "Let me guess. Dinero. Hold on, okay?" Then he saw the assailant's friend up in the bed of the El Camino trying to wedge open the shipping crate. "Hey! Alto! Stop!" and picking up his pace Ache began jogging to his car.

The guy with the knife stayed close by his side and grabbed Ache's arm. All the red gas cans tumbled to the ground and as Ache glanced down at his fallen purchase the man swung Ache's arm around behind his back and held the knife to Ache's throat. "No. No dinero. Mantequilla de maní."

"Seriously?" Ache asked. "You're holding me up for peanut butter?" Of course there was no indication anywhere on the crate that it contained mantequilla de maní. Ache instantly surmised that someone had tipped these jokers off. Probably the guys that he had lavishly compensated down at the dock. "Okay. Okay." Ache grumbled as the guy pushed him forward while twisting his arm harder behind his back. The razor sharp knife was less than a whisker away from killing him. "Okay. Mantequilla de maní. No problemo."

Suddenly and without any indication of a powerful counter attack, Ache executed a classic Krav Maga "defense against a knife to the throat from the rear" maneuver. With his free hand Ache instinctively grabbed the wrist of the hand holding the knife and violently yanked his assailant's arm down enough to thrust himself back and under, slipping his head out of the attacker's hold. The man must have known how sharp the knife was because once Ache had cunningly squirreled his way out of his clutches, the guy just kept backing away from his own blade, which he was still awkwardly holding but Ache was directing with brute force toward the guy's ribs. The two were both folded up in an origami-like lock grip. With arms and wrists bent so unnaturally it didn't take long for Ache to force the knife through the winter parka and into flesh.

"¡Carajo!" the defeated attacker exclaimed. The knife sliced the palm of his right hand as he attempted to block the fateful blow. Then, in rapid succession, Ache aggressively stabbed him again at least ten more times in the stomach. As the man was falling to the ground he whimpered, "Fuck." Clenching his wounds the man passed out, but Ache didn't notice. He had already turned his attention to the man attempting to break into the crate.

"Bolsa de ducha! Hey! Douchebag! Get your hands off my stuff!" he yelled, running over. The guy looked up but he didn't stop whacking the crate with a tire iron. In fact, he seemed to start smashing the crate harder and faster when he saw Ache was approaching. Just as Ache reached the El Camino the wooden crate cracked open, exposing the cases of peanut butter. The man snatched a case, jumped off the car, and ran toward the highway.

Ache chased him even though it did cross his mind to just let the poor slob have the friggin' peanut butter, but screw that; this guy's asshole friend was going to slit Ache's throat for it which meant that this guy couldn't be much better. Ache ran hard and overtook the man, tackling him to the ground. They both rolled down a dirt embankment and the case of peanut butter flew out of the thief's hands and tumbled onto the highway's breakdown lane. With cars swooshing by the two struggled and Ache spat out, "Who told you about the peanut butter?!"

Ache was just about to repeat the question more forcefully in Spanish when the guy replied in English, "I'll never tell, so help me God. Never!" With that, the man bit off what looked like a button on his winter jacket sleeve and instantly went flaccid in Ache's arms.

Confused, Ache released his grip. The man crumpled to the ground and did not move. Ache studied him. No movement. He checked for a pulse. Nothing. Ache grabbed the now certifiably dead man's arms and examined the sleeves of the jacket, looking for what the man had bitten. A little piece of black plastic was still stitched to the sleeve but it looked like a squished jellybean, deflated and just flopping around where a button used to be. *Cyanide?* Ache thought.

He looked at the cardboard box sitting in the breakdown lane and then back to the dead guy. He did a cursory pat down of the man and, finding nothing in any of the pockets, headed down the embankment to collect the box. With cars speeding by he was again thankful that Argentina was so poor. *No police,* he thought while picking up the box and running back up the embankment to the gas station.

The El Camino was still there with its broken cargo and beyond that the scattered red fuel tanks randomly stood their ground, but the man he had stabbed was gone.

CHAPTER SEVENTEEN

Later
Polk Correctional Institution
Polk City, Florida, USA
Cell Block 3

"SO, YOU IN LOVE WITH HER?" Abercrombie, the guy who was in for attempted murder, asked as he whittled at a bar of soap with a broken plastic spoon.

"Who?" Jerry responded, "The computer instructor?"

"Yeah." Abercrombie glanced up at Jerry lounging on the top bunk. "You keep talking about her and that class. I mean, you know the names of her kids, her dog, and where she went to high school. You really chatted her up. Is she hot?"

Jerry gave a sideways grin. "I guess, but she's totally not my type. She got mad at me for asking so many personal questions." He giggled. "That was right after I asked if she was married."

"Well, is she?"

"Nope. Divorced."

Abercrombie raised his eyebrows as he whittled away. "Maybe I should sign up for that class." He blew on his little sculpture and white flakes of cheap soap fluttered onto the floor and stuck to his orange jumpsuit.

Totally focused on his project, Abercrombie continued working while Jerry rolled over and stared at the ceiling, going through the day's events and wondering if what he had done was a good idea or not. Convincing himself that it really didn't matter at this point—*I mean, how could things get any worse?* He took a deep breath and then snickered about the teacher's password. He had tried it on a lark because it's one of the top corporate email passwords used in the United States, yet it made perfect sense that the prison's computer literacy teacher would use "FuckThisShit" as her password. He thought for sure it was going to be one of her kids', or even the dog's name.

Anyhow, he used the teacher's account that he had seen when she logged him into the class and "FuckThisShit" to get out and onto the main corrections department network and bounce himself over a few pathetic firewalls and then hurl himself into the wild expanse of the internet. The hardest part of the whole thing was the acting. He had been doing all this digital parkour while pretending not to know how to use Microsoft Word, and seeing as Microsoft really does suck, it wasn't impossible to appear discouraged and confused.

Once free-range, Jerry digitally ambled over to his home computer. He wanted to see if it was picking up the red wristband that he had slipped on the gun back at the Magic Kingdom. Much to his delight, it was! But he didn't have any concept of where the latitude and longitude were placing the gun, so he borrowed a pen and wrote the coordinates on his hand.

Then, out of some weird inspiration burst probably associated with not wanting to look like he had stolen the real guns or the cheap plastic guns, or more importantly the truck, he switched gears and snuck into the FBI network using the same exploit that he had recently used to contact Mark, only this time he didn't need the fancy footwork with the satellites. He had to admit that the satellites were primarily for flash, but still, it was wicked cool and he was glad he did it because he knew Mark thought it was cool too. Anyhow, Jerry typed Deputy Director Fitzgerald S. Crowley a short email before the class was dismissed.

Dear Deputy Director Crowley,

I know where the guns are. I didn't steal them or the truck. Someone who knows you came and picked them up. I also have your card safely stashed away and I will use it very soon.

Jerry

As Jerry lay on his bed he absently rubbed his stomach and wondered about the note. *Maybe I should have just asked him directly to get us out of here...* But Jerry really didn't trust Crowley. In fact, he felt a lot safer in jail than in the little witness protection program trailer they had set him up with. That's why he was so cagey in his note. He figured if he let Crowley know that he knew where the guns were, it might give him some leverage or protection or something. As he was analyzing his thoughts about personal safety and the effectiveness of his email, Abercrombie stood up from his plastic chair and gingerly held out his sculpted piece of soap for Jerry to see.

"So whaddaya think?"

"Aww, that's nice Abercrombie. What is it?"

"Can't you tell?" Crestfallen, Abercrombie stepped closer. "It's a crucifix."

"Oh...I see it now." Jerry leaned over the edge of his cot to really study it and was surprised to find every muscle and tendon of soap Jesus's anatomy precisely rendered. "Wow! You're really talented. That's pretty cool. And you did that with a broken spoon?" Abercrombie nodded. "But weren't you just reading the Koran?"

"I was reviewing my options." Abercrombie turned the little soap Jesus and looked at it. "You know Jerry, when I saw this bar of soap I knew there was something living in it and I had to pull away the mess that was burying whatever it was. I just let the soap talk to me, tell me what to do and, well, this was born."

"That's deep."

Abercrombie sighed as he looked at it. "Sure beats the covered wagon I did last week."

"So you whittle like this all the time?"

"Yeah," Abercrombie rubbed his neck with his free hand. "Usually I trade them for stuff worth more than the soap. Plus it gives me something to do while I wait for…"

"Release?" Jerry optimistically finished the sentence as he hopped off the cot.

Abercrombie pursed his lips and shook his head as he gently placed the soap Jesus on Jerry's pillow. "Release? Yeah, release…"

"Well, that's what I'm callin' it." Jerry took two giant steps, grabbed the bars and yelled out, "Mark! You home?!"

The cinderblock of the hallway bounced his voice around and wove it into a tapestry of mumbles and murmurs haphazardly embellished with exclamations. "Mark! I contacted Crowley!" Shouting over the din of the hallway he yelled, "CRR-OW-LEE! C'mon man! Talk to me!" Jerry saw Mark's orange jumpsuit move and he called out again. "Mark, don't be a jerk! Get up and talk to me!" Jerry waited in anticipation for Mark to respond or even move. He called out again. Someone laughed from far away but other than that, nothing but the perpetual hum of desperation.

Just as he was about to give up, the guy in the cell next to Mark started screaming and waving his arms through the bars of his cell. Mark sprung up from the bottom bunk and ran to the bars yelling something too. The big guy in with Mark stood up and came to the bars. Soon everyone was yelling. The wall of sound generated by the inmates was becoming more intense. The place was officially starting to go nuts. Jerry exaggeratedly made a confused face and mouthed the word "what?" over to Mark who was viciously pointing at him. Jerry pointed to himself and was still confused. Through the bars Mark gestured with his index finger as if he was swinging a lasso around. Now Mark's cellmate was yelling as if pleading with Jerry and pointing at him too.

"What's everyone freaking out about?!" Jerry yelled over his shoulder to Abercrombie while still trying to figure out Mark's hand motions. An ominous alarm blasted through the cellblock. Now Jerry was getting scared. All the locks on the cell doors clunked in unison and the alarm tone slowly died down, but the sound of the inmates got even louder. Jerry thought he heard someone yelling "Attica!" as random things were being thrown out of the cells at the four corrections officers racing toward Jerry. "Abercrombie, what the hell is going on?! Abercrombie?" Jerry turned fully around only to discover that his cellmate had hung himself.

"Oh Jesus!" Jerry rushed over to Abercrombie and grabbed him by the waist and with all his might tried to hoist him up, hoping to hold him up long enough so that Abercrombie could maybe breathe. The cell door clanked and swung open and two clambering corrections officers rushed in and squeezed themselves around the knocked over plastic chair. Jerry and the officers un-hung Abercrombie as the other COs stood out in the hall watching the action with hands resting on the teargas canisters on their belts. Soon an infirmary gurney rolled up to the door with more corrections staff and a nurse. Jerry watched helplessly as an unresponsive Abercrombie was efficiently transferred to it. Abercrombie was gray and his neck was unnaturally tilted to one side as the nurse carefully held an oxygen mask to his face.

"Oxygen? He's going to live?" Jerry asked one of the guards as the gurney got pushed away and the sounds of a potential riot subsided.

"If he does, he's gonna be all f'd up. You saw his neck," the guard commented. "He snapped it good." Jerry looked around the room trying to figure out what had just happened, and his eye fell upon the soap Jesus on his pillow. He would have maybe shed a tear had it not been for the guard trying to handcuff him. "All right, you're coming with me. This is a crime scene now."

Taken aback by the handcuff thing Jerry moved away toward the cell door, which was still wide open. "Dude, I just helped you guys. Why do I need to be handcuffed?"

"It's just protocol."

"You know what?" Jerry said as he sidestepped closer to the door, "Fuck this shit!" He bolted over to Mark's cell yelling at the top of his lungs, "I contacted Crowley!" Mark and his cellmate were wide-eyed watching Jerry approach. "I've got the get out of jail free card!"

he screamed, grabbing the bars to Mark's cell. "I know where the guns are!"

Instantly the uproar of impending riot reignited and ricocheted off the cinderblock walls. New buzzers and alarms rang out. Angry guards ran down the hall and the corrections officer Jerry had run away from quickly took Jerry down with a very painful non-bruise-inducing hold and handcuffed him. Much to the chagrin of the COs Jerry shat himself, and despite the awkwardness of walking with a stinky load of excrement in his pants while being escorted out of the block, he smiled broadly at Mark as he was led away.

CHAPTER EIGHTEEN

Meanwhile
Casa de Wolf

"WE NEED TO MAKE A PLAN," Jocelyn whispered to Margret in the dimly lit bedroom. The kids were cuddled up, fast asleep on the stack of blankets Margret had made for them on the floor. They had passed out from sheer exhaustion after Ethan left and hadn't woken since. "We've gotta get out of here. This is Crazy Town."

Making sure the kids were still asleep, Margret tucked a blanket around them and nodded. She whispered back to her daughter, "Honey, you need to recuperate. You need medicine and rest. That's the number one priority right now and as crazy as this is, maybe Ethan did make a good decision by bringing us here."

Looking at her mother in horror, Jocelyn whisper-screamed, "Mom! Are you out of your mind? This is nuts!"

Margret, rearranging the bottles of water she had snagged from the room service cart hours ago, little *con gas* bottles to the left and *sin gas* bottles to the right, quietly said, "Well, at least we have food and water Joss. You heard what Ethan said about conditions out there." She thumbed over her shoulder out the window to the moonlit mountains.

"Mom, the irony is, if we were back in the US and Ethan hadn't hauled all of us down here, food and water really wouldn't be much of a concern, now would it?" Jocelyn retorted as she grabbed one of the *sin gas* bottles from the nightstand, twisted off the cap, and took an angry gulp.

"Ethan made it sound like protecting all of us from whoever shot you outweighed the comforts of home. Plus, maybe this place isn't so bad," Margret said as she checked Jocelyn's tubes and the bags on the IV stand. "I'm going to find out if the results came back from the lab about that weird IV someone had you on. It will give me an excuse to take the kids out of the room in the morning and give you some quiet time. I think you need to just relax."

"I don't need quiet time." Jocelyn huffed but then she thought about it. "Mom, B.B. seems to like you. Have him show you around. He's the head honcho here. Do some reconnaissance."

Margret looked confused. "Reconnaissance," Jocelyn clarified, "you know, get the lay of the land. See what the deal is here. Find out where all the exits are; that sort of stuff. Oh, and try to find out where we are on the map."

Margret sighed as she rolled out the blankets on the floor and fluffed the pillow. "Jocelyn, I'm tired. I can't even think straight right now."

"I know Mom. I'm sorry," Jocelyn apologized and Margret gave a little nod but didn't say anything. "No. I am. I'm sorry I'm being so cranky with you. I'm really sorry you got dragged into all this. I can't believe this is even happening."

"Are you going to be able to sleep?" Margret asked as she laid down.

"I've got my morphine. Don't worry," Jocelyn quietly answered. "Why don't you get some rest? I'll keep an eye on the kids." Jocelyn carefully rolled to her side, making sure her IV tubes were just right, and shut off the light. "This is so messed up. Friggin' Ethan, I swear to God, Mom." Margret snuggled into her blankets and instantly fell asleep.

Meanwhile, although Jocelyn lay motionless in the dark, her mind was doing the equivalent of an Olympic gymnastics floor routine while wearing a bodysuit made of bubble wrap. All her effort was put into thinking of a plan of escape, but being hindered by the morphine her kinetic thoughts expanded and contracted with no logical resolution. Eventually, instead of being frustrated by her inability to reason, she shut her eyes and let her thoughts roll around in the bubble wrap, squishy and fun with little bursts of clarity and excitement. When all the little pops were expended she was asleep.

She looked down and saw with delight that she was wearing her red dancing shoes and a revealing dress. She was effortlessly spinning around as the dress ruffled like a red sine wave. The song was powerful. She didn't recognize it but she liked it. She stomped her feet to the beat and continued on with the prescribed dance steps which came easily. With her back arched and her arm outstretched, she was pulled in and spun into his arms. She gasped. The broken Christmas tree lights!

With their noses almost touching she dramatically looked away and their dance, a tango, continued along her line of sight. They moved as if a single machine. It was so mechanical how they were moving that the music began to change. It was now a tinny but sweet version of "Canon in D" by Pachelbel and Jocelyn realized that they were inside a Reuge music box. Their clothes had changed with the dance too. The dance was no longer a spicy Latin number with lots of fancy footwork, but rather a reserved classical thing of holding hands and gliding around in circles.

"What are we doing?" Jocelyn asked as she raised an arm decorated with embroidery and lacy frills.

"Appreciating art," the broken Christmas tree lights responded. He was wearing something out of the movie *Amadeus* and she realized that they both looked like they were in some sort of historical reenactment of European aristocracy in the 1700s. They both had massive wigs on. She might have laughed but didn't because it was all very serious, even with the twinkling of the music box. She continued with the Baroque minuet. One, two, three, and four, five, six controlled, ceremonious and graceful steps, but it was boring and exhausting.

"Why are we doing this?" she asked as they circled each other with their chins held high.

"To live," he answered simply. "This movement is life—the product of human processing of the life force. Any artifact of this processing is categorized as art." With that statement it was as if the rug had been swiped out from under her and she fell to her knees. Surprisingly it didn't hurt.

She looked up at him. He was now dressed in modern military desert camouflage. "Get up," he commanded.

"I can't," she gasped while attempting to push herself up. "I can't move my legs."

He looked disappointed and she was sad. The music stopped. "Then watch the art. Go where it takes you." Suddenly there was a scream in the distance. A child's scream. The camouflage morphed and wobbled, rendering him invisible in the sand dunes that now surrounded them. She sought out the broken Christmas tree lights as a focal point, but they were gone now too. The child screeched again, only this time she knew it was her daughter and she woke up.

The sun was shining intensely through the big picture window. It had snowed and the sky was making brilliant blue triangles between the white mountains. The bedroom with its race-to-space wallpaper seemed fresh with midday illumination. Blinking, Jocelyn saw her kids and mother standing with their arms outstretched. Two women were measuring them with yellow measuring tapes.

"Wha...what's going on?" Jocelyn asked as she rubbed her eyes. "Who screamed?"

"Oh! Mommy's up," Margret announced as Lilly grabbed a humongous stuffed teddy bear and ran up to Jocelyn's bed with it.

One of the measuring ladies glanced at Jocelyn and said, "Buenos," then unceremoniously got back to work measuring Will.

"Look what Mr. Wolf gave me!" Lilly gushed, presenting the nearly life-size bear to her mother. "Isn't he so cute!" she squealed.

"Did she wake you up?" Margret asked as a measuring tape circled her chest. "Lilly couldn't control herself when she saw it."

"They're taking our measurements," Lilly said matter-of-factly while clutching the jumbo stuffed animal.

"I see that. But why?" Jocelyn looked to her mother for the response.

"They're making our clothes for the party," Margret almost giggled.

"Seriously?"

"Custom made. I guess it's quicker and easier and just better than heading out to the city in this snow for something to wear. That's what B.B. told us this morning when he dropped off these clothes." Margret plucked at the sweater she was wearing and Jocelyn noticed for the first time that the kids had new sweaters and pants on too.

"Wow. That's just...wow," was all Jocelyn could say as she took in the scene with the seamstress, her mother and kids, and of course, the giant stuffed animal.

"Mom, should I name him Brownie or Blondi?" Lilly asked. "Mr. Wolf said his dad's dog's name was Blondi. What do you like better? Brownie or Blondi?"

"Oh, Brownie. Hands-down. Brownie," Jocelyn answered. "He's kind of a light brown so the name totally fits." Lilly enthusiastically hugged Brownie while Will, who had just finished having his inseam measured, bounded over to Jocelyn and pulled something out his pocket. "Look. I made this for you." He unfolded a piece of paper and handed it to her.

"Aww..." She kissed him on the head. "Thank you." Jocelyn took the paper and turned it around. "What is it?"

He leaned in close and said, "Nana told me to draw you a map. We walked all around this morning. See," he pointed, "these are the rooms. The doors look like this and these are the stairways." Having a new appreciation of the blue ink lines on the sheet of copy paper, Jocelyn patted the bed and the kids and Brownie all piled on to talk about the particulars of the map.

As soon as Margret walked the seamstresses to the door she

hustled over to join everyone on the bed. "They don't have the mystery IV lab results back yet." She shook her head. "I guess things just move slower here, but Joss, you've got to see this place! It's amazing," she happily reported while looking over Lilly's head to admire William's map. "He actually did a pretty decent job on that thing," she commented, pulling a road map out of her back pocket and unfolding it.

"Where did you get that?" Jocelyn asked, absolutely astounded that her mother and kids really did do reconnaissance work.

"Oh, this place is a winery. There's the tasting room," she pointed to William's map, "right here. We didn't get to see everything so Mr. Wolf is taking us on the wine tour later today. The tasting room is connected to a restaurant called The Wolf's Den," she sort of giggled, "We went there." Still pointing to the map she continued, "And they have tourist stuff sitting around. Of course, it's all in Spanish, but at least we can get an idea of the roads," Margret said, running her finger down one of the highways on her tourist map. "Looks like we're about 120 kilometers away from Mendoza International Airport. What do you think that is in miles?"

Jocelyn grinned. "You guys rock! Seriously. I love you all so much." As they tumbled into a group hug Jocelyn's gaze fell squarely upon the portrait of the woman, the one painted by someone inspired by Mary Cassatt, on the wall opposite her. She couldn't put her finger on it, but it spooked her.

CHAPTER NINETEEN

Parque General San Martín
Mendoza, Argentina

EXHAUSTED, ACHE CAREFULLY DROVE the El Camino through the massive French Renaissance inspired gates and was greeted by tall palm trees, heavy with snow, lining the park's main thoroughfare. He was tired, really tired, and the palm trees and snow didn't seem to jive. He blinked against the glare and adjusted his Oakley sunglasses. Last night's journey had been challenging mostly because of the weather and how the car was handling. He was grateful that he had that giant smashed up crate full of peanut butter in the back for weight, but still, it was tricky. What had made the thirteen-hour journey really miserable was that the car's heater simply didn't work, no matter how much noise it made.

Naturally, he had been on high alert all night because of the scene at the gas station, and since that time his field of vision had narrowed. He was laser focused as if looking through a drinking straw. His peripheral vision was gone. What he saw was what he saw. His body had neither time nor extra energy to waste on anything not directly confronting him. He had to make sure he double-checked everything, everywhere. This was not a new sensation. He had experienced all this before and it was oddly comforting. Somehow it felt like he was back in Kosovo. Kosovo with snow. Kosovo with snow and palm trees. Weird.

Everything was covered with snow and the park was alive with distracting dashes of colorful activity. Bright winter jackets, snow hats and mittens frolicking around, offset by the dazzling clarity of white snow, made the merriment of the Mendoza residents even more pronounced in contrast to Ache's involuntary fight-or-flight panic. Everything was vibrant and full of cheer but Ache was on edge, as if a giant elastic band was being pulled somewhere deep within him and getting ready to snap. Strange, because he was so tired but at the same time so jazzed and he was craving a gun. Just to hold it would calm him down and put everything into perspective, and not one of those cheap plastic toy things he was hauling around; a real gun, a real gun and a cup of super strong coffee.

Taking a deep controlled breath, Ache gripped the steering wheel. It was as if the snow day had created a municipal holiday or something. Mothers happily building snowmen with their children looked up when they heard the rumble of the El Camino slowly approaching. An errant snowball thumped against Ache's car, causing him to flinch and swear under his breath. He was breaking into a sweat despite the freezing temperature inside the car. He drove past the snowmen and snow angels to the little manmade lake, shiny with ice, and drove apprehensively through the arboretum toward Cerro de la Gloria, or Glory Hill. It wasn't manmade but it was small enough and manageable enough to be included in the footprint of the park.

Heading for the meeting place at the peak of Glory Hill, Ache noticed the pitch of the road beginning to rise dramatically and soon the El Camino was working a lot harder. The road was constructed to spiral around the landmass as it took him higher and higher to the summit. Precarious hairpin turns in the snow, slipping and sliding, on the edge of a cliff while commanding a vintage muscle car, in other words flirting with death, gave Ache purpose. Finally, after pulling around the last hairpin he saw, at the far end of the empty parking area, an impressive memorial monument.

Ache shut the engine off and made note of the stone steps leading even higher to the monument's prominent base. He scanned the contours of the bronze composition for hidden snipers and when somewhat satisfied that none were present, he took in what he was looking at. The base of the statue was covered with bronze reliefs depicting the struggles of the Argentinian and Chilean people as they supported their rebel armies, working together to drive out and defeat their colonial ruler, Spain. General San Martin, and placed lower in the composition, the Irishman General O'Higgins, each on horseback and flanked by the officers of their cavalry, supporting the central and most important feature of the sculpture, a raucous battle giving rise to a mighty winged woman. In victory she dominates, holding her hands to heaven, showcasing her broken shackles and chains. Even Ache had to admit to himself that the whole thing was a pretty powerful tribute to the first successful South American revolution for independence over two hundred years ago, but he didn't have time to appreciate the art.

He studied the terrain. Trees. Lots of pine trees covered with snow surrounded the parking lot. No visible footprints or evidence of other cars. Damn, he wanted a gun. It was creepy quiet not hearing the rumble of the engine after thirteen hours straight. He wiped his nose and as his view darted around the landscape, he debated whether he should get out of the car or lay down on the seat to avoid a headshot. He decided to lie down.

He was staring at the upholstery of the ceiling when a muffled, "Whaddaya takin' a nap?" blast such an enormous burst of adrenaline into his system that it would have killed an otherwise healthy individual. Ache instantly smashed the driver's side door open with a powerful two-legged kick, and the man who had been leering at him through the window was forced to stumble away, allowing Ache the opportunity to quickly exit through the passenger door.

Sweating and heart beating to break his chest, he rolled under the car and watched the winter camouflage boots slowly circle the El Camino. "Buddy, it's me. What the hell?" The man knelt down and peeked under the car. "You okay?"

Realizing it was Ethan a wave of relief bathed Ache's body. "No," he replied honestly, "but what's with the peanut butter?" he asked from beneath the car.

"What peanut butter?"

"The stuff I've been driving around. Someone tried to kill me for it."

"Seriously?" Ache nodded and Ethan sighed. "Well, you know how desperate these people are Ache, but I'm confused. I thought you had guns."

"I've literally got toy guns and peanut butter in that crate. The people who came after me are professionals." Ethan's brow furrowed as Ache continued. "One killed himself with what was probably cyanide. Another is at large and has stab wounds."

"What the hell?" Ethan glanced at the crate. "I guess that explains why it's all busted up." He pushed back the hood of his jacket. "Can you get out from under there?"

Ache shimmied out from under the car and brushed the snow from his pants. The two of them hopped up onto the bed of the El Camino to look at the contents of the crate.

"Oh, so now there's peanut butter involved?" Ethan groaned. "What the hell is going on Ache? We ordered up guns. Shit, there's enough real ones floating around. How did we end up with this?" With his fingers tapping a cardboard case of peanut butter he continued, "These were your people, your connections, were they not?"

"Yes." Ache nodded solemnly. "I don't understand either. These guys are seriously top of the line, globally recognized dealers. I requested the most powerful arsenal available and…"

"We didn't already pay for this crap, did we?" Ethan interrupted as he tossed one of the chunky little plastic guns back into the shipping box. Ache nodded yes. "Fuck."

While Ethan stood, looking forlorn at their purchase, Ache noticed Ethan's footprints in the snow and asked, "How'd you get here?"

"Huh?"

"There's no car. How'd you get here?"

"Oh, I climbed up."

"Impressive, but why?"

"I needed to confirm the coordinates of that place that sells the cell phones," Ache nodded like that was a logical answer to his question. "I got a ride to the park on a tour bus and then climbed up the side of Glory Hill. B.B. said he'd arrange for pick up. I guess he didn't want a load of guns driving through a wine tasting or something." Ethan pulled back his sleeve to look at his watch. "They should be here by—" but before Ethan could finish his sentence the wind picked up and the unmistakable batting of helicopter blades could be heard. A yellow Eurocopter Super Puma zoomed up and noisily hovered above them, clearing the snow in the parking lot.

Under the powerful blast of air, Ethan yelled to Ache, "You know these guys?!" Ache shook his head no. "Neither do I!" Still looking at the helicopter Ethan pulled his Sig Sauer P226 out of his jacket pocket and thrust it to Ache. "Cover me!"

Ethan whipped out his cell phone and began texting. Shielding his eyes with one hand, Ache kept the gun pointed at the underbelly of the Super Puma until it finally dropped two long, orange cables equipped with an assortment of bungee tie-downs and a roll of duct tape. Ethan tucked the phone into his pocket and giving the thumbs-up yelled, "Wrap it up!" Ache made sure the lid of the crate was securely in place with duct tape and Ethan started expertly slinging the cables and bungee cords around.

When they were satisfied that it was secure they both hopped up onto the crate and Ethan yanked the cable three times. Each holding the cable with one hand, they had their guns pointing straight up at the helicopter. The crate lurched and then slowly it and its hitchhikers rose up into the wicked, whirling wind. Ache, still holding his gun high and ready to fire, noticed the memorial statue below as it slid into his drinking straw vision. From this vantage point the magnificent bronze woman appeared to be offering her shackles and chains directly to him. Assessing that the statue wasn't a lethal threat he repositioned his gaze on the helicopter, but the image of that winged woman and the chains lingered.

Finally, they were within distance of the cargo hatch. Ache hurled himself into the helicopter and rolled to the rear of the craft while quickly surveying the dark interior for threats. Springing to his feet he locked both hands around his pistol and aimed it at the crane operator just as Ethan and his gun came flying through the hatch and landed in prone position in front of the crane controls. The crane operator didn't really look at either of them but stayed focused on the cargo he was managing. Once the cargo was safely on board Ache grabbed the crane operator, and quickly and aggressively patted him down. He nodded at Ethan and Ethan crawled into the cockpit. The pilot had an orange helmet on and didn't seem to notice Ethan's presence until the gun was jammed into the base of his neck. The man's shoulders visibly braced and Ethan, still holding the gun in position, came around to make eye contact with the man.

"What are you going to do? Kill me too?" the young, brown-eyed pilot with the thin little mustache sneered with an almost perfect American English accent.

Ethan studied the face and tried to place it. He took the gun away from the pilot's neck and, still keeping it trained on the man, sat down in the copilot's seat. It took a few seconds, but when Ethan finally figured it out he was impressed that the guy who had been scrubbing blood off the floor in Jocelyn's room knew how to fly a search and rescue helicopter. The cargo doors smashed shut and Ethan asked, "So where are we heading José?"

The Super Puma shot straight up and banked sharply south. "San Carlos de Bariloche."

CHAPTER TWENTY

Meanwhile
Polk Correctional Institution
Polk City, Florida, USA
Warden's office

WARDEN CALHOUN, wearing latex gloves and holding the specimen with what looked like salad tongs, was quiet for a long pause before he asked his secretary, "Who did the cavity search?"

"Barnes, sir," the secretary answered confidently while flipping through the file.

"Well, get him in here too." The secretary nodded, folded up the file and left the room. Warden Calhoun placed the specimen down and slowly began peeling off the gloves while looking disapprovingly at handcuffed Jerry. He casually tossed the gloves into the wastebasket and remarked, "You just opened a whole can of bullshit. You know that, right?" Steely-faced, Jerry did not respond.

A profound silence was trapped between the drop ceiling and the Home Depot area rug as the warden and Jerry braced for a staring match, but a hasty knock at the office door shattered the intense but short-lived contest and, as if pushed, Mark stumbled in. He was in his orange prison gear, hands cuffed, looking extremely tired and irritated. A beer bellied corrections officer directed him to the chair next to Jerry in front of the warden's desk.

"Thank you McGaven. You don't have to stay." The corrections officer nodded and exited, closing the door behind him. Mark and Jerry cautiously checked each other out.

Watching him as he uneasily plopped into the chair, the warden asked Mark, "Do you have anything you'd like to add to this little drama?"

"I want to see my lawyer."

The warden raised his eyebrows. "That's a pretty logical thing to say but I don't think that will be necessary."

"Red flag! Right there!" Jerry shouted as he hopped, still handcuffed, out of his seat.

"Calm the fuck down Apario!" the warden blasted back. "I'm getting really sick of your shit!"

"Yeah Jerry. Shut up," Mark added.

"No. I'm not going to shut up! This is bullshit. I produced the get out of jail free card and the next thing you know I'm in solitary and you're telling my friend not to call a lawyer!"

"You spent all this time in solitary?" Mark asked.

Ignoring Mark, Jerry continued, "Okay, then we don't want a lawyer. We want Associate Deputy Director Fitzgerald S. Crowley. Now!"

"I spoke to him."

"You did?" Jerry and Mark replied in unison. Calhoun nodded.

"Then, for God's sake, why are we still handcuffed?" Mark asked.

"You're being transferred to a federal prison."

"What?!" Mark and Jerry bellowed. Now Mark was on his feet.

"This is patently absurd!" Mark screeched. "We didn't *do* anything!"

"That's really not my concern right now. The feds will be here shortly to collect you." Jerry and Mark were aghast. It was at this very moment of "lost for words despair" that the door opened and CO Barnes walked in.

"You wanted to see me boss?"

Warden Calhoun nodded to Barnes and pointed at Jerry. "Did you do the cavity search intake on this guy?"

Barnes studied Jerry and nodded. "Yeah."

"You're fired."

"What!? Why?" Barnes quickly shot back.

"Damn it," Warden Calhoun griped as he stood up. "Now I've got to put these gloves on again. Hold on." He snapped on a new pair of latex gloves. Forgoing the salad tongs, he snatched up the sample sitting on the tray on his desk and held it up. "You mean to tell me you missed this during that intake?"

Barnes was seemingly confused but Mark knew exactly what the crumpled little tea-stained rectangle was.

"I…I guess so. What is it? A sheet of acid or something?"

"No! It's a God damn fucking business card! Now get your stuff and get out!"

"What? You're kidding, right?" CO Barnes looked at the two miserable handcuffed inmates standing by the desk for confirmation. When he didn't get any he spat out, "But Greene still has his job! The guy he did intake on had an actual shank jammed up his ass and I'm getting fired for a business card?" Barnes was trembling.

"This is different," Calhoun interjected.

"Bullshit! It's because I'm black. Isn't it?"

Calhoun shook his head. "No. Just get out Barnes."

"Oh, you'll be hearing from the union and the NAACP about this!" Barnes proclaimed as he started backing out the door. "If this fucks with my retirement, I swear to God Calhoun," he pointed at the warden, "I'll kill you myself! I haven't dragged my sorry ass into this hellhole for fourteen years to deal with skids just for the fun of it!"

"Goodbye Barnes."

Barnes stomped out waving a middle finger.

Jerry and Mark looked at each other while transmitting SOS signals telepathically to each other.

"Did you see what you just made me do?" Warden Calhoun said as he wiped his brow and sat back down in his Staples office furniture executive desk chair. "Barnes is a good guy and he lost his job because of you."

"Screw you." Jerry nudged the phone with his handcuffed hands. "I want Crowley on the phone right now."

"Yeah." Mark kicked the desk for added effect. "Right now!"

"You don't need a phone. I'm here." All heads turned as Associate Deputy Director Fitzgerald S. Crowley, outfitted in a bone-colored Brooks Brothers cotton poplin suit, strode in like he owned the place. Two corrections officers in federal prison uniforms followed him. Warden Calhoun jumped from his chair and hurried around the desk to shake Crowley's hand. Mark and Jerry, completely shell shocked, were silent as they watched the exchange of niceties.

"Thank you for holding these two until we could get the paperwork straightened out."

"Well, I'd like to say no problem, but this guy," Calhoun pointed to Jerry, "he's a real handful. Spent last night in solitary."

With hands on his hips and nodding thoughtfully, Crowley looked at Jerry and commented, "You don't say. Thanks for the heads-up. We've got them covered now." He cocked his head to the federal prison corrections officers. "Gentlemen, please escort these inmates to the bus."

"Are you fucking kidding me?!" Mark yelled as the feds instantly swooped down and locked up his ankles to Jerry's in chain gang style. After a few more pleasantries between the warden and Crowley, Jerry and Mark's prison-issued cheap black plastic shoes, inspired by the popular Crocs brand, shuffled out the door. Jerry appeared to be deep in thought with his head hung low and Mark was raging, "I never got a fucking phone call!"

As they walked they quickly learned that their stifled movements were more efficient if done in unison. Their tiny steps, controlled and ceremonious, were boring and exhausting as they trudged through the long, beige hall and out to the sweltering parking lot. One and two. Three and four. Five and six. Six, six, six ripples of heat rose from the pavement as the door on the big blue bus swung open to welcome them aboard with a heavenly blast of air conditioning.

Once settled on board, still cuffed together and miserable, Crowley hopped into the bus and dismissed the guards. Mark burst out, "Oh, is this where you just fucking shoot us?! What the hell is going on Crowley?!"

Crowley, leaning casually on one of the bus seats replied, "I could ask you the same question S. A. Witherall. Aren't you supposed to be searching for a missing woman? Suddenly you end up in jail with this guy?"

"Well, it's not like you didn't anticipate that eventuality. You gave him your card and told him it was, and I quote, a 'get out of jail free card.' Isn't that right Jerry?"

"Yeah. That's what you said."

"I gave the card to him, not you Witherall. I could have left you in there just now but I didn't, did I?" He threw each of them a large plastic bag filled with their pre-prison clothes and possessions. After Mark's bounced off his chest and Jerry's bag smacked him in the head Crowley said, "Guess what? Now you're free."

"So you gonna unlock us?" Jerry asked.

"In a little while. We just have to get some distance between this place and you roaming around."

"I'm not falling for it Crowley." Mark angrily shook his head. "There's more to this. I don't have a car. It exploded, as if you didn't already know. You're obviously in cahoots with Apario over there," he cocked his head toward Jerry, "and I just spent like forever in hell and now I have you springing me from jail with some psychological head trip that I'm supposed to be happy about all this?" Crowley looked as if he was going to say something, but Mark barreled on. "On top of that, has anyone been looking for Jocelyn McLaren this whole time?"

Jerry tore his gaze away from his reclaimed possessions bag. "Yeah. What's the deal with Jocelyn?" he wanted to know.

Crowley sort of shook his head no. Mark exclaimed, "Ta-ha! I didn't think so! This was all about keeping me away from that case!"

Crowley raised his hands, palms up, as if he was being held up at gunpoint. "Look, all I know is that I got an email, supposedly from

Apario, that said he knew where the guns were. If that hadn't rolled in, I wouldn't even have known you were here. So you can feel free to thank Apario for that. You guys are now going dark."

"What the hell does that mean?" Mark questioned.

"It means you're officially ghosts." Jerry perked up. "No one will miss Apario." Jerry feigned insult and Crowley continued while ignoring him. "He's already scrubbed because of the witness protection program, and you Witherall," he looked meaningfully at Mark, "your car blew up. You're dead. It's been listed in the all the relevant local papers. Closed casket ceremony. GoFundMe accounts set up to accept donations in lieu of flowers for the Mark Witherall Always Love Foundation."

Mark was at a loss for words. "The Mark Witherall Always Love Foundation?" he sputtered.

"It's how we're moving money for this operation. The fund is raising money for kids and their families affected by gun violence."

"What the…?"

"Standard procedure. Works really well with social media these days. Tax free donations come rolling in to support the cause, the money gets clean, and we get moving."

Mark shook his head incredulously. "But how…how can you do that?" Crowley gave Mark a "you've got to be kidding me" glare and Mark asked, "Does my mother think I'm dead?"

Crowley nodded. "We sent someone out to notify her, but she didn't attend the funeral."

"I…I don't believe this." Mark was reeling as he sat quietly processing the news of his death, imagining his mother spiraling down the alcoholic, whacky heartbreak slide and his father persuading her not to go to the funeral.

Jerry, on the other hand, was ready for action. "So what's the plan?"

"First you tell me about the guns. Where are they?"

Jerry looked at his handcuffed hands and held them up so that Crowley could see the faded ink scribbled on his palm. "I wrote the coordinates on my hand but now it's pretty faded."

Frowning, Crowley made his way through the school bus seats, grabbed Jerry's shackled hands, and examined them. "You don't have anything other than this to show me?"

From somewhere between annoyed and helpful Jerry replied, "Maybe if you'd un-handcuff us and let me get to my computer at my trailer…it will take like five minutes tops." Crowley studied Jerry as he considered this. “Seriously. It doesn’t take a lot of time if you know what the heck you’re doing.”

That last comment pushed a button and Crowley spun on his heels and exited the bus. Instantly, a federal prison guard’s shaved head popped up in the stairwell, the doors closed, and the bus sighed and hissed before driving out of the Polk County Correctional Facility parking lot with Jerry and Mark howling in protest.

CHAPTER TWENTY-ONE

Casa de Wolf
La Galleria y Sala de Fermentación

"OH, ISN'T THIS WONDERFUL kids?" Margret enthused while studying a five-foot tall acrylic painting of a Swatch watch. The kids, with Brownie in tow, were more interested in the life-size sculpture of a man with a briefcase constructed entirely of colorful plastic shopping bags entitled "Inversor de Angeles."

The place was deathly silent yet filled with light. The fifty-by-thirty-foot white-walled gallery they were meeting Mr. Wolf in had high ceilings and was primarily lit by daylight emanating through an expanse of plate glass, allowing for a view of the snow-covered garden outside. This panorama of the natural world dramatically contrasted with, and in a strange way very much complemented, the expertly displayed artwork inside.

"Don't touch anything," Margret cautioned the children as she wandered over in silence to a glass jewelry case centered below a series of gritty, large format, framed, black and white photographs depicting urban decay. Noticing that the artist had included a dirty and shoeless little girl with mussed up hair wearing a tattered Mickey Mouse shirt and eating a McDonald's hamburger somewhere in every shot, Margret leaned over and read the name of the series, "Big Mac Index," and wondered, *Who in their right mind would hang this in their home?*

She chose to avert her eyes and look at something else. Like a mouse, she was drawn in and captivated by the shiny contents of the case underneath the photos. Six brilliantly bejeweled butterfly pins by an artist listed as Carlos Delohim were perched as if ready to fly away.

"Stunning," Mr. Wolf commented as he noiselessly slid up behind her.

"Oh!" Margret gasped as she placed a hand over her heart. "You startled me," and then regaining her composure softly replied, "Yes, these butterflies certainly are magnificent."

Mr. Wolf, with eyebrow arched, huskily whispered, "I was not speaking of the jewelry." Margret blushed and bit her lip. Looking away, she fixed her hair behind her ear and saw the kids on the other side of the room watching her with Mr. Wolf. She called out to them.

"Guys, come over here and say hello to our host." The kids looked at each other and hesitantly started walking over. The sound of their footsteps on the battleship gray floor echoed as Margret turned her attention back to the jewel encrusted butterflies and Mr. Wolf. "This gallery is lovely. Very contemporary. Is this your personal collection?"

"No, darling." He smiled, shaking his head. "No. The work is curated by a friend of Tito's from Christie's auction house. The men, they change exhibits quarterly. Tito, in his brilliant mind, had the idea that this place would be a gallery for private viewings and he worked the deal for the space. They pay me to fill my world with art like this."

Impressed, Margret crossed her arms across her chest, surveying the place like a housing inspector, silently imagining what she would charge per square foot for rent.

"Of course," Mr. Wolf said, "if the sale was not to be going so well, the salesman might ply his client with more of our wine." He laughed, pointing to an illuminated glass case on the other side of the gallery displaying, as if crafted by a Renaissance master, bottles of Casa de Wolf Malbec. Margret politely smiled at his comment as the children approached and the sound of echoey footsteps stopped.

"This art dealer and many of Tito's other friends will be flying in for our party. It will be a very, very wonderful party," he said for the benefit of the children who were sheepishly standing behind their grandmother. "Is Blondi coming to la fiesta too?" Wolf asked Lillian.

"Brownie," Lilly corrected, fiercely hugging the stuffed bear.

William added, "She ended up naming him Brownie because he's brown."

"Ah, sí. Muy bien." Wolf smiled. "But William, do you not get to hold Brownie? It is gift for the two of you."

"That's okay. She needs Brownie more than me."

Nodding, Mr. Wolf considered what Will said. "You are a good brother. Come." He gestured for them to follow him to a set of double doors. "Let me show you how we make the wine." He pulled a big ring of keys out of his jacket pocket and unlocked one of the ten-foot doors. It creaked open as he pushed it and then he stood aside with his arm outstretched, ushering them in.

As the kids, Brownie, and Margret crossed the threshold and the doors shut behind them, they were hit with the smell of fermentation and a marked drop in temperature. With their eyes adjusting to the relative darkness, the hum of tiny electric motors might as well have been the opening salvo of the classic film *2001 A Space Odyssey*.

They all craned their necks to appreciate the massive, stainless steel fermentation tanks.

"Also we have cement fermentation," Mr. Wolf announced when everyone seemed to have had enough of tank gazing. "The winemakers have told me that it is better than the steel," Mr. Wolf said, pointing to a wall that looked like something out of a submarine covered with different sized hatches and embedded digital displays. They all snaked through the tall, steel tanks to get a better look at the wall. "We shall see if it is superior. We bought this when Tito first arrived years ago to create our most special wine to be released during the 2016 UN International Year of the Woman."

"Why, that's years away," Margret commented.

"Tito assured me it was worth the cost because this wine would most certainly be consumed in the US during celebrations of that year. But, I do not know," Mr. Wolf said, tapping his chin. "Do you make a big deal out of the United Nations in the US?"

"Not really," Margret shook her head almost in apology. "2016 is an election year though," she offered as consolation.

Wolf sighed. "Regardless, the grapes for this wine were all handpicked by women. Solamente women. The women, they are gentler with the fruit as they pluck it from the vine," he said, gesturing as if delicately holding a grape between his thumb and index finger. "The sweetness of the grape is preserved for fermentation and will allow for the extraordinary qualities of the Mendozan terroirs to express themselves." He sighed as if in ecstasy about the wonder of it all and continued. "The winemaker for this whole project is, as well, a woman. I am very interested to see how this wine presents itself, if it will be any different. We have invested greatly and put ourselves against the men."

"What do you mean?" surprised, Margret questioned. "Against what men?"

"The men we have always hired are angry for no work and complain that they cannot support their families. That this is somehow robbing them of their masculinity." Margret looked concerned and Mr. Wolf added, "This is the beauty of nature. Another crop is always coming. We will hire eventually the men again at the same price as the women."

They all stood in silence just looking at the wall. The fact that the women got paid less than the men was not lost on Margret but she didn't bring it up. Instead she mused, "I've never thought about how a company does its marketing so far in advance, and how it drives production."

"Oh, I know," Mr. Wolf responded. "That is why Tito was so magnificent. He knew of trends. I remember when he explained to me how new automobile colors were settled four years before the autos were released to the public. Same with the finishes of household appliances, many years in advance. Then that color pallet," he motioned with his hand as if plotting points on a timeline, "goes on to inspire the set designs for the entertainment industry and the many lines of clothing. It is absolutely amazing if you think of it," he tugged on his jacket, "all this reality being created years ahead of us, just waiting for us to simply buy into it. That is why campaigns, campaigns to win the market, are so integral and so fierce. Much has been invested. Sometimes, Tito told me also, that a campaign can be as long as a generation."

"Really?" Margret shook her head in disbelief.

"Sí, a very good bottle of wine can be aged ten years, perhaps twenty. That is why I remain skeptical of the new cement tanks. Why would wine taste better sitting in cement?" He sighed and they all looked at the submarine wall. "But, in my defense, it did take me a long time to adapt to the stainless steel," he said, placing his elbow on a ladder propped against the wall as he considered the towering steel tank.

Noticing that the kids were migrating to the oak barrels stacked up on the other side of the warehouse, Margret asked while pointing to them, "Do you still use barrels to ferment?"

"To age," he corrected her. "This is the traditional way to do it." Wolf smiled as he and Margret turned and walked toward the barrels and the kids. "The good old fashioned way," Wolf said, clearly proud of his usage of the phrase, "but no. We have used barrels from the French and North America in the past…"

"You're kidding me. Can't you make the barrels here?"

"We have never made them here. Argentina does not have proper wood for barrel. Since the steel tanks arrived, we age our wine without the oak. I still have barrels sleeping in the cellar holding wine waiting to be bottled though. I will show you."

Just then a steamy hiss and then a full-bodied BOOM! rang out startling everyone. In unison, they all spun around to witness an explosion of grape slurry, bursting forth from the top of fermentation tank number three like a grade school science fair volcano gone fantastically awry. Loud warning alarms rang out as if a nuclear meltdown was occurring.

Needless to say, Margret and the children were startled and Lilly was crying, burying her sobs into Brownie. William instantly jabbed his thumb into his mouth and stood like a jack-lighted deer watching the scene unfold. With William not in danger, Margret dashed to Lilly's side and began soothing her by rubbing her back. Leaving his confused guests to simply watch him, Mr. Wolf casually walked over to number three. Margret was embarrassed for the man as he lovingly patted the vomiting beast while getting pelted with purple rain.

"El respiradero en la tapa!" he shouted to Margret over the whooping siren and not knowing what that meant, she smiled weakly. He walked behind the tank and she lost sight of him until the alarm stopped.

The freakishly impressive display was quickly reduced to a sickly drool sliding down the side of the tank. When he emerged with wet matted hair, a bald spot was visible and Margret noticed his hearing aids for the first time. His clothes were splattered and obviously stained. Wiping his eye as he approached, Margret offered, while still rubbing Lilly's back, "I'm so sorry this happened." But before Wolf could respond, Lilly unexpectedly let out a frightened wail and Margret immediately picked her up. "This must be thousands of dollars' worth of wasted wine," she commented without missing a beat while balancing the child and a big stuffed animal on her hip. "Can any of it be saved?"

Mr. Wolf motioned as if throwing a used Kleenex over his shoulder, "*C'est la vie.* I probably deserve it. Come." He started walking toward the door and Margret and the children followed.

"You're just going to leave it?" Margret asked. "We can clean it up." Then looking at the state the kids were in added, "Maybe we should we call someone?"

Mr. Wolf snorted. "I would rather die than to see a woman such as yourself to clean this place. The tank is exploded because of gas created during fermentation and the lid and vent had not been adjusted properly. We must let this room air out." He made a shooing motion with his hand. "The cleaners will be here before the guests arrive for la fiesta."

"But shouldn't this be handled now, before it attracts pests or something?"

"Por favor, please," he begged. "It will get taken care of. Let us not think of this again." Following Mr. Wolf, they all hustled toward the double doors leading back to the gallery. As she walked with William and still holding Lilly, Margret kept one eye on tank three until she entered La Galleria. Mr. Wolf then double-locked the door.

CHAPTER TWENTY-TWO

Meanwhile in Jocelyn's room

"YOU ARE DONE," the good doctor said as he rolled the IV stand away. The sound of the plastic wheels rumbling over the hardwood floor surprisingly made Jocelyn want to cry. She sucked back the tears and continued to apply ample pressure to the gauze which was hiding what she imagined to be a giant, gaping hole where the IV port had been. The doctor rummaged through his backpack and produced a sort of bright green, clingy Ace bandage material and tightly wrapped the gauze to her hand. "Like new," he proclaimed as he patted her good shoulder.

Jocelyn, studying the wrap, asked, "Did you happen to find out what they were originally giving me? You know; the medicine that was making me so silly?" When he didn't answer, she looked up and added, "I'm asking not so much for me but for my mother. She gets anxious. You know how moms can be."

The doctor took a breath through his nose and after a heavy exhale answered, "No. I have not heard of results."

"Oh."

"Do not worry. You are healing very good." Jocelyn forced a smile. "Let me fix the rest of you." Jocelyn carefully boosted herself up in her bed and Dr. Fernandez created a makeshift splint for her injured shoulder. "These big stitches, I will remove them soon. The other stitches you have are on your insides and will dissolve. We simply need to keep the shoulder supported as it heals." He finished off the project by wrapping her upper chest, shoulder, and splint just as tightly as her hand with the bright green, clingy material. He stood back to admire his work and Jocelyn adjusted her flimsy hospital gown.

"This is quite the fashion statement," Jocelyn remarked, comparing the neon green bandages to the industrial phthalo green of her gown.

Dr. Fernandez forced a smile and said, "Please walk to the water closet." Jocelyn looked confused and the doctor pointed to the tiny bathroom. "Walk there and return. I am fearing for the muscles. They are weak. You must move. Move and eat. We will make you fat."

Jocelyn smiled because of how concerned the doctor seemed. Raising herself to the challenge, she carefully lowered her unshaven legs over the side of the bed and stood up. Immediately it was apparent how emaciated she had become. When her bony, bare feet hit the little hooked rug, she stood up straight, hesitated, and then sat right back down on the bed. "You can do it," the doctor encouraged. "Imagine as if you are marching." He demonstrated a slow marching motion.

"But what if I can't," she mumbled while smoothing the neon green on her hand. "I mean, I feel off balance and very heavy, like I have lead boots on. What if the MS is acting up?" she added almost hopefully. The doctor looked at her quizzically. "No really. Even on my best days I stumble around. Multiple sclerosis stinks," she huffed but in reality she didn't know why she was even looking for an excuse not to walk. She wanted, with all of her heart, to escape this place, to run!, but she found herself all sorts of depressed, not wanting to exert herself in any way, and feeling the need to throw a pity party for herself in front of the doctor.

"Ah, the white woman's disease."

Taken aback Jocelyn replied, "Excuse me?"

"This is what we call this. We do not have this disease here," he scratched his chin, "or at least we did not until very recently. Tú madre made me to be aware of your condition."

"I figured she would talk to you about it," Jocelyn sighed.

"This phenomenon is specific to white-skinned, northern Europeans and their descendants. Women have always reported the symptoms, modern men too are afflicted. Unfortunately, the condition has flourished in the United States. As of right now, no specific gene has been identified to show that this multiple sclerosis is a genetic disorder, although there may be a gene complex that when not working properly creates an opportunity for this disease. Perhaps, rather, this condition is because of an unknown virus, or exposure to chemicals; or the patient lacks some vital nutrient? Or maybe it is a combination of all creating the disease in a specific group. We do not know. Not yet."

He looked at her sympathetically and offered, "Projects to map the genes and the mechanisms of the brain are vigorously underway all over the world. These studies are of great value. Neuroscience is undoubtedly the most important field of scientific study today. Billions and billions are being invested. So maybe, someday soon, mind and brain," he made a show of uniting his fingers as if in prayer, "and their intimate connection to the rest of the body will not be as mysterious and you will feel better."

"Interesting, but I still can't walk."

"You did not try."

"What if I fall?"

"What if you do not?"

Jocelyn smirked and shook her head as she stood up again and took her first tenuous step off the hooked rug and onto the chilly, hardwood floor. Assessing the situation, she realized that mostly she was afraid of falling. She took another cautious step with her hands held out as if balancing on a tightrope. And then another, and another, and another. Noticing the bloodstain, she decided to raise her chin and focus on the little blue painting as she moved toward it, sort of like when she was a kid at dance lessons and had to keep her eyes focused on one spot to spin around more gracefully. It worked! She got all the way to the bathroom, turned around, and came back to the bed and sat down.

The doctor clapped and exclaimed, "Muy bien! Very good!" Then he sternly looked at her, "You must do that every hour you are awake and you must eat as much as you can, whenever you can. ¿Comprende?"

"Sí."

"It will get easy and you do it more and more. Now," he said as he reached into his pocket and produced an amber pill bottle, "this is most important. You are to take one of these pills, just one," he stressed as he held up the bottle, "and no more than one, every six hours for pain should you need it." He solemnly handed her the amber bottle and she accepted it like a sacrament.

"Gracias Dr. Fernandez. Muchas gracias."

CHAPTER TWENTY-THREE

Somewhere in Florida, USA

JERRY, STILL HANDCUFFED, was using his fingernail to etch a map into the Naugahyde of the bus seat. They had already turned right at the gas station and were awkwardly cutting through a shopping plaza parking lot. Jerry didn't know where he was exactly. He knew that they had been on this bus, heading south, for about an hour before exiting the highway, then traveling on bumpy back roads, and ending up here. Over the sound of the diesel engine the Cell Phone Shoppe, Discount Wine and Liquors, Big Daddy's Gun & Coin, Payday Loans, and a restaurant proudly advertising four different types of chicken wings slowly slid by. The Dollar Store was across the street.

The bus angled around the dumpsters and turned onto an access road that led to a dismal, well past its prime, residential road. Jerry, marking that on his Naugahyde map, glanced across the aisle to Mark who was gingerly exploring the contours of his face with his handcuffed hands. Jerry winced when he saw Mark's mangled not yet black eye but he said nothing. In fact, he stayed absolutely silent. He didn't want a repeat performance of that bald prison guard literally crawling over the seats like a monster king crab to give him a smack down too. *Sure, Mark had been mouthy, but jeez...,* Jerry ruminated and turned away.

With his focus back outside he watched as the sun-bleached ranch-style homes featuring vintage decorative concrete blocks and car ports got shabbier and shabbier until it appeared as if they were driving through some sort of 1950s or early 60s ghost town. Lawns were either mini overgrown weed fields or burnt-out dust patches. They passed an old church that had a cinderblock circle arch adorning the path to the front door. Jerry remembered a long forgotten photograph of his grandparents, holding hands, smiling, walking under one of those things. A weird nostalgia set in, but that was quickly replaced with curiosity when he noticed the peacocks wandering around. He craned his neck to look at the small flock of exotic birds, two of which were strutting by with their vibrant tails fully fanned out.

Where the heck did they come from? An old zoo? Jerry contemplated as the bus roared down the street. He was becoming painfully aware that there wasn't any other traffic on this road. None.

Soon a sad town center sprung up around them. An old, abandoned gas station, an empty drug store, and a barber shop with a broken window and a candy striped sign frozen in time greeted them. Almost as if in celebration of the bus's arrival a pack of skinny, mangy dogs barked and gave chase until the effects of starvation and exhaustion kicked in. With the sounds of the yelping dogs fading in the distance, the bus slowed down and pulled into the parking lot of a deserted tire store. The place looked like it hadn't seen a customer in decades given the faded, bluish posters hanging in the window.

As the bus idled they waited in silence. Jerry, still looking out the window, noticed a newer model white Mustang speeding through the heat waves, up the road toward them. He leaned over, got Mark's attention, and pointed to it. The two watched as the Mustang skidded to a stop next to the bus and a bleached blond woman hopped out. The door of the bus swung open and the king crab prison guard scuttled out to meet the lady. The two shook hands and the guard gave a thumbs-up to the driver.

Mark was intently watching the scene while Jerry scratched the Mustang's license plate number into the Naugahyde. Eventually the driver shut off the engine and joined the blond lady and the guard. Now it really was quiet and they could hear the muffled ebbs and flows of the conversation outside. No one, on or off the bus, was smiling.

Eventually the blond opened her car door, ushering the bus driver into the tiny back seat. The bald guard nodded, trotted back to the bus and threw something in. The bus door slammed shut and he ran back to the Mustang. As soon as the bald head was in the car the Mustang whizzed away.

"What the..?" Jerry said as he clumsily jumped up, encumbered by the ankle cuffs, and scooted out of his seat. He and Mark were still connected by chains and with Mark out in front, they nosily schlepped down the aisle. "Dude! Did you see that?"

"Yeah." Mark huffed. "How much you wanna bet her hair will be brown tonight and that bald asshole will have a buzz cut soon?" The metallic, sloshing sound of their chain linked steps stopped when Mark squatted down and picked something up.

"A key," he said, flipping it over with his fingers. "The guy threw us the key," he announced, presenting it to Jerry.

"To the bus?"

"No, to the cuffs." Excited, but trying not look like it, the two of them unlocked each other. The feeling of emancipation was tremendous and, grinning wildly, Jerry started stripping off his orange prison gear.

"Whoa, whoa, whoa!" Mark raised his hands as if pushing the sight away.

"What?" Jerry questioned, kicking off his pants. "No self-respecting ghost runs around in prison duds." Although Mark had to agree, he made a conscious effort to look at anything other than Jerry's naked body as he headed back to his seat. Ripping open the big bag of pre-prison clothes, Jerry whistled and commented, "This smells like hell." He held out the bag for Mark to smell. "Aren't they required to wash our stuff?"

"I can't believe you're even asking that." Mark glared at him with his one good eye, angrily riffling through his bag to find his phone. He quickly found it and after fiddling with it proclaimed, "Figures. Out of juice."

"Probably scrubbed too," Jerry added, pulling up his civilian shorts. "Don't bother to turn that thing on," he instructed, "they'll just use it to track you."

"Oh, like this thing?" Mark snatched the red Adidas wristband that Jerry had given him out of the bag and threw it at him. It bounced off Jerry's shoulder. "Seriously. This is a God damn joke. You're in on this."

"Huh?"

"I know you are. Well, guess what?"

"What?"

"I'm done. You can tell whoever you're working for that I'm going home. I'm done. My father always said I wasn't cut out for this."

"Jesus Mark, I'm not in on anything and what does your father have to do with it?" Jerry asked, pulling his stinky shirt over his head. "You gotta calm down. That's why that guard beat you up."

"Oh, so now you're on his side?"

"No. It's just that you shouldn't yell at people, or worse yet, make them feel like complete idiots, when you are trying to get them to understand the truth of the matter. People are predisposed to defend their version of the truth. You need better diplomacy skills."

"Just shut up Jerry, okay?" Mark retorted while angrily tucking his perspiration stained white polo shirt into his Banana Republic khaki shorts. "Seriously. Shut up." Jerry shrugged, sitting down to tie his sneakers. Mark was inspecting his wristwatch when his shoulders fell and he actually started crying. "This isn't supposed to happen to someone like me," he lamented, a tear trickling out of his puffed up eye."

"What? Getting smacked in the face?"

"No! This whole friggin' thing! I was supposed to be in the cybercrime unit and now I'm officially dead and in some weird black op." He shook his head. "My father was right. I can't handle this."

"This is the second time you've brought up your dad. What's he got to do with anything?" Jerry wanted to know. "You think he's behind this? Like some sort of elaborate prank or something?"

Mark shut his eyes, took a deep breath through his nose, opened his eyes and replied, "Nah, he's a friggin' cheapskate. He wouldn't part with the damn money. He's just a dick. But seriously though, I didn't sign up for any of this!" His bottom lip quivered. "Mom always had my back but Dad… shit." He wiped his good eye. "I just want to go home and lead, you know, a normal life."

"What? You mean like all the people who lived in those deserted houses we just drove past?" Mark sort of nodded so Jerry continued. "Yeah? Well, you're an American, go for it, but you know who else wants to lead a normal life?" Mark sighed and shook his head no. "Jocelyn!" Jerry shouted. "She's hanging on for dear life and now I'm finding out that she's been kidnapped. That you were the one who was supposed to find her and suddenly you're a giant wuss! Man up! Pull yourself together. I'm not giving up. Let's do this thing!"

"Jerry, last I heard you were supposed to find guns," Mark commented, wiping his nose with his prison shirt.

"Yeah well, that's the easy part."

"But that has nothing to do with the McLaren case."

"And this affects me how?" Jerry called over his shoulder as he headed to the front of the bus, kicking their discarded chains under the seats on his way. Mark just stared at him and then busied himself putting on his belt. "Yes! I don't have to hotwire this thing!" Jerry excitedly exclaimed and Mark rolled his eyes. "The keys are still in it!"

Eagerly plopping himself into the driver's seat Jerry started the engine. It rumbled to life. "Sweet." With cold air blowing at his face he yelled to Mark while looking at him in the mirror. "The air conditioner's on!" From the mirror, Jerry saw Mark heading down the aisle toward him.

"Jerry just let me off. I want out," Mark said, planting himself next to the driver's seat at the top of the stairs to exit.

"Aww, c'mon."

"I'm serious." Mark took a step down the stairwell. "Open the door."

Jerry sighed and was about to open the door but then realized that he had no idea how to do it. There was no big lever handle like he remembered on the school buses he had ridden on as a kid.

"Open the God damn door."

"I don't know if I can."

"Oh, screw you!" Mark started pushing on the hinged doors to no avail.

"No, really. I don't know how to…oh, wait. What's…" and that's when Mark punched through the glass. Naturally, it was at the very same moment that Jerry found the door lever by his left armrest under the driver's side window.

Cringing, Mark shook out his fingers and studied the blood dripping down his cut hand. "What the heck Mark?!" Jerry shouted as he loosened his grip on the door lever and pointed to the shattered window. "Stop being crazy! There's nothing here except maybe those rabid dogs." The two surveyed the situation from their unique vantage points.

Jerry shifted the bus into drive. "Come on, let's just get out of here." Holding the big steering wheel at ten and two o'clock and looking left and right, he commented, "Pretty funny us ghosts driving around in a prison bus." He kind of giggled, took a deep breath, and eased on the gas. Suddenly, and without warning, the front of the bus, in a tremendous cacophony, smashed to the ground. Jerry's body was instantly flung against the steering wheel and Mark slammed onto the windshield as the now angled blue bus lurched forward, grinding up the pavement. Finally everything was quiet and Jerry thought to take his foot off the gas.

"What? What the hell?" Mark breathlessly asked as he pushed himself up and scaled the tilted stairs up to shell shocked Jerry. "You okay?"

"Not really," Jerry responded, spitting out blood. "I think I chipped a tooth."

Not saying anything, Mark reached over Jerry and pushed the door lever. The tilted, broken door squeaked open and with the Florida heat hitting him hard, he carefully exited the bus. "You've got to be kidding me!" he exclaimed from outside.

"What?" Jerry yelled back, extracting his legs from beneath the steering wheel. He held his ribs as he made his way over the incline plane of the aisle and then down the crooked stairs.

"Someone stole the friggin' front tires!" Mark announced as Jerry hopped out.

"How did...?" Jerry started to ask but then he saw the fallen emergency jacks laying in the wake of the bus.

The two battered men, both looking as if they had survived some sort of post-modern *Fight Club* match, were completely perplexed. They were considering the disabled carcass of the bus when a voice, dark like tinted glass, uttered, "Welcome to the jungle." Jerry and Mark slowly turned around to face a heavyset man in overalls chewing the stub of a cigar. "They left you, huh?" the man asked. Jerry, still holding his ribs, nodded. "This is the third time they'd gone and done that after I've told them I'm not havin' it."

Jerry and Mark glanced at each other and Mark took a step forward and extended his hand.

"I'm Mark Witherall."

The man just looked at Mark's hand and the cigar slid to the other side of his mouth before he said, "So, you've got a name. That's nice." Mark, still standing there with his hand out, nodded yes. The man sighed and replied. "I don't wanna know it."

Mark withdrew his hand and asked, "Do you have a name?"

The man laughed as if responding to a cruel joke. "See, this is exactly why I don't want them doing this. It's not fair to me or to you guys. What's the next thing? Water? Food? A place to stay?" Jerry and Mark were unsure if these were rhetorical questions. "Money?"

Jerry piped up, "No. No. Of course not. We're not asking for money or any of that other stuff. But do you have a cell phone charger?"

The cigar stub slid back to its original position. "Son, you're a special type of stupid, aren't you? I'll give you exactly sixty seconds to get off my property before I shoot you in the ass."

Mark was nodding and mumbling thank you while backing away from the man while Jerry, conversely, headed back onto the bus shouting, "Hold on! I've just got to get something! Sixty seconds and I'll be gone! Hold on!" He ran up the crooked stairs and up the incline plane of the aisle, back to the seat he had been sitting in. He felt around for where the upholstery had been stitched, but not finding anything he just kicked the bottom of the seat and the entire cushion, stapled to plywood, popped up. He grabbed it, ran down the aisle, and fell down the stairs landing on his Naugahyde seat cushion.

Mark, completely aghast, looked over at the man with the cigar and apologetically offered, "He really is a special kind of stupid."

The man, unimpressed, tossed the cigar stub from his mouth, took out his Smith & Wesson .45, and fired it into the air before hollering, "Get the hell off my property!" Mark instantly bolted while Jerry scrambled up, grabbed his seat cushion, and, hugging it, ran after Mark. The sound of the .45 blasting off behind them inspired both to run faster than either thought possible considering the searing heat.

CHAPTER TWENTY-FOUR

Off the coast of San Carlos de Bariloche, Argentina
Huemul

THE YELLOW SUPER PUMA HELICOPTER swooped between snow covered mountains and buzzed over the town. It had been about five hours straight of hard, noisy flying and Ethan, chomping on a piece of beef jerky, was surprised when he looked up from José's aeronautical map to find that it appeared he was about to land in Switzerland. The architecture nestled in the Patagonia foothills of the Southern Andes was clearly Alpine inspired. They flew over the Swiss chalets made of wood, their heavy, sloping roofs frosted with snow. Then, dropping altitude and zooming away, they raced just meters above the chilly cobalt waters of Lake Nahuel Huapi toward an island called Huemul. To Ethan, this island looked eerie and mysterious in the middle of this idyllic lake. The remains of ruined concrete structures littering Huemul stood as witness to post World War Two secret projects and greeted them as José headed in for a landing.

Ethan turned in his seat to look at Ache, who was sitting cross-legged at the rear of the cargo hold cradling the P226. "We're getting ready to land, brother!" Ethan called out over the noise of the engine. Ache didn't move so Ethan stood up and gestured with his hands. The message was received and Ache gave a thumbs-up. He hopped up and positioned himself by the cargo door, nodding to the steely-faced crane operator whom he had frisked at the beginning of the journey.

The Super Puma touched down with a thump and a rattle. The blades were still noisily whirling around when the crane operator began the process of unloading the cargo. The door swung open, and with pupils adjusting to the snow cast daylight, Ache, after hours of near darkness and not being able to sleep and not so conveniently highly strung out on PTSD adrenaline, was unsure of what to do as a gang, fully outfitted in baggy CBRN (Chemical, Biological, Radiological, Nuclear) gear hungrily descended on the busted up crate like ants to a sugar cube.

"Alto! Hey! Back off! Basta!" he shouted, pointing the gun at everyone and no one. When that didn't work he shot the gun above everyone's heads into the air. CBRN activity stopped immediately.

José burst from the cockpit and grabbed Ache's arm. "Don't shoot! You might hit the blades!" he yelled, pointing to the settling machinery that was now beginning to slump down like a wilted wildflower.

"Do we need to get decontaminated?!" Ethan anxiously shouted to the CBRN guys below. When no answer came, José, equally as concerned, hopped off the helicopter and shouted the question in Spanish. After some conversation José motioned for everyone aboard the helicopter to follow him. As soon as Ethan, Ache, and the crane operator jumped off the Super Puma the CBRN activity resumed.

Pushing his way up to José, Ethan asked, "So what's the story?"

"They don't know for sure. Told us to check inside." While the little group walked toward one of the blown-out buildings, Ethan watched the contents of the crate being quickly transferred to a weird looking, white Humvee snowmobile type vehicle.

He leaned into Ache as they trudged over the snow and quietly asked, "We did pay for all that, right?" Ache nodded in the affirmative. "So what's going on?" Ache didn't answer but his jaw was set and his finger was on the trigger.

Following José and the crane operator to the dilapidated property, Ethan held his gun with both hands and cautiously stepped over the battered threshold. Ache followed him, sweeping the space through the sight of the P226. There wasn't much to look at inside. In fact it was pretty dismal. Baby stalactites hung from the ceiling of the concrete hallway and a dripping sound could be heard. "You know, this would be a perfect spot for an ambush," Ethan cautioned.

"They told me there was an elevator in here," José replied. Sure enough, through the dimness, not ten meters away they spotted a stainless steel wall panel. They all walked to it with Ache and Ethan on high alert with their weapons.

"Okay, fellahs, what's the deal?" Ethan asked while marching down the hall, his gun following his line of sight. "Who exactly told you to pick us up and bring us here?"

"Wolf," José said as he pushed the button for the elevator.

"Oh, for shit's sake! He could have filled me in on this part of the plan," Ethan spat out in frustration. He grabbed for his cell phone, and with Ache still at the ready with his gun, Ethan started fussing around with the tiny phone. "Perfect. There's no friggin' signal," he growled. "I swear to God…" A tiny 'ding' punctuated his thought and the elevator door opened. Ache was already on task, squatting down on one knee, pointing his gun at the interior of the open elevator. He gave the clear signal and José, followed by the crane operator, cautiously entered.

"You guys coming?" José asked. Ethan and Ache looked at each other for confirmation then stepped in. The stainless door began silently sliding shut. At the same moment they felt the floor of the elevator gently easing them downward. Ethan noticed that there were neither buttons to push nor any indication of what floor they were heading to. Having nothing to look at, they all stood uncomfortably staring at the wall and/or checking each other out. The awkward silence was reaching the point of unbearable when finally, like a breath of fresh air, the surface of the wall opposite the one they had entered through slid open, revealing an enormous, brightly lit work space.

Ache, still wielding the gun, was out first and the others followed, curiously absorbing the new setting. Seemingly deserted, the place had a mid-twentieth century Nicola Tesla power station vibe going but it was completely modernized. The concrete walls were pristine white and the stainless steel tables holding test tubes and slick computer monitors were all shiny in contrast with the oxidized heavy pipes and vintage machinery embedded into the concrete structure.

"Hello!" Ethan shouted, still holding his gun but nowhere near as ready for combat as Ache. "Anybody home?" Just then, emerging from behind a wall of machinery, a CBRN suited person shuffled toward them and waved. José waved back and a flurry of Spanish came issuing out of his mouth. Ethan, having no idea what was being said, inched in next to Ache and asked, "Do you know what they're saying?"

Ache sort of winced and replied, "They're talking too fast. It's Argentinian Spanish, so it's tricky. It might be code."

With José still deep in conversation, Ethan, waving his gun at the crane operator, quietly barked, "You!" The young man looked his way. "What are they saying?"

"José is asking after the man's family."

"What!? You're kidding me." The crane operator shook his head and Ethan marched directly up to José, ignoring the CBRN suited person, and flatly asked, "Do we need to be decontaminated or what? Everyone's got HAZMAT suits on for Christ's sake."

"They don't know yet what exactly is in the shipment," José answered, clearly irritated by Ethan's interruption.

"Well, neither do I. It was supposed to be guns but obviously we got involved with something else," Ethan said, running his gaze obnoxiously over the CBRN guy, and then glaring at Ache who had followed him. "What is this place?"

The CBRN guy, who apparently knew English, answered in a

muffled voice from behind his hermetically sealed hood. "You are in my private laboratory."

"Nice setup," Ethan said. Turning his attention to the man and making a show of looking all around he added, "I like what you've done with it." Now Ethan knew this guy had juice, meaning he was important and probably had money, and that he was connected to B.B. so he asked, "What's your name?" while reaching out for a shake.

Accepting Ethan's offer with his heavy, space-age polymer gloved hand, the man whom Ethan was just realizing was pretty old, very cordially replied, "Maximillian Juan Carlos De todos los Santos-De los Cobos y Huraño de Mendoza Castile Raubal-Ortiz de Ruldoph de Habsburg."

Ethan had stopped the handshaking motion somewhere around "all the saints," or as they say in Spanish "todos los Santos," and was finally able break away from the man's grip with, "Nice to meet you Max," ignoring José who looked like he was about to have an aneurysm. "I'm Ethan. Ethan Lowe. My associates and I paid for that shipment. It belongs to us. I just want you to remember that."

"Why of course. This is not an issue. In fact, I prefer that there is no record of me or this lab at all. I am simply here to help."

"Uh-huh," Ethan uttered, highly suspicious of the man. Ache was still scanning the area for possible threats and the innocuous crane operator was staying silent when José stepped forward to contribute, "Ethan Lowe is, of course, the man who famously attacked Meister Jonas Ledergerber."

Ethan wasn't sure if José sharing this information was a plus or minus so he braced himself as Señor Maximillian de Habsburg studied him through the plastic hood. Ethan watched in anticipation as a smile slowly spread across the elderly man's wrinkled face, until eventually Max was laughing hysterically. Once he regained his composure he heartily patted Ethan on the shoulder, letting out a gregarious, "Oh, bravo! Ledergerber, that moron! Is he dead?" he asked hopefully. Ethan wasn't sure how to respond so José shook his head no. This was followed by more giggles.

While Ethan was processing the news of Ledergerber's fate, he was taken off guard when Maximillian put his CBRN suited arm around his shoulder and hugging him, giddily offering up through the plastic face shield, "Better luck next time my boy! Do you know how badly I wanted to kill him myself recently in Monaco?"

"I can only imagine," Ethan said, forcing a smile. Ache, hearing all this, sought out José who simply raised an eyebrow as if silently transmitting: you guys have no idea who you're playing with.

"So tell me Max," Ethan asked after the hysterics and backslapping had calmed down and the two had essentially bonded like anonymous drinking buddies perched on pub stools, "what is it that you do around here? Looks pretty high tech."

"I have been pursuing more effective weaponized mycoplasma."

"Oh, interesting. Is there a market for that, or is this just a hobby of yours?" Ethan asked, attempting to keep the conversation moving in a positive way. He didn't know what mycoplasma was but he sure as heck knew what weaponized meant.

"There is always a market for my work. You'd be surprised. But to answer your question, I do indeed enjoy what I do. Look up Punta Gorda, Florida, USA and chronic fatigue syndrome. That was me!" Max said excitedly thumbing his chest.

"You had chronic fatigue?" Ethan asked.

"No, I created it!" he proclaimed proudly. "It was when I was a young man, up in Canada..." He sort of sighed thinking about it. "Come," he said waving his arm for all of them to follow. "Let me show you." Ethan and Max led the pack and Ache followed up at the rear providing cover for Ethan.

They all shuffled up to a glassed in area that looked like a kennel but instead of dogs, it was full of monkeys. "I've been working from the patented work of Dr. Shyh-Ching Lo, a senior researcher at the US Armed Forces Institute of Pathology and one of America's top mycoplasma researchers. Dr. Shyh-Ching Lo reported that the disease agent I have been using, a crystalline bacterial toxin extracted from the brucella bacterium, causes illnesses such as cancer, Crohn's colitis, Type I diabetes, multiple sclerosis, Parkinson's disease, Wegener's disease, and collagen-vascular diseases like rheumatoid arthritis and Alzheimer's, not to mention AIDS and of course," he added with pride, "my chronic fatigue syndrome."

"So you're not into killing people. You're into making them suffer. I get it," Ethan said, nodding like it was cool while surveying the monkeys behind the soundproof glass wall.

"The US and Russia have always been very eager to test my work and call it their own. Of course, the medical companies associated with their militaries will release treatments. Stock prices go up. Everyone is happy. One saltshaker of my pure disease agent in a crystalline form is capable of wiping out the entire population of Canada. It is absolutely deadly, not so much in terms of killing the body but disabling it."

"So basically, the whole point is that the enemy can't fight back but lives to see you dominate them, and being sick and humiliated your victims end up buying your cure when you take over?"

"Well, I wouldn't call it a cure, more like a maintenance plan which, in reality, is much more profitable. The US and Russia have such surplus population they are not worried so much about testing unsuspecting citizens. Look at Operation Big Itch in the US where they have an almost unlimited supply of disposable stock. It now appears that your government pays, in a roundabout way, their test subjects to continually breed. The Germans and the Japanese were some of the first to experiment on prison populations but have since calmed down and the Chinese, well, they have so very many people...But you are correct, it cripples armies."

"And superpower militaries are really using this stuff?"

"Of course! Once the mycoplasma gets into the cell, it can act right away or lie there doing nothing, sometimes for ten or twenty years, so this can also be implemented for long-term projects. However, if a trauma occurs like an accident or a vaccination that doesn't take, the mycoplasma can become triggered. The US was spraying the crystalline form of mycoplasma on the Chinese and North Koreans and later admitted brucellosis was linked with multiple sclerosis when they publicly stated after the war, and I quote," he cleared his throat and recited as if it were the Lord's Prayer, "'Veterans with multiple sclerosis, a kind of creeping paralysis, developing to a degree of ten percent or more disability within two years after separation from active service, may be presumed to be service-connected for disability compensation. Compensation is payable to eligible veterans whose disabilities are due to service.'"

He stomped his rubber CBRN boot and clapped his gloved hands. "Ta-ha! Yet they continue to pretend that they don't know what causes it! And of course the treatment plans get sold. I always invest in the treatment drugs when they arrive on the market."

"Smart move," Ethan quipped, then noticing that Ache had become fixated on an open doorway at the far end of the laboratory he repeated, "Smart move."

"There are two hundred species of mycoplasma. Most are useless to me. There are only four or five that are pathogenic. The strain I had been working with, mycoplasma fermentans from the incognitus strain, comes from the nucleus of the brucella bacterium. The confounding thing about it is that the disease agent is not a bacterium or a virus. It is a mutated form of the brucella bacterium combined with a visna virus, from which my mycoplasma is extracted. It is a hybrid type of DNA. Of course, many of us have been experimenting with herpes and the very popular and easily accessible common cold, coronavirus strains too. Attempts to marry any one of the herpes virus strains to the bacterium became more common after the Vietnam War."

"Fascinating," Ethan said, laying a hand on the glass wall and squinting to peer in. The monkeys in their cages were exhibiting various states of misery ranging from rage to vacancy to obvious physical impairment. Because Ethan couldn't hear the animals it was as if he had been granted private audience to some sort of strange, silent, pantomimed performance of *Dante's Inferno*. Some of the monkeys, who appeared either asleep or dead, or on their way to being dead, were hooked up to IVs.

Max continued, "The pathogenic mycoplasma used to be nearly benign, but biological warfare research conducted between 1942 and today has resulted in the creation of more deadly and infectious forms of mycoplasma. Dr. Maurice Hilleman, chief virologist for the pharmaceutical company Merck Sharp & Dohme, stated that this disease agent is now carried by everybody in North America and possibly the rest of the world since they weaponized it and began testing it on the unsuspecting public."

"You don't say?" Ethan remarked watching the monkeys, captivated by one hooked up to an IV. Its legs were twitching. If he hadn't been so fixated on the animals Ethan might have noticed that the crane operator appeared horrified while José remained stoic and Ache was just about levitating because of ridiculous levels of natural adrenaline coursing through his veins.

"It's true," Max continued, seemingly appreciative of this newfound captive audience lined up at the glass wall. "Despite reporting flaws, there has been a marked increase in the incidence of all the neuro/systemic degenerative diseases since World War II and especially since the 1970s when they started the widespread marketing of vaccines." He kind of cleared his throat and continued, "Now that, my friend, is a profitable business. The vaccine industry basically utilizes the entire continent of Africa as an open laboratory. However, it will come to an end. Genetic modification will eventually make vaccination obsolete. The better long-term investment is in identifying critical genes. While I have some money tied up with that I have shifted my personal focus and am now working on newer, more precise applications of my past work. I find myself completely consumed by the possibilities available via nanotechnology. That bad boy right there," Max said, tapping on the glass wall and pointing to the zonked out, twitching monkey Ethan was looking at, "is one of my most recent test subjects. I'm trying out a new type of nanobot from Russia. I don't know if this will be successful given the compromised immune system of the creature, but since I have all this damaged stock, I figured I might as well give it a go."

Ethan turned away from the monkey and asked Max flat out, "What's a nanobot?"

"A tiny robot made of organic and/or inorganic material," Max replied. "It's at the nano scale." Ethan looked confused so Max elaborated. "One nanometer is about the length a fingernail grows in one second, or more precisely, a nano is one billionth of a meter."

"That's literally invisible."

"Yes. It's an incredibly minuscule robot that can swim right along with the blood cells."

"Shut up! Seriously?" Ethan exclaimed causing Ache, still holding his gun with both hands, to twitch and blink his tired eyes. Max grinned and nodded yes.

"And what do these robots do?" Ethan asked.

"Anything they are programmed to do," Max replied, folding his arms across his chest. "The US National Institutes for Health put out a paper in 2008 extolling the virtues of how critical this technology would be, specifically for the military. Nanorobots integrated with nanobiosensors can transmit real time information, using international mobile phones for wireless data transmission through satellite communication. That's what the paper was talking about in 2008. They have figured out how to do that but now recognize that they need much faster cell phone connections for optimal performance. Communications companies will be doing everything and anything to make this work."

"So, that's where this is going, eh? Cell phones connected to nanobots?"

Max grinned. "No. That's just a step toward the ultimate goal. During the next two decades the impact of neuro devices in nanoscale will be profound. Absolutely profound. You see, precise mind control started in the 1960s in Spain when Spanish scientist José Delgado implanted an electrode into a bull's brain. The bull charged at Delgado but was instantly stopped, remotely by the implant."

"Oh, I think I sorta remember seeing a clip about that on YouTube or something."

"It's a very famous experiment. Delgado was subsequently hired by the US CIA. Another pioneer in this area is Doctor Jacobson from Norway. He was also hired by the CIA. This technology of mind control is a military project and has been well underway since the 1960s. It is now nearly perfect. Today it is called 'Full Synthetic Telepathy,' meaning they are able to read your thoughts. They are able to see through your eyes and maintain direct conversations with your thoughts. They may even induce images, short films, sequences, directly into your brain. The Swedish Military Research Agency is also involved in this development. All this is made possible with nanotechnology. Machines can be made at about fifty nanometers and can interact through streams of photons. They can speak to and decode the neurotransmitters in your brain, so they can communicate directly with the brain."

"You're blowin' my mind here Max," Ethan said, shaking his head.

Maximillian de Habsburg, with arms still crossed, leaned back, admiring his lab specimens. "I know. I am just as fascinated by the whole thing as I was fifty years ago. I never stop learning. Neuroscience is the study of the brain. With advances in chemistry, computers, engineering, medicine, and other disciplines, neuroscience now includes aspects of molecular, cellular, structural, functional, evolutionary, computational, and medical aspects of the nervous system. Neuroscience has crossed a threshold and has become a key element in the national security apparatus of the world. Presently three hundred and fifty colleges and universities in the USA have Pentagon research contracts in this area."

"Whoa. I had no idea," Ethan gasped, looking over at the others who, from the expressions on their faces, had no idea either.

"I would imagine most people do not. Even the people working directly on it probably don't realize the full scope of their work. However, remote neural monitoring is already in use in the United States, the UK, Spain, Sweden, Germany and France. Electromagnetic emissions of the brain can be decoded into actual thoughts or images and sounds in the subject's brain. Brains can be stimulated so that the subject hears sounds and smells things that just aren't there. Audio and visuals can be transferred straight to a subject's brain. Twenty years ago they had to introduce the implants through the nose or neck. Even then it was almost impossible to see the scar, but today all you need is injection into the blood."

He pointed to the monkey's IV bag. "I amalgamate the nanobots into the hydromorphone so that the subject sleeps while the nanobots get acclimated to the host environment. Look at his little legs!" Max excitedly pointed out. "It's like he's dancing! I can only imagine what he's dreaming about," Max said, smiling beneath his CBRN hood.

Ethan swallowed hard and wiped his nose. José was standing like a statue watching the animal's spasms and the crane operator, looking like he was going to vomit, turned away from the soundproof window. Ache was still fixated on the door.

"This is the danger of nanotechnology, because when the bot enters the bloodstream it travels through various types of frequencies; later it passes through the brain and binds to specific frequencies. Frequencies and vibrations in the body are very important for this type of communication. We can inject many thousands of nanobots through the blood and this is how you get connected.

"To who? Who do you get connected to?"

"Right now, most probably the Defense Advanced Research Projects Agency in the US. Synthetic telepathy is, hands down, the dominion of DARPA. It's when you talk with your thoughts, not with your voice-based language. That's why you need human subjects for this. My little monkey is not equipped to fully exploit synthetic telepathy. When fully implemented they can read your thoughts and you communicate back just by thinking.

"In the future, when all this is declassified, the wealthy will be able to get implants to clone memories. It will be the equivalent of saving a photograph or home movie but with all the sights, sounds, smells, thoughts, and gut-wrenching emotions intact. Currently there is a project devoted to cloning the contents of an entire human brain directly onto a supercomputer. It's called the Soul Catcher and it was created by British Telecom. This research has received billions and billions of pounds in support. The desired end product of Soul Catcher is, of course, to have an implantable chip in the brain which will ultimately allow for immortality."

Just as Max concluded his jaw-dropping soliloquy a group of five CBRN outfitted people armed with little suitcases and small rifles wandered through the door that Ache had been obsessed with. Ethan spun around, gripping his gun, ready for action, but was diverted when the elevator door slid open revealing another crew of five CBRN suits, all armed with much more intimidating firepower.

"Look assholes!" Ethan shouted. "How you gonna shoot straight wearing—" and that's when Ache threw over a table and dove behind it while squeezing off a bullet toward the door, thus unleashing a bona fide firestorm.

With bullets whizzing all over the place from the heavy automatic rifles coming from the elevator and glass smashing, people were dropping. Ethan was flat on the floor rolling behind one of the Nikola Tesla cast iron antiques when he saw José grab the still unidentified crane operator and use the guy as a human shield. Unfortunately the human shield promptly got shoot. Blood was dribbling out of the kid's mouth as José dragged both of them behind some sort of 1950's out of commission furnace.

Ethan crouched down and took aim at the guys coming at them from the elevator. That's when he realized that they were carrying American made Colt submachine guns. That's also when he confirmed his hunch that they weren't very accurate shooters. The glass from the soundproof wall shattered and fell away and instantly the crazed cries and howls, not to mention the distinct aroma, of the primates filled the air adding to the palatable chaos of the situation. Three escaping monkeys angrily bound out over the broken glass and began screaming and jumping around amidst the gunfire and bloodshed.

Ethan shot the guy who had shot out the window and as the CBRN suit crumbled to the floor, one of the monkeys hurled itself onto Ache, who was now lying prone behind the table because he had just shot one of the small gun guys coming through the doorway. The monkey viciously bit Ache on the back of the neck. Ache, howling like an incensed grizzly bear, tore the monkey off his back and shot the animal point blank in the face. It was right then, when Ache was covered with splattered monkey brains, that Ethan noticed Max trying to corral the two surviving escaped monkeys back into the kennel with the other animals. Recognizing that this was his opportunity, he took it.

Dashing out among the flurry of bullets, Ethan grabbed Max. Holding him close he pumped a bullet into the air hoping to get attention. Then, with his hot gun pressed firmly against Max's CBRN protected temple, Ethan bellowed over the screeching monkeys and the rat-tat-tat of the ARs, "Stop! Or I'll fuckin' kill Habsburg!" Just as he shouted one last emphatic "STOP!" someone fired off one more round, but that was it. Everything was silent except for the screeching monkeys hopping around. Ethan, with the gun still stuck to Max's head, surveyed the writhing wounded and barked, "José! Translate for these motherfuckers! Tell them to drop their weapons!" José emerged, his hands and clothes covered with the crane operator's blood, and translated the essence of Ethan's message.

With the guns now on the floor Ache started collection. He started with the SMGs over at the elevator and then headed to the doorway where the smaller guns and briefcases were. His neck was bleeding and Ethan noticed it as Ache passed by. Ethan squeezed Max's fragile frame, and drilling the gun deeper into the elderly man's temple asked, "Is he gonna get AIDS?"

"What?" Max confusedly responded.

"AIDS! The God damn monkey bit him. Is he gonna get AIDS?!"

"Probably not. None of my animals come from US military labs where that disease was created." Relieved, Ethan eased up the pressure on the man but kept the gun right where it was. "He might get Crohn's colitis though."

Just as Ethan was pondering the definition of Crohn's colitis, Ache marched up holding one of the little hard shell suitcases and waving a little plastic gun. "These are our toy guns from the shipment."

"Those aren't toys," Max commented.

"Well, what are they?" Ethan wanted to know, giving the man another meaningful hug.

Gasping for breath, Señor de Habsburg managed to sputter, "Let me go and I'll show you."

CHAPTER TWENTY-FIVE

Casa de Wolf
Uco Valley, Argentina

"MOM, YOU GUYS HAVE BEEN GONE literally all day. I was getting really, really worried." Frowning, Jocelyn reprimanded her family as they filed into the room like some sort of spa-based cult. They all had big white towels wrapped around their wet heads and were wearing white, fluffy slippers and bathrobes. The oversized robes were dragging on the floor behind the kids as they shuffled into the room.

"Mom's out of bed!" Willy excitedly exclaimed.

"Oh, honey!" Margret sighed. "This makes me so happy!" She put her hand on her daughter's good shoulder. "Can I hug you or will that hurt?"

"It might hurt, but okay. Just be careful." Everyone was ecstatic that Jocelyn was out of bed and off the IV. She handed the amber pill bottle to her mom to inspect and showed the kids how the doctor had wrapped her up with the green bandage. The kids were giddily hugging her hips when the towels slid off their heads and littered the floor. Finally she had to sit and settled herself down on the bed next to the bags.

"Oh, good! The clothes are here," Margret said, noticing the six shopping bags sitting on Jocelyn's bed. "B.B. mentioned that he'd have someone bring everything we needed." Margret began eagerly digging into the clothes. She pulled out a Bottega Veneta, dark merino wool pullover turtleneck with contrasting red detailing. Holding it to her shoulders she remarked, "This would fit you hon."

"That's nice. I'd wear that. But Mom, where were you?" Jocelyn demanded. "You left hours ago and I was getting really scared."

"Oh, we went swimming."

"Seriously? There's a pool here?" Jocelyn asked.

The kids nodded their wet heads and William said, "It's heated."

"And it's skinny," Lilly added.

"Skinny?" Jocelyn looked to her mother for clarification as Margret rummaged through the bags and handed clothes out to the kids.

"It's B.B.'s personal lap pool in the basement," Margret said like it was no big deal. "It's not open for guests, but there's a shower and a sauna down there."

"You've got to be kidding me. Really?" Jocelyn said, thoroughly impressed. "That's...That's pretty cool. You can put that on the map you were making Willy." Then directing her comment to her mother, "B.B. went—sorry," Jocelyn corrected herself while looking at the kids. "I mean Mr. Wolf went swimming with you guys?"

"No," Margret answered before the kids could respond. "I don't think he intended for us to go swimming at all, but since we were all stinky with wine he—"

"Wait," Jocelyn interrupted, "You and he were stinky? You were drunk?"

"I was stinky too!" Lilly chimed in and Jocelyn raised her eyebrows.

"No," Margret laughed, pulling the towel from her head and tussling her wet hair. "We weren't drunk. We were getting a tour of the fermentation room and there was some sort of explosion—"

"What?!" Jocelyn burst out, nervously looking at everyone. "Like a bomb?"

The kids nodded their heads emphatically and Margret said, "No. B.B. told us it was a malfunction of a tank or something."

"And we got splattered with wine!" Lilly excitedly contributed.

"Jeez, you guys had an interesting day. I thought getting off the IV was a big deal."

"But honey, it is!" Margret looked up from the shopping bags and smiled at her daughter. "That's so promising! You'll be up and around soon. I just know it."

"You should smell Brownie," William said. William was sporting an Arsenal Fútbol Club sweater and wrestling with a pair of Burberry Kids blue jeans. "He's all stinky now." Lilly frowned.

Watching her kids get dressed Jocelyn asked, "Mom, why do you think B.B..."

"Mr. Wolf," Lilly corrected, pulling a Hello Kitty sweatshirt with something written in French on it over her head.

"Right. Thanks Lilly. Why do you think Mr. Wolf is being so nice to all of us Mom? He doesn't know us and next thing you know he's got you guys swimming around in his underground pool, buying us clothes, and has basically set up a recovery room for me."

"Oh, he's just being hospitable," Margret replied from inside the little toilet closet. Her back was to everyone as she pulled on a Ralph Lauren Black Label cashmere, floor-length, turtleneck sweater dress. "We're from New England and people just don't act like this there." Stepping out and turning around to face Jocelyn she ran her hands over her hips and asked, "How do I look?"

"You look like a model Mom. You look great," Jocelyn said, self-censoring comments about her mother going bra-less.

"B.B. has such refined taste," Margret gushed as she inspected a Jimmy Choo shoebox. "Jocelyn, you really should see the gallery attached to the fermentation room. You would absolutely love it! It's like a little museum or something."

"Are you kidding me?" Jocelyn questioned with disbelief. "There's a gallery here too?"

William replied, "There was a statue of a man made out of plastic bags…"

"And a big painting of a watch," Lilly completed her brother's sentence as twins are apt to do.

"Interesting."

"Joss, when you start feeling better I'll bring you there," Margret offered while slipping on a suede high heel. "I guess they change exhibits quarterly."

Jocelyn slowly nodded and then noticing the time on the little clock on the nightstand, she picked up the amber pill bottle. "Mom, I mean seriously," she pressed and twisted off the cap, "this guy is spending way too much money on us. Look, I even have painkillers! I don't care how rich he is. No one just does that."

"I don't know sweetheart. Ethan told you not to worry about money, to focus on getting well. I think this is a really nice place to be doing just that."

Squinting her eyes and shaking her head, Jocelyn popped a pill into her mouth and washed it down with some *sin gas* bottled water. "I don't know either, Mom. There's gotta be a catch. This is too easy." She put the water bottle to her mouth.

"I don't think so," Margret said. "Look at how far we all flew to be here. Ethan probably did make a smart decision. This place is fabulous!"

Involuntarily spraying water out of her mouth, she wiped her face and exclaimed, "Mom! We need to get home!" Then hushing herself, "This is crazy. Ethan kidnapped us. There's got to be a reason Wolf's being so generous."

Completely ignoring her daughter's comment, Margret responded with, "Here, let me help you get dressed. It will make you feel better to get out of all that hospital stuff." Jocelyn sighed and shook her head in disbelief at her mother, but complied.

While Margret was helping her daughter disrobe and put on a

what was essentially a really expensive designer potato sack because Jocelyn couldn't move her arm well enough to put on the formfitting sweater with the red piping, little William held up a knife. "Look!" he exclaimed. "Look what was in the bag!"

"You be careful with that young man," Jocelyn cautioned as her son began pulling apart all the different tools tucked away inside the red Victorinox Swiss Champ. "That's sharp you know. You could cut your finger off."

"I know," William replied without looking up. Lilly, in her Hello Kitty sweatshirt, was smooshed right up next to him, curiously observing what he was doing and Margret instantly slid up behind the two in order to keep a watchful eye on the proceedings.

"Do you think this," Margret said, pointing at what was going on with the various blades jetting out all over the place, "is a good idea?"

Jocelyn kind of shrugged as she secured a five-inch wide, dark leather belt around her skinny waist, giving the tea-length, with a slit up the side, Armani potato sack some definition. She decided that the outfit was really quite stunning if not for her sasquatch-like unshaven legs. "I wouldn't have gotten that for them, but since they found it, let them check it out. They're gonna come across one of these things someday anyway."

It was when William discovered the little wire crimping tool that there was a knock on the door and Mr. Wolf poked his head in. "May I enter?"

All heads turned and suddenly any danger of a gaping flesh wound from the Swiss Army knife disappeared and Margret floated across the room in her floor-length cashmere dress answering, "Sí, sí, yes, of course," as she opened the door wide for Mr. Wolf.

Jocelyn and the kids watched as Mr. Wolf made a show of being completely overwhelmed by the presence of Margret. Visually taking in her whole body and arriving at her chest, he tapped his fingers on his torso as if calming his feeble heart and whispered, "Dios mío, eres hermosa."

Margret bit her lip and smoothed her damp hair. "I don't know what that means," she replied, batting her eyelashes.

"My God, you're beautiful," Jocelyn obnoxiously blurted out but her mother didn't seem to mind.

"Es verdad. It's true," Mr. Wolf said, gazing deeply into Margret's eyes and then taking her hand and kissing it.

This time Jocelyn wasn't laughing uncontrollably, instead she cleared her throat. From the bed, barefooted and wearing a designer potato sack she said, "Señor Wolf thank you very, very much for taking such good care of us. What you have done is amazingly generous." Tearing his gaze away from Margret, Mr. Wolf turned toward Jocelyn as she spoke. "I don't know how we can ever possibly repay you for the hospitality you have extended."

Mr. Wolf replied, "Oh, but there is no need to repay! I so enjoy having, how do you say, 'fresh blood' a mi casa. It can be very lonely here in the valley." He looked again at Jocelyn's mother, "Especially during the long, cold, winter nights." Jocelyn almost gagged but Margret looked as if she was actually swooning and might topple over in her Jimmy Choo heels.

"Gracias for this," William said, holding up the Swiss Champ, shattering the moment.

Margret turned to look at Willy and his knife and happily exclaimed, "Did you hear that Joss?! He said gracias. The kids really are learning Spanish!"

Mr. Wolf smiled and Jocelyn cringed. "De nada," Mr. Wolf said, walking over to William. "I wanted for you to have that because your sister got for the present the animal toy and you needed something just for you."

"But Brownie's all stinky now," Lilly whined. "I wanted to take him to la fiesta with me."

Margret caught Jocelyn's eye and pointing to Lilly mouthed the word "fiesta" while giving a thumbs-up.

"Brownie will have a bath and be all clean para la fiesta. Do not worry sweetheart," Mr. Wolf assured Lilly.

Margret swooped in next to Mr. Wolf. "I don't know B.B. Maybe this knife isn't the best idea for a child."

"Nonsense. William is most equipped to handle this. You North Americans underestimate the mind of the children. As you have just seen, they absorb everything. Whatever you put in front of them they will take as their own. William is smart. You need not worry." Margret looked skeptical. "And if he hurts himself he learns the hard way, as they say. Is that not right William?" Jocelyn watched as Willy nodded and carefully began flipping some of the blades back down. "If you give respect with this knife it will last many years. In fact, I always carry the one my father gave to me."

Wolf reached into his trouser pocket and pulled out a bronze colored pocketknife. Flipping open the four-inch blade he said, "See how she works," while showcasing the tool. William stood up to look more closely at Mr. Wolf's knife. "It has also two small blades," Wolf said as he flicked one out. "Mine is old and cannot do as much as yours." William was captivated and Mr. Wolf offered it to him to examine.

Jocelyn was watching Willy weighing the difference between his and Mr. Wolf's knife when William said, "Mom, his is heavier than mine."

"Oh, let me see," Jocelyn replied, trying to focus on anything other than the newly acquired affected mannerisms her mother was exhibiting.

Willy, with Lilly right behind him peering over his shoulder, came up to the bed and handed Jocelyn Mr. Wolf's knife. "Look how fancy it is."

Even before the thing was in her hands she saw it. "Oh...," she sighed. Jocelyn wasn't quite sure what to say as she held the heavy knife emblazoned with a swastika. "This *is* a special piece of history, isn't it?"

She looked up and made eye contact with Mr. Wolf who raised his chin and said, "Yes. I keep that with me always. My father was not married to my mother and I saw him rarely." Pointing to the knife Jocelyn was holding he continued, "He gave that to me when I was about William's age. His associates made sure to remember me when he died. This is how I have come to own this place."

"Interesting," Jocelyn said, holding out the folded knife for him to collect.

Mr. Wolf strode over, plucked it out of her hand, shook it, then using it to point at the painting of the woman on the wall next to Jocelyn's bed said, "That is a portrait my mother despised." All heads turned to look at the oil painting. "I am told that this painting, should it ever find its way to market, would fetch millions. This is the only woman my father ever loved."

"Who is she?" Margret asked, sliding up next to Mr. Wolf and gently placing her hand on his arm.

"Angela Maria Raubal," he said, staring at the portrait. "Geli was what my father called her. The two were inseparable." Margret sighed and gave Mr. Wolf's arm a loving squeeze. "She was in medical school when she killed herself after my father came to find she wanted to marry with another man."

Margret gasped. "Oh, that is so tragic. Was it a forced marriage?" Wolf shook his head no. "But that doesn't make sense," Margret mused. "You'd think he would be the one to commit suicide if he was so heartbroken." Jocelyn scowled at her mother and mentally willed her to stop talking.

Tucking the pocketknife away and still staring at the portrait, "Not only was she the love of my father's life, she was also my father's niece. So I am related to this woman."

It was quiet as no one knew exactly what to say. Jocelyn leaned back and, changing the subject commented, "It is very well painted. When I first saw this painting, I don't know why, but I thought Mary Cassatt might be the artist."

"Oh! You are close!" Wolf burst out. "The man who for Mary Cassatt was inspired by and tried to emulate painted it, Degas. Very good! You have a good eye."

Needless to say, Jocelyn's jaw dropped. "This is a real Degas?" Wolf nodded. "Seriously?" Even though it was awkward and uncomfortable she crawled over the bed to get a better look. She stopped herself from touching the fragile layers of oil paint. "I don't remember seeing this particular painting in any of my art history classes," Jocelyn skeptically commented. "I remember Degas mostly for paintings of ballerinas and fancy dances."

"Sí. However, this was forever in my father's personal possession. He traveled with it always. It was not ever in the salt mine in Merkers." Jocelyn did know what the salt mine comment was about but remained fixated on the painting. "Of course, you must recognize this artist," Mr. Wolf said, holding out his hand, palm up, and turning his whole body to feature the little painting on the wall by the bathroom.

Without even turning to look at it and keeping her eyes fixed on the mystery Degas, Jocelyn confidently replied, "Picasso from his Blue Period."

"Correct!" Mr. Wolf exclaimed like a game show host. Margret, happily amazed by her daughter's fine art acumen, walked up to behold the Picasso. Now knowing it was worth thousands, if not millions, of dollars, she leaned in to study it as if it was a private viewing at the Louvre and not some random thing stuck to a wall next to a closet with an emergency toilet installed in it.

Jocelyn turned around to face Mr. Wolf. "Was that your father's too?" she asked, pointing to the little blue painting.

"No. He detested that picture. I suspect that is why my mother loved it so."

"Interesting," Jocelyn commented while carefully sliding off the bed. Walking barefoot, off-balance as if drunk, past the kids who were sitting on the floor flipping open the blades of the Swiss Champ and making sure to avoid the bloodstain she said, "You have a room decorated with artwork that both your parents didn't like."

"Sí. The passion of the two is with us here."

"And that's what this is?" Jocelyn asked while stopping and running her finger over the race-to-space wallpaper to the bullet hole. "Passion?"

"No." Mr. Wolf shook his head. "A fatal mistake. I leave it to remember. This room is as it was when my mother died."

Jocelyn took a deep breath and swallowed the questions but Margret didn't. "How did your mother die?"

"Of a broken heart, I am sure." Jocelyn watched as Margret squeezed Mr. Wolf's arm again. Wolf, as if pulled physically into his memory, continued, "US dollars arrived from the bank when the news of my father's death came. Mother also found from the man that accounts had been set up for me, but none for her. I now understand that this insult is what drove her ultimately insane." Mr. Wolf shook his head. "I have been told that Mother came from an impressive family line that passed along specific, how do you say, genetic traits. That it wasn't anyone's fault what happened."

He closed his eyes as if willing the memory to go away and after a long pause opened his eyes and solemnly said, "May both my parents rest in peace." Margret made the sign of the cross over her chest and bowed her head. Jocelyn wasn't sure what to do so she just nodded sympathetically.

Finally, Lilly asked, "Are we still having la fiesta?"

The question snapped Mr. Wolf back to the here and now. "Yes, por supuesto! Of course, little one."

Lilly and William smiled at each other.

CHAPTER TWENTY-SIX

Meanwhile
Somewhere in Florida, USA

"I AM SO THIRSTY," Jerry whined. "I can't remember when I was ever this thirsty." He had his shirt off, like he had at Disney, but this time he was balancing the bus seat cushion on his head, holding it in position with one hand, and using it as giant sun visor. He hugged his ribs with his other arm as he trudged along. "I honestly don't think I've been this thirsty in my entire life."

Sunburned and exasperated, Mark didn't say anything but just kept walking. His white polo shirt was completely saturated with perspiration; even the collar was damp. His puffy eye was in full bloom so he couldn't see out of it. His right hand was stiff, swollen, and caked with scabbed up blood.

"Dude, seriously, have you ever been this thirsty? This is crazy."

Rolling his one good eye, Mark finally stopped and turned around to face Jerry. "Look, we've already established that it's hot, so I'm going to attempt to be diplomatic. Okay?" Jerry nodded. "You doing up that map and bringing it with us was a good idea." Jerry smiled. "A really good idea. I'll give you that, but you going on and on about being thirsty isn't exactly helpful right now, especially considering what we're walking through." He pointed to the abandoned carports and houses with their decorative cinderblocks and the faded notices hanging on the doors warning of radioactive water. "Why don't you quietly focus on something else right now?" Jerry agreed and they silently continued their trek.

They had been walking down the deserted street for what seemed like forever when Jerry had the novel idea that he and Mark were ghosts walking past and through ghosts of the former residents of this street. Bittersweet optimism about the future lingered and swirled around the abandoned architecture as Jerry's heart, not to mention feet, became very heavy. "I have to stop," he said, holding his ribs.

Mark, who looked exactly like a lightweight prizefighter who had just lost a match, turned back toward him and said, "Come on man, you can do it. We're almost at the chicken wing place."

"I don't know." Jerry sighed, dropping the naugahyde seat cushion on the ground and slowly sitting down on it. "I think I really did break some ribs."

"Yeah, you probably did," Mark commiserated, picking a scab off his beat-up hand. He was going to sit but the pavement was too hot, so he just squatted down next to Jerry.

"I know you don't want me to bring this up, but I really need some water," Jerry commented. Mark was going to reply but out of the corner of his eye he saw something moving down at the end of the street. At first he thought it was one of those crazy dogs they had seen earlier, but in actuality it was really a bird, like a turkey, sauntering through the yard of a seemingly out of place two-story brick house.

Mark pointed to the bird. "Now, how's that thing getting water?"

Jerry looked up and smiled, "Oh, that's one of the peacocks I saw on the drive in. There's more of them around here too."

"Really? That's a peacock?"

"A girl. A peahen. The boys have the showy tails. I saw two males and a few females," Jerry said as he hoisted himself off the bus seat cushion to get a better look at the gray feathered female. While arduously standing back up he caught a glimpse of the fingernail etched map and said, "Gosh, we really are close to the chicken wings place," then he gave his full attention to the peahen. "I bet the others are nearby."

"Where'd they come from? They're not native to Florida."

"That's exactly what I thought when I first saw them!" Jerry replied, watching the bird and then adding as two more peafowl waddled out from behind the brick house, "Yeah, how are they surviving?"

The house the peacocks were pecking around looked different from the other houses they had been walking past. This one was impressive and had tall, skinny, rectangle windows and a big front porch. It was made of old, red brick in contrast to the cinderblock 1950s ranch-style neighborhood they had passed through. Being on a corner lot it had much more land than the other houses in the bad water zone. It even had two elegant tall trees in the yard and exotic flowers, whereas the other houses had little, postage stamp size yards and brambly bushes. "I bet all these other houses were built on what used to be one big estate," Mark commented.

"Do you think anyone lives in there?" Jerry wondered.

"I don't know, but it's got trees and shade. Let's go sit there." Mark reached down and picked up the bus seat. "I'll carry it for a while if you want." Jerry, holding his ribs, seemed grateful and with sweat beading off both their brows they headed toward the brick house.

The shade was amazing. They entered the yard and Jerry gratefully eased himself down on the rough Florida grass under a tree dripping with Spanish moss. Mark remained standing and noticed that the backyard was fenced in by a four-foot-tall brick wall and a fancy iron gate. Ivy and bougainvillea spilled out from the enclosed area. Mark was drawn to the gate and walked over to it.

"This place must have been really nice back in the day," Jerry commented while looking at the spalled bricks and damaged shutters. "I'd live here."

Mark was just about to open the garden gate when a male peacock hopped up from behind the wall and perched itself onto it, nervously unfurling its massive display of blue and green plumage. This caught Mark completely by surprise and he jumped back, shouting over his shoulder, "Jerry! Check this out!"

Jerry, still dreamily staring at the house, turned to look and gave a whistle. "Now that's a good-lookin' bird. Watch out, they bite."

The peacock jumped off the gate as it was being opened by an old man with a leathery face and sporting a pathetic little gray ponytail. He was wearing a Pan Am T-shirt and a shark tooth necklace. His look was completed with mangy cargo shorts and hemp bracelets. The patchouli scent and Birkenstock sandals further amplified the impression that this guy had survived many a Grateful Dead concert. "Damn junkies! Shoo! Get off my lawn!"

"We're not junkies sir. I know this doesn't look good, but I swear…We really need water," Mark said, instinctively patting around at his pockets. "We don't have any money but we'd do anything for something to drink."

The man's eyes were squinting with suspicion when he asked, "Anything?"

Jerry yelled from under the tree, "Yes! Anything!"

Mark could almost physically feel this man's gaze running over his sunburnt, puffy black eye. The visual inspection was going on way too long but Mark didn't budge. "We just need water. We'll gladly pay you back however we can."

The man, still highly apprehensive of the two, shook his head and sighed. "Why do I get the feeling I'm going to regret this." He held the gate open for Mark who waited for Jerry to get up, collect the cumbersome bus seat map, and join him.

They stepped into the garden and were pleasantly surprised.

Although the square garden was not very well maintained, it had good classical bones and lots of interesting, mature plantings bursting into bloom tucked in all over the place and, in some areas, choking each other out. In the center of the space was a water garden full of water lilies and tall ornamental grass. As they walked over the crunchy pea-stone path the splashy plop of a frog diving for cover could be heard.

"This is really nice," Jerry commented. "Where'd the peacocks come from?"

"Pakistan," the man said simply. "Birthday gift for my mother back in '73."

"Do you need a special license to keep them?" The man didn't answer but kept walking up the stairs to the house. Jerry and Mark followed.

They entered through a screened-in porch that had two ceiling fans slowly spinning around, a perfect vista to enjoy views of the garden. Patchouli man opened a French door and ushered them into an outdated kitchen where there was a big water cooler set up by the refrigerator.

"Have at it guys," their host said, shakily passing each of them a paper cup. "Don't make yourselves sick now." Neither of them were at all concerned that the water might contain aborted fetal cells at this point and they voraciously descended upon the water cooler. It did cross both their minds to just drink directly out of the five-gallon bottle but they controlled themselves. They took turns relentlessly filling up their tiny cups and chugging the contents. They were so fixated on consuming as much water as possible that they didn't notice that the man had left the room.

Eventually, Jerry noticed a whirling sound and realized that the man was missing. Still holding his little paper cup he wandered into the adjacent living room where the man was watching a cable news channel on a modest television while riding an exercise bicycle. The high ceilinged room in which the bike was awkwardly positioned featured a big, dusty, oriental rug, past its prime furniture, and an eclectic mix of artwork hanging on the walls including but not limited to: carved, wooden tribal masks; incredibly detailed horticultural illustrations; sepia photographs in oval frames; rectangle diplomas in mahogany frames; and an assortment of varying quality watercolor and oil paintings. The placement of the pieces on the walls was much like the situation in the garden where all the fascinating plants were competing for space and attention. To further complement this aesthetic, there were big piles of newspapers and manila folders stacked up against the wall.

"Hey mister, thanks for the water," Jerry called out to the man, raising his little cup. "I think you literally just saved our lives. We owe you one."

"Oh, good. I'm glad we're all in agreement on that. Come on in," the man offered, flicking his fingers toward a 1980s mauve couch. "Take a load off. You too," he said to Mark who had followed Jerry in. While Jerry and Mark were making themselves comfortable and checking out what was on TV, the man stretched his arms and reached down to a cup holder attached to the exercise bike. He pulled up a little neon green plastic bong with a dancing bear sticker on it. Still pedaling away, he put the water pipe to his mouth, sparked up his lighter, and with the sound of bubbles percolating took a deep breath. Upon exhale, followed by a brief coughing fit, the distinctive, pungent scent of marijuana permeated the air and he asked, "So what's your story?"

Jerry and Mark were speechless so he offered the bong to Mark, who raised the eyebrow over his one good eye and declined. Jerry, watching the exchange, took a sip from his dainty cup. He seemed as if he was considering taking a hit when Mark nudged him, causing him to gasp and grab his ribs. "No takers? Okay," the man said. "I could tell by the way you two spoke that you weren't redneck junkies." Inserting the bong back into the cup holder he kept pedaling. "Look," the man began while staring at the TV, "as you can probably already tell things have really changed around here. See that?" He pointed to a mahogany rectangle. "That's my law degree." Jerry and Mark looked up and saw three diplomas all displaying elaborate, painstaking, curlicue calligraphy spelling out the surname "Stephens." "The one next to mine is my father's and the one next to that is my grandfather's."

"Oh, you must be Clifford," Jerry surmised from the graduation dates.

"Cliff. You can call me Cliff." Jerry nodded and was about to introduce himself, but the guy kept talking and pumping the pedals. "This place you're sitting in," he huffed, "this has been my family's home since it was built one hundred and fifty-seven years ago. Back when we were fighting the Seminoles." Bearing down on the handlebars, Cliff pumped faster. "This whole area used to be called Stephensville. That is until the accident. God damn sinkhole. That blew everything to hell."

"That sucks," Jerry added, not knowing what else to say. Mark was still processing the image of an elderly Dead Head lawyer smoking pot from a green mini-bong while riding an exercise bike. He was trying to reconcile what he was looking at. It was completely messed up but at the same time weirdly making perfect sense.

Cliff randomly started giggling an old man's type of cackle, and then sitting up straight on his bike seat started pedaling slower with his hands sliding up and down his thighs as he worked the pedals. For a seventy- maybe eighty-year-old he was in very decent shape. The only thing that gave away his age were the worry lines indelibly etched into his wrinkly face and evidence of arthritis in three of his boney fingers; otherwise, he had a runner's body type.

"Yeah. They're saying it was a freak accident, an act of God. But oh, noooooo. I don't think so. That sinkhole drained millions of gallons of acidic water laced with sulfate and sodium from the fertilizer company's discharge pool." Cliff was going on as if Jerry and Mark knew exactly what he was talking about. "Of course, there was gypsum involved, a fertilizer byproduct. Radioactive, naturally. That spilled into the darn sinkhole too. A certifiable disaster."

Even though Jerry was afraid Cliff might have a stroke or something, he was most impressed by how well this guy was articulating himself while being stoned and riding an exercise bike.

Cliff grabbed the handlebars and leaned into his movements. "The sinkhole turned out to be almost three hundred feet deep and that's why this place cleared out. It contaminated all the drinking water!" Cliff took some deep breaths before continuing. "Meanwhile, a Texas-based oil company was cited for illegal fracking in Corkscrew Swamp Sanctuary. That's a nesting site for wood storks."

Mark was gritting his teeth. He couldn't believe he was being forced to listen to the plight of wood storks. He was consoling himself by rationalizing that the whole experience was the price of the water.

Cliff continued, "The Florida Department of Environmental Protection sanctioned and fined that company twenty-five thousand dollars for fracking without a permit." Cliff was now heaving deep breaths as his soliloquy rambled on. "I'm convinced that the Stephensville sinkhole is because of fracking. But you know how it goes when you question the official narrative." He glanced meaningfully over his shoulder to them then turned his attention back to the TV as he pedaled furiously. "I've spent nearly three million dollars of my own money figuring out how this happened. To fight this thing in court." *inhale.* "I was hell bent on making it illegal to frack. Finally I said enough's enough!" *inhale.* "Three million? Someone else needs to carry the torch and fight the good fight!" he screamed. His pedaling slowed down. "My plan is to enjoy what's left and let everyone else go to hell."

He stopped pedaling. The whirling noise stopped and, breathing heavy, Cliff leaned over to grab a glass of water resting on top of the TV. "You know, less than a thousand humans have had genuine lasting impact on civilizational memory beyond their lifespan and most of the ones that we remember are remembered for doing nasty shit." He shook his head. "I finally realized that I can't save the world. Hell, I can't even save the neighborhood my father built."

Still shaking his head he raised his glass to the two of them, "Here's to simple pleasures!" Mark with his messed-up eye and Jerry holding his ribs watched in dumbfounded silence from the couch as Cliff gulped down the water and finished it off with a big "Ahhhh" of satisfaction.

"What the hell?" Mark whispered.

"What?" Jerry whispered back. "I thought that was very poignant." Ignoring him, Mark stood up and pointed to the TV. A swirling "breaking news" logo swooshed over the screen and the camera rolled to a woman smiling from behind a podium. The footage abruptly cut to the same woman sort of whimpering and then cut again to a map of the United States where yearbook class pictures of children were falling like raindrops on the map.

"What's up?" Jerry asked Mark who was completely captivated by the television. Mark waved at Jerry to be quiet. Cliff got off the exercise bike and stood back to watch Mark and what he was so enthralled with. The screen was now filled with statistics about gun violence and then the original woman, captured with a warmer type of lighting and a defusing camera lens filter, was sitting cross-legged in a wingback chair. There was an orchid plant placed strategically on the end table to her right and it showed up as a colorful dab of purple on the screen when the camera zoomed in on this woman's smiling face. She looked so happy, in fact, that it appeared she was receiving a direct revelation from God or was perhaps heavily drugged. Mark was frozen. The news piece ended with a busty female anchor shaking her head as if in pity and then gently and reassuringly nodding while announcing how people could make donations to the Mark Witherall Always Love Foundation.

Stunned, Mark slowly sat back down on the couch as Jerry jumped up and exclaimed, "Dude! Was that your mother?!" Mark nodded yes. "What the? They already have a logo for the foundation

Mark! They already branded the darn thing!"

Mark was quiet and Cliff offered, "If they're taking donations as a nonprofit organization that tax paperwork takes time to set up, so they probably got the graphic designer working back..."

"Before I was dead," Marked completed the sentence.

"Cliff, do you have a cell phone charger?" Jerry anxiously asked.

Cliff, who was staring quizzically at Mark, replied, "No, but I've got a fax machine."

"Oh, that's great, but I don't need that right now. Do you have any sort of computer here?" Jerry hopefully inquired.

"No," Cliff said thoughtfully, "but the kid over at the cell phone place, down at the plaza by the Dollar Store, always lets me send email from there when I need to."

"Okay, let's go," Jerry eagerly announced, heading toward the door. Mark, still stuck to the couch, was rubbing his chin, staring at the TV.

"First, you guys had better get cleaned up," Cliff suggested. "Patchouli can only do so much, you know."

"Yeah, I guess you're right," Jerry said, sniffing his underarm.

"There's a shower upstairs," Cliff offered.

"But what about the radioactive water?" Jerry wanted to know.

"For a quick shower, it's probably okay," Cliff said and then stifling a giggle added, "The odor you're effusing is definitely more deadly." Jerry sniffed his underarm again.

Mark looked away from the TV and asked, "What about clothes?"

Controlling his laughter Cliff replied, "I've got some things you can borrow. The clothes you've got on we might as well burn. There's no fixing that." Touching his shirt, Mark had to nod in agreement. "Go get showered up," Cliff directed. "It's upstairs to the right. When you're done, I'll drive. I'm hungry and I want some chicken wings anyway. Come on," Cliff encouraged, clapping his arthritic hands. "Chop-chop! Four different types of wings. I'm buying!"

CHAPTER TWENTY-SEVEN

Meanwhile
Huemul, Argentina
In the laboratory

"IRONICALLY, IT IS DISGUISED as a toy gun to get the technology across international borders," Maximilian de Habsburg explained.

"Actually, that's pretty smart," Ethan responded with arms crossed over his chest, still holding his handgun. Max was now without a face shield because Ethan had yanked it off earlier, arguing that if he had to be in this lab without a suit getting exposed to some debilitating pathogen, then Max did too. The absence of a shield not only revealed the full resplendence of Max's prominent jaw, it also made quite obvious how elderly the man was. He looked to be at least ninety years old with his long pointy nose which harshly contrasted with his rectangular jaw. His angular face was gaunt with a smattering of age marks and moles running across his wrinkled, papery flesh. To his credit, he had ample amounts of white hair.

The monkeys were hooting and screaming and the injured scientists were moaning pathetically in the background as Max, with Ethan watching, began disassembling the toy gun with the speed and alacrity of a circumspect tree sloth. He very slowly and methodically unscrewed the stock, carefully placing it to the side. Then, twisting the cheap plastic trigger mechanism like a key, a little, clear plastic container resembling a mini 35 mm film canister slid out of the barrel onto the table. Max twisted the trigger all the way around to its original position and then twisted it again. Ethan watched as another little plastic container slid out of the barrel. This time, it obviously held a green microchip.

Ethan pointed to the little containers with his gun. "That looks pretty easy to sneak through customs. Why the big production? Just put it in your pocket and walk through the scanners."

"Firstly, it's against the law to transfer this type of technology. Secondly, this is stolen technology. Most importantly, I am almost certain that going through a scanner would destroy this thing," Max responded.

"Well, didn't it get zapped with all sorts of rays and stuff coming in from wherever it came from?"

"Yes, and that is why, if you look closely at the barrel where the chip is nested," he picked up the barrel and showed Ethan where he had unscrewed the stock, "it is lined with a fine layer of lead specially designed for optimal baffling of incoming rays. The barrel acts like a chambered sarcophagus keeping the chip and its accompanying documentation completely sealed off from outside corruption. That's why these things are much heavier than they appear," Max said, slowly heaving the barrel of the toy gun like a barbell.

"Okay, so what does it do?" Ethan asked.

"I don't know." Ethan was gearing up to pistol whip Max when the man added, "This is the brain of the nanobot fleet before it swims away."

"Fleet?"

"Basically, this is the blueprint for a singular repetitive operation to be done by one tiny machine. In our case we have plenty of tiny machines to do whatever this task is. The machines have to work together to complete the mission." Max raised his skinny index finger, "Remember, you can fit seven oxygen atoms spinning in a row within the length of one nanometer. We are operating at the smallest scale currently accessible to man. At this scale, whatever it is will take quite a long time to accomplish unless you have many bots working together. The more the better."

"So, this," Ethan waved his hand over the clear canisters, "tells all the nanobots what to do?" Max nodded. "And every toy gun we brought here has these things in it?"

"I would assume."

"Do you think all these guns contain the same exact chip for the same exact task or do you think whoever sent this to us had a more complex operation in mind with different nanobots doing different things?"

Max sighed. "I don't know but I would assume the latter because this is an enormous shipment."

"Let me guess, the nanobots are hidden in the peanut butter?" Ethan said, holding up and studying a jar.

"Again, I would assume, but we should check. I'm fairly certain they used peanut butter to avoid scrutiny because security dogs have difficulty detecting even cocaine when packed carefully inside a jar of peanut butter. I also think it's quite clever that they used peanut butter considering all the bluster about nanobots and gray goo." Max chuckled.

"Gray goo?"

"Oh, it's a made-up term coined by nanotechnology pioneer Eric Drexler in his 1986 book *Engines of Creation*. It's a hypothetical apocalyptic scenario involving out-of-control self-replicating nanobots that end up consuming all the biomass of Earth while creating more of themselves." A screaming monkey barreled past the stainless steel table. Noticing Ethan's concern as he watched the marauding primate, Max added, "It's a bit farfetched, but it's within the realm of possibility."

"Uh-huh. Okay. So," he pointed the gun at the little plastic canisters, "what's this brain going to tell the nanobots to do?"

"Ah, we have a problem," Ache interrupted. He was outfitted with the automatic rifle he had reclaimed from the guy Ethan had shot. He had been rounding up and keeping all the CBRN guys in what he and Ethan were calling the "monkey pit," or the original specimen kennel before the soundproof glass got blow away. Two dead and one critically injured were also conveniently stashed away in there thanks to Ache and his ability to effectively coerce the surviving to carry the fallen.

Ethan turned and replied, "Yeah, what is it?"

"What are we going to do with that guy that isn't dead?"

"They're all PhDs. Let them deal with it." Nodding, Ache turned on his heel and headed back into the noisy monkey pit. "You were saying?" Ethan directed to Max. "What exactly are these nanobots going to be doing?"

"That depends on the point of origin. If these are from the United States, the UK, Spain, Sweden, Germany, or France they will probably be useful for synthetic telepathy."

"God damn it! I don't need synthetic telepathy," Ethan barked. "I need firepower! The ability to kill on demand. Your diseases sounded better than this."

"Let's find out where our package came from, shall we?"

"Yeah, sure, why not?" Ethan grumbled. He glanced over to the monkey pit and saw all the CBRN guys coalescing around the injured man Ache had alerted him about. They were cutting the man's CBRN suit off as Ache, flanked by José who was also holding a big black rifle, oversaw the proceedings. José appeared to be interpreting for Ache.

Max meanwhile was opening one of the little plastic briefcases that the guys coming in through the door had been carrying. Ethan watched as Max, still moving at his unhurried pace, pulled out what looked like a strange, oversized jeweler's loop; a small tablet computer; a pair of tweezers; a USB cord; and three black plastic things about the size of thick pencils. Max rested himself on a stool then hooked the USB cord to one of the computers on the table and connected it to the tablet computer. He then snapped open the first little plastic film case and very methodically collected the square chip it contained with the tweezers. It looked like a piece of plastic confetti. He held this material very carefully with the tweezers and placed it at the center of the tablet computer screen. As he worked the two free-range monkeys were still going bonkers, hopping all over everything.

"Is there any way to get these monkeys to shut up?" Ethan wanted to know.

"Why do you think I installed that soundproof wall?" Max said without looking up. He snapped the pencil things into the jeweler's loop, creating a little tripod with the big loop thing resting at the top. "These field kits are fantastic in a pinch," he commented while cautiously placing the tripod over the tablet computer. "I own the full-size machine, of course, but it appears to be out of commission," he said, motioning with his chin to a bullet riddled piece of equipment. He then clicked the on/off button on the tablet three times and a perfect stream of light instantly burst down onto the chip from the jeweler's loop on top of the tripod. He leaned over and snapped the big flat-screen computer monitor to life. Silently studying the monitor he sighed and then burst out laughing, a giddy type of laugh.

"What?" Ethan asked, "What's so funny?"

"Oh, this is priceless!" Max exclaimed, holding back a spasm of hilarity and pointing to the monitor which was filled with long, tedious lines of code and text. "This was commissioned by the Vatican."

"What?!" Ethan spat out, walking over to look back and forth between Max and the computer screen. "That's completely insane!" With a furrowed brow he looked to Max for clarification.

"Pontificia Academia Scientiarum," Max giggled.

Confused, Ethan watched Maximillian de Habsburg laugh. Finally Ethan spat out, "Okay. I'm done." Pointing the gun at Max he said, "The Vatican? Really? Is there anything else you wanna say before I shoot you in that big ass chin of yours?"

Instinctively raising his hands Max confidently explained, "Its members include some of the most respected scientists of the twentieth century, Max Planck and Niels Bohr among others. It's Latin for Pontifical Academy of Sciences and it was established by Pope Pius XI. It's the modern descendent of the Vatican's first scientific advisory, Accademia dei Lincei or 'Academy of Lynxes.' That was started up in 1603 and boasts Galileo among its members. Accademia dei Lincei survives to this day as a completely separate institution. In fact, I was a member until I was expelled."

"Why were you kicked out?" Ethan wanted to know.

Max lowered his hands and shrugged his shoulders. "There were accusations that I was unethical or something along those lines."

"Uh-huh." Ethan studied Max and lowered his gun completely. The monkeys were still at it but Ethan, ignoring their antics, asked, "Why would the Vatican, of all places, be interested in nanobots?"

"Oh, you'd be surprised by what they get themselves involved with over there. They own and operate some of the most advanced telescopes on earth because they're looking for alien life. They even got involved with something called Lucifer at their observatory on Mount Graham in Arizona, USA. Interestingly, the Vatican Observatory is built on a Native American sacred site," Max replied absently while studying the information displayed on the computer monitor. "Why wouldn't they be interested in nanobots? They have all different fields of inquiry at the Pontifical Academy of Sciences."

He looked back up at Ethan. "The life sciences are one of but eight areas of study and that is further broken down into research and experimentation in," he counted off on his fingers, "agronomy, botany, zoology, genetics, molecular biology, biochemistry, the neurosciences, and surgery. They are into absolutely everything. The specially selected scientists chosen to participate do not have to follow the church. They could be Satanists for all they care. Probably how the telescope in Arizona got the acronym LUCIFER..." he giggled and then trailed off momentarily. "Anyhow, that's how badly the Vatican wants to be on top of the game. As I've told you, nanobots are going to have an enormous impact on everything on this planet. It makes perfect sense that they would be handing out grant money for nanobot research."

Ethan bit the inside of his cheek and then asked, "Max, are the nanobots blank slates? You know, can we program them to do whatever we want?"

"No. Well, I take that back. Not likely. The little machines are designed with a very specific task in mind. From what it says here these nanobots are part of something called the LAZARUS project."

Just then a stinky wad of monkey dung came hurtling toward Ethan and smacked him on the back. Taken totally off guard, he swung around and shot the monkey. Everyone in the monkey pit looked up. The monkey stumbled then fell. Red blood was pooling up around the creature on the cement floor when Ethan shouted, "See! See what I did right there? That's exactly what I thought I was getting, not some bullshit microscopic robots! I want guns God damn it!" The other monkey was hopping around near the elevator, screeching and beating its chest when Ethan shot it too. "Fuck this shit. Seriously."

He grabbed Max and yanked the man off the stool, dragging him into the monkey pit where the CBRN suits, José, Ache, and the critically injured guy sprawled out on the floor greeted him with frozen looks of fearful anticipation. The infected monkeys in their cages were going absolutely insane, thrashing around, hooting and screeching. The sound was echoing off the concrete walls as Ethan pushed Max into the crowd with everyone else. He pointed to Ache and Josè and motioned for them to stand next to him.

"You all have a choice," Ethan said. Then raising his voice he shouted, "I'm giving you a choice! As I'm sure you are all aware there is a significant shipment of technology that just rolled in. My associates and I own this! You have a choice of working with me or against me. You!" he pointed his gun at the near-naked injured man on the floor that the CBRN suits had all been attempting emergency triage on. The man looked up at Ethan as he asked, "Do you pledge your allegiance to me?" When the man did not answer, Ethan took a deep breath and shouted, "Translate!"

José stepped forward with his rifle and yelled above the caged animals, "¿Prometes tu lealtad a este hombre?"

Looking confused the injured man shook his head and said, "No."

"That is completely your choice. I want you and everyone here," Ethan said, pointing the gun at each of them, "I want you to remember that I gave you a choice." Then he casually shot the injured man smack dab in the center of the forehead.

Ethan, with the help of José translating, very cordially asked each person in the monkey pit to join forces and pledge allegiance to him, and of course each person did. That was until he reached Max, whom he had purposefully left for last.

"Max, I feel like we've bonded here today. I very much respect your knowledge and think you would be an incredibly important addition to my team."

"Gracias," Max said, bowing his liver-spotted head and folding his hands as if in prayer. "Thank you very much." Raising his chin he looked Ethan in the eye and continued, "I know you are going to ask me to swear loyalty to you. That is not an issue for me. I will." Ethan grinned and the monkeys screamed.

"My work is my life and I will continue to do what I do until the day I die regardless of any new king, or government, or tyrant sweeping into power. What I do take issue with is your statement that all of this technology, all these new nanobots and their code belongs to you and your associates." Ethan stopped smiling. "Well, where do you think all the anonymous bitcoin that showed up in your wallet came from in the first place?"

Ethan squinted his eyes. A long pregnant pause ensued while everyone in the room anxiously watched and waited to see what Ethan was going to do. "You," Ethan snarled. "So you're saying it came from you?" The two men engaged in an extended stare down and Ethan finally broke the terse silence with, "You have guns here don't you Max? I mean, your men were carrying Colts. Are there more guns here?"

"Yes," Max replied.

"And ammunition?"

"Yes."

"Good. We'll take all that." Still staring at Max, Ethan yelled, "José!" José walked up and stood next to Ethan. "Please formally welcome Max here to the team. Then let everyone know we have to pack up." He picked up one of the toy guns and studying it said, "We have a party to go to."

CHAPTER TWENTY-EIGHT

Stephensville, Florida, USA
8:05 p.m.

"SWEET RIDE," Jerry commented, crossing his arms over the "Long Strange Trip It's Been" graphic on the T-shirt Cliff let him wear. "I like how there's a little analog clock right there at the bottom of the tachometer." Pointing to it he said, "That's pretty cool. You just don't see that anymore."

"I know," Cliff replied, inserting the key into the ignition of the midnight blue 1984 Mercedes 300D Turbo. The car made an extended buzzing tone and as soon as it stopped Cliff twisted the key. With the diesel engine chugging to life he proclaimed, "I'm tellin' you, this is the best money I've ever spent," and gave the steering wheel an appreciative pat. "Straight from the factory and 242,000 miles later she still runs like a champ." He turned on the headlights and popped a tape into the cassette player. Mark, who had opted for a simple white T-shirt from Cliff's collection, was sitting in the back seat trying to catch a glimpse of his swollen eye in the rearview mirror from over Cliff's shoulder when the springy electric guitar riffs of "Sugar Magnolia" filled the interior of the car. The song seemed a fitting accompaniment to the sky and clouds swabbed with sunset colors.

The car was still really warm from the day's heat and Cliff adjusted the air conditioning before he edged the boxy Mercedes sedan out of the carport and onto the deserted road. "A benefit of living here is that directionals are optional," Cliff giggled as he took a left turn onto another abandoned street.

It wasn't long before the Dollar Store sign loomed in the distance and they were pulling into the brightly lit shopping plaza's parking lot. "How 'bout you guys go do what you gotta do and I'll order up the wings? Everything should be closing up by nine." Jerry and Mark agreed and hopped out of the car with cell phones in hand.

"Hey!" Jerry yelled and Cliff turned to look at him. "Are they going to ask for money to charge the phones?"

"Nah," Cliff shook his head. "Just tell them I sent you." Jerry nodded and they headed out on their respective missions.

Cool air, a high pitched **ding*,* and a panoply of different iterations of the latest cellular communications technology welcomed them to the store. "Hello!" Mark shouted, once standing at the counter.

A young man, tucking his Cell Phone Shoppe polo shirt into his khaki pants, emerged from behind a wall festooned with balloons celebrating "no activation fee" and racks of reconditioned cell phones. "Oh, hi. Sorry about that. What can I help you with?" he asked, obviously taken aback by Mark's messed up eye.

"Cliff Stephens said we could charge up here," Jerry said, waving his phone.

"Stephens? Is he here?" the kid asked, craning his neck to look out the window.

"He's over getting some wings."

"Oh, Christ. Kim! You gotta go!" Mark and Jerry watched as a young woman emerged from behind the same wall, fixing her hair with an elastic. The girl glanced at them while smoothing her jean miniskirt and then darted out of the store, leaving a piercing **ding** in her wake.

Mark, with his one good eye, watched the girl trot across the street to the Dollar Store. Jerry wiggled his eyebrows as if giving a congratulatory "good for you" to the young man, but noticing that the guy wasn't making eye contact he asked, "Where can we charge our phones?"

"Right here," the shopkeeper said, nervously taking a package from the wall and ripping it open. He handed a charger to Jerry who plugged in his cell phone. Mark got a tap on the shoulder and, tearing his gaze away from the girl entering the Dollar Store, he passed his phone over to the blushing shopkeeper who plugged it in. "You can leave them here and come back later if you want. It takes time to fully charge."

"No," Mark said flatly. "We should stay with these phones."

"You don't want any wings?" Jerry asked.

"Yeah, I want wings, but I'm not leaving these phones unattended."

Jerry scratched his head and said, "You're right. I'll go tell Cliff that we'll be here for a while."

"Can you get me some ice?" Mark pointed to his painful eye.

"Sure. I'll be right back."

Mark called out over the **ding** of the door, "And don't forget my wings!"

Jerry instantly spotted Cliff as he swung open the restaurant door which also **dinged** like the Cell Phone Shoppe's. Cliff was reading a newspaper under the fluorescent light in a booth on the left side of the sparsely decorated little establishment. The place featured a lot of yellow and orange formica and checkerboard linoleum. There were two wall-mounted TVs quietly broadcasting sports commentary as Jerry slid into the booth facing Cliff. "Mark and I are going to be hanging out next door until our phones are charged up." Cliff put the paper down. "I just wanted to let you know."

"That's okay. I don't have anywhere I have to be," Cliff said, folding up the newspaper and placing it to the side. Smiling, he called out to the approaching waitress who was hauling a serving tray loaded with platters of chicken wings, "Just in time!"

"Is all this for us?" Jerry asked, looking around the empty restaurant. Then, not getting an answer and assuming it was, he grabbed the newspaper to make room for the wings. Cliff tucked a napkin into his T-shirt collar and rubbed his hands together. Jerry very happily followed suit. He was just about to take a bite of a "3x HOT" buffalo chicken wing when the newspaper headline caught his eye.

About fifteen minutes later...

"I don't know. She said it's not me, it's her..."**ding** Mark, lounging in a cheap, white plastic, stackable lawn chair, turned away from Cell Phone Shoppe guy's unrequited love story and saw Jerry marching through the door with a styrofoam cup, a take-out box, and a folded up newspaper tucked under his arm.

"Dude!" Jerry slammed the take-out box and cup onto the counter and whipped open the newspaper. "Look!"

"What am I looking at?" Mark asked.

"Here!" Jerry pointed to the headline: *Suicides Plague Prison System*. "Look who they're talking about."

"Your cellmate?" Mark guessed as he stood up, tipping the styrofoam cup to inspect the ice cubes it held. "These for me?"

"Yes and yes," Jerry answered. Mark plucked a frozen cube from the cup and held it to his swollen eye. "And guess who else?" Jerry continued. Mark flipped open the take-out box and hungrily grabbed a wing with his non-ice holding hand as Jerry announced, "CO Barnes, and—ready for this?—Warden Calhoun!"

The ice cube popped out of Mark's fingers like a spent bullet shell. Snatching the newspaper from Jerry's hands he exclaimed,

"When was this published? We were just there for God's sake!" half his face contorting with concern and the other half remaining paralyzed, puffed up and painful. "This doesn't make any sense." Mark stopped flipping the paper around and uttered incredulously, "Barnes. That's the CO that did your intake?" Jerry nodded.

Mark studied the paper as Jerry spoke, "Yup. They're suiciding everyone who knows we're actually alive."

The Cell Phone Shoppe guy slowly eased out of his stackable lawn chair. Framed by a colorful backdrop of balloons and cellphones he said, "Look, fellahs, I don't know who you are or what your story is, so I'm just gonna leave now. Help yourself to anything you need." And with that, he bolted out the door which, of course, belched an electronic **ding** upon his exit.

Watching the young man running for his life under the parking lot lights Jerry muttered, "Smart move, buddy," while placing his hand on his sore rib.

"They certainly got this into print with the quickness," Mark commented. "Why do I get the feeling this is for our benefit?"

"Oh, paranoia comes with the territory," Jerry answered, still looking out the window.

"It says right here," Mark announced, "that Barnes shot himself in the mouth with a shotgun, purportedly because he was so upset about getting fired—"

"See, I don't believe that," Jerry spun around to face Mark. "I think that guy was way into taking the whole thing to court to get his pension and maybe a little extra too."

"And Calhoun…" Mark continued, "oh, dear God…are you kidding me?!"

"I know. Right? Calhoun must have really pissed someone off. I didn't get the vibe that he'd be the type of guy into erotic asphyxiation."

"There's no physical way! Like he went straight home from firing Barnes and seeing us out the door and then immediately got busy on himself and they had time to find him dead, report it, and print this up?" Mark angrily shook the paper.

"Journalism in the digital age," Jerry commented while walking behind the counter to stand next to Mark. "You have to remember, they did have a logo ready to roll for your nonprofit…" Mark angrily pursed his lips and shook his head. Looking over Mark's shoulder Jerry pointed to the part in the article about his cellmate Abercrombie. "On the bright side he's not dead. He's in a coma."

"Uh-huh..." Mark mumbled as he scanned through the article.

"Read down. To the left." Jerry pointed, "That little gray box there. I didn't realize he was actually in the slammer because someone had reported seeing him carrying lots of guns into his garage."

"And he went to jail for that?" Mark questioned. "It's Florida. I'm surprised anyone even noticed."

"It says there were over one hundred and eighty guns in there."

"Yikes."

"Mostly ARs. Some handguns too. Basically the dude had an armory in his garage. The guns weren't registered and he wasn't a registered arms dealer or anything."

"I guess Abercrombie thought whatever was waiting from him outside was worse than being in prison," Mark mused. Just then a **ding* alerted them that Cliff had wandered in.

"You enjoying those wings, Mark?!" Cliff called out, pointing to the take-out box as he approached the counter.

"Not to their fullest. Not yet," Mark answered. "But thank you though."

Jerry nodded at Cliff and picked up his cell phone. "We're dealing with some pretty heavy stuff here Cliff."

"I can see that. You're behind the counter. Definitely in a position of power," Cliff giggled. Then turning serious, "Where's the guy who runs this place? He and I have some business to attend to before closing."

"He literally just ran out," Jerry said, pointing to the window.

"And left you two alone with the cash register and all his inventory?" Cliff asked. Mark and Jerry nodded. Cliff frowned. "Is he what they call a millennial? I keep hearing about how they don't have any work ethic."

"Yeah," Jerry answered, "he's a millennial Cliff, but so is Mark here."

Jerry and Cliff looked over at Mark, who was grimacing back at them from behind his puffed-up eye. "Well, that's comforting. Open the register," Cliff demanded.

"Huh?" both Jerry and Mark uttered in surprise.

"You heard me. Open the register. That kid now owes me three months' back rent for this space. He's officially out as of right now and I'm taking what's in there and shutting this place down. I've given him ample opportunity to make things right."

"Wait. You're the landlord?" Jerry asked.

"I own this whole sorry town Jerry. I can't find a buyer for any of it. Radioactive water does that, as I'm sure you can imagine."

"I don't know if stealing is the appropriate way to settle his rent, Cliff," Mark offered.

"I don't really care. The kid is not fulfilling his half of the contract." Cliff's eyes wedged into suspicious slits and he said, "I can't imagine you would care seeing as you're both obviously running from something. Could it be the law?"

"We've been kind of set up—" Mark started to explain.

"You don't say?" Cliff replied sarcastically. "Well, I think I'm being set up with you two wandering into my life. You guys said you'd do anything for some water. Well, here's your chance. Jerry, open the cash box," Cliff ordered.

"Would you mind saying all that directly into the microphone for me?" Jerry held up his phone and pointed to it. "You know, so that when we're finally able to come out and prove that the whole freakin' FBI framed us, we don't get thrown back in jail for something stupid like breaking into a refurbished cell phone shop's cash register."

"He's right, you know," Mark added, grabbing his phone to maybe record the whole exchange too, but when he clicked on his phone his brows furrowed. "They didn't scrub it."

"What?" Jerry blurted.

"All my pictures, they're still here."

"You're kidding me." Jerry leaned in close as Mark tapped through the photos of the toy guns and the white box truck pulling out of the Disney parking lot. "Okay, that's actually freaking me out. Why didn't they get rid of that?" Jerry questioned.

"Will wonders never cease?!" Cliff mockingly interjected. "But excuse me, I'd like my money," he said, wiggling his crooked index finger toward the register. "Then you guys can be on your way. Oh, and don't worry about the water and the wings," he huffed.

Jerry sighed. "Look, I'm not about to steal, okay Cliff? But if you want at it, give it a go. I'm not having any part in that," and he backed away from the cash register. As Jerry stepped away he noticed a little office behind the wall covered with the balloons. Specifically he noticed the computer sitting on the desk. And even more specifically his vision zoomed in on the modem on the floor beneath the desk. "Yeah, I'm not a thief."

"Fine. You're not junkies and you're not thieves. What are you?" Cliff wanted to know.

"I used to be in the FBI," Mark answered as Jerry wandered into the office, "and then my car exploded and next thing you know Jerry and I are in prison and people who saw us in there are now either dead or in a coma," Mark explained as he laid the newspaper out on the counter for Cliff's perusal.

"We're ghosts!" Jerry yelled out from behind the ballooned wall.

Cliff, still studying Mark, reached around to his pocket and pulled out a little package of rolling papers and a plastic sandwich bag full of weed. "So you guys are the Grateful Dead and the FBI threw you out on shake down street, huh?" He began rolling up a joint on the counter next to the take-out box.

Mark scratched his chin. "You could say that." Then giving it some thought Mark added, "Do you get a lot of people like us wandering through, Cliff?"

"Not a lot but enough to know there's something going on." Then cradling his creation with his fingers, Cliff licked the edge of the paper and finished wrapping the marijuana cigarette. He offered the joint to Mark who shook his head.

"No. No thanks. What type of lawyer were you Cliff? Where did you work?" Mark asked as Cliff popped the joint into his mouth and then dug around in his pockets.

"I was working for…shit…" Cliff anxiously patted his front and back pockets. "You don't have a lighter, do you?" Mark shook his head no. "All right, I've got one in the car," and he plucked the joint out of his mouth. "I'm sorry. What did you just ask me?"

"What type of lawyer were you? We saw your law degree. Where did you work?" Mark asked again. "Or are you still working?"

"Good question," Cliff said as he absently rolled the joint between his thumb and index finger and inspected it. "If I had to put something in the *Who's Who*, I'd document my work on the Drugs Act, 1976."

Mark let out an involuntary chuckle.

"You think I'm kidding?" Cliff cleared his throat and recited, "An Act to regulate the import, export, manufacture, storage, distribution and sale of drugs." He paused and added, "Even homeopathic ones. They made a big deal to include *The Homeopathic Pharmacopeia*."

"Seriously?"

"The act still extends to the whole of Pakistan," Cliff said.

"Hey!" Jerry called out from behind the colorful ballooned wall. "That's where you told us the peacocks came from!" Mark raised his good eyebrow and Cliff nodded.

"That's right Jerry!" Cliff yelled back, and then speaking for the benefit of Mark. "But of course, now Pakistan is the heroin addict capital of the world. Their pathetically poor population spends more than two billion US dollars a year on the stuff. Pakistan, along with Iran and Afghanistan, produce something like ninety-five percent of the world's opium, a.k.a. opioids in polite company and a.k.a. heroin for everyone else, and over half of it gets smuggled out through Pakistan."

"Wow. I didn't know that. So you worked for…?"

"Officially the Department of State but really I was working for the drug companies and the military. You know; the whole military-industrial complex enterprise. The British were heavily involved in creating this act too." Cliff looked down and shook his head. "My curse is that I can see what has been done and I'm not able to do anything about it."

The tanned wrinkles on his face fell into deep valleys as he frowned. "The CIA runs a four hundred billion dollar drug trafficking business, mostly heroin from Afghanistan moved through Pakistan, but they also have cocaine from South America and Asia. They have labs that produce more heroin there, transported through diplomatic channels and NATO/US bases. US soldiers are guarding everything, including the poppy fields. One of the key locations for this whole operation is Bondsteel in Kosovo, a Muslim enclave in the heart of Serbia, established by Bill Clinton and NATO when they destroyed Yugoslavia under false pretexts. This base is a main trafficking hub for weapons, human organs, and children. The money is laundered through US and UK banks like HSBC. Honestly, drugs are one of the easiest and biggest sources of income for them. The whole Bondsteel operation is an integral part of the 'war on drugs' and 'the war on terrorism,' and mainly it constitutes a war against the truth."

He closed his eyes and ran his hand over his face, ultimately rubbing the corner of his eye as if getting the sleepy dust out. "The critical fact remains that I'm a broken man because of it. I'm done. I'm just done. I see it. I know it, but there's nothing I can do. I feel deeply cursed and as I look back, that's probably why I was fighting so hard over that damn sinkhole."

"I see," Mark commented thoughtfully as he took in everything that Cliff had shared, but not wanting to get diverted he asked, "and you're sure you're not still working for anyone?" Cliff appeared baffled by the question. "I ask because I think it's very odd that you would blatantly ask us to steal."

Just as Mark finished his statement he noticed two police cars slowly pulling into the shopping plaza parking lot.

At the very same moment Jerry yelled out, “Okay! I know where my gun is!”

“Wonderful,” Mark mumbled, still looking at the police cars.

Jerry excitedly hopped out from behind the balloon wall and noticed the police cars through the window. His face fell. “Aw, shit,” he sighed and looked at Mark to make sure he saw them too. “I’m not into dealing with this right now.” He reached out and grabbed three cell phones, a bunch of SIM cards, and some airtime cards from the wall.

“I thought you weren’t a thief,” Cliff smirked.

“And I thought you weren’t a snitch,” Jerry shot back as he stepped up to the cash register and began hastily ringing up the purchase of the airtime and SIM cards in order to get the activation codes.

“Oh, I didn’t call them,” Cliff retorted as he stashed the joint in his wallet and tucked it away in his back pocket. “The police and I have something of a ‘don’t ask don’t tell’ relationship.”

“Could have been the kid we scared out of here,” Mark said, still watching the cop cars circling under the lot lights like aquarium sharks.

“You still need your money?” Jerry asked Cliff as he scanned the cards and tapped the register keys. “The drawer will be open in thirty seconds.”

Mark was still watching the police cars when he heard the register drawer slide open and he asked, “Is there a back way out of here? An emergency exit or something?”

“Yes,” Cliff answered as he greedily grabbed what little cash was in the register and Jerry collected up the sales receipts with the activation codes on them. He stuffed the receipts into a plastic shopping bag with the phones.

“There’s an exit in the office,” Jerry said, thumbing over his shoulder as more receipts pumped out of the machine.

Mark jogged to take a look. Jerry, clutching his bag of loot, trotted up next to him. “Is an alarm going to go off if I open this thing?” Mark asked, pointing to the sign that clearly stated: Fire Exit Only. Alarm will Sound.

“I don’t think so,” Cliff answered as he rounded the ballooned wall. “It goes out to the alley.” Just then they heard the piercing electronic *ding* of the shop door. They all held their breath as Mark pushed open the emergency exit. Instantly an apocalyptic blast of fire alarm horns blared as he swung the door fully open to reveal the front end of a police car and a confused looking policeman urinating next to a dumpster. Needless to say Mark and Jerry were equally confused.

"Nichols!" Cliff shouted over the sharp whooping of the alarm. "Would you mind not pissing all over my property!?" Officer Nichols hastily zipped up his pants just as another breathless policeman skidded into the office, inadvertently popping some balloons on his way.

"What the hell is going on?!" the balloon popper yelled at the three who were stuck like deer in headlights at the threshold of the door. "Move! Let's go!" he ordered.

Mark and Jerry uneasily wandered out into the darkness toward the dumpster, carefully avoiding any puddles, but Cliff turned around and waved the balloon popping policeman away. He marched directly through the earsplitting sound waves to the alarm box next to the circuit breakers and punched in a code. The silence fell like a guillotine.

"There's no fire," Cliff assured the balloon popper as he secured the cover to the alarm. "Nichols, get in here!" he shouted. Nichols pushed his way past Mark and Jerry who stood dumbly between the police car and the dumpster.

Cliff shook his head as Officer Nichols approached. "Find a toilet next time," Cliff admonished. "That's just rude and disrespectful." Nichols and the balloon popping officer glanced at each other and Nichols produced some cash. Cliff took the money, counted it, and gave him the sandwich bag of marijuana he had stashed away in his cargo shorts pocket. Nichols opened the bag and sniffed it. "It's all good," Cliff guaranteed.

"This is so messed up," Mark whispered over the prevailing scent of urine. Jerry nodded.

"Now kindly get out of here," Cliff advised, shooing the two uniformed policemen away with his hands. "People will be talking."

The men nodded, marched menacingly past Jerry and Mark, and drove off in the police car.

"Well, how was that for a drug deal gone completely awry?" Cliff asked the astonished pair as they reentered the office.

"Yeah, that was something else," Jerry commented, purposefully positioning himself in the chair in front of the brand new Gateway computer sitting on the little desk. A corkboard with a calendar and photographs of the girl they had seen running out to the Dollar Store were the only things adorning the office. Mark closed the emergency exit while Jerry began furiously clicking away on the keyboard.

Turning to face Cliff, Mark asked, "So that's how you sustain yourself, is it?"

"There's not a lot of options for me these days," Cliff replied. "I do what I have to do."

"Uh-huh."

"And speaking of doing what I have to do, I have to ask you both to leave now."

"Wait!" Jerry piped up. "My gun. It's moving!"

CHAPTER TWENTY-NINE

Casa de Wolf
Jocelyn's room

"THIS IS HOW THEY SLEEP IN JAPAN," Margret had cheerfully explained to the kids while assembling the bedding hours ago. Jocelyn pushed and twisted the cap then angrily swallowed another pain pill. Her frustration and unfamiliar night sounds weren't letting her sleep like the kids and her mother, all happily tucked away Japanese style in their beds on the floor. She was sick of being bedbound. She was sick of essentially being held hostage. Looking at the pathetic reflection of herself bouncing back to her from the black mirror the window had transformed into, she tried to mentally lasso all the things that didn't actually suck about her whole experience:

Her mom and kids were with her.

She was warm.

The sheets had gotten changed and smelled like lavender again.

She had a seemingly unlimited supply of *con gas* water.

She had an expansive view of the outside world during the day.

She was alive.

She wasn't on the IV anymore and could think better.

She could sort of walk.

But that was all she could come up with. Food, although there was lots of it, didn't make the list because there's only so much medicinal herb-infused gazpacho, bread dipped in olive oil, and soupy yogurt a person can handle, and it seemed from the selection that was rolling in that Argentinians really only ate raw slabs of beef and chunks of pungent cheese, and again, there's only so much a person can take of that. Even the delightful looking pastries were disappointing. They weren't sweet. It was as if someone had forgotten to add the sugar. Nothing was sweet enough for her American tongue. The situation with the orange juice in the mornings...well, that was like TANG gone way wrong. She just wanted food that she was used to and even though she rarely ate it, she was surprisingly craving a McDonald's cheeseburger. She'd even settle for some cheap pizza or chicken wings or something.

As she lay in the dim light cast by her night side lamp fantasizing about dipping a buffalo chicken wing into a ramekin of blue cheese dressing, Willy's floor plan of Casa de Wolf somehow called to her from the bedside table. She reached over and plucked it from between the bottles of water and the leftover bread her mother had scavenged from supper and purposefully wrapped up.

The carefully rendered map was nearly incomprehensible to Jocelyn, but William had showed her how he had drawn the doors and stairs and she marveled at his determination to document everything for her. The intention of his mark making is what made the drawing so exceptional. Studying his deliberate lines she couldn't help but be filled with love for the kid. She looked down upon him, curled up with his sister. The two were nestled like yin and yang as she imagined they must have been in her belly before they were born.

She wanted to just squeeze them both up and run, but physically that wasn't going to happen, at least not yet. She touched her neon green bandages and resolved to…to…to do what? *Shit.* She didn't know. She was trapped and tears were welling up. Blinking them back and wiping her nose she focused on the painting of the only woman B.B.'s father had ever loved and wondered, regardless of whether it really was a Degas, what sort of life that woman had to deal with. Then looking at the bullet hole in the wall, the Picasso, and the shadowy bloodstain spilled out on the floor next to her family, things got real. Very real.

Outside the box Joss. Think outside the damn box, she mentally coached herself. Then another little phrase, ringing somehow familiar, popped into her head. *Watch the art. Go where it takes you.* This resonated in her sleepy head and, carefully placing Willy's drawing face-up for inspiration, she reached for a pencil and the doctor's notebook that was kept next to her bed. She started scribbling, just sort of absently writing at first. Eventually her handwriting got really fast and she flipped the notebook to continue writing at that pace upside down on the page.

With layers of illegible text written over and over and over she started making independent lines that were not connected to words. Shapes magically emerged that demanded definition. Smearing the pencil with her fingers for shading naturally turned her hands into a big mess and then she set in with the eraser, which left another big mess of disintegrating pink rubber. Turning the notebook around to look at her creation from all different angles and not finding what she was looking for, Jocelyn tore the page out and started the process again. But her pencil was worn out. So she broke it in half and picked the wood off the core of the pencil. Clutching the fine tube of mark making material too tightly, it snapped and she was left with little shards to work with. Undeterred, she began using her fingers like tweezers to draw and her index fingers to push around the little pieces. She kept going. Jocelyn did this again and again until finally there was no workable graphite left. Her hands and forehead were all smeared with gray and the pencil eraser was now in tiny little chunks, like cookie crumbs scattered all over the bed with her.

Feeling worn out and defeated she fell asleep only to be awakened in, what seemed to her, a matter of minutes.

"My God, Jocelyn. What happened?" Margret asked, picking up the drawings strewn on the floor next to her bed. The kids, still in pajamas, were huddling around the room service cart that had just been rolled in. "You look a mess."

The room smelled heavy, like morning. With gray light bouncing off the cloudy mountains and into her room Jocelyn blinked awake and said, "I feel a mess." She was sore and strenuously rolled over to reach for the pain pills. "When was the last time I took one of these?"

"I don't know Joss. That's why the doctor left this notebook," Margret said, shaking the empty but for one page composition notebook, "so you could keep track of your meds and your progress."

Jocelyn grunted and popped two pills in her mouth. She didn't even use water to swallow them.

"Oh, for cripe's sake Joss. The sheets were just changed and now there's crud all over the place," her mother fretted, brushing away the fallout from Jocelyn's nocturnal creative emission. "What the?...There's little pieces of wood in here!" Margret exclaimed, picking a splinter out of her finger. "Jocelyn, how did you even get this dirty? Look at you," she scolded. "The doctor will be here soon and it's like Ash Wednesday in an exploded coalmine."

"That's a good one Mom," Jocelyn quipped with a sideways smile as her mother fussed around with a napkin and some bottled s*in gas* water.

"Let's at least get you cleaned up," Margret said, before leaning in and not so gently scrubbing the grime off her daughter's face. Meanwhile the croissant nibbling kids set to work making a tent with the bedding.

"This is gonna be good," Lilly said as she tossed some pillows and William tucked the corner of a blanket under Jocelyn's mattress. "Wait till you see it Mom." Jocelyn smiled through dabs of wet napkin.

"Guys, can we please not make more of a mess?" Margret asked over her shoulder to the kids. "I just folded all those blankets."

Unmoved by their grandmother's comments the kids continued with their tent building.

Margret was still busy washing Jocelyn's face when Dr. Fernandez gently knocked on the open door.

"Buenos. May I enter?" The kids stopped what they were doing and immediately scrambled for cover.

"Sí," Margret quickly answered while folding up the moist napkin. "Yes. Please come in Doctor."

Watching the kids' little bare feet disappear under the bed, Dr. Fernandez asked, "How is our patient today?"

"She had a hard night—"

"Mom!" Jocelyn blurted out, glaring at her mother. "I believe he was asking me the question. I'm fine Doctor. Thank you."

Dr. Fernandez eyed the two of them while pulling out his stethoscope. "Tú madre says you have a bad night. Why?" He leaned over to listen to her heart and lungs.

"I don't know how she can even comment," Jocelyn replied between taking deep breaths. "She was asleep the whole night."

"And you were not?"

"Not really. I was drawing."

Instantly Margret's hand holding the drawings appeared on the scene. "These were scattered all over the floor when I woke up."

"Ah," the good doctor nodded, acknowledging the drawings. The hand receded. "So you are feeling better, no?"

"I feel beat up." The doctor looked at her quizzically so she tried saying it another way. "I feel sore and tired."

"I see," Dr. Fernandez said, inspecting her bright green bandages. "When was the last pill taken?"

"Eleven minutes ago," Margret quickly answered as her hand again slid into view, only this time holding the one page notebook. "She used all the pages in this to draw and didn't document when she took the pill before last."

"Gracias," the doctor replied while still fussing with the green bandages.

"Yeah. Gracias Mom. Thanks."

"Have you eaten yet?"

"No," Jocelyn and Margret answered in unison.

"Mom! Please!"

Margret stepped away as the doctor stood back to look at Jocelyn. With hand on chin, still studying her, "Have you been to the toilet today?"

Giving her mother a preemptive warning glare, Jocelyn answered, “No.”

“Please, you go. I will observe as you walk.” Jocelyn carefully slipped out of bed and began moving toward the Picasso. Her steps were not as deliberate as the day before. She was still off-balance and stiff, but moving more naturally. “You have been practicing, yes?”

“Sí,” Jocelyn answered.

“Muy bien,” Dr. Fernandez said, nodding approvingly. She entered the little bathroom and shut the door. “She is progressing nicely, yes?” he asked Margret, who nodded solemnly.

“Doctor, is there any new news?” Margret asked hopefully. “You know, about the test results from that IV bag?”

“No.”

In disbelief Margret exclaimed, “Look, this is getting ridiculous! And you know what? I want her back on her copaxone!” She smacked her hand down on the night side table. All the little glass water bottles rattled and Jocelyn’s drawings fell to the floor. Dr. Fernandez and Margret stood in dumbfounded silence as they beheld the collection of images Jocelyn had drawn. The doctor squatted down and laid the drawings out in long rows then stood up to study them. He was so engrossed that he didn’t notice Jocelyn hobbling toward him.

“Oh,” Jocelyn moaned when she saw what her mother and doctor were up to. “Those are junk. I was just messing around and…”

“¿Que es esta arquitectura? ¿Una catedral?” the doctor asked, pointing to the second picture in the row. “Architecture. What is this building? A cathedral?”

“I’m not sure exactly. Really, I was just messing around.”

“And this?” Margret asked, pointing to the first drawing.

“Mom, this is so embarrassing.” Jocelyn said, fidgeting with her hair. “Seriously, I don’t know. It’s nothing.”

“It’s a monkey,” came from under the bed.

“No. It’s Mickey Mouse,” Lilly’s muffled voice responded.

“That’s not Mickey Mouse,” William debated. “Mickey Mouse has bigger ears and doesn’t have a tail like that.”

“Well, that’s the castle at Disney Land.”

“Why don’t you two get out here?” Margret reached down and pulled up the kids’ tent.

The doctor was now squatting down again looking at the drawings. “Hola,” he said to the kids as they poked their heads out from under the bed. They shyly grunted back. “Jocelyn, at what hour were you making this art?”

“I don’t know. Everyone was asleep. It was probably a few hours after midnight.”

Dr. Fernandez scratched his head then asked, “What were you thinking about when you were to draw these?”

“I wasn’t thinking. I was drawing.”

“This picture,” Margret said, pointing. “Is this a monkey with a gun or Mickey Mouse?”

“Oh, for goodness sake!” Jocelyn huffed. “This is mental. Seriously, I don’t know. Can we just throw those things out?”

“This one is clearly a crucifix. So maybe that one really is a cathedral,” Margret reasoned. “It does resemble St. Peter’s Basilica in Vatican City.

“I think it looks like the White House,” Lilly offered.

“No, the president doesn’t live there. You’re thinking of the Capitol Building,” Margret corrected.

“I like these. They’re all different,” Willy commented, pointing to pages and pages filled with repetitive patterns of circles, obviously labored over while some appeared hastily executed and smudged. “I like how the circles turned in a figure eight.”

“Or the symbol for infinity…”

Jocelyn angrily hauled herself back into bed and shouted, “Everyone stop! I just want to go home!” and pulled the covers over her head.

Everyone was quiet and Dr. Fernandez collected up the drawings. When he was done he stood next to her holding the pages. “Jocelyn,” he said, and she didn’t move. “Darling. You are becoming well. Tu arte es maravilloso.” Still she didn’t move. “You must continue to eat and practice walking and I want for you to continue to draw. This is therapeutic,” he said, shaking the drawings.

“Do you mind if I take these with me? I will return them. I would like to study them.”

“Sure. Take ‘em. Throw ‘em out,” Jocelyn huffed from under her blanket. “I don’t care.”

“Gracias,” the doctor nodded in appreciation while picking up his bag.

Just as the doctor was walking out the door Jocelyn popped out from under the covers and shouted, “Doctor!”

Dr. Fernandez turned to face her, “Sí.”

“Can I pick out the supplies for my drawings? You know, the right paper, and pencils, and charcoal, and good erasers and stuff.”

The doctor nodded. “Por supuesto. Of course.”

"I know a good website we can order from, or at least I can show you what I want."

"Very good," Dr. Fernandez nodded thoughtfully. "A laptop computer can be had. I will make for you so that it is promptly here. Remember to eat and walk."

Jocelyn grinned. "I will," she responded, and then adding as he headed out the door, "Muchas gracias." Turning to her kids and pointing to the room service cart, "Guys, would you get me a croissant and some of that…" and before she could even finish her sentence her mother was at her side offering her a full plate of breakfast.

CHAPTER THIRTY

Casa de Wolf
The vineyard

A MANLY EUROPEAN STYLE HANDSHAKE with a kiss on each cheek and a clasp of the shoulders. "You are a moron," Maximillian Juan Carlos De todos los Santos-De los Cobos y Huraño de Mendoza Castile Raubal-Ortiz de Ruldoph de Habsburg declared succinctly in English to Brunhold Bertram Keller Wolf during the rigamarole of disembarking the helicopter and being welcomed to Casa de Wolf. B.B. didn't seem at all bothered by the comment but instead took frail Max, who was still wearing most of his CBRN suit, by the elbow and led him to the limousine.

Battle weary Ethan and blood splattered José were carefully observing the exchange from inside the Super Puma while handing the guns down to ultra-exhausted Ache, who had his monkey munched neck bandaged and wrapped in a plaid winter scarf. Over puffs of their frozen breath and moving without talking, they watched the black streamlined limo drive away past skeletal grapevines toward the vineyard compound.

With everything offloaded José began preparing to close the cargo bay doors. "José, you're not going anywhere," Ethan said, throwing the last box of ammunition down to Ache. "You heard what B.B. said. We—as in you, me, and Ache—have to dispose of the guy I shot."

"Oh, you mean my partner?" The world stood still. Ethan watched José's frosty puff of breath dissolve like a dream and Ache inconspicuously reached down and gripped his pistol. "You didn't know that, did you?" José spat. Ethan cautiously shook his head no. "Of course not. You're the classic definition of a loose cannon." José grumbled and ran his fingers over his thin mustache and morning stubble. "You don't know much, do you?" Ethan stood completely still. "Do you?!" José screamed. Standing steadfast Ethan didn't blink, but his fists clenched and Ache noticed.

"Look buddy," Ethan finally said, "this whole thing sucks and it's gonna suck more. I want you to—"

"Oh, don't tell me what to do!" José snapped back. "Here's what I want you to do: shut up and stop playin' around. You have no idea what type of operation you just disrupted."

“Then why don’t you educate me?” Ethan responded.

“Uhm,” José feigned thinking about it. “How ‘bout no! I’m not telling you shit ass wipe. Now get off,” and he pushed Ethan with both hands toward the open cargo doors. “Go!” Stumbling back, Ethan grabbed for the handle next to the open doors and steadied himself before hurtling himself like a slingshot back at José. The men fell over in a flurry of fists and grunts.

Ache watched the two grapple as he wearily crawled back up into the Super Puma. “He’s right you know,” Ache said calmly, standing with arms crossed next to the sprawling fight that was now rolling to the tail end of the craft. “We don’t know what we just stepped in.”

“You just gonna watch?!” Ethan called out to Ache over the furious sounds of winter camo scratching up against shiny polyester and boots squeaking. Ache took a deep breath, and like some sort of super cop, subdued José by jamming his knee into José’s back while grabbing his arm, yanking it backward, and skillfully applying pressure to a select spot on José’s shoulder. Rolling out from under José, Ethan wiped his nose, took a deep breath and sat back on his hunches. “Whaddaya mean he’s right?”

“I mean,” Ache said as he lashed a bungee cord around exhausted José’s wrists like handcuffs, “eighteen million US dollars gets moved *weekly* through sixty-two little companies via Wolf Enterprises.”

“Ya, you told me the guy had dough…”

“Oh, he’s personally a bottomless pit of money. No doubt,” Ache explained as Ethan stood up and brushed himself off. “Wolf Enterprises isn’t valuable because of B.B.’s money though. It’s important because it’s a discreet hub for CIA black money movement. B.B. just happened to be born at the right time for…” Ache yanked on José’s restraints, “his handlers at the CIA to capitalize on this.”

Jabbing José in the chest Ethan asked, “So, does B.B. know you’re a company guy too?” José sort of smirked and rolled his eyes. “Making you wash up Tito’s blood?” Ethan shook his head as if in pity. “That’s just cold.”

When José didn’t respond Ache answered for him. “I’m pretty sure B.B. is the lucky recipient of a twist of fate. I’m also pretty sure he doesn’t have a clue about his complete portfolio or the particulars of Wolf Enterprises or the people he’s surrounded himself with.”

“From what I’ve seen of him I think he likes it that way,” Ethan commented.

José, still bound, spun around to face his captors. “Excuse me jerkoffs, but I am from a lineage of people who fought against the

Ottomans and most recently dealt with Communist left fascists. You," he said with disdain, "you 'Americans,' as you call yourselves, are too dumbed down to know history or to observe the philosophical value of freedom."

Tucked within the cold shadows of the Super Puma's cargo hold, Ethan and Ache looked at each other in confusion. "I'm sorry," Ethan said to José. "I thought you were with the US Central Intelligence Agency. What the hell are you talking about?"

José shook his head and spat. "I *am* talking about intelligence you idiot and guess what? You don't have any!" He forced a laugh. "Bloodlines. If God didn't hold bloodlines in high regard then why is the Bible filled with chapter upon chapter of who begets whom?" José shook his head again. "You don't understand." He sighed. "But you must know—you have to know—history is the story of one empire taking over and either destroying or merging with another. The personalities that show up on the scene are almost inconsequential. It's the philosophies, the belief systems, born and accepted during the times of turbulence that shape reality for those participating in it for generations to come."

"Man, he speaks English a lot better than I thought he would," Ethan obnoxiously commented.

Glaring at Ethan, José continued, "9/11 will happen forever. In every lifetime 9/11 will happen. It will never not happen. Life is a record. It starts, plays itself out, ends, begins again, and does this for literally all of forever and ever more. It's in your DNA. Your parents and their parents, and their parents before them signed the contract and you keep signing it."

In frustration, Ethan was rubbing his eyes and pinching the bridge of his nose, but Ache recognized something in what José was saying and it wasn't *The Fourth Turning* by Strauss and Howe. José was talking about something much deeper than that. "Was Tito interested in this story about the record?" Ache asked.

"Of course. That's why I am here," José snapped. Ethan stopped rubbing the bridge of his nose and glanced up at José and then Ache.

"You said Tito was your partner," Ache questioned. "But you aren't a CIA agent, are you?" José shook his head no. There was a long pause while Ache looked him over. "He was your lover?"

Raising his chin, José proudly said, "Yes."

"Oh, what the hell," Ethan grumbled.

"You have a problem with that?" José snarled.

"Look, I'm all for love wherever people can find it and I'm really sorry to have offed your friend there, but—"

"But what?! Tito was my reason for being!" José started to tear up. "My soul mate." His voice cracked. "We were brought together against all odds for a higher purpose and you, *you!"* he screamed. "You murdered him…" Whimpering, José's bottom lip quivered, his hands still bound behind him.

Ache stepped between exasperated Ethan and grieving José. "Okay. Okay. If it's all a record like you said it's all going to come around again, right?" Ache put his hand on José's shoulder. "Maybe Tito was here this time around to bring all of us together to play this through."

Blinking back tears José looked at Ache and seemed to be considering what he said. "You *are* here for a higher purpose," Ache consoled. "We all are." Ethan rolled his eyes. Ache noticed but continued, "Tito needs you to be strong. Stronger than you have ever been in your life."

Dim gray winter light filtered in through the open cargo entrance, rendering a graceless quadrilateral on the helicopter's floor. José collapsed to his knees sobbing, his wrists bound behind him in an awkward backwards prayer.

Ethan, still fixated on José's drama, grabbed Ache by the arm and led him up to the cockpit. "For fuck's sake," he whispered violently, "why are you pussyfooting around this guy? Is it because he's gay?" He glared at Ache. "If it is, well, fuck that shit."

"He's our translator," unfazed Ache whispered back while carefully adjusting his ponytail and the scarf wrapped around his injured neck. "We have to keep him close. He knows who the players are. He knew what Max was all about and how to speak to him. He even knew Ledergerber wasn't dead. We need him."

Ethan sighed, eyeing weeping José through the cockpit door. "We don't know shit about this guy and for someone who said he wasn't telling us anything he seemed pretty eager to spew an ass load of useless bullshit."

"He's got skills. Flew us all over the place and didn't screw up once. Not even when he was armed. He stayed classy." Ache, glancing out the cockpit door, leaned in close and whispered, "Keep him close."

Ethan considered it while rubbing the scruff of his chin. "But what the hell is he talking about with the record thing? Is he in some sort of cult or something?"

"I'm not sure but he's into royal blood and those bloodlines usually equal pipelines of money. We need him if you want to keep this going."

Ethan nodded. "You're right," he concluded. Then studying Ache's stoic features and dark tired eyes he added, "But brother, you look like shit. You gotta get that monkey bite fixed and catch some sleep before everyone starts rolling in for Tito's memorial thing that B.B. wants to throw."

Just then José, still kneeling in the back of the helicopter, yelled out over his sobs, "I want to see him!"

Ache raised his eyebrows and Ethan yelled back as he made his way out of the cockpit, "You're in luck José! That's where we're heading right now. Let's go."

Keeping him restrained, Ache helped José to his feet. All of them jumped off the helicopter and squeezed into the jeep, which was heavy with guns and ammo. Ethan, of course, took the driver's seat. They barreled over the crunchy, frozen earth, down the snow dusted dirt road intersecting the rows and rows of colorless, leafless grapevines, and headed directly to the garage door of the fermentation room.

Ache jumped out and rolled open the big garage door and Ethan drove the jeep up to tank number three. "Where is he?" echoed over to Ethan as he hopped out and grabbed a twelve-foot ladder leaning against the wall.

"In here," Ethan called back to Ache over the hum of the fermentation tanks. He hoisted the ladder onto the hardtop roof of the jeep and crawling up himself proclaimed, "In this one." Tank number three was sticky and smelly with lines of putrid grayish purple staining its sides. From the roof of the jeep Ethan noticed the same grayish purple splattered all over the floor.

With his footsteps echoing ahead of him Ache took in the messy scene. "What happened?"

"I'm not sure," Ethan answered, confused. "The place didn't look like this last time I saw it."

"Let me out!" José yelled from inside the jeep. Ethan gave Ache a "sure why not" shrug and Ache opened the car door. Bound José stepped out of the jeep and looked up at Ethan. "Tito's in there?" he asked incredulously as Ethan placed the ladder against the tank and started climbing up

"That's what B.B. told me," Ethan said, holding onto the ladder with one hand as he ran his other hand over the edge of the tank's lid. "You heard him. We've got to get rid of Tito and clean this place up."

Leaning his whole body against the ladder and using both hands he threw the lid open. A powerful whiff of noxious fumes made him blink back tears and instinctively turn his head away from the tank.

"Is he in there?!" Ache called up.

Tucking his chin into his winter camo coat, Ethan tugged it up over his nose and, controlling the urge to vomit, looked in. A barely recognizable grayish purple Tito looked up at him with open, stained eyes through the gently bubbling, reddish purple soup. His now permanently purple lab coat rippled behind him like a cape as he floated lifeless with his broken arm extended, frozen in a fractured salute. Ethan was too nauseated to speak so he gave a thumbs-up.

"Can you get him out?" Ache called up.

Considering the situation Ethan yelled down, "Can we drain the tank? Is there anything below that opens up that's big enough to pull him through?"

Ache walked around the base of number three as José stood dumbly by the jeep. "Just a spigot!" Ache answered.

"How did B.B. even get him in this thing?" Ethan wondered aloud as Ache stepped away from the tank and looked up at him. "The old man said he put him in here by himself," Ethan reported. Frustrated, he was about to crawl down but Ache shook his head and pointed up. There was a large pulley, like something you'd see on a clothesline but much bigger, hanging over the tank. Seeing it Ethan grinned and thought, *Tricky old bastard.*

"Okay! We need some rope!" Everyone looked around and instantly, from his vantage point, Ethan saw it neatly coiled in the corner. "There!" he pointed. Ache wearily trotted over, grabbed it and hauled it over to the jeep. "Tie it to the rear fender or something. Then toss the other side up to me," Ethan instructed while scrambling down the ladder to better catch the rope. Ache tossed the line up to him. Ethan missed it and caught it on the second try. He started climbing back up but then stopped. "Someone needs to hold this ladder," Ethan realized. "I'm going to the top of this thing."

Ache looked at José who was numbly staring at tank three. "It's going to be okay," Ache consoled. José blinked back a tear and nodded. Ache forced a weak smile and then crawled up on the roof of the jeep and held the ladder in position. Ethan continued his ascent to the very top of the ladder. Like a professional circus performer, Ethan balanced himself only two rungs down from the top with his knees braced against the ladder while threading the rope into the pulley. With yards of rope splashing down and now trailing into the tank,

Ethan started his decent back down the ladder, glancing again at Tito on his way.

Finally placing his foot firmly on the jeep's roof Ethan said, "Someone has to go in and fish that guy out."

Sighing, Ache said, "And you can't?"

"Umm, no," Ethan said simply.

The two looked at each other in silence for a long time and finally José called out from below, "I'll do it."

Oh, thank God, was mentally transmitted between Ethan and Ache, and Ache hopped down to unlash José's bungee cord restraints.

"You can do it," Ache said patting José on the back. He helped him up onto the jeep and then nodded to him.

"Take the rope that's in there and tie it around his chest," Ethan explained. "Ache and I will pull you both out. Just hang on to him. You can do this." José nodded and took more steps up the ladder as Ethan held it. The revolting scent of fermenting death grew stronger and stronger as José climbed. Finally, José looked into the tank and gasped. Ethan and Ache waited in silence as José stood frozen with white knuckles, stuck to the ladder.

"You need to give him a proper burial!" Ache shouted up to José, hoping that would motivate him to action.

"Yeah, we can do that!" Ethan added while grabbing the rope tied to the jeep with his left hand. "Bring him out!"

Ethan and Ache watched José's shoulders shaking. Ache was just about to yell another piece of encouragement when José unzipped his coat, threw it to the floor, and dove off the ladder into tank three. The ladder, despite Ethan holding it with one hand, wobbled then tumbled to the floor because of José's powerful lunge. The reverberations of the metallic clanging shattered the stillness of the echoey fermentation room. When it stopped the sound of José splashing around and gasping for breath was all that could be heard. Then it was silent.

"You all right?!" Ethan yelled. Still silent. Ethan glanced down at Ache who was now hanging out of the driver's side window of the jeep looking uncharacteristically nervous. "If you can hear me, yank the rope!" There was no yank and Ethan waited. He waited some more and then muttered, "Shit. I should have just done it myself."

Preparing to get off the jeep to collect the fallen ladder, Ethan heard the watery sounds of life splashing inside the tank and the rope twitched. "Well, alright José! Hang tight mister!" Authentically happy and patting the tank Ethan shouted, "Ache! Start the car! Drive away *slowly* on the count of three! One. Two. Three!"

The jeep rumbled to life and, hanging onto the rope, Ethan jumped off the roof. His weight pulling down yanked soggy José up out of the slurry. As soon as Ethan hit the floor Ache eased the jeep away, pulling José and the broken body he was clutching completely out of the fermentation sludge. “Kick yourself away from the tank!” Ethan directed, waving his arms to one side as drips of rancid wine fell from the macabre piñata. Once José and the remains of Tito were clear of being dipped back into the tank, Ache, with Ethan’s assistance, eased the two down to the ground.

With the piñata on *terra firma,* Ache jumped out of the jeep and joined Ethan. The two watched as José, soaked through with fetid wine and his own tears, knelt on the cold cement floor and lovingly smoothed Tito’s wet hair away from his vacant eyes. “Ya te extraño,” José whispered and then, awkwardly angling himself around the stiff broken arm, he leaned in to kiss Tito on the lips.

Ethan loudly cleared his throat. “Okay. That’ll be enough of that,” he said, rubbing his nose. “You did good José. Real good,” and he patted José on the shoulder. “Ache, why don’t you take José here and give Tito that proper burial you were talking about? I’ll clean this place up.”

Ache started laughing.

“What?” Ethan glared at him. “What’s so funny?” José was now glaring at Ache too.

Fighting back giggles Ache shook his head. “You…” he pointed to Ethan and burst out laughing. Then composing himself, “The ground’s frozen and…” and he couldn’t contain his hysterics. Tears streamed down his face as he gasped for breath between laughs. Ethan and José watched him in disbelief. “I can’t… I’m sorry José.” He shook his head apologetically as more inappropriate laughter burst out of him.

“What the fuck is wrong with you?” Ethan questioned.

Wiping back tears and gasping for breath Ache chuckled, “I’m so…so friggin’ tired and…I don’t even…I think I might be hallucinating…” he held out his hands and studied them.

“Great,” Ethan huffed. “Then you’re closer to dreamland where all those Native American Indian spirits live. Now go harness those ghosty motherfuckers and get rid of Tito.”

A huge grin, the likes of which Ethan had never seen before on Ache’s face, grew until an uncontrollable wave of maniacal laughter overtook Ache and he doubled over. Ache kept laughing until he realized that he had wet his pants. He sort of calmed down, but still quaking with sleep deprivation giggles he asked, "How?"

Ethan reached around in his pocket and pulled out a stainless steel Zippo lighter and handed it to him. "Go do a rain dance or something."

Ache nodded. Then walking over to José he said, "Sorry man."

"You pissed yourself," José pointed out from his position curled up on the floor next to his lover's pickled corpse.

Still fighting the urge to burst out laughing, Ache was unsure if José meant that statement to be hurtful or helpful, so nodding, he said, "Yeah. I don't think Tito cares."

Meanwhile, Ethan was angrily unfastening the rope from the bumper. "Get movin' you two!" Ache reached down and grabbed stiff and stinky Tito under the arms, leaving a trail of purplish gray leading to the back seat of the jeep. "José! Help Ache!" Ethan barked. "Go around the other side and pull Tito through!" José, who was also saturated and dripping putrid wine slurry, got up, walked over, and opened the back door opposite Ache. He crawled in and, reaching out, he and Ache wedged stiff-as-a-board Tito into the back seat. It was José's yanking that ultimately revealed the tattoo on Tito's abdomen.

"Uhm…Ethan!" Ache, now devoid of any hilarity, called out. "You need to see this."

Disgruntled, Ethan grumbled, "What?!" and marched over to join Ache. Surveying the dead body he remarked, "Yeah, so? Nice ink," when he saw the dinner plate-sized tattoo of a snake eating its own tail centered over Tito's solar plexus.

"Remember I told you someone tried to stab me and that he's still running around?" Ethan nodded. "That guy had this same tattoo but smaller on his neck."

Ethan nodded again and slowly walked around the jeep over to trembling José, and quick as a viper lashed out and tore open José's wet and stinky shirt. José did not have the tattoo. Further questioning with a well-placed pistol to the temple revealed that the tattoo was indicative of successful initiation and that José was very much looking forward to receiving his ink. José, shivering and with teeth chattering, also willingly added that the person who had tried to stab Ache was probably part of the same Circle Snake group that he and Tito had been involved with; however, José did not know who the person was or any specifics of the attack. Because of this information Ethan, at the insistence of Ache, decided to keep José alive.

CHAPTER THIRTY-ONE

Jocelyn's room
Casa de Wolf

EVEN THOUGH THEY WERE ON THE OTHER SIDE of the world, Jocelyn knew right away this person was an I.T. guy. It wasn't just the yards of gray LAN line looped over his shoulder and dragging on the floor behind him or even the MacBook that gave him away, it was the winning combination of Drakkar Noir men's cologne intermingling with the smell of factory fresh electronics. He wore a too short, blue and white, horizontal stripped tie that Jocelyn suspected was a clip on, with an out of season, thin cotton, white button-down shirt that faintly revealed the presence of a dark *Star Wars* T-shirt underneath.

Jocelyn and her mother tried to communicate with him but he only responded with sheepish smiles and seemed to not want to look anyone in the eye. The kids meanwhile made a production of noisily "driving" the room service cart under the Picasso to make space for blue tie guy as he offloaded the looped LAN line from his shoulder and deposited it directly onto the bloodstain.

Margret, in either an attempt to help or, more likely, to keep the room as spotlessly clean as possible, leaned over and picked up the thick plastic cord trailing through the door. "My goodness. How long is this thing?" To her surprise the gray line traveled not only down the hall but also down the stairs. The guy didn't answer and proceeded to hook the laptop to the cord. He sat down cross-legged on the floor between Jocelyn's bed and the heavy spiral he had just dumped. Everyone silently watched him pecking around on the keyboard of the computer until he nodded, apparently pleased, and looked up at Jocelyn.

"Okay. This," blue tie guy said, holding the open laptop with one hand and presenting it to Jocelyn. "This, it works. This for you solo una media hora." Nodding, she gratefully accepted it. Holding up his index finger, blue tie guy repeated in English, "Only one half hour."

CHAPTER THIRTY-TWO

One hour later
Stephensville, Florida, USA
The Cell Phone Shoppe

"ISN'T THERE A WAFFLE HOUSE or something around here?" Mark asked as he picked through the crusty, leftover chicken wing bones in the take-out box. He and Jerry had been awake the entire night partaking in a good old fashioned hack-a-thon and everything around them just screamed it, down to the popped balloons and the persistent scent of Cliff's tiny roach of a joint sitting next to some long empty Red Bull cans. "I could really use some food right now," Mark sighed, rubbing the corner of his good eye. His other eye had settled into a textbook presentation of a "big black eye" and he didn't bother with it.

Last night, after the drug deal debacle, Mark hadn't initially believed that Jerry had pinpointed the location of the Adidas wristband tagged gun. At first he was actually pretty pissed that Jerry was messing with him and had assumed that it was some stupid old GIF thing on par with the early video game Pong that Jerry had scooped off the internet. It was only when Jerry began explaining how the satellite system was so old that it should have fallen out of the sky like five years ago, and how it still worked, and how he had hacked into it to track the wristband that Mark slowly accepted the fact that he was in the presence of a master.

Even Cliff who had absolutely no idea of the complexity or technicalities of the situation had been totally enthralled by what Jerry was saying and that's when Cliff went back out to the Mercedes, got his lighter, and enjoyed the joint he had stashed away in his pocket. Naturally, he offered the roach to Jerry and Mark but they both declined. Instead they helped themselves to the Red Bulls and bottled water in the little office fridge. They had work to do. Cliff, meanwhile, spent a long time happily watching a little dot twitch every fifteen seconds on a very rudimentary, green on black, ASCI art image of the globe. They all agreed that it was very strange that the gun, or at least the wristband, was in Mexico.

Eventually Cliff fell asleep on the floor. He woke up a little after midnight and told them they could stay and he'd be back in the morning with food after he officially evicted the owner of the Cell Phone

Shoppe.

But now after the long night, Jerry was hungry and asked, "Is the wings place open yet?" while hooking up yet another cell phone to a long chain of phones. "They gotta have coffee. But more importantly where the heck is Cliff? Did he or did he not tell us that he'd bring breakfast?"

"Yeah, he did," Mark answered, "but I'm not banking on it anytime soon. Can't count on stoners," he said disparagingly while throwing a crusty chicken bone back in the box. Looking around the little office he realized how much of disaster their late night cyber hoedown really was. After Cliff had left, the store had turned into a virtual beehive of activity. Wires were running all over the place and the Gateway had basically been rebuilt. The naked green motherboard was now married to other little computers scavenged from the bellies of the Cell Phone Shoppe inventory, making the humble Gateway desktop computer a much more formidable and evasive thinking machine although it wasn't very pretty. In fact it was big mess.

Jerry and Mark had worked well as a team, cobbling stuff together and then trying out different ways of tackling the code while attempting to break into Mark's files at the FBI. They got nothing. All Mark's points of entry, not to mention his files, appeared to be on at least triple lockdown and they knew that just by doing what they were doing the FBI knew they were there. But that didn't stop them. They kept working.

The only bit of friction between the two as they plowed on had been the music they had cranking over the Cell Phone Shoppe's in-house stereo system. Jerry had been really productive while listening to the 1990's digital hardcore assaults of Atari Teenage Riot and The Lords of Acid, "Voodoo U," but Mark was more of a classical hacker and preferred the logical, mathematical melodies of Mozart, Bach, and Beethoven. He attributed his musical inclinations to the fact that his mother while pregnant with him would put headphones around her belly and blast him *in utero* with the stuff. She had read somewhere that it made kids smarter and better at math. Mark wasn't sure it had actually worked but he did like classical music, especially when he was "in the zone" with a computer. Eventually they agreed to just shut the music off.

"Alrighty, let's see if this RAID works," Jerry said as he leaned back to admire his creation. He tapped around on the keyboard and after a long silence grunted. Mark walked up behind Jerry to see what he was doing. He had given up hope, at least for now, on breaking into the FBI and was curious.

"What level RAID are you doing?" Mark asked.

"It's a CRYPTO softRAID on OpenBSD. It's good for more confidentiality but it doesn't provide redundancy," Jerry offered while still studying the computer screen. "In the early 2000s, OpenBSD got DARPA funding and that's why I got interested in it in the first place. Plus I like its puffer fish logo." Mark rolled his eyes and leaned over to optimistically shake an empty Red Bull can. "I don't get why it's not working." Jerry frowned as he surveyed the row of cell phones. "I mean I've done this before…"

"You have?" Mark asked while collecting up the empty Red Bulls and throwing them in the wastebasket.

"Oh, sure. I did this for my ChemTrailTales website. I'm gonna go back and see how I set that up. I don't know what I'm doing wrong."

"Uh-huh," Mark mumbled as he wandered out to the front of the store, keeping a lookout for Cliff and breakfast. Through the front window the bright, late morning light scratched his tired, caffeine buzzed brain. He looked over the empty parking lot and scanned the abandoned intersection with its non-working traffic light. The Dollar Store lot across the street had only two cars parked in it. The heat waves weren't rippling up off the pavement yet and the greens and blues of the landscape still looked friendly.

"What time is it?!" he shouted back to Jerry while studying the shadows laid by the tall parking lot light poles. When Jerry didn't answer, he schlepped back to the office looking for his watch or phone to check the time, and rubbing the stubble on his chin he griped, "Cliff better get here soon. I'm freakin' starving."

Rounding the balloon wall, he saw Jerry with his scruffy unshaven face and crazy hair, fully fixated on the computer screen and trembling. "The Red Bull getting to you?" he asked while glancing at the time. Jerry, in his Long Strange Trip T-shirt, didn't even look up. "Why are you shaking like that?" Jerry didn't answer. Bending over to look at the screen that had Jerry so entranced Mark read:

> I hope this website is still active. I know the person who started it. I used to work with him. If you know where he is tell him I'm in Argentina. At a vineyard. I'm sort of ok. My mother and kids are with me. We don't know if we can get out of here. None of us have a passport. I only have this computer for a few more minutes. We are in a place that looks like that famous Frank

Lloyd Wright house 'Falling Waters' I think it's called. Mr. Wolf is the owner and everyone has been very kind to us. But we are trapped. Please let the owner of this website know this. If you, or he, or anyone who sees this can pass this information along I would sincerely appreciate it. I want to come home.

Thank you.

Jocelyn

"Is this a joke?"

"I don't know…"

"Well ping it."

"Yeah. Yeah. Okay…" Jerry typed and Mark watched. Jerry raised his eyebrows. "This is being spoofed."

"Figures," Mark grumbled.

"The IP address shows that it's coming from Russia."

"At what time?" Mark questioned.

"Uh," Jerry rubbed his nose, "about thirty minutes from now. Whoever this is, they're ahead of us."

"Bullshit."

Pointing to the screen Jerry countered with, "This says it was sent at 10:52 a.m. today."

"What's up with the clock on your server?" Mark asked, flipping his phone over to look at the time again. "It's 10:20 a.m. here."

"My server's clock is in perfect synch."

"Wait. Is Argentina in a different time zone? Russia certainly is."

"I don't know."

"Well find out! Jesus!" Mark demanded, pacing back and forth behind Jerry as he typed. Mark ran his fingers through his hair. "Do you think it's really her?"

Jerry pursed his lips and shook his head. Still typing he whispered, "I hope so."

Just then the piercing tone of the door let them know someone had arrived. "That better be you Cliff!" Mark shouted. Conflicted because he wanted to be there with Jerry, Mark marched out from behind the ballooned wall.

"What the hell happened to my store?" the three months late on his rent proprietor of the Cell Phone Shoppe gasped. Seeing Mark and his big black eye coming at him from out of the office the young man shouted, "Oh, my God! You're still here?!" Mark sighed. He was more disappointed that it wasn't Cliff with the promised food than anything else. "That's it!" the kid, outfitted in Cell Phone Shoppe gear yelled as he whipped out his phone. "I'm calling the cops!" Then, with a sudden burst of reserve Red Bull energy, Mark bolted over and smacked the cell phone out of the guy's hand.

"You don't want to do that," Mark said. "The cops were here last night and they're the last thing we need right now." Cell Phone Shoppe guy's face was set with determination as he dove for his phone to call for help.

"Yeah!" Jerry called out from behind the balloons as Mark kicked the young man's phone out of reach like a jinxed hockey puck. "Argentina's an hour ahead of us! That means the message was sent like, what? Forty-five minutes ago?" Jerry breathlessly announced while jogging out of the office as Mark and the owner of the store wrestled.

Mark's mini-melee in the middle of the racks of reconditioned phones and assorted accessories took Jerry by surprise. He was about to say something to break it up but was interrupted by the penetrating *_ding_* of the door. He looked up and saw Cliff ambling in looking well-rested, clean-shaven, and holding a box of pastries in one hand and in the other a carryout tray of large plastic cups filled with iced tea.

This, of course, quickly diverted Jerry's attention. "Oh, hey Cliff."

"What are they doing?" Cliff asked, motioning with his chin to the struggle behind the rack.

"I'm not sure," Jerry replied, taking the beverage tray from him and inspecting the cups. "Thanks. Any of these with sugar?"

Cliff reached into his pocket and tossed some sugar packs on the counter. "Come on kids! Stop your fighting. I brought sustenance." At the mention of food the sparring stopped. Mark was clearly the victor as he was left holding the prize phone.

"Mr. Stephens! Thank God you're here. These guys trashed my store," the young entrepreneur whined while taking one last unsuccessful swipe at Mark in an effort to repo his phone.

"Well, you haven't paid rent in over three months so we're both feeling a little violated right now, aren't we?" Cliff said. Then, offering the open box of pastries, he asked, "Would you prefer a cheese Danish, glazed doughnut, or a croissant with your eviction notice?" Cliff then produced a legal-size envelope with the name "Trevor Hathaway" on it and handed it to the young man.

Reaching across the stunned former tenant, who was fumbling around with the envelope as he tore it open, Mark grabbed the cheese Danish.

"But…but…my stuff. My inventory. Can I just leave it here for a while until I find a place?"

"No."

"But…"

"But no. The fellas here," Cliff motioned with his arthritic finger to Mark and Jerry, "will help you move everything out. The van should be here any minute now," he said while consulting his watch.

"Woah, woah, wait a minute." Mark swallowed his pastry hard. "We're movers now?"

"You did say you'd do anything for some water," Cliff reminded him and counted off on his fingers, "I've given you water, chicken wings, iced tea, and pastry as well as a safe place to stay, a shower, and some clothes. I think I've more than held up my end of the bargain."

Jerry, holding his sweet tea like an office manager, looked over at Mark before speaking. "Yes, yes you have Cliff. But see, we're in the middle of something right now and we just got our first real lead."

"That's great Jerry!" Cliff exclaimed before taking a sip of iced tea. Just then the moving van rolled up and noticing it, Cliff announced, "Oh, it's here. Chop-chop everyone! Let's get this place cleared out!" A communal groan emanated from the group as Cliff waved to the guy in the van.

Jerry put his plastic cup down and sprinted back to the hacked up computer in the office and started scribbling the Jocelyn message in a notebook. Mark, wiping his sticky cheese Danish fingers on his shorts, hustled in. "Can you believe this? The old man shows up and needs us to be his moving company right in the middle of this?"

Jerry, still scribbling sighed, "I know. Figures."

"Did you try and ping it again?" Mark asked, reaching out for the keyboard.

Jerry shook his head. "No. Just write down the coordinates of the wristband," Jerry instructed as he wrote. Mark pulled out his cell phone and took a picture of the simple map with the blinking light then got back to trying to figure out where the Jocelyn message came from. Jerry sighed, "Dude, just write it down." Glancing over at the blinking light on the flat earth he hastily jotted down the coordinates at the top of the page he was working on. He was just about to gather up his cell phone RAID when a bloodcurdling scream rang out.

"What the hell did you do to my computer?!" Trevor Hathaway screeched. "Do you know how much that thing cost?!"

"Yes," Jerry and Mark answered in unison.

"Well then pay me for it!"

Jerry and Mark looked at each other and, thinking fast, Jerry held out his notebook and pen. "Here. Write down your address and we'll send you compensation."

"You?" Trevor questioned, pointing at each of them. "I'm going to give you two my address? I don't think so."

"Then put down a P.O. box or the chicken wings place's address. I don't know," Jerry urged. "Just put something down and we'll send you something. We're not thieves."

"Yeah, we're not criminals," Mark added, still staring at the screen while typing. Trevor smirked, obviously studying Mark's black eye.

"Okay boys! Let's get moving!" Cliff yelled. "We have boxes out here!" Trevor huffed and scribbled an address in Jerry's notebook, then noticing it was his own notebook, he tore the page out that had the address on it and handed it to Jerry, tucking the notebook under his arm.

"Uh, can I get the page I was just working on?" Jerry asked.

"No."

"Seriously?" Jerry and Trevor glared at each other and then Jerry lashed out and grabbed for the notebook. "But all I need is one page!"

"And all I need is my phone and my computer!"

Still stuck in a stare-down with Trevor, Jerry conceded, "Mark, give this kid his phone."

Mark walked up and, holding the phone in front of Trevor's face said, "Just give him his piece of paper and I'll give it back."

"You guys are assholes," Trevor grumbled while angrily tearing the Jocelyn message page out and handing it to Jerry. "You know that, right?"

"Yeah, I know," Jerry said as he looked over his scribbles; then, folding it and putting it in his pocket, "Thanks."

"Let's go!!" Cliff yelled and a cardboard box tumbled into the office. "I'm paying for that van by the hour!"

Two and half hours later...

"I really thought you guys could have cleared this place out in fifteen minutes," Cliff complained as he counted the money in his wallet. "All you had to move were some little cell phones—"

"Cliff," Jerry interrupted, "but there were a lot of them and did you see that rack system that the phones were hanging on? There were tools involved."

"There was a mini-fridge I had to carry out too," Mark added. "Plus, you had us vacuuming."

Cliff shook his head in disgust. "This generation is doomed. Come on guys, let's go."

"Where we going?" Jerry asked as Cliff hung the "For Lease" sign up in the window.

"To the airport," Cliff replied, securely locking the Cell Phone Shoppe's door.

CHAPTER THIRTY-THREE

Meanwhile
Jocelyn's room
Casa de Wolf

"THERE'S A FIRE ON THE MOUNTAIN," William reported, pointing out the window.

"What? Like with flames?" Margret, donned in a striking Marchesa Notte floor-length embroidered floral dress, asked as she pushed her way past the catering cart, piles of clothes, and shoeboxes so that she could stand next to her grandson by the window.

The typically tidy bedroom had devolved into more of a babysitter be damned type scenario as soon as the gray LAN line had been collected up and the IT guy heroically made his exit. Jocelyn attributed this environmental shift to her mother's complete and total preoccupation with getting everyone dressed and presentable, meaning sponge baths and hair brushed, just in case Mr. Wolf should drop by to say hello. This had obviously redirected Margret's energy from her former housekeeping efforts.

Lillian, meanwhile, scrambled out from under the tent hanging off of Jocelyn's bed. A pigtail sprouting out of each side of her head, she was wearing a frilly Monnalisa jean jacket featuring a real fur collar. Resembling a curious chipmunk, Lilly wanted to get in on the fire spotting action too.

Squinting, Jocelyn strained to look out the window. "I don't see fire," she commented from her reclined position. "I see smoke though." Propped up with pillows, she was wearing her oversized designer potato sack because it was pretty much the only thing easy enough to get into and out of considering her condition. Not being able to see much of anything because of her nearsightedness, Jocelyn instead watched Lilly pressing her little hands up against the window, leaving smudges and fingerprints all over the glass.

"Where?" Lilly asked. "I don't see the fire."

Squatting down, Margret wiped the window with her sleeve and directed Lilly to the suspicious smoke. "Over there."

"Ohhh," Lilly said.

"What do you think it is?" William asked. He was the only person in the room who had yet to be manhandled by Margret so he didn't look like he had tumbled out of a fashion show. He was barefoot and still wearing the little gray sweat suit he had worn to bed.

"Probably someone burning garbage or something," Margret theorized. "The fire certainly won't spread with all the snow but it is weird," she said, watching the smoke billowing up to the clouds, creating a striking black pillar in contrast to the white terrain. "It's in the middle of nowhere."

"Maybe it's a smoke signal!" Lilly excitedly concluded. "Maybe someone else is trapped here too."

"Mom! We could do that," Willy offered. "I know how to start a fire."

"You do?" surprised, Jocelyn asked, and William nodded. "That's actually not a bad idea but come here." She waved for them to come to her. They walked over and around the littered landscape of pillows and plates of half-eaten food scattered on the floor by their makeshift tent. Gathering up her kids into a big group hug, Jocelyn said, "You guys are so smart. I love you both. You know that, right?" The kids kind of grunted and Jocelyn continued. "And William, I do not want you playing with matches. You know that too, right?"

"But Mom…"

"No buts," Jocelyn said sternly, "but I love you. No playing with matches. I don't know what I'd do if you got all burnt up." She squeezed them as tight as she could and felt like she might cry. "We're gonna get home. Don't worry," she said more for herself than for them. Then pulling herself together she asked, "Do you know what I did?" They looked at her with questioning eyes and shook their heads. Jocelyn leaned in to whisper to them.

At first the kids seemed confused but then William burst out with, "Oh, you remember him Lil. He smelled really bad when we first met him. Remember? But then later, he smelled better and we built a fort."

"Ohhhh," Lilly nodded. "I remember. He was cool."

Margret, in her resplendent embroidered dress and framed by the window, folded her hands, silently watching her daughter and grandchildren. "Who are we talking about?" she asked.

Turing to her grandmother Lillian answered matter-of-factly over her fur collar, "Jerry Apario. Mom emailed him and told him to come get us."

Margret, not recognizing the name, shook her head and looked to Jocelyn for clarification. That's when Jocelyn and the kids took the opportunity to tell her all about Jerry and because of this William somehow avoided the sponge bath; but he did have to help straighten up the room, get dressed, and have his hair brushed—just in case.

CHAPTER THIRTY-FOUR

Meanwhile
7 kilometers away

"BUT DON'T YOU HAVE TO KEEP SIGNING the contract if the whole thing just keeps repeating itself over and over?" Ache asked as he threw more gasoline on the fire.

Transfixed by the blaze José finally absently answered, "The whole thing folds over on itself and starts again." Ache nodded as if he knew exactly what José was talking about. "Everyone and everything has its own specific pattern, an algorithm, that has to play out. I called it a record before but the best way to describe this is more like a 3D hologram of a fractal set. It won't play unless you've permitted it to because you create it. That's why I used the word contract, I guess. I translated it poorly." Ache, still eyeing the fire, carefully put the gas can down next to the jeep which had its doors wide open in an attempt to air it out.

José continued, "Our bodies are like clunky old computers, good computers though," he stressed, "but they can only perceive part of a massive whole. We assume that what we are dealing with is all there is but there is so much more. We create elaborate lies, en masse mind you, to make sense of the unseen forces that are also working through their part in the fractal set as they constantly interact with us." José, with arms across his chest, rubbed his upper arms as if bracing himself for the cold despite his winter coat and the sweet smelling heat. "With these scraps of the whole," he stopped rubbing his arms and gestured as if displaying the scraps, "we are creating and living in an illusion, a popular illusion. We all reinforce each other's made up world." Then, after looking at his invisible scraps for a while longer he shrugged, put his hands back in his pockets, and just looked at the fire.

Everything was quiet for a long time and Ache was noticing how the snow was melting and retreating from the heat, exposing the frozen earth and bent, now thawing, brown grass. It looked sloppy and disrespectful and recognizing that this was the zoned out phase of his trip he noted that it was interesting and kind of funny how his mind was bouncing between microcosms and macrocosms with sleepiness and hyper-vigilance pulling him in both directions at the same time. If he had been the type to drink alcohol this would have been the perfect time to imbibe, but he had learned that lesson a long time ago. Never. Not even if it was the last drop of fluid on the planet. Just don't do it. He was sane enough to know *that* about himself.

José broke the silence of Ache's internal dialogue and continued with his previous thought. "Actually, nothing that most people are concerned about is real. Nothing. The bloodlines, or rather, the DNA, you know, the families that rule the planet, are fully aware of this. This is ancient knowledge and they exploit it to the fullest for continued success of their line."

As the fire danced Ache let everything José had just said percolate in his brain. He knew he was officially trippin' from exhaustion sprinkled with a healthy dose of PTSD and he was comfortable with that. At least he knew, not like the other vets who didn't know and were just bat shit crazy, drunk assholes devoid of self-respect and self-control. Nope, that wasn't him. He was under control. Sure he had pissed his pants but he was still in control here. He had to roll with it. He'd been in this mental state before with Ethan and they had gotten out, so it was possible. Nothing was impossible. He just had to stay loosey-goosey and roll with it. So he did. He scanned the mountains. No incoming threat. Everything was still except for the random pops of the fire that seemed to happily punctuate his scattered thoughts about blood and ancient knowledge.

Ache studied José's matted, stinky hair and for the first time fully appreciated how well José was holding up considering everything the kid had just lived through. "Why?" he finally asked and José looked over. "Why haven't you killed me or Ethan? Or at least even tried? You've had the opportunity but you've helped us. Why?"

"Tito told me to."

"Oh." *Yup, I'm trippin'.* Ache heroically fought back the urge to bend over and let out a hearty belly laugh because, after all, he was in control and that wouldn't be the right thing to do, so he rubbed his tongue over the insides of his cheeks before he spoke. "When?"

"Oh, years ago…"

And José and Ache coiled down a memory hole back to when José's parents had been killed in Chile and José had been lucky enough to be taken in the by the church's orphanage. He didn't remember his parents at all and the church was his family. But he did remember getting duct taped, naked, to a crucifix at age seven and feeling special that he had been included in the late night religious worship service. He remembered at age eight how nervous it made him to drink the holy water to rinse away the flavor of sin left by the priests. By age eleven he was aware that he wasn't like other children. That something was clearly off. He knew because he felt it. Something was wrong and he became severely depressed because now he looked forward, in a weird way, to the late night services.

It was when he was thirteen, wearing the same vestments as the priests, when new trusting and terrified little children were introduced to the service that something snapped. He didn't like it anymore. He realized that the priests must have been used like the little ones at some point. That this was all they knew. It was somehow normal for them. It was normal for him and he didn't like it anymore. He was on his way to becoming a priest but no amount of holy water could wash away his sins and he escaped and ran away.

He left his church family and was sad especially since he had no one, and more importantly no food. He worked picking grapes and vegetables but was essentially a stray dog. Wintertime was the hungry time and then by some miracle of God a group of drunk men stumbled upon him while he was panhandling. It was a frigid July day, he remembered. July fourth. And the drunk men took him to a fabulous party. It was so fancy and loud with the music and dancing! There was delicious food and everyone was so happy. The night wore on into the early morning hours. The drunk men were falling asleep on the couches embracing each other, hugging and kissing. It was there that he met Tito and from that point on Tito would be everything to José.

It was Tito who encouraged him to join the army and Tito who had helped him by creating new paperwork so that he could be a solider—the safest place to be. He was very young and took much abuse in the army but they fed him and he stayed and worked hard doing the most menial of tasks as his body developed into strong manhood. Eventually he learned to repair and fly helicopters and when he was done with all that, Tito gave him work and a place to stay and they became devoted lovers. Tito supported him and told him to learn everything he could about being an angel of war because Tito himself was doing God's work. It was a noble calling.

The two traveled together. They studied the Circle Snake and Tito told José that there would come a day when he and all the others in Circle Snake would be called upon to serve. That everything he had lived through and learned, and was currently learning, would culminate, manifesting during an epic, globally felt repositioning. That the USA would arrive and so would the Chinese. They would come and they would either slay or be saviors and how José had debated that with him because he had been certain the British would be the ones, but Tito was steadfast in this and told him to do everything he could to be of help to the North Americans so that they wouldn't kill him. Tito had explained many times the sheer power, advanced weaponry, and most importantly the *magic* the USA had access to.

As Ache's overtired mind bumbled around, arduously organizing and filing away the information José had just shared with him, he poked the glowing embers with a sick. Tito's charred remains hissed, crackled, and popped as the black smoke unostentatiously turned white and silently spiraled its way up to heaven.

CHAPTER THIRTY-FIVE

3:00 p.m.
An abandoned airfield
Somewhere in Florida, USA

"COULD YOU HAVE TAKEN A MORE TWISTED ROUTE to get here?" Mark griped as Cliff rolled the Mercedes over the brambly, overgrown field at the very end of a short, beat-up cement runway that had weeds growing out of its cracked, sunbaked surface. They had been driving around in what seemed like circles and then backtracking for the past two hours. Uncharacteristically, Cliff reached over and shut off the music.

"It's called evasive driving," Cliff responded while tapping the steering wheel and watching the northern sky. The air conditioner was still humming but it couldn't fully mask the sound of the idling diesel engine.

"You know we have phones, right?" Mark questioned, holding his up. "Someone knows exactly where we are." Jerry nodded in agreement.

"Where you're going you won't need those." Jerry's eyebrow twitched with that statement and he and Mark looked at each other with palatable concern. "Might as well leave them here with me," Cliff said, still searching the sky. "Besides, those things give you cancer." Cutting through the uncomfortable silence, a speck emerged on the horizon heading in for final approach. "Oh, there it is now," Cliff pointed. "Let me do all the talking."

Jerry and Mark had given up trying to get Cliff to talk to them about anything regarding their fate fifty miles ago. The man's lips were sealed and he had taken every opportunity to say pretty much exactly that many times during their circuitous journey. Interestingly, to both Mark and Jerry, Cliff wasn't high. They hadn't seen him smoke any marijuana all day. Cliff seemed focused but edgy, so they sat in relative silence until the chugging of the yellow and black Maule M-7-235B bush plane's engine was upon them.

They all watched as the fixed strut tail-dragger circled around the airfield once and then noisily descended. The surrounding tall grass and swampy foliage aggressively waved and panicked birds darted away as the plane glided in for a landing. The front wheels touched down and the plane bounced and skipped its way over the distressed runway until the little tail wheel finally touched ground. Hitting the brakes, the pilot swung the plane around to face the Mercedes just in time as to not disastrously drive and then dive into the swamp at the end of the airstrip.

Cliff repeated while popping the trunk and opening his car door, "Let me do the talking."

"Do you want us to stay here or come with you?" Jerry asked while keeping half an eye on the airplane's hypnotic, and potentially deadly, spinning propeller.

"Just stay here until I wave for you!" Cliff yelled over the noise of the plane. He took a deep breath and then, stepping out of the car into the knee-high grass teeming with crickets, moths, snakes, and of course mosquitos, he slammed the door behind him. His baggy linen dress shirt and wisps of fine gray hair not slicked back into his scraggly ponytail flapped in the hot wind as he waded through the grass.

"Well, this should be interesting," Jerry commented over his shoulder to Mark. "What do you think this is all about?"

"Probably his drug dealer," Mark grumbled, leaning on the armrest.

Soon an unsmiling, sunglasses-wearing pilot crawled out of the cockpit and shook Cliff's hand. Through the heat waves, Jerry and Mark watched the pilot pass Cliff a large manila envelope which Cliff carefully opened and inspected the contents of. Upon nodding to the pilot a big, blue, beach party-sized cooler with biohazard stickers and an orange notice stuck to its side came tumbling out of the plane.

"There's someone else in that plane," Jerry observed.

"Probably armed," Mark reasoned. Cliff signaled for them to join him.

"Are we supposed to look tough or friendly?" Jerry nervously asked before opening his car door.

"I don't know. Just be yourself," Mark said as he grabbed for the door handle. "On second thought, just look like you don't care about anything."

"Got it," Jerry replied. They both stepped out and were instantly blasted by the hot wind that smelled of aviation exhaust. Mark headed directly to meet Cliff. Jerry, however, still holding the car door, yelled, "Hey Cliff! Want me to turn the car off or leave it running?!" Mark grimaced but kept purposefully walking toward the plane. Cliff put a hand up to his ear and shook his head, so Jerry yelled again while gesturing with his hand as if twisting a key and pointing to the steering wheel.

"What's his problem?" Cliff asked as Mark gave a manly, unspoken "what's up" with his chin to the pilot who was not so inconspicuously sliding his Aviator sunglasses down his nose to get a better look at Mark's black eye.

"He wants to know if he should shut the car off."

"Oh, for goodness sake," exasperated Cliff huffed. Looking directly at Jerry, Cliff shook his head no. Jerry gave a thumbs-up and, making sure to leave a wide margin between himself and the propeller, he jogged over to meet them. Meanwhile, Mark was studying the bright orange sticker on the cooler that was lying on its side not far from Cliff's Birkenstock outfitted feet. It read:

LIVE HUMAN ORGAN / TISSUE
FOR TRANSPLANT
TIME SENSITIVE
HANDLE WITH EXTREME CARE

Taken completely aback, Mark gulped and pulled in a short, quick breath as Jerry, huffing and puffing, jogged up and shook the pilot's hand.

"Okay. What's the plan?" Jerry eagerly asked Cliff.

"After you two get this in the trunk," Cliff pointed to the cooler, "you guys are going with him." He pointed to the pilot.

"Oh, hell no!" Mark exclaimed. Surprised by Mark's sudden outburst, Jerry looked questioningly at Mark who in turn responded, "I'm not getting my organs harvested. No way." The pilot, meanwhile, was scratching his eyebrow and appeared to be holding back laughter.

"Who said anything about getting your organs harvested?!" Cliff, still holding his manila envelope, angrily questioned. "I just asked you to carry this to the car."

Shaking his head Mark pointed to the bright orange sticker. "Come on Jerry, let's go," and he turned to leave.

"Go where?!" Jerry called out. "We're in the middle of a swamp!" Mark, still walking down the runway, slowed down and then, with shoulders slumped, stopped. With Cliff and the pilot watching on, Jerry jogged up to him. "C'mon man, all we have to do is haul that cooler to the car and we're outta here."

"Yeah, but where are we going to end up?"

"I don't know, hopefully somewhere we can focus on the case. I mean, we've got two solid leads here Mark, and I don't know about you but I really don't feel like trudging through freakin' swamplands. I mean, there's got to be actual gators in here and they can run faster than a racehorse when they attack." Jerry scanned the place for lurking alligators as he smacked a mosquito in mid-bite. "What better way to get out of here than to fly up and over it? Remember the walk to Cliff's house?" Mark nodded. "That sucked and that was on a sidewalk. Let's just get out of here, even if it's with these medical couriers."

Still highly skeptical Mark nodded and followed Jerry back to the patch of shade underneath the wing of the plane. Cliff, still holding his manila envelope, shook his head disapprovingly and pointed to the blue cooler and then to the still running Mercedes. "Just haul that thing over to the trunk of my car and then you're off."

With sideways glances to both Cliff and the pilot, Mark and Jerry each grabbed a handle of the cooler and picked it up. It wasn't heavy with the two of them carrying it and they began walking. Weirdly, the pilot and Cliff followed them. Glancing over their shoulders as they walked, Mark leaned in and in a hushed voice said, "We can make a run for it. The car's still on." Jerry nervously chewed his cheek, considering it. He looked over his shoulder again and saw the person who had thrown the cooler hop out of the plane and stretch. This person was unmistakably a woman with her brown hair in a pert little ponytail, wearing khaki cargo shorts, a nondescript white T-shirt, hiking boots, and requisite Aviator sunglasses.

"Dude, there's a chick back there," Jerry said in an equally hushed tone. Mark, nearly snapping his neck, instantly looked back and saw not only the female back at the plane but Cliff and the pilot hot on his tail, glaring at him from about ten feet away as they all marched off the runway to the car.

About five feet away from the popped trunk, Mark asked, "Are we running?" Jerry, looking totally conflicted, sort of nodded his head yes but then shook his head no. Mark, seeing only what he wanted to see, dropped his side of the cooler and his end smashed to the ground. He bound to the driver's door and tugged the handle. The door was locked and suddenly the car alarm was blasting everywhere. Hidden birds shot up, fluttering away as Jerry was left awkwardly holding half the unbalanced cooler. Cliff smirked and held up his car keys. Panicking, Mark looked at everyone then bolted.

"He's the smart one?" the pilot asked, pointing to Mark who was arduously fighting his way through the abundance of flora and fauna lining the runway that was growing taller and taller with each step.

"No. The other one. That guy running is the one with the mother on TV." Cliff sighed while pressing the button to shut off the alarm. It chirped and over the new silence Cliff mumbled, "What's with these guys and alarms? I swear to God…"

Hearing that, Jerry carefully put his half of the blue cooler down and turned to face Cliff. "Oh, so you've obviously told this man," he pointed to the pilot, "all about us but you won't tell us anything about them. Not to mention why you would have the two of us," pointing with his chin downfield to Mark, "dragging human body parts around." They all watched as Mark tripped over something, fell, got momentarily lost in the overgrowth, hopped back up, and then kept running. "This is pretty twisted Cliff. What the hell?"

"Jerry, for all you know, that cooler is filled with a case of Budweiser." Cliff walked over and with a key, sliced open the packing tape on the cooler's lid. "Don't believe everything you read. Okay?" and he threw open the cooler. "It's called a diversionary tactic."

Confused, Jerry leaned over to study the contents. "Bags of ground coffee?" He picked up one of the red, five-pound bags labeled "Timothy's Classic Columbian Blend" that were neatly jammed into the cooler. "There's got to be like, what? Twenty? Thirty bags in here?" Jerry surmised "It's chock full of ground….ohhh…" Jerry's eyebrows went up and he looked at Cliff. "Drugs?"

Cliff nodded.

"I thought so!" Jerry snapped his fingers and pointed to Cliff. "You know, the first thing I thought of when I saw all this was *Beverly Hills Cop* when Eddie Murphy discovered the ground coffee."

Excited and smiling, Jerry cupped his hands around his mouth and yelled across the field, "Mark! Mark!! Come back! You were right!!" He waved his arms. "It's just drugs! They're not gonna kill you and take your organs! You were right!" Mark stopped in his tracks and turning around, Jerry called out again, "Come back!" waving him on. "It's drugs!"

"You mean to tell me *this* is the smart one?" the pilot skeptically asked Cliff who was rubbing his brow and sighing.

Everyone watched as Mark made his way back. His black eye was the perfect crowing complement to the newly acquired mosquito bites, dirty stains, and fresh scratches running up and down his legs.

"Nice of you to join us," Cliff sarcastically greeted Mark. "Jerry here brought up a good point. Maybe if you fellahs had known who we were meeting this wouldn't have happened. Mark, Jerry, please meet Ryan Thomas." The men assessed each other. The tanned, sunglass-wearing pilot appeared to be older than Mark but not as old as Jerry. "He and Laura back there," Cliff thumbed over his shoulder to the woman with her hands on her hips watching them, "work for an old friend of mine over at the NRO."

Blank stares as both Jerry and Mark scoured their mental rolodexes. "National Reconnaissance Office," Cliff helpfully added. The mental rolodexes transformed into mental Legos as Jerry and Mark attempted to snap this information together with any preexisting knowledge their brains might contain. Nothing was clicking.

"This office was completely dark before its declassification to the public in 1992, but rest assured it's been chugging along since its inception back in 1961." Looking wistfully back to 1961, Cliff recollected, "Those were good times. In September of that year President Kennedy tactfully announced the NRO without actually naming it at a UN general assembly meeting in almost the same breath as his mention of the United States' intention of harnessing global weather, purportedly for better world wide communication. Ultimately satellites and weather control and intercontinental communication would lead to world peace. It was such an amazing time to be alive. There wasn't anything the US couldn't do but, of course, now we all know it didn't quite work out as peacefully as expected…" Discouraged, Cliff trailed off.

"Right. But what does the NRO have to do with this?" Mark questioned, pointing to the open cooler and bags of coffee.

"That's his payment," Ryan answered, his eyes darting over to Cliff. "We offered BTC but he refused. Wanted this instead."

Cliff suddenly became defensive, as if Ryan had picked at a wound inflicted during an earlier battle. "No one knows what the heck bitcoin is, how to use it, or even who invented it. I opted for a more tangible, completely understandable, more widely accepted and much less traceable currency," Cliff argued.

Ryan, shaking his head as if in pity for the old man, whipped out his cell phone and was about to show Cliff how simple the BTC app was when Jerry interrupted.

"Wait a minute. What exactly does the NRO do?"

Ryan, still holding his cell phone answered, "Oh, we're basically in charge of developing and maintaining all the satellite assets for the US intelligence community. That's why Mr. Stephens contacted us."

"He contacted you?" Mark asked while noticing Jerry's reaction to the definition of NRO. Jerry was rubbing the back of his neck, biting his bottom lip, and curiously looking like he might have to go to the bathroom, shifting his weight from leg to leg.

"Yeah, Stephens told us about the stuff you two were up to. We need to talk," Ryan said, looking directly at Jerry.

"I don't even know what you're talking about," Jerry responded, shaking his head and shrugging his shoulders.

Staying quiet, Mark weighed whether he should jump in with his FBI credentials and spill the beans about everything he and Jerry had been living through, highlighting how Jerry had been essentially bragging about using a (dot)Mars email account to break into the FBI's phone system and then, later, the blinking red blip on the ASCI map at the Cell Phone Shoppe and how Jerry had explained that he had been using old satellites to make that happen.

But then Mark's mind changed gears. What if Ryan checked with the FBI and Mark Witherall didn't even appear on their records? He was a ghost after all. Or worse yet, what if Ryan had seen his mother on the news hawking the Mark Witherall Always Love Foundation? Obviously Mark knew Jerry was bluffing and afraid, but he didn't say anything. Instead he just watched Jerry squirm.

"Jerry, we can offer you immunity," Ryan said.

"Nah, I'm good. Besides, I really don't know what you're talking about."

"We'd like to hear about the vulnerabilities you're working with."

At this point, Mark noticed the woman trudging through the tall grass toward them.

"What's a vulnerability?" Jerry asked, looking confused. Ryan, and even Mark, groaned at Jerry's response.

"Okay. This isn't going to work Mr. Stephens. Your man's not talking. Laura!" he waved, "let's get the cooler back to the plane!"

"Now wait a minute," Cliff retorted, "let's not be hasty here."

Laura wandered up and pointing to the open cooler said, "It's still full."

"Yeah, deal's off. Mr. Stephens didn't deliver."

"Why, yes I did!" Cliff objected and turning to Jerry he beseeched him, "Tell them what you told us last night. You know, about how you got that signal. You know. The old satellites..."

While Cliff groveled around begging Jerry to share even the tiniest of details Laura studied Mark. "Hey, didn't you go to Wentworth? I feel like I've seen you before."

Mark, still keeping his eyes on Jerry, sort of grunted, "Yeah."

"So did I! Were you ever at that pub at the bottom of Mission

Hill, right off Huntington, with a woman named Britney?" With the mention of his old girlfriend, the one who had disastrously broken up with him during finals, Mark blinked and was suddenly off-balance. It was as if a meteor traveling many times the speed of sound had fallen out of the sky, pulverized the world around him, and left only his heart, conveniently wedged into his esophagus. He turned to look at Laura. He didn't recognize her.

"It is you!" she beamed. "You look…uhh," she hesitated and kind of winced, "good. You look good. "

He wanted to recognize her but he didn't and he wondered if this was a trick. Some sort of Jedi mind trick used during interrogations. Blindsided like this, he played along. "Laura? Jeez, I didn't recognize you. Did you have a different hairstyle or something back then?"

Laura laughed. "No, I got a nose job." She turned to feature her new profile. "After that volleyball tournament my parents sprung for a new nose for me. Funny thing is Brit ended up getting implants…" Mark's eyebrows showed his concern. "You know, breast implants," she winked, "from the same surgeon that did my nose. Dominic got them for her after she finished nursing the kids."

Pausing with finger on chin, Laura asked. "Wait a minute. Did you know about him and her back in school, or no?" Naturally, Mark was completely speechless. When he didn't answer, Laura didn't skip a beat and rambled on. "Anyway they got married after Dom graduated with his PhD from MIT and had settled into his position over at Gilead heading up the research department for their catalogue of HIV/AIDs drugs…" Mark swallowed and nodded absently as the heart that had formerly been wedged uncomfortably in his throat fell like an industrial sized anvil down to his gut. "Brit doesn't have to work these days. She's busy with the twins and helps out at the daycare center. Plus, her parents basically moved in with them over at their newly remodeled Victorian—it's huge. So she's got that to deal with too."

"Oh, she has twins?" Mark mumbled, sensing that his ex-girlfriend might have known Laura and maybe had mentioned her at some point. Heck, he probably did meet her but Mark honestly had no real fixed recollection of this person pre-nose job and he certainly didn't know this Dominic guy. *Britney was right; all I thought about was my grade point average. I didn't know her friends. Come to think of it, I didn't have any friends…*

While Mark inwardly chastised himself for being too self-absorbed, Laura rambled on. "I got in here at NRO senior year as an intern and well…," she continued and Mark, like a robot, smiled numbly, "it puts that Wentworth degree to good use, I guess. I don't have kids or any of that so I don't talk to Britney that much anymore, you know, different lifestyles and all, but I'll make sure and tell her I saw you," Laura said with a big smile and then with eyes alight asked, "So, how's things going for you?"

Now feeling completely emasculated and still not one hundred percent positive about the origin of Laura, Mark began a tired rendition of, "Oh, you know, things are good…" when out of nowhere Cliff, waving his manila envelope, was screaming. There was a scuffle. Ryan, Jerry, and Cliff were all on the ground and before Mark could do anything to break it up he saw Jerry roll out of the fray and begin running. Running for his life through the tall grass that had given way to the really tall grass.

Mark glanced back at Cliff who was incoherently shrieking at Ryan, something about his '"rotator cuff." Mark didn't want to lose sight of Jerry but that's when he noticed Ryan sit up into a kneeling position and whip out what looked like a pistol. A pistol with a fluff of fluorescent pink and then *BANG!* The tall grass that had been all a-shuffle because of Jerry stopped moving.

"What the…? You shot him?!" Mark exclaimed in horror and instantly began galloping through the grass, following the bullet to find Jerry. With the soggy ground squishing beneath his sneakers, the green blades cut his arms and face as he pushed his way through. He found him.

Jerry was on his belly, face-down on the ground with a tranquilizer dart hanging out of the center of his back. Mark yanked it out and rolling Jerry over asked, "Buddy?" He slapped Jerry's cut up and muddy face. "Buddy? You all right?"

Jerry, in a daze, blinked and upon recognizing Mark whispered with a tear rolling down his cheek, "Tell…tell Jocelyn I love her."

Mark smiled. "You can tell her yourself. They hit you with a tranquilizer dart. You're gonna be okay," he assured Jerry, kneeling on the squishy earth next to him.

"Oh, that's why my rib feels better…"

Mark watched as Jerry slowly closed his eyes and that's precisely when Ryan, the pilot, tore through the curtain of grass, slapped the handcuffs on Mark, and yanked him up onto his feet. Jerry's eyes snapped open to witness the whole thing and struggling over his thick tongue he managed to blurt out loud enough for Mark to hear, "You were right. Someone really does own those networks and satellites. I don't think they're messing around." Then Jerry promptly fell asleep.

CHAPTER THIRTY-SIX

Everywhere and Nowhere

@SirLanceALot, @billistic, @0317028180604,
@aceofspades, @SullyMan, @ReddingInterna-
tional, @timmythatsrighttimmy, @hardcore-
christian, @hardcoremuslim, @StevenBrownn,
@hardcorebuddhist, @Paramountsolutions,
@hardcorebullshit, @letsroll, @greenscreen,
@rogerkingsly, @Finlandorbust, @concretesup-
ply, @Tim1010101, @Microsofthomebase, @hap-
pydays, @facethemusic, @fckoff, @serenitynow,
@citadel11, @StevenBraunn, @glitchgrl. @Fair-
field911 @0418028180604, @tellyourmom-
shelefthershoesatmyplace, @creaminmycoffee,
@mcoshea, @heartbreaker, @grandmamoses6,
@0518028180604, @bingonightbonanza, @simp-
lyputYankeesSuck, @StevenBrown2222,
@abcdefghijklmnoprstuvwxyz, @minime, @Landed,
@boyscouttroop754, @Chicagooooo, @spelling-
beewinner, @0618028180604, @JeffMcNutty,
@beachcomber @StevenBrown4000, @thisisstupid,
@killerbees, @StevenBrown2017,@privatehedge,
@hellsbells, @0718028180604, @Steven-
Brown1212, @OLDGlory, @holdthephone, @Ga-
torsFan75,@finlandiaicecream, @battlestar,
@orareyoujusthappytoseeme,@landlocked,
@0818028180604, @StevenBrown+1, @rogerroger,
@independentcontractor, @LibertyStreetLand-
Line, @jizzonufaz, @cinamonswirl, @paper-
splease, @0918028180604, @TimmysKid,
@battman, @phantomoftheopera89, @whuteva,
@millivanillee, @orbitalsolutions,
@taxidriver78, @StephenBrown, @totallyinvisi-
ble, @rogerthatgreensmoke, @rainydayfund,
@painfulrectalitch, @StevenRogerReadding,
@oakventurecap, @0317038180604,@HomeCooling-
Solutions,@SBrwn,@houseofredemption,@mother
father,
@Powerman,@TimothyRedding,@thingymajigy,
@777, @thatswhatshesaid, @landshark

```
assemble NOW.
32.8895° S, 68.8458° W
stop. offline. page 3 key 2. go.
```

Double-checking the coordinates, Ethan pressed send. Located at 32.8895° S, 68.8458° W was a nondescript store in Mendoza near Independence Plaza he had done reconnaissance on before meeting up with Ache. That place sold money orders and did currency exchange through a bulletproof glass window. It also sold cell phones, cheap snacks, newspapers, and bottled water. Everyone on the team knew to follow those coordinates, buy the least expensive, in other words disposable, Samsung cell phone, and locate page three of the "User Agreement" buried deep within the bowels of the phone. Everyone on the team also had been issued a set of digital "keys."

These keys in simplest terms were like personalized electronic slices of Swiss cheese that when overlaid on the User Agreement revealed a short overview about payment, mission objectives, and specific actions. Ethan had devised this encryption while working for the Conglomerate and had used it ever since even though the code and process were now technically the intellectual property of the Conglomerate. It was because of that Ache had recommended that they create planB, a slightly more advanced encryption method just in case they got cracked or the Conglomerate decided to get litigious.

CHAPTER THIRTY-SEVEN

B.B.'s office
Casa de Wolf

ETHAN STRODE INTO B.B.'S OFFICE like it was cool. His hair was all matted down, his five o'clock shadow was taking on a life of its own, and more pressingly, everyone smelled him before he even cracked the door. The heavy scent of bleach followed him as they all briefly looked up, inspected him, and then continued with whatever it was they were doing.

"I was watching you," B.B. commented from his 1980s office chair that was rolled up to the window overlooking the fermentation room. Ethan grunted; he was more interested in the three men conspiratorially clustered around the flat-screen monitors.

"Who are these guys?" Ethan asked, flopping himself down in the worn chair in front of B.B.'s desk.

"Mis hombres financieros," B.B. replied, looking tired and bored. "They are telling me that I must move money and, as you know, I have no concept." And he made a hasty yet very natural flourish with his onyx pinky ring clad hand, clearly depicting an untethered thought fluttering away.

"Did you invite them or did they just show up?" Ethan wanted to know, looking over his shoulder at the suits and clean-shaven faces—two Europeans and one obviously from the US as evinced by his posture, facial features, slightly higher body mass, and an inexplicable aura of impending heart disease and/or diabetes.

"They arrived ten minutes ago. I did not invite them but this is not unusual. They are waiting to hear from—" There was a knock on the door and B.B. shouted, "Ven!"

Dr. Fernandez appeared holding some papers. He held the door open like a soldier and waited patiently for Maximillian Juan Carlos De todos los Santos-De los Cobos y Huraño de Mendoza Castile Raubal-Ortiz de Ruldoph de Habsburg to enter. Chairs scraped against the floor as the suited men quickly stood up.

Ethan noticed that Max had changed out of his CBRN suit and now looked every bit the old-money specimen he was, attired in a green, satiny, dragon brocade smoking jacket and three hundred dollar Herring Monarch velvet slippers. With his geriatric, sloth-like movements, Max slowly ambled into the room as the suited men stood at attention. When Max was about halfway to the men he motioned for them to sit back down. They all did and eventually Max fell in with the group by the computers. Dr. Fernandez, meanwhile, nodded to Ethan and approached B.B.'s desk, upon which he laid the papers he was clutching.

"¿Qué es esto?" B.B, asked, pointing to the pencil drawings now covering his desk.

"An anomaly," Dr. Fernandez replied with arms crossed over his chest. Ethan leaned up in his chair to get a better look. B.B. shook his head, not understanding, and began leafing through the drawings as the doctor explained. "Some elements of the transmission appear to have reached the target, others then failed. We suspect some type of interference as is shown in the artwork, despite our best efforts to control the environment."

"Your woman is a talented artist," B.B. remarked, tossing a page down and when Ethan realized that comment was intended for him he eased himself out of the chair and cautiously approached the desk.

"Jocelyn drew all these?" Ethan asked, taking in the expanse of smudgy sketches on the desk.

"There are more," Dr. Fernandez replied, "these are but a sample." Then looking directly at B.B. the doctor said, "Based upon all," waving his arm over the drawings that Ethan was now handling and examining, "Señor de Habsburg is to advise the financial men and—"

"Wait," Ethan interrupted. "Max is making trades based on Jocelyn's drawings?" The doctor appeared very concerned, almost confused by this statement and shot a glance at B.B. Ethan clarified, "You know. Him. Hapsburg. Max," pointing to the little man, hunched over in his green satin smoking jacket, taking on the attributes of a Japanese beetle captured by the glow of flashing Asian indexes.

"No! No, you moron," Max crankily snapped, holding onto the armrest of the chair with one hand and pointing to the monitors with the other. "The Shanghai Composite! Not Hang Sengin! That's in Hong Kong for goodness sake! Everyone knows that."

Ethan was actually surprised by how excited and animated Max appeared.

"Where is Taiwan?" Max snapped. One of the men mumbled a response and Max burst out, "I know *that* you idiot! Which *screen* is Taiwan on?" The man pointed and Max squinted. "Fine. Now go over to Mumbai Sensex and the Nikkei." The suited men appeared unperturbed by Max's direction and continued tapping away on their keyboards as the monitors blinked and arrows went up and down and numbers scrolled by.

Ethan, still holding a drawing of a weird mouse, tuned back to face Dr. Fernandez. "Well?" he asked, shaking the drawing for emphasis, "What does this have to do with all that?"

"Señor de Habsburg has made for us a final assessment of Jocelyn's therapy by analyzing her drawings," the doctor explained, "and can now prudently invest."

Holding Dr. Fernandez in an uncomfortable death grip of a stare, Ethan finally nodded and said, "I see." He carefully put the drawing back down on the desk and B.B., in an obvious attempt to change the subject, started complaining about the limited selection of caviar and oysters that had been ordered for the party.

"They should get all of my critical items here overnight," B.B. whined. "DHL, FEDEX? Is that not at the core of their business?"

"Yes," Ethan answered still looking at the doctor. "Yes it is. And speaking of overnight results did that test result ever come back? I forget. Was it morphine or hydromorphone in Jocelyn's IV?"

Looking uneasy, Dr. Fernandez replied, "Hydromorphone."

"Oh, okay, that's really all I need to know. I'll see you guys at the party," and he turned and left the room.

CHAPTER THIRTY-EIGHT

Meanwhile

NO *WAY!* Jocelyn giddily thought when she realized she was wearing black DocMartin combat boots with red laces. It made sense; she was at a club, or something, and people were mushing up against her. It was dark and the place smelled like an ancient beer stain with cigarette and marijuana smoke but the music was by far the most overwhelming sensation. Not only did she hear it, she could feel it. It vibrated and moved her. Everyone was fiercely into it, hopping around and punching the air. A joyful anger to a relentless battle cry. Heavy drums and electric bass lumbering like an army of mountain climbing pachyderms held the song's primal elements in steady time as an electric guitar soared above it all like a phoenix, when suddenly she felt the familiar sting of broken Christmas tree lights on her back. She stopped dancing and, turning to face her old friend, the music faded into the background. She asked, "Where have you been?"

"I'm here. I've always been here. I'm forever here." He was still wearing the desert camo she had last seen him in. He looked dusty and weary but pleased to see her. "I'm your only true friend now."

The bass and drum sounded muted as if she was outside in the parking lot or something but it didn't matter; she only saw the broken Christmas tree lights. "What do you mean? I have friends. Just look at my Facebook page."

"Oh, I have. But they, they will betray. I'm your dream. I make you real." And taking her hand he turned it over and slowly ran his dirty index finger across her wrist.

"Uh-huh, whatever," she replied, not knowing if what he was doing was supposed to be sexy or not. "Let's go. I wanna see the band." And suddenly they were up on stage, stacks of big Marshall amplifiers, bright lights, sweat, deafening drums and cymbals with a writhing faceless crowd below.

Her only true friend grabbed her shoulders and with frantic urgency uttered, "I'm your dream."

"Yeah, you said that…"

"I'm your pain when you can't feel and you, you are my eyes when I must steal."

"What?!" she shouted over the music.

"I am you!" he yelled back and with that he let go of her shoulders and punched her in the face. It didn't hurt and falling back in super slow motion, she the landed softly on the faceless crowd, who via some sort of shock absorber crowd-surfing mechanism transported her back to her bed.

Jocelyn rolled over and blinked. The bottles of water on the night side stand and the pill bottle greeted her. She was sad the dream was over, and not wanting to deal with anything she pretended to be asleep.

CHAPTER THIRTY-NINE

Outside
Casa de Wolf

WITH JAW CLENCHED AND CLEAR HEAD, Ethan moved through the wintered over garden toward the main house with his footsteps following behind him in the snow. He knew he couldn't stop. Not now. He was *en fuego*, hot with purpose, and that purpose was to end a system that enslaved the entire planet. It was funny, but not really, how when people or even entire nations resisted being absorbed into this system they were automatically marginalized as backwards thinking, moronic, uneducated heathens, or worse, something akin to swine flu infected pigs worthy of slaughter. This message was repeated so often and in so many subliminal and overt ways that the western world's general population didn't even know it was religiously being brainwashed. To add insult to injury, the messaging for those already ensnared, caught by the system's trawling net and flopping around like a soon to be fried fish, was hauntingly similar to what rape victims are often forced to endure, namely, that they had done it to themselves.

Ethan shook his head as he walked, realizing the hardest part of what he was going to do was having to deal with the folks who ardently believed that they needed this artificial system which had been foisted upon them literally since birth. He tried to imagine what it was going to be like when the people he was trying to save turned against him, and although he wasn't religious he knew the story of Jesus Christ and empathized with the guy. He knew the targets he was aiming for never fought their own battles. Never. Instead they sent in their fully outfitted armies, or their silent hit men, or their lawyers and tax collectors, depending on how sadistic they were feeling on any given day.

Sure it was a huge undertaking, but the good news was that he wasn't the only one working on it. At this very moment there were untold legions of people all over the world inspired by the same general idea and they were armed with everything from rocks and machetes to smuggled surface-to-air missiles or backpacks filled with explosives. Ultimately though, it would be him who would actually break it all down and claim victory. He was convinced of that. It was just a given that the name Ethan Lowe would someday be printed in the history books. He knew he had set the bar pretty high for himself but it was possible. Things like this had been done before, heck, many times before in human history. This was nothing new. It wasn't like he was reinventing the wheel.

Arriving at the garden's edge, Ethan began pushing his way through brittle skeletons of ornamental shrubs and headed for the main house. Trudging through snowdrifts it dawned on him that the best thing that had happened to him since Jocelyn had gotten shot was that he could think straight. This newfound clarity mixed with the urgency of the situation kept his train of thought from jumping off the rails. Especially now with what he had just witnessed in B.B.'s office. His thinking was laser guided and obsessive, unlike in the past when he was simply post traumatic stressed out with pinhole vision and bumbling around like an ass.

Now it was obvious. He saw everything and what he saw was crystal clear and squeaky clean because it made perfect sense. This was definitely meant to be. It was basically a chess game and he was good at chess; plus, the darn pieces were actually coming to him! Now that José had showed up on the scene with his cult, or whatever it was, he had a bishop in play and, of course, Max was a castle. The knights, pawns, and all the logistic support that always accompanies an army had been alerted and were now positioning themselves on the board. It was up to him to effectively move all the pieces around in order to save his queen and topple a well-guarded and heavily cloaked opposing king.

Sliding his phone into his pocket, Ethan double-checked his gun in its holster and began brushing the snow off of the hatch at his feet. This entry to the main house would have been a glaring building code violation back in the States, but for those who built it after WWII here in Argentina it was clearly a bonus. It was basically a bomb shelter. He yanked the heavy iron square open and descended the stairs.

Stepping down, he pulled the hatch closed over his head and secured it. As soon as it was locked up tight, lights snapped on and Ethan followed the path of the tunnel. The passageway was hewn from an enormous boulder that also served as the foundation for most of the house. He turned a corner and the tunnel abruptly widened, revealing shelf upon shelf of provisions and folded up cots. It was a comfortable temperature down here and it was bright enough so as not to be creepy. Not looking at anything he kept moving through the thirty-by-fifty-foot room and soon the chiseled walls contracted around him and it was just a simple stone tunnel again with little lights running along the cement floor. When he got to the end there was another heavy, locked door. He grabbed for his pistol, punched in the code, and swung the door open.

The gentle bubbling of the water filter greeted him as he panned his gun over the long, skinny, rippling lap pool. The chemically treated, aquamarine blue water glowed, illuminated from lights embedded below the surface, and refracted ripples danced on the ceiling in the otherwise dark room. It was almost magical, completely relaxing, and if he hadn't been doused with bleach from his fermentation room cleanup effort he would have smelled the chlorine.

Carefully shutting the door behind him he eyed the door opposite him at the far end of the lap pool. With his hand still on his pistol he headed toward it. The echoes as he moved were somehow even more pronounced and menacing in here than in the tunnel and Ethan theorized it was because of the dimness and the water and the weird lighting effect. He made sure this door was locked too, and once satisfied it was secure he grabbed a neatly folded, fluffy white towel and headed over to the shower.

Kicking off his boots, he reached into the blue tinted glass shower stall and turned on the tap. Jets of water burst out of the showerheads as he shimmied out of his winter fatigues and removed his bulletproof vest. Carefully placing his gun on top of his towel, he stepped into the steamy stall. Letting the hot water pelt his tense neck and shoulders as he lathered up. All the friendly demons from the hell storm he had just summoned were in there with him too and he took extra care to remember exactly their positions on the chessboard while vigorously scrubbing his scalp with sandalwood scented shampoo.

He was triangulating the timing and placement of the Steven Brown and Timothy regiments when he thought he heard a clunk and muffled voices over the hissing and splatter of the shower. Still sudsy and with water raining down upon him, he dropped to the lapis lazuli tiled floor and cautiously pushed open the glass door. Seizing the opportunity, he quickly rolled out of the shower stall, grabbed his gun, and hopped up into shooting stance just as all the lights in the room flicked on.

Startled, exhausted José and flat-out hallucinating Ache froze in their tracks. With mouths agape they took in the sight of a stark naked, dripping wet man holding them at gunpoint. The bubbles and suds still crowning Ethan's head were slowly sliding down his glistening neck to his well-defined chest and abs and Ache burst out laughing.

Sighing, Ethan lowered the gun. "How the in the hell did you guys get here?" The question was amplified as it reverberated throughout the cave-like pool room. José pointed to the door that Ethan had just made sure was locked while attempting, but not succeeding, in making it not so obvious that he was taking full inventory of Ethan's manly attributes.

"Take a friggin' picture," Ethan grumbled when noticing the visual inspection going on. Wiping soapy water from his eyes with one hand and waving the gun at the door with the other Ethan said, "That goes up to B.B.'s suite. You came through his room?"

"And you didn't?" José asked, implying impropriety.

"Oh, for fuck's sake. No. No I didn't," Ethan answered. "I came in through an emergency exit." He pointed his gun to a heated towel rack on the wall. Now that the cleverly camouflaged door was closed he realized that he'd probably never see it himself if he didn't know it was there. Ache and José squinted at the towel rack. "I'm staying in there."

"Where?" Ache asked, confused and convinced he was going out of his mind.

"That's the entrance to a fallout shelter. It's a great hiding place," Ethan explained. "B.B. thought it was better that I crash in there."

José curiously approached the towel rack to inspect it, and Ache rubbing his temples offered, "We came down a stairway off a hallway from the kitchen. Some housekeeping lady that he knows," Ache thumbed over his shoulder to José, "showed us the way and gave us the code."

"I'm sure she was mortified by how badly we smelled," José added, motioning with his chin to Ache's urine stained pants. "Delivery people coming and going. She just wanted us out of there."

"Interesting," Ethan remarked, then thinking it through asked, "Where are the guns?"

"Still in the jeep," Ache answered and holding up his hand in anticipation of Ethan's next question, "we camouflaged it. It's not far from the fermentation room."

Ethan nodded. "Okay, you guys hit the showers. You're staying with me. We all need sleep. I'll do first watch since you guys are toast." Ache and José looked at each other, unsure of what to do. Ethan opened the shower stall door and stepped in. With water cascading down upon him he loudly proclaimed, "Time to renew that commitment to personal hygiene fellahs!" and as his statement echoed throughout the room he shut the glass door and proceeded to finish rinsing the suds out of his hair.

CHAPTER FORTY

Jocelyn's room

"GET YOUR HANDS OFF YOUR SISTER!" Jocelyn shouted and downed two more pain pills. "I'm so sick of you guys messing with each other. Just leave her alone already!"

"But Maaa..." William whined.

"Seriously, no buts! I mean it," Jocelyn scolded her son as he rolled out of a poorly executed wrestling hold on his sister. "And you! Lilly! Stop provoking him for God's sake." Lillian, still wearing her fur collared jean jacket, pouted and began explaining why she had to stick her finger in her brother's ear. "You're asking for it if you keep doing stuff like that. Just stop. I can't take it!" Jocelyn barked and shook her head, hot with frustration.

"You guys are just bored," Margret said while organizing the water bottles on the room service cart for the third time. There was only so much "let's-make-a-game-out-of-cleaning-the-room" stuff she could come up with. "Come here Lil," she called, waving her granddaughter over. "I'll do your hair a different way."

"No."

"Oh, for God's sake Lilly. Go get your hair done!" The bedroom was closing in on Jocelyn. The smell of the place with all the new shoes and clothes mingling with the scent of more damn raw meat on that catering cart they kept rolling in made her queasy and for the first time in her life she wanted to punch and smack her kids so hard. Even her mother flouncing around in those Jimmy Choo's and full-length dress was pissing her off and she fantasized about jumping out of bed and just going nuts on everyone's head and how great that would be to have them finally out of her face so that she could sleep. Sleep and go away. Sleep and go away and not hurt. Sleep and go away and not hurt and just disappear—maybe die. It didn't matter.

She was overwhelmed and bursting with an emotion she had never felt before. Some sort of prickly, angry rage but she didn't know what to do with it because she was so uncomfortable, which didn't even make sense because she had taken two pain pills. *Two was better than one, right?* But was it pain? Whatever. It didn't matter. This sucked and she hated Ethan. She hated everyone. Mostly she just wanted to get the hell out of this room with the friggin' bloodstain taunting her, making her nauseous, and—

"Aaaghhh!!!" An unexpected, primal scream gurgled up from her belly and grabbing a *sin gas* water bottle from the night side stand she threw it at the bloodstain on the floor. It smashed and everything was quiet. Everyone, including Jocelyn, was shocked and after a tenuous silence Lilly immediately began crying.

"Jocelyn! That was completely uncalled for!" Margret yelled over Lilly's sobs while leaning down to carefully pick up shards of glass. "The kids are barefoot for Christ's sake."

Rubbing her temples, Jocelyn mumbled. "I don't know what's going on. I'm sorry Mom but...I...I just want... I want to..." Then jumping out of bed she screeched, "KILL EVERYONE!" neon green bandage trailed behind her as she ran, or rather attempted to run. Ultimately she ended up falling flat on her face, bruising her chin. Checking to see if she had chipped a tooth she tasted blood and spat as both her terrified children circled around behind Margret. Poking out from behind folds of embroidered fabric, the kids fearfully watched their mother.

Appearing dazed, Jocelyn blinked at her kids and mumbled, "What was that?" Lying on her belly she hoisted herself up onto her elbows and shook her head. "I feel sick Mom." Now this was Margret's call to action and she swooped over to help her daughter, her luxurious dress billowing out behind her making a swooshing sound as she moved.

Succumbing to maternal instinct Margret squatted down and began fussing over Jocelyn, who unbeknownst to her had collected a big chunk of broken glass. "Here Joss, let's get you back up to bed," Margret consoled, attempting to lift her daughter while balancing on her Jimmy Choo heels; and that's when Jocelyn unexpectedly lashed out like a rabid, cornered animal and slashed her mother's face with the razor sharp glass. Dropping Jocelyn with a horrified gasp Jocelyn flopped to the floor and grunted as Margret's hand flew up to touch the wound on her cheek.

Still tightly clutching the glass and with blood trickling through her cut fingers, Jocelyn began belly crawling toward the kids. Frozen with fear, both kids were too freaked out to scream as they watched their mother huffing and puffing, arm over arm, pulling her useless legs behind her across the wooden floor like a solider belly crawling under a tripwire in Vietnam.

Lilly spun around and sprinted away. Will was close behind and they scuttled into the tiny water closet, slamming the door behind them.

"Jocelyn!" Margret screamed. "Stop! Stop what you're doing right now! Those are your babies!" Jocelyn stopped. Turning her head she looked confusedly up at her mother and the fine red line and smudged blood. It extended from Margret's cheek to her chin. "You don't want to do that," Margret calmly said and repeated, "Those are your babies. Remember when they were born? I do. They were so tiny and so healthy. You did such a great job. You were holding them both, one in each arm, when I came to see them for the first time at the hospital. Remember that?"

Jocelyn blinked and her nostrils flared but she appeared blank, vacant, like nothing was sticking until a tear rolled down her check. She mumbled, "I'm so sorry Mom," and she began viciously slashing her own wrist with the chunk of glass. She didn't hear her mother yelling for her to stop. She didn't feel her mother tearing the glass out of her fingers. She was fascinated with how her blood squirted out in time with her heartbeat. That amazed her and she didn't notice that Margret, reverting to her emergency room nursing days, had grabbed the large cloth napkins from the catering cart, or how her mother had kicked off her heels and knelt down on the floor to tightly tie the cloth napkins around Jocelyn's arm like a tourniquet. It was only the mighty cinch of the final knot that drove Jocelyn back to noticing that her mother was at her side and she wanted to cry but somehow she wasn't able to. She felt numb. The angry prickly feeling was still there in the distance poking at her but she was dizzy and some sort of natural flush of adrenaline, or maybe it was blood loss, made things strangely okay.

Margret dressed Jocelyn's wrist with gauze and the sticky neon green Ace bandage. "We need the doctor stat," she said with such seriousness that it kind of scared Jocelyn. "He has to surgically repair this. It won't heal by itself."

As Jocelyn sat, looking forlorn at the new addition of neon green to her collection, there was a knock at the door. "Final fitting."

"Huh?" Margret answered and then called out, "What?!"

"Final fitting para la fiesta." There was a pause and Margret and Jocelyn looked at each other. "Your clothes. They are done. We need to make that they fit."

Margret, still applying pressure to the wound yelled, "Not now! Please get the doctor!" The door cracked open and a woman holding a big armful of clothes peeked in. Margret looked up at the woman revealing not only the cuts on her bloodied face and hands but the scene on the floor with Jocelyn. "We need the doctor. It's an emergency." The seamstress's eyes opened wide as she quickly tapped out the sign of the cross. "Emergency! Go. GO NOW!" Margret shouted.

The woman nodded, dropped the clothes, and ran off. "That was lucky timing," Margret said, attempting a smile. "Someone's looking out for us." She reached out and stroked her daughter's hair. "It's going to be all right honey. Keep pressure on it," she instructed, noticing how Jocelyn was holding her bandaged wrist. "The doctor is coming. Everything is going to be okay," but Jocelyn didn't believe her.

CHAPTER FORTY-ONE

Patrick Air Force Base, NRO headquarters
Florida, USA

"WHY AM I HANDCUFFED?" Jerry asked, groggily studying the shapes of an unfamiliar face filling his entire worldview.

"So that you don't run away again," Laura said. "He's handcuffed too." Her face shape receded, leaving him with just a profile and a pert little ponytail. She pointed to Mark who smirked at Jerry from the confines of the wheelchair that he was bound to. Jerry closed his eyes and felt himself comfortably sliding back into his own skull when, like an egg timer unexpectedly going off, the harsh realizations of *That wasn't Jocelyn!* and *That wasn't a dream!* smacked him awake.

Snapping his eyes open, he willed himself back to full consciousness. "Wait! Where am I?!" Jerry shouted in a panic, yanking at the handcuff that was keeping him stuck to the sloping wooden armrest of a slick 1960s NASA blue couch. Jerry noticed that the couch was pushed up against a beige wall, facing a big window on the opposite side of the room. Framed black and white photographs of suited up airmen standing next to C130s or assorted rockets holding banners were mounted on the walls. A long walnut table was positioned between him and the big window. All eight chairs at the table were pushed in and upside down water glasses were placed at each empty seat.

"Conference Room Delta," Laura said calmly, taking a sip from a styrofoam coffee cup. "Ryan and Director Gribbin will be back soon. They're dealing with the paperwork." Then, noticing Jerry struggling with the handcuff, she said, "Oh, and don't break that couch, okay? That thing is like vintage, an antique or something."

"Director?" Jerry asked, taking time to check out the thing he was sitting on. "The director of what?"

"OSL. Gribbin is in charge of the Office of Space Launch at NRO. He came in from the launch pads over at Cape Canaveral Air Force Station, but with what Mark just told us they need to get someone from GEOINT, SIGINT, and SCO in here. Just hang out."

"Oh, that's cool," Jerry said as if knew what she was talking about and hadn't a care in the world. Sighing, he laid back and rubbed his Long Strange Trip clad chest as he studied the placement of the recessed can lights in the drop ceiling. "What did you tell them Mark?" he asked.

Looking penetratingly at Jerry through the slit of his black eye Mark grumbled, "Everything."

"Oh," Jerry replied.

Laura, still holding the styrofoam cup, turned and walked past Mark to lean against the wall next to a pathetic potted ficus tree and the expansive window that overlooked the airfield. Jerry watched as she reached over to water the tree with the contents of her cup, then crushing the cup she tossed it into a little wastebasket.

"Did they rough you up or something Mark? Why are you in that wheelchair?" Jerry asked.

Mark ran his tongue over the inside of his cheek before he spoke. "Oh, you missed the best part Jerry. They had to do a full-scale emergency medical air-evac to take *you* and Cliff to the VA."

"Oh, really?"

"Yeah. Apparently Cliff had some sort of shoulder surgery or something last year and it got all messed up when you guys were fighting. So you now have assault and battery charges being filed against you."

"And that's not all," Laura smartly cut in, "you're also looking at resisting arrest, not to mention violations of the state of Florida's 'unauthorized access' laws, as well as the federal CFAA stuff for exceeding scope of authorized access. That's a criminal statute and that allows for lawsuits. You're screwed buddy."

"Uh-huh." Unfazed by Laura's attempt at intimidation Jerry asked Mark again, "So why are you in that wheelchair?"

"I threw out my back helping lift *you* out of the grassy swamp and over to Ryan's plane. That's when they called in the pros and a real air ambulance came in. We had to listen to Cliff screaming in pain for a good twenty minutes before they arrived and sedated him."

"Probably closer to an hour," Laura added.

"How come you didn't just shoot him with what you shot me with?" Jerry wanted to know.

"Oh, we thought about it," Laura answered, "but that would have been pretty grisly. Shooting an old, skinny guy at close range like that; at least you've got a little meat on your bones."

With his non-handcuffed hand on his belly Jerry had to agree and Mark continued, "Yeah, well, after the VA hospital ran me through the MRI—"

"Wait. You had an MRI? At the VA? Good Lord. How long have

I been out?" Jerry asked, seriously concerned.

"Oh, forever," Laura answered. "I was sure you were dead."

"Yeah, but he wasn't," Mark snidely directed over his shoulder to Laura. "Anyhow, to answer your question, after they shot me full of steroids they gave me this," he patted the wheelchair, "which Laura here," he pointed in the general direction of Laura and the potted ficus, "felt the need to handcuff me to. I'm supposed to go in for physical therapy next week."

"Damn," Jerry shook his head. "That sucks. It's all about the legs when you're lifting—"

"Shut up!" Mark snapped, thoroughly pissed off.

The whole room, filled with a weird antiseptic type of anxiety, was silent for a long time and finally, with the sound of an F-16 booming by outside, Ryan popped his head into the room and nodded to Laura. Seeing him, Laura reached around behind the ficus and flipped a light switch, activating a little motor. It started purring and a screen started chugging down the wall at the far end of the room at the same time as a shade slowly slid down to cover the window. The hidden motor stopped with a muted clunk when everything was in position.

With his eyes adjusting to the new lighting situation Jerry watched two older men, one completely bald, the other with gray temples and a brow stuck in a permanent scowl, march in with laptops tucked under their arms. The bald guy looked curiously at Jerry as he passed by to his seat. The permanent scowl guy didn't even look at him. He just sat down and whipped open his laptop.

Meanwhile Ryan, holding three cans of Coca-Cola and a Diet Dr. Pepper, followed them in and sat in the seat closest to Mark's wheelchair. Holding the Diet Dr. Pepper out toward Laura, she took the can and settled in at the table too.

"Okay, let's get this party started," the permanent scowl guy announced, banging a button on his computer. The NRO insignia suddenly lit up the big screen. "Are you with us Massey?"

"I'm here," came in through tiny speakers mounted in the corners of the room and Massey's big head and receding hairline showed up on the screen. Massey repositioned himself for the camera as another participant in the call appeared in another frame on the screen.

"Good to see you Director Gribbin," the unsmiling, middle-aged, female newcomer said as she adjusted her glasses

Permanent scowl guy nodded and said, "Hello Sheila. The gang's all here. What's systems integration have to say about all this?"

The bald guy, typing on his laptop, looked up and sighed. "Well, it looks like we have five satellites still up there that *might* contain such a vulnerability." Jerry's eyebrows went up but no one noticed.

"When are they slated to come down?" the receding hairline asked from on-screen.

"They really should have been down already but, you know, they built the things like armored tanks back in the day so it's anyone's call. The latest model we've identified was released off the space shuttle."

"Which contracts are we talking about?" Shelia wanted to know.

"Uh...here," the bald guy said, clicking around on his laptop. "I just sent the spreadsheet over to all of you." The room was quiet and Jerry looked over to Mark who was obviously ignoring him. Laura, taking advantage of the fact that no one was saying anything important, popped the top of the Diet Dr. Pepper and as she poured it into the readily available water glass the gurgling and hissing sounds made Director Gribbin look back at her and scowl some more.

"Want your Coke?" Laura asked, sliding the can down the table to Gribbin who shook his head no, but grabbing it, he opened it and took a gulp anyway.

"Okay. Three of these clients aren't going to be a problem. The other two are," Shelia remarked. "What are our options if we just shoot them out of the sky and say it was a meteor strike?" A contemplative silence spread over the room which was immediately overtaken by everyone talking at once.

Fifteen minutes later...

"Hell no! Not on my budget! No way! I've already got something like forty thousand dollars going to this whole snow job, wacky-tobacky scheme. I'm not even counting any upcoming legal issues because of the assault." Swiveling in his seat, Gribbin threw a disparaging glance at Ryan and Jerry.

"Look," Jerry argued, still handcuffed and leaning forward on the couch while thumbing over to Mark, "he'll pay for all that."

"Who? Me?!" Mark burst out. "I'm not even sure I'm employed."

Undeterred Jerry continued, "If you'd all stop arguing about whose budget I fall under and just let me touch a computer," Jerry begged, "I'll show you what I'm talking about. You have way more than five compromised satellites up there."

"Oh," Laura blurted, "so you're admitting you've touched our stuff."

"No. I'm not admitting to anything Laura."

Ryan, continuing Laura's line of thought, added, "But you *are* saying that our IT guys, not to mention a slew of world-class engineers, totally missed some fatal flaw?"

"Yes. Would you please just let me—"

"Okay," the bald systems integration guy interrupted. "Here." Shutting the lid of his laptop and speaking more for the benefit of his peers than for Jerry, "I, for one, would like to see what he's talking about." Standing up he grabbed his computer and, walking over to Jerry, he handed it to him.

"Thank you," Jerry said and his handcuff scraped the armrest as he reached out to accept the laptop.

"Hey!" Director Gribbin barked. "Watch that damn sofa!" Looking to Laura and Ryan he ordered, "Get him out of those cuffs before that thing," he said pointing to the couch, "comes out of my budget too." Laura hopped out of her seat and quickly unlocked Jerry.

With the computer on his lap Jerry rubbed his wrist and said, "All right, great. But before I do anything I want it all agreed upon that I have permission to touch your network and to go on and off that network while I do this." A communal grunt of approval came from the room. "And that you are specifically requesting that I do this. That I'm not uninvited." Another round of mumbled consent. "That I am not responsible for any weird stuff that might happen to this laptop after I touch it."

"Oh, for Christ's sake Jerry," Mark hissed. "You've got your computer now just get on with it."

"No Mark," Jerry responded. "This is important. This is important not only for national security but for your career." If confused, arching eyebrows made sounds it would be pretty noisy in Conference Room D. "I want it known that what I'm about to show everyone was developed and discovered by Special Agent Mark Witherall. He can confirm all this with the photos he has on his phone that he sent in to the FBI as the event was unfolding. He was clever enough to place a GPS transponder on a shipment of guns that I had been tasked to deliver to Disney Land." Something between a grumble and a gasp filled the room.

"Disney World," Mark corrected.

"Right!" Jerry blurted. "See! See that?!" He pointed to Mark. "His attention to detail is unparalleled." Mark rolled his eyes but let Jerry keep talking. "This shipment of guns was then collected from the two of us and that's when we were made into ghosts and the funding for the operation began. Agent Witherall's mother, of all people, was even involved in the laundering of the money for this. So it goes without saying that he is making a huge personal sacrifice here by exposing it."

"What the hell?" Gribbin commented under his breath but loud enough for everyone to hear.

Scratching his forehead Mark groaned and Massey asked from on screen, "What's he talking about?" Shelia in her digital rectangle winced and shook her head, confused.

"It was only through his exceptional ability to multitask that he was able to collect evidence of any of this," Jerry continued. "He was and still is, I should add, simultaneously working on an international missing persons case. Now, I'm no expert, but what I suspect is going on is completely shady and SA Witherall here has all the evidence he needs to blow his case wide open."

"This is fascinating, but how does this relate to the vulnerability of our satellites?" Director Gribbin asked. "That's really all we're interested in."

"Oh, let me show you what he showed me." Jerry stood up with the laptop and approached the conference table. "Wanna put it on the big screen so everyone can see?" he asked.

"Sure," Gribbin grumpily responded. "Why not?"

"I thought the guy in the wheelchair reported that it was this guy who was hacking in," Shelia questioned as she and Massey's rectangles shrunk into squares and the bottom half of the big screen as it filled up with code.

"Can I get one of those Cokes?" Jerry asked while pressing "enter." "I'm dyin' over here."

Ryan looked to Gribbin for approval. Gribbin nodded and Ryan handed Jerry the can. Jerry popped it open, took a swallow, and started vigorously typing. "Okay. As you know, there are well over a thousand active satellites hanging in orbit. But it's not those you have to worry about, as SA Witherall was happy to show me."

Looking nervous, Mark bit his lip while everyone sat watching the black screen being populated with white text.

"Should someone be recording this?" Shelia asked.

"Yeah, probably," Massey answered. The text Jerry was working on continued to scroll under them.

"In addition to the one thousand active satellites it looks like there are over two thousand junk satellites, dead ones, just floating around up there doing nothing. Those junkers are the ones that can easily be hijacked."

"Yes, but those don't do anything," the bald systems integration guy interrupted. "They don't have any hardware of relevance on them."

"*Au contraire!*" Jerry exclaimed as he clicked himself over to a German server and signed in. The black area on the screen filled with white text and split into two columns. Everyone, especially Mark, was fixated on the screen. Jerry dug deep into his pocket and quickly pulled out a piece of notebook paper that he had folded up so completely that it looked like a thin mint. As the text was seemingly self-generating and taking over the bottom of the screen, Jerry opened the paper, looked at it, and typed in an IP address. Mark recognized the address. The split bar of text moved up to the center of the screen. Shelia and Massey got smaller and a third black bar now extended across the bottom with a white cursor blinking and ready for action. Jerry typed in more code and that area magically split into two columns so that now there were four areas actively running code.

"Obviously, this is a nonlinear sort of attack here," Jerry commented. He took another gulp of Coke and continued typing. Mark, thoroughly engrossed, was nodding. "When Special Agent Witherall showed me this I was really quite astounded. The brilliance of his approach is that not only can we pinpoint exactly which of the three thousand plus satellites are vulnerable, but we can use these satellites to our advantage without leaving much of a trace. Watch."

Needless to say, every person in the room was now completely captivated by what Jerry was doing. "You're recording this, right?" Shelia asked, and Massey nodded.

Jerry did some sort of Control/Alt thing and everything currently running on screen blinked and divided up again. Shelia and Massey were now very small compared to the eight blocks of code. All the visual activity of the white text racing against the other blocks of running text was dizzying. "Okay, this is the most dangerous part, but I bet we won't have a problem given where we're coming in from. I'm just glad this laptop's got a good processor and decent amount of memory." Cracking his knuckles, Jerry took a deep breath and like a virtuoso concert pianist attacked the keyboard.

One of the blocks of text froze and started flashing. All the other text was still furiously running. Biting his bottom lip Jerry split the screen again and, poof, Massey and Shelia were too small to be seen. Jerry was now touching a server in India and he used that to slingshot himself over to Russia. When the top two-thirds of the screen still running code blacked out and were replaced with a grainy video feed of a snow-covered compound of buildings out in the middle of some sort of agricultural field, the audible sound of people sitting up straighter could be heard.

"What are we looking at?" Director Gribbin questioned and Mark, leaning forward in his wheelchair, squinted at the image on the screen. Jerry didn't say anything and continued typing. The video feed got smaller and the screen split in half. Now the other half of the screen was filling up with the flat Earth map. A red blinking light was slowly flashing on and off over the northeastern Mexico/US border.

"This would be a lot better if I had more than one monitor to work with," Jerry commented. "However, as you can see, it was very easy using the technique that Special Agent Witherall shared with me. Basically, anyone could hack into one of what Witherall estimates to be a little over three hundred vulnerable satellites."

"Jesus Christ! You've got to be kidding me," systems integration guy gasped while running his hand over where his hair used to be. Turning to Mark he asked, "Three hundred? Really? Can you confirm this?" Mark sighed, shrugged his shoulders, and nodded.

"More or less," Jerry said, taking a swig of cola and looking at the big screen.

"I'm calling BS," came from a disembodied female voice up in the corner of the room. That's not Mexico. The map and the image don't relate."

"Exactly!" Jerry proclaimed. Pointing to the screen, "That's exactly what I'm talking about! Do you see how Special Agent Witherall was able to not only find where the guns were located using the outdated satellites and simple GPS hardware but he was also able to hone in and geolocate the exact origin of an email that he suspects was sent from his missing person. That email had been spoofed for goodness sake. This man is a genius! An unsung American hero!"

Before anyone could object or even comment an F/A-18 Hornet zoomed past the big window and the shade rattled.

"That's great. But where the hell does that leave us?" Gribbin asked over the rattling shade.

"Someone recorded everything I just did and, as Ryan mentioned earlier, you've got teams of talented engineers to explain it all to you," Jerry replied. "Right now we absolutely must get to that house," he said, emphatically pointing to the screen. "There's an American woman named Jocelyn McLaren being held captive there. She was kidnapped from the hospital in Tampa recently and—" Another F/A-

18 Hornet blasted by outside, rattling the window shade again. Three withering leaves fell off the ficus tree.

"He's right. Look," Mark interrupted, holding up his cell phone. "Right here. Here's the email that was sent. I took a picture of it." He passed the phone to Ryan who glanced at it and handed it over to Director Gribbin. "I firmly believe that message was sent by Jocelyn McLaren and that she's there," he said, pointing to the screen, "at that...," he swallowed hard, "at that place."

"What *is* that place?" Massey asked from the speakers.

"More importantly," Gribbin cut in, "what's chemtrail tales?" he asked, pointing to Mark's phone. "This email was sent to something called chemtrailtales.com."

Mark started rubbing the bridge of his nose and Jerry didn't miss a beat. Clicking around on the keyboard he replied. "Oh, that's one of the websites I was webmaster of a while ago. It's just conspiracy theory stuff that kids are into, no big whoop. But to answer your question Massey, that place..."

"Dr. Massey," came from the speakers.

"Of course. My apologies Dr. Massey. That place is located at exactly—"And at that very moment a giant whooshing sound, different than the sound of the other jets that had flown by, gobbled up what Jerry said. In fact, Jerry wouldn't have even known it was an aircraft creating the disturbance had the ficus tree not shed more leaves.

"God damn it! What the hell?! Are they holding an airshow today? I can't hear a God damn thing!" Director Gribbin howled. "Laura!"

"Yes, sir," Laura instantly responded.

"For future reference I only hold my conferences in Alpha. Got it?"

"Understood, sir."

"Don't worry Director Gribbin," Jerry soothed, "I've made a note of the coordinates and a link to the satellite feed. Everyone here has to access it. I'm all about transparency in situations like this. Most importantly though—and this is above everything else—we need to immediately extract Ms. McLaren, her children, and her mother from this location."

"I'm sorry," Gribbin snidely replied. "We're National Reconnaissance. Not the friggin' marines."

"Oh, I'm sorry too," Jerry calmly shot back. "The way you're all operating right now, you know, carting forty thousand dollars' worth of illegal drugs around—that's what you said, right? I'm not making that up. We all heard that, right?" Jerry looked around the room. "And seriously discussing blowing up privately owned satellites—I mean, really, who does that? I guess it only makes sense if you're shooting innocent people with tranquilizer darts—and that's on record now too at the VA. I don't know. This all seems more like how I imagine the CIA might operate rather than the NRO, at least to me anyway."

Jerry dramatically shrugged and the room was stunned silent. "Anyhow, I bet people will look into all this, especially when everyone finds out about the vulnerabilities of the satellites under your care. I mean, other agencies actually pay you from their budgets for you to keep track of their stuff up there and I'd be happy to report all this to the appropriate authorities. Who knows? I might even leak the actual exploits out to all the hacker forums should we not get the help we need. No problem."

Yet another loud, angry jet furiously blasted by. A single leaf snapped off the shedding ficus and silently fluttered to the floor. Mark, with his black eye twitching, shifted his weight and shrunk back into his wheelchair as Jerry and Director Gribbin remained locked in an intense, jaw-clenching stare down.

CHAPTER FORTY-TWO

The bomb shelter
Casa de Wolf, Argentina

"I CAN'T SLEEP."

"You want me to punch you out?" Ethan quietly offered.

"You wish," Ache grumbled back, shaking his head as he lay on the cot, staring at the ceiling. His dark Sioux hair, woven into two long braids, writhed like snakes slithering over his terrycloth-covered shoulders.

The manmade cave they were in was dimly lit and maintaining a steady 19.4 degrees Celsius, perfectly suited for sleep but Ache's body, out of whack from war, wasn't having it. "Coffee," he grunted. Rubbing his eyes he threw his legs over the side of the cot and pushed the first aid kit, or rather, the Tupperware storage bin of a medicine chest that he had pilfered to deal with the monkey bite, out of the way with his foot. He had already gobbled down painkillers and some nighttime cough syrup and that wasn't helping his sleep situation one bit. Maybe it was because of this that an untouched hypodermic needle and a brand-new vial of morphine included in the generously appointed medical kit grabbed his attention and held it for longer than it should have.

Ethan, sitting on his own cot in a plush white bathrobe and chomping a granola bar, lowered his cell phone. He couldn't text on the thing in here anyway so he watched Ache, with the back of his neck bandaged, quietly get up, cinch his bathrobe belt, and slink past José who was curled up on a cot and sleeping like a baby.

Previously, while they had all been setting up the cots after the showers, José had shared his suspicion that the pool was the reservoir for this shelter. He had made the connection upon recognizing the brand name of the reverse osmosis filter system and the pre treatment stuff. Ethan and Ache were skeptical until he walked them through the memory of Tito being uncharacteristically agitated about attempts to filter pool water. This was significant to José especially since, at the time, he had no idea what pool Tito was even talking about or that this shelter existed. Somehow the memory of his deceased lover freaking out about pool maintenance supplies and potable water seemed to soothe José and he had been the first to fall asleep.

José's cot was tucked up close to the expanse of shelving which was stocked with the equivalent of a survivalist's dream bunker give-away sweepstakes grand prize. Ache, hunching over, was perusing the contents of the shelves looking for coffee. Among other things like a selection of books and a completely out of context, absolutely gorgeous, inlaid with gold and ivory chess set, the shelves were stocked with commercial sized sacks of rice, stacks of canned beans, and jars of pickled vegetables; a crate of Argentinian Army MRE's (that's where Ethan had snagged the granola bar); ten gas masks and little boxes of IOSAT (tablets of potassium iodide in case of a nuclear attack); lots of special toilet paper that had a picture of a sailboat on the packaging which happened to be stacked right next to bags of kitty litter, boxes of baking soda, and a very modern looking five-gallon potty chair thing; capsules of diphenoxylate and atropine (antidiarrheal medication) and bottles of bleach and hand sanitizer; biodegradable trash bags; matches and candles; a portable emergency stove with boxes of fuel pellets; twenty ten-gallon plastic barrels of water (presumably plan B if reverse osmosis wasn't working); and finally the following, arranged as if for a still life drawing class and enclosed in a gilded display frame: one Glock 17 handgun, vintage probably 1982. Its bullets, still in the yellow cardboard box, leaned against a recently assessed at ninety-four thousand dollars bottle of Glenfiddich Janet Sheed Roberts Reserve 1955 Scotch whiskey. The only thing missing was a little mallet and engraved plaque that said "break in case of emergency." Regardless of the missing mallet the overall message "your final option" was immediately understood by anyone lucky enough to find themselves in this underground bunker.

"I don't know if that's a good idea Ache," Ethan cautioned and Ache, still rummaging around, didn't answer. "You know; coffee. You gotta get some sleep brother. We've got T-minus thirteen hours before we start rollin'."

"Powdered milk and sugar..." Ache grumbled, picking up stuff to inspect and angrily putting it back down.

"Look in with the MREs," Ethan instructed and absently pointed to the case he had gotten the granola bar from. Ache would have seen this if he had normal peripheral vision and wasn't struggling to see through PTSD drinking straws. "Maybe there's some instant in there, but seriously," Ethan begged, "would you please just get some sleep? You gotta be at the top of your game. The Winning Numbers are coming and they don't fuck around. I'm pretty sure I saw one of the Liberty Street cell members working on the computers in B.B.'s office."

Ache spun around, his vision zeroing in on Ethan. "You did? Already?"

"Yeah, was there with some Euro financial guys doing stock trades with Max. Stuck out like a sore thumb." Lost in thought, Ache absently nodded and Ethan continued, "If everything is going to plan, each one of our contacts has already sent the message to their three contacts and those three contacts forwarded it out to their three contacts…"

In actuality Ethan had no idea who exactly he had contacted, well, at least not all of them. He just knew that Ache had given him the Winning Numbers; that's what he and Ache were calling the series of very similar numerical contacts. Those guys were a faction composed of Israeli Black Cube cyber mercenaries that Ache had bumped digital elbows with over the course of his career. The Winning Numbers had essentially defected, gone underground, and were strictly contract based. They only emerged for the highest bidder. Two of them had actually helped build the US National Security Agency from the ground up back in the day. And one of them was last spotted working for Unit 8200, aka Israel's NSA.

Anyhow, this gang was NSA but way sketchier. They often worked in tag team style and they were in it to win it and because of that they were not loyal to anyone or anything, so obviously they were to be handled with extreme caution. Ethan and Ache figured that the Winning Numbers probably only agreed to be involved with Ethan's whole scheme so that they could be out in front on the impending incoming threat calls. This way they could milk their other customers and create new customers by selling fixes to the thing they had just built for Ethan that was mysteriously jamming up systems all over the world. Also, having this sort of inside knowledge was extremely valuable. All of the Winning Numbers reportedly had made fortuitous, if not highly suspicious, stock trades and were multimillionaires.

The Winning Numbers were not to be trusted. As previously mentioned they were in it to win it and thus cheating was just a technique. Ache knew this and had created elaborate—oh, let's just call a spade a spade here—"fuck-with-me-and-I'll-rip-your-heart-out-and-eat-it-while-raping-your-wife-kids-and-dog" digital tripwires for this group. Sure it sounds harsh but those guys could handle it. If Ache didn't do this then how could the Winning Numbers possibly respect him? They were from the Middle East after all and Lord knows that although they considered themselves more sophisticated than their neighboring Arabs they were just as Code of Hammurabi, "eye for an eye tooth for a tooth"-oriented if not more so.

Ethan had also taken the opportunity to alert some mercenaries he had worked with. Those guys were perfect because they had the ability to not give a shit about taking money from any old source while somehow still making their murderous behavior seem necessary, or patriotic, or at least in their own minds, legit. One of them had officially served on the US Stryker Infantry Brigade based in Kandahar Province in southern Afghanistan. He didn't get busted like the rest of his brigade because his father knew a guy and had pulled some stings, but he fit in perfectly with the gang Ethan had thrown together. These were the type of men who chopped off your finger while you were still bleeding out and took the time to craft it into something to hang fashionably from a belt loop. Basically homicidal psychopaths who had found their niche.

Naturally, not all of the people that Ethan had contacted were as clinically messed up in the head. Most were just really, really good at their job. Professionals. They tended to stay to themselves, get the job done, pack up, and just leave. They trusted that final payment was coming because if it didn't arrive within a reasonable time, like immediately, they could easily eliminate the non-paying party on principle and everyone involved would understand.

All the other contacts that Ethan had alerted and were now mobilizing fell under the same basic operational premise, namely some sort of financial function since all armies need money to continue their campaign. The Greens, Browns, and Timothys were income generators, moving drugs mostly for the US Central Intelligence Agency but they could easily be coerced to help raise funds. They had reputations to uphold after all.

LibertyStreetLandLine was the financial hub of all the economically savvy terrorists and this band of specialists was probably the most ruthless of them all. Ethan gained instant street cred with this group the minute he had stabbed Ledergerber in the throat. He personally knew none of them, which was fine. Ethan didn't need to know these people but they all knew him. Narcissistic pure power is all this group dealt with and this was the group that Ledergerber often relied upon.

They had literally no qualms about blowing up a private airplane or commercial jet packed with innocent people to snuff out their target in order to bump a stock price up or down. If you ever saw a news story about a high profile banker jumping—no, make that getting pushed—off a skyscraper, or a story about a white collared, cufflinkwearing executive committing suicide with a nail gun, that was most definitely the Liberty Street crew.

As far as Ethan could tell money wasn't even the point for these people. They had access to tons of it. They were diabolical and all about flaunting power but they weren't very creative and often used the same time-tested techniques to achieve their aims. These guys reveled in domination over others, hence LibertyStreetLandLine being virtually on speed dial at the New York Federal Reserve and the Dow Jones which, as you might recall, is right down the street from 9/11 Ground Zero.

"It's on, brother."

Ache rubbed his bottom lip with his thumb and decisively said, "Okay. Knock me out."

Ethan crumpled up the granola bar wrapper in his hand, making a fist, and stood up. "You sure?" he asked, navigating his way around Ache's cot. Ache nodded. "This is gonna hurt me more than it's gonna hurt you. You know that, right?" Ethan commented and Ache smirked. "Oh, and where exactly are the guns again?" Ethan wanted to know. "You had said in the jeep somewhere by the fermentation room."

"José knows where they…" and as Ache glanced over at sleeping José, Ethan immediately delivered a devastating lead hook, hitting right below the ear, knocking Ache into a sparkling, dizzy free fall. In other words, a perfectly executed controlled demolition. Ache wobbled and his legs collapsed under him. He landed awkwardly against the shelves causing two cans of beans and a variety of assorted spice canisters to clang to the floor. Ache was out cold.

Conversely, José was suddenly fully awake. Clutching his robe he sputtered, "Wha…What's going on?"

"Oh, Ache just needed some help getting to sleep."

"But he's not in bed," José prudently observed.

"Yeah, well, why don't you help me get him up there?"

Cautiously, José got up off his cot, keeping his eyes on Ethan as he made his way over to Ache who was haphazardly splayed out on the floor. The two bathrobed men hoisted the other up onto the military grade collapsible bed.

While José examined unconscious Ache to make sure he wasn't actually dead, Ethan snatched a little envelope off the shelf and tore it open. He unfolded the contents and shook out an emergency thermal blanket that looked like a sheet of silver mylar and carefully spread it over Ache. "Get some sleep buddy."

Then addressing José he said, "I'm going to catch some z's too. You're in charge of getting some decent clothes for us tonight. What do people wear to something like this?" José shook his head. "We want to look like we fit in with the crowd. Who are these people?"

José looked down at Ache one more time, then turned and answered Ethan directly. "I'm assuming most will come from the important cities so they'll be dressed as metropolitans would. Some deal with guns, human trafficking, and much, much worse. These people have become the 'earners' in their families. They wear very fancy suits and live with luxurious accommodations. Some of them have been given a title. I know that some of these men have changed names, buried inconvenient parts of their past, and more often than you would care to imagine have become the local bank moving money around their respective territories. Therefore, Ethan, it's only natural that they will detest you regardless of what you show up wearing tonight."

"Good to know," Ethan commented as he picked up his bulletproof vest. Taking off his robe he slung the vest over his shoulders and began securing it. "I have full faith that you'll get us looking sharp." José looked concerned so Ethan elaborated as he slid his robe back on. "I mean, you're a gay guy. The best person for the job. I'm counting on you to make us look presentable."

Done with the conversation Ethan made himself comfortable on his cot and shut his eyes. As an afterthought, and with his eyes still closed he added, "Oh, and make sure you bring us some real coffee from the kitchen. Ache said you knew someone in there. We're all gonna need it."

CHAPTER FORTY-THREE

Jocelyn's Room
Casa de Wolf

FROM THE FAR CORNER OF THE ROOM, high above the bullet hole and skimming the ceiling, Jocelyn watched with interest what was going on with the surgery. Mom and the doctor were cleaning up now. The little clock on the bedside stand showed that they had been working for almost two and a half hours to repair the artery that she had sliced. She could stay or go. It really didn't matter, but this little corner of the room seemed to hold her like a magnet so she remained and watched.

The doctor, with a cell phone balancing on his lap, kept massaging her hand and fingers to make sure blood was reaching all her little capillaries and Mom, in her white nursing uniform and cap from the late 1960s, was hustling around making sure the surgical instruments were counted, collected, and documented on the chart.

Comfortable with the fact that she was just floating there weightless, Jocelyn struggled with the idea that she was also timeless. Sure, the clock kept twitching away the time signatures of the current scene in play, but that didn't account for the other figures in the room. They weren't there all the time. Every so often they would appear and then just as suddenly disappear. Maybe she just wasn't paying enough attention? No. They were snapping in and out. They always assembled during what felt like a weird electrical surge, a super slow strobe light going on and off, allowing her to catch a glimpse of them. A woman and a boy, but now they were gone.

Jocelyn was becoming bored just watching her body lying there. She knew there was no eminent danger. Her mother was there after all, but it was curious that Mom was wearing that nursing uniform and looking so well rested, young, and downright beautiful. But that was okay because Mom was beautiful. It made sense. What didn't make sense was the sometimes here kid wearing green lederhosen silently sobbing.

Insatiable curiosity took hold and Jocelyn willed herself to see what the heck was going on with this boy and the woman in the gray, belted, long-sleeve dress with the crisp white collar and cuffs. The dress, circa 1945, was cut right below the woman's knee and Jocelyn noticed that there must have been shoulder pads involved and maybe even a petticoat because of the way the dress puffed out just a little. Jocelyn also surmised that the woman's short, dark hair must have been set with rollers considering the way it framed her face with curls. The woman's shoes weren't very remarkable as far as Jocelyn was concerned. Regardless, she knew that this was the boy's mother. It was just obvious.

The more Jocelyn wanted to see these two the longer they stayed away. The freaky thing was that when she became distracted by some arbitrary, mundane, totally un-noteworthy event like Margret in her nursing uniform folding towels, the boy and his mother would phantasmically reappear then disappear with the throb of the super slow strobe light as if teasing her like a cat—Schrödinger's cat.

So Jocelyn waited. The boy and his mother would be back. It wasn't like she had anything else to do. The little clock on the night side stand kept ticking like a metronome in perfect syncopation with the doctor and her mother-the-nurse's movements.

Jocelyn decided to focus in on the clock and the second, or had it been a minute? Possibly an hour? It didn't matter. The actual time wasn't the issue. Anyway, by the time she started focusing in on the clock the boy and his mother snapped back onto the scene. It was like another piece of film had been overlaid on the footage of her surgery. The doctor was rubbing her fingers, Mom was folding, and this kid was right underneath her crying.

She wanted to know why the boy was crying. She couldn't hear him. She just saw him and his thin, little legs and his scratchy wool socks. Hands over his face with shoulders quaking, clearly he was sobbing. She didn't feel the need to go hug him or anything but she was worried about him. Jocelyn looked down and **snap*,* the lights did their flashing thing again and the boy was gone. Interestingly, Jocelyn's mother was now wearing her bloodstained, luxurious, floor-length, embroidered gown. Her hair was a mess, gathered up into a bun. She looked tired and worn out. The big cut on her face had been bandaged up. Jocelyn could hear her mother talking.

"I'm just glad I had that emergency room and surgery experience in nursing school and that it all came back when I needed it."

"Sí. Nicely done, calling in that memory. That was very helpful. Muy bien."

"So, she's going to be all right, right?" Margret wanted to know, using the ample folds of her designer dress to nervously wipe her hands. The doctor didn't say anything. "When do you think she will be waking up?"

The doctor still didn't say anything and Jocelyn noticed a singular, fantastically shiny, glistening tear bead up in the corner of Margret's eye. The tear slid down Margret's worried face and as it dripped off her chin time slowed down, way down, almost to a veritable stop. Jocelyn was right there with the little droplet of water as it wiggled against atmospheric pressure, wobbled with the forces of gravity, and began what seemed like a million mile journey down to the floor as it assumed the properties of an undulating ball of mercury. Soon, or maybe not so soon considering how slowly things were moving, more mercurial tears were falling and cataclysmically exploding upon impact, splattering off into hundreds of minuscule silver orbs which also divided upon impact.

This went on and on and on, and Jocelyn could have gotten lost following the infinitesimal smallness of it all until she realized that these weren't coming from her mother's tear. These were the tears violently pouring out of the lederhosen boy as he shakily leaned over and withdrew a gun from his mother's well-manicured, dead hand. Meanwhile, the doctor continued massaging Jocelyn's cold fingers unaware of the tiny sliver ping pong balls bouncing around in slow motion or the red tide creeping in around him emanating from the woman in the gray dress on the floor.

"Vorsichtig. Gib mir das." Two new men, looking very official, appeared on the scene. They were here now talking to the weepy boy. One warning the boy to be careful and to give him the gun. The little boy, sucking back tears, carefully handed the revolver to the man with the mustache. It was a funny little mustache but the man was so serious, so heavy with the weight of the world bearing down upon him, or as the Germans call it *"weltschmerz,"* that there was absolutely nothing comical about it. As the man with the mustache emptied the bullets from the gun's barrel into the palm of his hand, shook them around like shelled peanuts, and stashed them away in his pocket, he let the boy know that his mother had done the right thing. "Deine Mutter hat das richtige getan. Sie war sehr krank." That she was sick. Jocelyn watched the man lovelessly tussle the kid's hair, telling him that it wasn't his fault. "Das ist nicht deine schuld." The man produced a pocketknife and handed to the boy.

The child took it with both hands and held it to his heart. "Danke papa." Then, with his head down, the little lederhosen boy waddled toward the door and as he did the strobe lights went on and off and the energy in the room realigned. The dead woman and the men were gone and the child passed right into and was absorbed by the form of another man entering the room. A man Jocelyn recognized, Brunhold Bertram Keller Wolf.

"Oh! Dios mío!" B.B. gasped, swooping into the room and hugging Margret. He seemed instantly overwhelmed and appeared to be blinking back tears. Holding Margret's shoulder he ran his finger gently down the bandage on her face then kissed her on both cheeks. He looked past her to the doctor, who seemed irritated, and then he studied the unresponsive Jocelyn. Returning his attention to Margret and almost in a panic B.B. asked, "¿Donde están los niños?"

"Niños?" Margret repeated back.

"Children. Where are the little ones?"

"Oh, they locked themselves in the bathroom." B.B. looked concerned so Margret strode over to the restroom door and knocked on it. "Kids, you can come out now." They didn't answer. "Please come out. Mr. Wolf is here." She smiled weakly at B.B. while holding the doorknob and leaning in toward the door. "He'd like to see you." No answer.

"You never told them," the doctor said, still rubbing his patient's hand. "They don't know." B.B.'s chest heaved and he turned around to address the doctor, but just as he did a very old man in a green, satiny jacket slowly shuffled into the room.

Shakily waving his arthritic finger at the doctor and patient the old man crankily asked, "Why is she wearing a potato sack?"

"I have no idea," the doctor replied. Then continuing in Spanish which Jocelyn high above the scene could easily understand but it was clear that her mother could not, "She is not stable. The readings are all over the place." The doctor handed the cell phone that had been on his knee to the old man.

"Fascinating..." the old man remarked as he studied the phone. "Why is this level so high?" he asked, turning the phone around so that the doctor could see the screen.

"She overdosed."

"Find out precisely by how much then dispose of all this." B.B. audibly gasped and Margret, still holding the bathroom doorknob, looked quizzically at him as the doctor and the old man continued in Spanish.

"Dispose?" The doctor seemed either confused or surprised.

"She will die I presume. I do not need further testing on this subject."

"But if I were to give her a full blood transfusion. I have universal donor blood on the way..." Just then the bathroom door squeaked open and Lillian with her disheveled pigtails and real fur collar jean jacket and William with his puffy, pink-lined eyes and tear streaked cheeks appeared. Both barefoot, they shyly tiptoed out and gathered behind their grandmother's full skirt.

Noticing the children the old man sighed and smiled, but Jocelyn knew from her vantage point that it was not a benevolent smile. Margret, however, obviously did not possess the same awareness and returning the smile offered, "These are my grandchildren. Jocelyn's niños." Proudly adding while placing a hand on each child, "They're twins."

"Twins!" the liver-spotted old man with the pointy nose and oversized square jaw cried out. "Why Brunhold! You told me nothing about twins. Have you no clue as to how unique an opportunity this is?"

That was it. With that comment Jocelyn was done hanging out in the corner of the room. Recognizing that she was the equivalent of a sprawling electrical scribble she drew in all of her tendrils into a big, dense knot and hurled herself back at her near lifeless body. Whizzing at the speed of light past the doctor was the easy part. Smashing into herself was another story. The weight of impact caused her to sharply pull in a deep, sandpaper breath and she experienced the taste of pain once again.

Margret instantly noticed a change in her daughter and pointing, alerted the doctor. Meanwhile, the dense knot that was Jocelyn began untangling itself and started expanding and flowing like spilled golden milk, flooding into all the familiar corridors of her abandoned and distressed home. Her toes wiggled and her good shoulder twitched. The doctor started rubbing her hand and fingers with more vigor. That's when Jocelyn, still not yet conscious, yanked her hand away and rolled to her side.

Keenly aware of her daughter's movement and forgetting her grandchildren, Margret nearly leapt over to Jocelyn's side, leaving William and Lilly awkwardly standing with B.B., facing the grinning old man.

"No," B.B. said softly while shaking his head. "Estos niños no son para ti." And he stepped behind the children, protectively placing his hands on Willy and Lilly's trembling, tiny shoulders.

CHAPTER FORTY-FOUR

Meanwhile
Patrick Air Force Base, Department of State Hangar
Florida, USA

"INITIAL HERE, HERE...," Laura instructed, pointing to the highlighted areas in the bound ream of paper she was awkwardly cradling. Leafing through to page one fifty-seven, she placed the document on a gray metal desk tucked in the back corner of the enormous, empty hangar and smooshed her index finger definitively down on a bright yellow line. "And here." The hangar's florescent lights buzzed and the pigeon-be-gone system chirped through the rafters at regular intervals like electronic fingernails on a chalkboard. Grabbing the pen Jerry nodded, and Laura continued, "Most importantly don't forget to date and sign your full name with your social security number on that page with the little yellow sticky." She flicked the yellow tab hanging out of the document.

"Got it," Jerry replied, and he hastily began flipping through the pages scribbling his consent, thus legally binding himself and anyone in his immediate or extended family, even any tangentially concerned party, to not sue or seek damages should he die, go crazy, attain any level of disability, or...he stopped and reread the part about possible infertility and erectile dysfunction and then initialed there too.

Then, continuing to breeze through pages jammed with legalese that didn't have any highlighted areas, he jumped ahead to specifically sign away any possibility of public speaking engagements. This included commenting to the press and appearances on any and all social media platforms. He also agreed to forego pursuing a book or movie deal. A dozen pages were then dedicated to him not communicating with foreign nationals, which he initialed on each page. The next two pages were a standard non-disclosure agreement—signed and dated; no problem. The very last chunk of paperwork consisted of legally recognizing the penalties he would face should any of the vulnerabilities he had demonstrated back in Conference Room Delta somehow find their way out to the world. He didn't bother to read any of that and simply jotted his now nearly illegible initials at the designated spots.

"You sure you want to do this?" Laura asked, peering over Jerry's shoulder, watching him write his social security number on the appropriate highlighted line. "People practice and weight train and do breath control exercises for something like this…" Jerry absently nodded and visibly concerned Laura added, "for years. They train for years Jerry. This isn't a video game."

"Yeah, I know," Jerry said, smacking his pen down on the metal desk. The noise of his triumphant completion reverberated throughout the barren hangar as the sound of approaching footsteps on concrete grew louder and louder.

"Sir?" echoed through the all-things-aviation-infused climate controlled air. "T-minus fifty-two minutes."

Puffing up his chest, Jerry braced himself and looked to Laura for a clue. But she didn't look up. She was fully focused on reviewing the paperwork he had just signed and even though she was avoiding eye contact with Jerry, he could have sworn that she was on the verge of tears.

"Time to gear up," the unsmiling, graying at the temples man said with a slight Texas accent as he abruptly stopped in front of Jerry.

The two men sized each other up. The newcomer was in civilian clothes—khaki shorts, a white polo type shirt, and running shoes. His posture, physical fitness, clean shave, along with the big class ring, aviator wristwatch, and the way his shirt was perfectly tucked into his belted shorts led Jerry to suspect that this person was actually in the military, or at least had been in the military. They shook hands without exchanging names and not looking back at Laura, Jerry and the mystery man left the building.

The steel door slammed behind them as they made their exit. Walking into a wall of humid heat Jerry was grateful for the natural light and the muted acoustics of fresh air. He noticed that the sun would be setting, probably within the hour. It was later than he had anticipated, and taking in deep breaths as he walked Jerry surveyed the long, tidy, parallel rows of white runway lights and the curves of the blue taxiway lights as the rotating beacon slowly spun out its welcome at the far end of the airport.

Jerry followed his guide through the letters and numbers of the tied down small planes and two parked private jets while overhead a flock of seagulls glided east. Other than that, the place appeared deserted. The solemn crunching of their feet on the expanse of Kennedy era concrete was all Jerry heard and to break the uncomfortable silence he asked, "So, is fifty minutes going to be enough for an orientation?"

"I'm not briefing you about anything," the man said, still looking straight ahead while purposefully walking. "Just suiting you up. After you're outfitted I'm passing you off as was outlined in your contract."

"Oh," Jerry replied. "Right," and they headed toward a modest, cinderblock, two-story building at the edge of the airfield. When they got there the man held the door open for Jerry and followed him in.

"Walk this way, please," the man instructed.

Moving in silence down a pale, almost minty green cinderblock hallway with a well-worn but highly buffed linoleum floor, they stopped at Room 107. The man unlocked the door and ushered Jerry in.

Entering, Jerry noticed that it was a lot like a doctor's examination room with metal cabinets on the wall and blue naugahyde all over the place with thin rolls of paper to cover it. It smelled sterile, like ammonia and rubbing alcohol. What looked like snow boots were lined up in the corner and a big oversized digital wall clock blinked steadily toward T-minus zero.

"Have a seat, please."

Jerry nodded and opted for the stool in the center of the room instead of the examination table and sat down. That's when, from out of nowhere, came the clippers. "Woah! What's the deal?" Jerry's hands, with fingers outspread, reflexively popped up. "I didn't realize I'd be getting a haircut."

"It was in your contract."

"It was?" Jerry's hands slowly fell back to his side. The man nodded and his thumb clicked the hair buzzer into action. Chunks of Jerry's dark, naturally wavy, overgrown locks were falling to the floor and for the first time in his life he appreciated his hair. Feeling kind of sad that it was getting all buzzed off he consoled himself, *It will grow back. I'm doing this for Jocelyn.* The buzzing stopped with a click and, running his hand over his "new recruit" bald head, Jerry was shown the white tiled restroom.

He was assessing his new haircut in the mirror when the man ordered, "Empty your bladder and bowels then put this on, please," while holding out a Depends adult diaper. Seeing this in the mirror behind him, Jerry cautiously turned around and apprehensively accepted the thing. The door was shut and moments later Jerry emerged.

With arms crossed over his chest the man assessed the physique of the bald IT guy wearing a Grateful Dead T-shirt and diaper standing before him. He shook his head as if in pity or disappointment, Jerry couldn't tell which, and the man sighed, "Okay, time to get suited up." He reached over and pulled a bright orange, heavy-duty, one-piece flight suit decorated with American flag patches off a hook on the wall and held it open for Jerry to step into. "This jumpsuit is insulated and has sensors embedded throughout," the man explained. Jerry cautiously slid his right foot into the pant leg. "It will be monitoring and recording your vitals."

"Wow. How much did this thing cost?" Jerry asked, placing his other foot into the suit.

"Not as much as the helmet," the man said while shimmying Jerry's pants up. "Now, start securing the suit." Jerry did as he was told and as he did a stiff, plastic, neck brace was slipped around his neck.

"This is like one of those things they give you for whiplash," Jerry commented while touching the neck brace with his fingers. "I had to wear something like this after a car accident once." The man didn't respond and efficiently connected another piece to the brace. It had two plastic tubes, one very small in diameter and the other thicker and crimped, hanging off of it. "What's this for?" Jerry asked.

"These are for your oxygen mix and vomit."

"Oh."

The man quickly and expertly patted Jerry down, making sure all the connections were secure. "Okay. Get your boots on." And he pointed to the boots lined up on the floor in the corner of the room. "One of those pairs should fit you."

Jerry nodded and, wedging his foot into a boot, decided it was too uncomfortable and tried the next size up. As he did, he watched the man go back to the examination table and fish a key out of his pocket. Bending down, the man unlocked the storage door under the table and carefully extracted a white, almost luminescent, plastic cube. The cube was a little bigger than a milk crate and its eight vertices were smooth and rounded. It could have passed for a piece of modern art or some sort of children's toy, especially with the little cartoon skunk printed on the upper left corner.

Jerry, of course, immediately noticed the cartoon and excitedly asked while pointing, "Is that the Skunkworks logo?" The man nodded while sliding the lid off the cube. "Are you kidding me?!" Jerry blurted. "That's from Lockheed Martin's Skunkworks?"

"Yes."

"Where they build all those ultra-top secret planes that everyone thinks are UFOs?"

The man sighed and his shoulders fell in exasperation. "Didn't you read your contract?"

"Oh, of course, but I guess I missed that part."

The man's eyebrows arched with skepticism before he quietly turned his attention back to the contents of the cube and pulled out a sheet of white cardboard with lines of little blue dots on it.

"Skunkworks and the late, great Clarence Kelly Johnson." Jerry swooned and dreamily shaking his head added, "What an inspiration. He's one of my biggest idols ever."

"May he rest in peace all of eternity for building God's air force," the man said with great reverence as he plucked a dot off the cardboard. "Bow your head, please."

"Huh?"

"Look at your feet. I have to apply these to your head," he said, raising his index finger with the blue dot stuck to it. "These are like the ones they use for EEGs. Just stickers. It doesn't hurt. Now bow your head, please," he repeated.

"Oh, sure," Jerry said, dutifully looking down.

The man systematically began fixing about twenty dots in straight lines up and down and across Jerry's head. When he finished he stood back to appreciate his work.

"Can I touch them?" Jerry asked, about to run his hand over his head.

"No."

"Oh, okay," Jerry mumbled and then asked, "These work with that Skunkworks helmet?"

"To be clear, Skunkworks did not make the helmet. An Israeli company did. Skunkworks designed and built the aircraft and contracted out for the helmet. But to answer your question, the sensors I just applied to your head will work to pick up how you are processing the experience. They monitor the electrical signals in your brain. Ideally, your brain would be interacting with the helmet, sending your impulses directly to the craft for execution."

"Seriously?" Jerry questioned. "You mean the pilot could just think about something, like turn left, and the plane would just do it?" The man nodded. "No way. That's pretty awesome!" Jerry blurted out incredulously.

"It's something like that," the man clarified. "Right now it has more to do with tracking your eye movement over the interface on the screen. But considering you have no flight hours logged the control function has been disabled. This is simply to monitor you. However, you should be able to see the pilot interface through your visor once you're belted in."

"Okay. That makes sense." Jerry nodded. "It's probably pretty easy to track eye movement now that I think about it," Jerry commented, getting lost in thought. "You know, I've always wanted to work at Skunkworks. That would have been my dream job," Jerry rambled, "flying in and out of Area 51, but you need a college degree and, uhm…I dropped out."

"Really?" the man asked as he pulled a strip of velcro off of something inside the Skunkworks box.

Jerry sheepishly grunted and nodded.

The man seemed to do a double take and, penetratingly staring at Jerry commented, "Interesting." Then shaking his head as if hearing an ironic old joke, "I guess it's only fitting that you tickled COSMIC TALENT KEYHOLE. Some of the best never went to college. Congratulations," the man said while lifting a shiny, silvery gray hybrid of an astronaut helmet meeting a jet fighter helmet out of the cube. It resembled some sort of space-age insect head. "Technically, you're working for Skunkworks right now." The digital clock silently flicked the red countdown to T-minus zero as he placed the helmet, with the visor up, on Jerry's polka-dotted head.

Jerry's chest swelling with pride made him forget his question about the cosmic thing; and he stood at full attention as a thermo-insulated type of specialty scarf was placed around his already braced neck and the man double-checked the tubes and the oxygen mask again and presented him with a one-hundred-dollar bill, tucking it into a little velcro pocket on his sleeve. "For the steak dinner when you get there." Jerry smiled as the helmet securely locked into position, and being patted down entirely yet again Jerry was just about giddy putting on the big thermo-insulated gloves. Slapping him on the butt the man said, "Looks good. Let's go."

The two exited the room with the man leading the way. Jerry walked down the long well-buffed linoleum hallway with a newfound sense of pride. He felt as if he was in the movie *The Right Stuff*. But this wasn't a movie. This was real life and Jerry's heart was beating hard and fast. He knew he couldn't screw up. He was aware of everything from the minty color of the walls to the slippery squeakiness of the floor to the plasticky smell of the oxygen mask that was pressing somewhat uncomfortably against his sweaty chin. He was in cognitive overload and consequently couldn't do much of anything other than blissfully, albeit purposefully, march along after the man guiding him.

Because of the insulated suit Jerry didn't feel the difference in temperature as they stepped out of the cinderblock building and into the night, illuminated by cones of light shining down from poles in the parking lot. A golf cart was conspicuously parked right outside the door and the man, hopping in on the driver's side, motioned for Jerry to join him.

With Jerry in his astronaut suit and silver bug helmet, the two buzzed across the tarmac, cut behind the State Department's hangar, and then hit the access road. They were heading to the very farthest point of the runway, diametrically opposed to the dutifully spinning rotating beacon.

Finally, when they reached the end of the runway the man shut off the golf cart and asked, "How are you doin'? Feeling all right?"

"Yeah," Jerry answered, his voice muffled by his oxygen mask that wasn't hooked up to anything other than some floppy tubes slung over his shoulder. "I'm all right," he shouted through the mask while cautiously adjusting the visor. "What are we doing way out here?"

"Your bird will be here in...," glancing at his big aviator wristwatch the man said, "approximately seventy-two seconds." He looked up. "This baby needs a long runway so you're gettin' on out here."

"Oh. Makes sense. Sure." Just then Jerry heard what sounded like two big booms. Sonic booms.

"Yup. That's her. She'll be here in bit. Just hang tight my friend," the man said.

Leaning way back in his spacesuit, Jerry strained to find the source of the booms in the night sky. He saw a few twinkling stars and the telltale strobes of commercial jets heading into and out of Orlando, but other than that nothing remarkable. He took a deep breath and rubbed his gloved hands on his thighs. It was quiet. Very quiet. Anticipation was bubbling over as he imagined what they could possibly be using to shuttle him over to Jocelyn. *One of those jets the Blue Angels use, an F/A-18 Hornet? How cool would that be?* he wondered. *Nah...they wouldn't have me wearing this astronaut getup...*He rubbed his hands on his legs again and the man noticed.

"You sure you're all right?" the man asked.

"Yeah, just getting pumped. You know, it's not every day something like this happens." Jerry noticed that his oxygen mask was getting all spitty from talking, or maybe it was sweat. Jerry wasn't sure and the man nodded. Suddenly flanks of super bright floodlights lining the runway snapped on, startling Jerry, and he squinted. He just wanted to take the darn helmet and mask off so he could see or, more correctly in this case, hear. It was that weird, all-consuming HVAC sound that he had heard in Conference Room Delta. It didn't sound at all like a mighty jet engine. It sounded like a really low humming air conditioner, or better yet, one of those white noise machines. The tone seemed to swallow sound rather than produce it and soon Jerry saw it.

The winged craft, as if laser guided, was descending and barreling directly toward them as they sat vulnerably in their little golf cart at the end of the runway. The plane had no landing lights. No navigation lights. Nothing. It was completely dark. As Jerry watched its perfect approach and landing he could discern the sound of wheels hitting the pavement and reverse thrusters bursting into action, but this was simply because he saw it happening. If he hadn't witnessed it he probably wouldn't have known what those sounds were because everything was so oddly muffled and it wasn't just because of the helmet.

Still fixated on the dark plane racing toward him, Jerry was taken by surprise when a brand-new, white Ford pickup skidded to a stop next to the golf cart. The truck had its headlights pointing at the little plane and Jerry could now see that the craft was painted black on the bottom and silvery gray on top, the same color as his helmet. Its stubby little wings were slung back sharply, sort of like a stealth bomber, but this craft was much, much smaller than a bomber. Most notably, it didn't have big engines hanging off its wings, just two very small ones, integral to the design of each tiny wing. *Probably the reverse thrusters,* Jerry theorized, and thought it appeared to be more of a winged rocket on wheels. Just as the thing was rolling to a stop in front of them a young man wearing a white baseball hat and holding a large metal L-shaped crowbar thing hopped out of the truck parked next to Jerry.

"Howdy!" the young man called out, all smiles, over the winding down sound the plane was making. Tapping his first two fingers to his brow in a casual salute to the driver of the golf cart, he strode over and, slapping Jerry on the shoulder, exclaimed, "Well all right! We have our first human volunteer!" He held his hand out for a shake and Jerry instinctively shook it. "Pleasure to meet you, sir. Thank you for your service." Jerry didn't quite know how to respond so he just nodded. "I'll take him from here Fred." White hat wearing Howdy said, "Mommy will be here shortly."

Jerry glanced over at Fred who nodded solemnly and said, "Godspeed. Until we meet again."

Jerry didn't know why, but at this moment he felt like he wanted to hug Fred. He resisted that urge and instead said, "Thank you," and shook the man's hand. Fred motioned with his chin for Jerry to get out of the cart. So Jerry arduously removed his space suited body from the golf cart and Fred stepped on the gas and hightailed it away.

"Ready to get tucked in?" Jerry nodded. "Great! Let's do this thing!" Howdy exclaimed and gave Jerry's helmet a friendly tap. "Lookin' good buddy!" Gripping the metal piece and waving his arm enthusiastically for Jerry to follow him, they traversed the gravel and weeds at the end of the runway. Arriving at the plane he said in a tour guide voice, "In the 1950s we had the highest flying airplane, the U2. And in the '60s we developed the fastest airplane to this day: the SR-71. In the 1970s it was all about stealth and the '80s was all about thrust vectoring. Nineties was guided missiles then drones. Put it all together and you get this," he proudly recited with arms outstretched to showcase the tiny black plane.

It wasn't much bigger than a little four-seater private airplane. Jerry guessed it no more than thirty feet long and maybe twelve feet wide including the wingspan. "An aircraft with insane speed. An unmanned, highly maneuverable, stealth aircraft. Hyper-X Scramjet Hybrid. It's a combo of a ramjet for Mach 2 and 3 and a scramjet for Mach 5, with the cruising and final stages powered by antimatter. Now we're going to see if it can successfully deliver human cargo."

Jerry was totally geeked out, beholding the creation from behind his oxygen mask. "Are you kidding me?" his muffled voice squeaked. "Antimatter?"

The guy in the white hat nodded. "Yeah, that's what makes this project so freakin' expensive. Antimatter is a bitch to produce and store. We had to get this particular batch done up over at CERN."

"How fast does this thing go?" Jerry wanted to know.

"Without cargo, about MACH 10."

"Holy shit…Ten times the speed of sound?"

"Yup. Can get around the world in about three and half hours if it has to. NASA and everyone else, mind you, have been officially working on perfecting this since 1997. Our team has been specifically tweeking the sustained antimatter propulsion. Theoretical projections have this baby goin' between Mach 12 and Mach 24, which is near orbital velocity."

Jerry shook his helmet protected head and through the plastic tasting, spitty humidity of his oxygen mask remarked, "This is real *X-files* stuff. I mean, this is incredible."

"You bet it is. The antimatter reaction basically creates a stream of nano-sized black holes and that's what propels this thing. So there is no pollution pouring out of it. It's really remarkable."

"Actual black holes?" Jerry asked with concern through his oxygen mask. "Wouldn't that be, like, way worse than pollution?" But the white hat man didn't hear him or at least seemed like he didn't hear him and laughed.

"Come on. Mom will be here soon. This craft has to be launched from a moving, in-flight plane. Let's get you strapped in before the rest of the crew arrives." The young man took off his white hat and purposefully plunked it back on his head with the brim facing in the opposite direction. Then, squatting down like a car mechanic, he used the L-shaped piece of metal he had been toting around and cranked opened a hatch in the belly of the plane. What looked like a big, beefy missile clanged noisily onto the ground and it split open the long way. "Okay, hop in. I'll hook up those tubes so you can breathe."

Now this is where Jerry clumsily ripped off his oxygen mask, and with it flopping around he screeched while pointing, "You want me to get in that?! That's how I'm getting there?! At MACH 10?!"

"Well, yeah," the guy in the white hat confusedly answered. "Didn't you read your contract? It's pretty explicit about how this is gonna go."

"Nah, screw this," Jerry balked. "This is suicide. I'm out. I'm calling it off."

"I'm afraid not, brother." The L-shaped tool clanged to the ground and the man pulled a gun from a concealed holster, training it on Jerry. "I don't think you realize the kind of Pandora's box you've opened. You can't just walk away. There's a lot at stake here. You signed the contract."

Just then two military jeeps and some sort of big, boxy airport vehicle outfitted with what appeared to be a folded up crane on top of it, pulled in. The four guys getting out of the jeeps drew their guns and circled around Jerry, surrounding him. The guy in the white hat said, "Look, we have a mission here. You are getting in that thing one way or the other. You might as well make it easy on yourself and just crawl in. It's as safe as it could possibly be. Believe me; we all want this to be successful." The jeep guys were slowly closing in on Jerry. "You'll be able to follow everything by watching what is going on in your visor. It's basically a flat-screen monitor and you'll see everything the remote pilot is seeing. You can even hear the conversation with command and control. You'll be there in no time. Heck, you might really enjoy this."

Looking over his shoulder at the jeep guys closing in, Jerry's heart raced and ached, not so much because he was having a near heart attack, nor because he was scared to death of wedging himself into a hollowed-out missile shell which was clearly a ready-made casket, but because it wasn't going the way he wanted it to and he was disappointed. That's really what was bumming him out. He had imagined his arrival to rescue Jocelyn to be heroic and epic, more exciting, like the cool parts of the movie *Top Gun* with "Highway to the Danger Zone" pumping in surround sound rather than the less than satisfying ending of the film *Dr. Strangelove*. Jerry closed his eyes and put his hands up as if surrendering just as an enormous B-52 bomber touched down. The smell of burning rubber and aviation exhaust wafted toward them as its wheels skid and squeaked, leaving a new set of black marks on the runway.

"Okay, Mom's here," the white hat guy announced as the B-52 noisily rumbled directly toward them. The jeep guys jammed the muzzles of their guns into Jerry's back and sore rib. "Let's go!"

Jerry didn't move and that's when someone punched him in the gut. Jerry doubled over and the four jeep guys pounced. Restraining him as he moaned, they jammed him into the missile shell, holding him down while the backwards hat guy hastily hooked up the oxygen and vomit tubes. White hat guy then secured Jerry's oxygen mask, flipped down his visor, and pressed a button. Patting Jerry on the shoulder he said, "Good luck buddy. Just know that you're doing something good, okay?" and he slammed the lid of the missile shell down over Jerry like the hood of an old car.

It was dark in there. Pitch black. Jerry could hear his heart pounding in his ears. Panic was taking hold. Huffing in the cool oxygen mix he lay with his arm crossed over his chest as if he really were in a casket at a funeral home or, because it was so dark, buried in the ground at a cemetery, and he started to cry. He couldn't wipe away his tears because he was so jammed in and even if he could move his hands up to his face, it was covered with the visor and he wouldn't be able to prop it open anyway. So there he lay, all soggy and hyperventilating in the dark when suddenly the missile shell was violently yanked around from side to side and he heard muffled metallic clanging noises.

He stopped crying and realized that they were now hoisting him upwards, coupling the little black plane to the B-52, and this is when Jerry had to give credit where credit was due. The people who had created this delivery method had taken the time to thoroughly insulate and pad the tube he was trapped in. The space-age polymer foam cushioning he was encapsulated in was expanding and actively form fitting his body, hugging him securely. He squeezed his eyes shut tight as the B-52 Mom with the tiny baby strapped under its wing proudly rolled through the blue lights of the taxiway, getting back into position for takeoff.

Oh, Jocelyn. I'll be there soon. You have no idea how much I love you. And he talked to her like that until the enormous weight of acceleration paralyzed even his thoughts and his visor lit up with what looked like a video game. Shortly thereafter the vomit tube proved invaluable and he effectively passed out.

CHAPTER FORTY-FIVE

Meanwhile
Wakulla Suites
Cocoa Beach, Florida

"MOM, IT'S ME." Mark, swollen with anticipation for this conversation, gulped back emotion. He'd been trying to reach his mother for the past five hours and she was finally answering! "Mom, I'm—" *Click.* The line went dead.

Disappointed that he couldn't have his made-for-TV moment of revealing that he hadn't actually been killed, he examined his phone. It had decent reception. He pressed redial and waited for his mother to answer. It rang and rang. He hung up and called again. Nothing. She wasn't picking up. "Figures," Mark grumbled. "She's friggin' drunk," and he despondently tossed his phone onto the couch. He was done. Completely and totally over this nonsense. His back hurt, his eye was still all messed up despite the ice he had been applying, and he couldn't even cry anymore.

He had been pent up here, alone, in this cheesy, circa 1970s Polynesian-themed oceanfront hotel seven miles away from the fraught meeting in Conference Room Delta for way too long. When the meeting in Delta had morphed into serious negotiations mode he had been rolled out of the conference room and whisked away to "wait for his people." The uncomfortable wheelchair that he had been handcuffed to during that meeting sat empty next to the couch and he crookedly stood, stunned and motionless, at the bottom of his mental pit surrounded by annoying abstract hotel art; a dusty, plastic Bird of Paradise flower arrangement; a mini coffeemaker accompanied by a mini microwave oven; menus and event calendars strategically placed around the room featuring tiki heads, pineapples, and surfboards; and, of course, the omnipresent din of home improvement shows and commercials emanating from the oversized flat-screen TV.

Realizing that he had been trapped on all sides by wallpaper with pink flamingos standing on one leg while he had been scrolling through a mind-numbing blue screen of cable listings where a random click delivered custom chop shop motorcycles as freedom, real estate investment as contest, and capturing rouge alligators lurking in suburban swimming pools as a legit career path, Mark unexpectedly laughed. A weird crazy laugh. The strangeness of his laugh surprised him and it made him laugh even more.

The whole scene was classic millennial metamodernism but more maniacal. Alliteration aside, earlier generations would have called what Mark was experiencing "a nervous breakdown." But Mark, triggered by the tiki heads and pineapples, naturally and comfortably associated his situation with the cartoon SpongeBob SquarePants and his whole universe became absolutely hysterical. The wheelchair. Hilarious. The dusty plastic Bird of Paradise. Hilarious. The mini coffeemaker and so on were equally hilarious, nonsensical and surreal, heavily laden with what he perceived as irony making it all the more funny.

Take Gen X's sarcasm, flip it on its head, add the flavor of Adderall, then cut and paste everything onto any random, preferably some 1980s video game screen shot, and the joke made perfect sense to anyone born between the years of 1981 and 1996. For Mark's grandparents this might be the equivalent of watching a Fellini film dubbed with a laugh track while taking an illicit toke, but this was way deeper, more absurd, and darker than that and consequently a real sidesplitter. The laughter issuing out of Mark was of monumental physical relief from the unbearable lightness of bullshit. He was essentially living a real-time internet meme. No, this wasn't an emotional breakdown. This was a generation's coping mechanism.

Uncomfortably splayed out on the couch and still snorting back giggles, Mark didn't hear the door click open and was taken completely off guard when his much despised boss, Fitzgerald S. Crowley, sauntered in wearing a light gray linen suit, and picking up the phone, ordered room service like it was no big whoop.

"Want anything?" he asked, tipping the hotel phone down below his chin.

"Yeah," Mark sputtered in disbelief that Crowley had personally come to collect him. "I wanna go home."

"From the menu," Crowley clarified, holding up the tiki head trifold that Mark had read a million times.

"The veggie burger," Mark instantly replied, working to contain his emotions and trying to plot the impending argument with his boss. "The veggie burger and some lemonade," he said, wiping his nose and sitting up straight.

The unexpected room service call was a good thing because at this point, despite the laughing fit, Mark really was incredibly angry and he wanted to get what he needed to say right so this gave him time to think.

Propped up on the couch with pillows supporting his back, Mark had a plate full of potato chips and the hotel's overpriced, signature grilled Hawaiian teriyaki veggie burger balancing on his lap. He carefully patted the corners of his mouth with his napkin and began. "Do you know what you've just put me through?"

Crowley, sitting at the glass topped bamboo executive desk by the window which overlooked the drained pool and construction of a new Hawaiian themed waterslide, stopped chewing his luau lomi lomi salmon patty, which incidentally bore no resemblance whatsoever to its traditional Hawaiian namesake, and looked up.

"Well, do you?" Mark waited for an answer and Crowley didn't respond. "This whole thing," Mark complained. "I swear to God!" Having anticipated instant engagement, Mark was befuddled. So he quickly snagged a potato chip and munched it while glaring at Crowley. "I have a degree in computer science."

The chip was tasty and with Crowley still not saying anything, Mark took the opportunity to crunch down a quick couple more then blasted out, "What you just put me through is completely and totally not in my job description and definitely illegal!" Crowley remained silent. "You know that, right?!" Mark thought it was weird how he wasn't gaining any traction here. "I never, not in a million years, signed up for any of it!" Crowley kind of raised his eyebrows and started eating again. "I was in the middle of the Jocelyn McLaren case and next thing you know you have me and that guy Apario—"

Crowley dropped his fork. "No." He stood up and, approaching the couch with index finger extended said, "I didn't do this to you. You did it to yourself." That comment really irked Mark and if he hadn't been partially incapacitated because of back pain inflicted while trying to help Jerry Apario he would have jumped off the sofa and faced off with Crowley. But, of course, he didn't, so he just clenched his jaw and maintained full eye contact as his boss advanced toward him.

"Did you ever get any orders to engage with Apario?" Mark didn't answer. "No. No, you did not. Did you ever report to anyone that Apario had contacted you before you met with him? No, you didn't. There's a reason why we have binders full of official procedure available all over the place. In fact, there's probably one in your desk right now and you, my friend, didn't follow any of it. Apario was on a completely different budget and—"

"Ah-ha! So the two of you were working together!" Mark blurted out. "I friggin' knew it!" With his outburst potato chips slid off his plate and he quickly grabbed for the burger, making sure it didn't end up on the floor too.

"Apario is in the witness protection program and had a delivery job," Crowley calmly explained. Mark took an angry bite of the veggie burger and scowled at Crowley as he chewed. "You were tasked with a missing person case. How was I, or anyone for that matter, to know that the two of you would end up here? Seriously, watch yourself kid. Now everyone, across multiple agencies, is dealing with mountains of paperwork because of you and Jerry Apario."

Studying Crowley's demeanor and realizing that something was very off, Mark gobbled down his food and changed his approach. "Okay, but what exactly was Apario delivering and to whom?"

"That's classified."

"Really? You can't disclose this even though I was there during the deal?"

"Look, all Apario had to do was drive the truck from point A to point B," Crowley said, using his hands to illustrate moving from point to point.

"Okay. But how many deliveries was Apario making between point A and point B?" Mark wanted to know. "He claims that he was delivering toy guns. I witnessed something the ATF would be interested in and it's obvious you were interested too. You were pretty darn direct in ordering Jerry to find out where those guns were. You know, after we were arrested and thrown in jail and you put us on the prison bus to hell!" Crowley rubbed his temple.

"And speaking of hell, what the hell was going on over there?!" Mark pushed his plate off his lap and stood up. "That wasn't the first time something like that's gone down, is it?!" Mark snarled. "Oh, you better believe you owe me more than a 'that's classified!' I mean, everyone at that damn prison who saw me and Jerry is dead!!" Crowley stood up straighter and Mark thoughtfully added, "Or are they all dead like me? You know, totally faked?"

Crowley, appearing completely conflicted, said, "Look, look, the toy guns really have nothing to do with me. Nothing."

Somewhat surprised that he got confirmation that the toy guns really were real, Mark clenched his jaw and nodded. "Go on."

"I don't even know what they're for. Our guys got them in a raid. They were included with a shipment of peanut butter of all things and instantly another agency claimed that they were theirs and—"

"Which agency?"

"That's highly classified." Mark rolled his eyes and Crowley continued. "No. It's true. I don't even know. Everything was black lined by the time the paperwork got to me. This agency claimed they were theirs. Higher-ups confirmed. They offered to make a deal and since we were just going to dump the things anyway we made the trade."

"So you traded them for real rifles and then you moved those?"

Crowley nodded. "Might as well get something for our time and effort."

"I see," but Mark wasn't completely buying it. "So what about the guy who collected the rifles from us? He worked for you?"

Crowley sort of shrugged his shoulders and said, "Technically a contractor."

"Uh-huh."

"Look, you don't need to know any of this but the bureau is currently tracking two suspects. Everyone is looking for them. This is a multiagency effort. They are the last of seven accused of murdering a border patrol agent six years ago." Mark had no idea about this manhunt but continued staring as intimidatingly as he could back at Crowley.

"That shooting blew the doors off Operation Fast and Furious." Mark nodded. He knew about that because he knew about the *Fast and Furious* movies. He had seen them, and so the headlines about the 2009-2011 Bureau of Alcohol, Tobacco, Firearms, and Explosives and their partner agencies' plan of letting two thousand illegal gun sales just slide so that they could track the buyers and sellers who were believed to be connected to Mexican drug cartels had definitely made a lasting impression on him, or at least the movies had. So, not that he knew the details, at least he knew what Crowley was talking about.

"The whole thing is getting insane with the elections coming up. It's turned into a God damn circus so we had to pull out all the stops," Crowley explained. "We needed to make one last gun run. All Apario had to do was simply drive the truck." He re-pantomimed the point A - point B movement with his hands.

"Did Apario know any of these details?"

"Heck no! I'm just happy to have that guy out of my hair." Crowley shook his head with disdain and Mark watched him turn and walk back to his luau lomi lomi salmon patty.

As Crowley passed the little hotel refrigerator next to the TV he tapped on it. "This a cash bar?" he asked, and Mark couldn't help but focus on all the little one-legged pink flamingos on the wallpaper as he processed the question. He would have laughed if he hadn't been so preoccupied with what Crowley had just disclosed about the guns.

"Yeah," Mark said while gathering up the remains of the pineapple ring from the grilled Hawaiian teriyaki veggie burger, which appeared to be the only thing that had actually been grilled. "I ate the bar snacks but someone left a bag of ice in the freezer."

Crowley opened the fridge door and Mark asked, "So, what about Apario? Did he find your rifles?"

"There's a team moving in on the location he provided right now," Crowley said as he inspected the label on a little bottle of whiskey. "The coordinates he provided place the guns in Mexico within Los Zetas cartel territory."

"So, he really *was* working for you the whole time?"

"Not exactly," Crowley replied over the sound of ice clinking into a glass, "but I was hoping that maybe he'd have some details from that cellmate of his, Abercrombie. That's the guy who led us to the toy guns." Pouring the scotch over the ice he let out a deep sigh and added, "Abercrombie really thought those plastic guns were lethal and that he could use them to work some sort of plea bargain." He screwed the cap back on the whiskey bottle. "What an asshole." He took a long swig of his drink and looking fairly satisfied added, "When Apario's map and the coordinates came in, someone, somewhere, snapped on the green light. And well, I've never seen anything like this. DOD says that the maps and coordinates were from their NATO COSMIC TK files."

"NATO?"

"Yeah, all NATO's top secret stuff is tagged COSMIC with the DOD."

"What's TK?" Mark wanted to know.

"TALENT KEYHOLE." Mark shook his head, not understanding. 'TALENT,' is an overarching code word for top secret aerial intelligence-gathering assets, such as the SR-71 Blackbird and U2 spy planes, and 'KEYHOLE' covers intelligence-gathering satellites. So they just use the abbreviation 'TK' because the missions overlap all the time."

Mark nodded. "Okay, so who flipped on the green light?"

"I told you. I don't know. This is a friggin' cluster fondue." Crowley said, holding up his scotch on the rocks as if offering up a toast. "People have no idea what I'm dealing with." He shook his head and took another gulp of his drink. "No friggin' idea." Then scratching his forehead he seemed to reminisce. "Back in 2002 when e-government was just rolling out the Treasury, Department of Defense, the National Finance Center at the Department of Agriculture, and NASA were the only departments important enough, or digitally savvy enough, to be tracking and verifying each other's purchases electronically."

"That's a weird combination," Mark commented. He didn't know where Crowley was going with all this but something told him to pay attention as he fussed with the remains of his veggie burger.

"No. No it's not. Agriculture's National Finance Center is a huge bank. Huge. And it all comes under critical infrastructure, hence national security," Fitzgerald Crowley said matter-of-factly. "The money, especially the money moving through the DOD and Space, now *that* has a life of its own. If someone wanted to, those agencies could siphon millions off their budgets and funnel it into some unknown black hole. Heck, billions and no one would know." Crowley glanced up. The Hawaiian waterslide construction work lights had snapped on and an eerie halogen glow illuminated the window by the bamboo desk he had been sitting at. "This BS they're putting everyone through right now…Shit, it's not like this border patrol guy is the only one who ever got whacked on the US/Mexico line." Studying his drink he grumbled, "Diverting attention so that the money can move where it's supposed to…Once you get your head around that, everything falls into place. They'll do it again."

Before Mark could respond a high-pitched, singsongy voice called out, "Hell-ooo?!" The hotel room door clunked shut and a woman rushed in, a floral silk scarf fluttering in her wake.

"Mom?"

"Oh! Sweetheart! I am soooo proud of you!" she gushed as she ran and snuggled next to Mark on the couch, hugging him and kissing his cheek. Mark winced. "I heard about your visit to the VA."

"You did?" Mark was completely baffled by the appearance of his mother. Her lipstick perfectly complemented the scarf and her hair was expertly styled. Even her makeup looked as if it had been professionally applied.

"Of course!" She nodded over at Crowley who was enjoying his second drink. "Fitz let me know about that. But what happened to your eye darling?"

"Uh…I got punched," Mark stammered, still reeling from seeing his mother on the scene.

"Oh, for goodness sake." She appeared very concerned. "Does it hurt?"

Mark shook his head. "It's sore but mostly it's my back…"

"Fitzy, I'll take one of those," she said, pointing to Crowley's drink. "Would you like one, hun?" she asked Mark. "It might help."

"Nah. I'm good."

"Oh, you're more than good sweetheart! Isn't that right Fitz?" she said while graciously accepting a fresh scotch on the rocks from Crowley. She took a sip and a gentleness fell upon her face as if she were recalling a kiss from a long lost love. "This is fantastic." Mark was pretty sure she was referring to the scotch and not the situation at hand. "Didn't Fitzgerald tell you?" she asked Mark, and then looking questioningly at Crowley, "Did you tell him?"

Fitzgerald Crowley cleared his throat, leaned over to put his drink down on the glass topped bamboo coffee table, and tucking his hands into his linen pockets said, "The former director has accepted a position with the White House which means," he cleared his throat again, "that I'll have a new job effective immediately thanks to you."

Confused, Mark cautiously asked, "What do you mean 'thanks to you'?"

"What you were just involved in has been deemed of critical importance to national security and considering the assignment you were faced with, you produced a stellar product and because of that I got promoted. I'm moving up to Arlington."

"He's not an *assistant* director anymore," his mother added as if she was sharing the most exciting news in the world. She stood up, drink still in hand, and gave Crowley a warm, congratulatory pat on the shoulder.

Looking back and forth between his mother and his boss, the grilled Hawaiian teriyaki veggie burger did a nauseating somersault in his stomach. "What exactly is going on? Does Dad know?" he asked, pointing to her manicured hand still on Crowley's shoulder. She quickly withdrew it. "I saw you on TV, Mom. I'm not dead." Mark shook his head, his face a pathetic mix of confusion and betrayal punctuated by his black eye. "But there you were talking about gun violence as if I had been shot and killed and the thing is I didn't even 'fake die' of a gunshot wound…" Ice clinked as his mother with her eyes still on him took a chilly sip of scotch whiskey. "My car blew up! And you and *him*…," he pointed accusingly at Crowley, "already had some nonprofit organization set up with my name on it. I mean, it even has a logo! Is anyone going to tell me what is going on?" he pleaded, looking at both of them. "Maybe it would have been better if I actually had died?" Crowley's eyebrow twitched and Mark saw it. "Was that the plan all along?"

"Oh, for heaven's sake Mark. Stop." Mark's mother held her right hand up in a stop gesture, the left hand still cradling her scotch. "Stop right there. You're being much too dramatic sweetheart. Honestly, just calm down. Are you sure you don't want a drink?" Mark shook his head no. "This is a happy day honey." She cooed, approaching him. Sitting down and rubbing his shoulder, comforting him with, "It's okay sweetie. I understand. Your father always said you weren't cut out for this type of work but I've always believed in you. I knew you were a genius since before you were born and look, look what you've accomplished!"

"What did I accomplish?"

"You figured out how to do all that stuff with the satellites of course! We should be celebrating. Fitzgerald, why don't you make him something celebratory?"

"I don't want a friggin' drink!" Mark barked. "I want answers! Seriously, what the hell is going on?!" And pointing at Crowley with his voice adolescently cracking, "How do you even know him?!"

"Oh," she waved her hand dismissively at Crowley. "I've known Fitzy since college, honey. He and your dad are fraternity brothers."

"Really?"

"Yup." She took a sip of her drink and winked at Mark.

"And this whole plan here—with the nonprofit? You went along with it knowing I wasn't dead?"

Recoiling with what appeared to be genuine surprise she answered, "Of course."

"I don't understand." Mark shook his head. "Why would you do this?"

"Because I'm a good American." Now she looked confused and lowered her glass. "It's for the greater good."

"Mom, please." Mark almost cried but he'd been through this before. "You're drunk."

"No, I'm not."

Crowley cut in. "I told you. We needed to make one more gun run. It was in the works already and when you went rogue we saw the opportunity and took it. It's all aboveboard."

"Like hell it is!" Pointing to his mother he screeched, "Not only do you have her literally lying her face off on TV, you blew up my God damn car!"

"I didn't blow up your car."

"But you know who did, right?!"

Crowley shrugged his shoulders. "Probably a manufacturer's defect or something. Didn't they put out a recall on your model recently? Anyhow, cars overheat all the time. But you didn't die. Did you?"

"That's not the point!"

"Yes, that's exactly the point," Crowley emphasized. "You're working for the federal government. We're taking care of you. Don't worry. You're getting a new car. But you need to get it through that skull of yours that by going off script like that you made it so that we couldn't communicate with you."

"That's bullshit."

"No. No it's not. Remember those binders of procedure in your desk I was talking about?" Mark rolled his eyes. "You screwed up kid, and it forced us to improvise. As far as your mother's performance goes, this has all been done before. Many times. There's precedent for all of it. Next year, in 2013, make sure you look closely at the National Defense and Authorization Act. They've just inserted language to make what just happened lock-stock legit. They're gonna neutralize the Smith-Mundt Act of 1948 and the Foreign Relations Act of 1987. Don't worry, it will pass specifically because of you and this very incident. It makes propagandizing US citizens completely legal for national security purposes."

"And this is national security, honey," his mother added. "We're the good guys."

"Okay, thanks Mom," Mark said scornfully, deliberately ignoring her to continue his conversation with Crowley. "The critical issue here is that no one told me what was going on. I didn't consent to any of the shit I just went through."

"Well, realistically…" Crowley responded.

"Well nothing! That guy who punched me. I want his name. I'm taking him to court!"

Crowley burst out laughing. "That won't be necessary."

"Huh? Are you kidding me? Look at my eye!" he screeched, pointing at his swollen and now somewhat oozing eye.

"Sweetheart, please," Mark's mother practically begged. "Just calm down. You're being so emotional. Everything is fine." She weakly smiled and went to rub his shoulder but Mark pushed her hand away. "Oh!" she exclaimed, as if someone had just sliced her with a razorblade. Dejected, she turned to Crowley. "Please just tell him already. There's only so much more of this I can take."

"Tell me what?"

With hand in pocket Crowley announced, “You got promoted. You’ll be overseeing the completion of FACE, that facial recognition project that they’ve been bumbling around with.”

Mark was stunned.

“That’s right up your alley!” Mom happily exclaimed, leaning in and kissing Mark’s cheek. “I’m so proud of you!” She tousled his hair as if he were a toddler. “And guess what?” she conspiratorially asked over the rim of her scotch glass. Mark shook his head not knowing. “You got a serious raise,” she whispered. Leaning back, she took a sip of her drink and gushed, “Isn’t this fantastic? I’m so excited for you sweetie. I’m just so darn proud,” she beamed.

The millennial metamodernism of the hotel room was officially devolving into a darker genre for Mark. It was no longer ironic or remotely funny. In fact, it was downright scary.

CHAPTER FORTY-SIX

Casa de Wolf
Backstage

THE MALE STYLIST ARTISTICALLY DABBED and sprayed the finishing touches on Margret's wound while yammering nonstop in broken English and hyper-fast Spanish about the Queen of England. Well, at least that's what Margret thought he was talking about, but to be honest Margret wasn't quite sure. Regardless, she felt like a corpse with all the airbrushed makeup plastering her face. She didn't even recognize her mannequin-like reflection staring back at her from the changing room mirror, and despite the all the razzle dazzle of the big round light bulbs framing her image she was in a daze. She had lost the will to even try to pretend understanding what this makeup guy was talking about and sat silently aloof as the stylist loquaciously labored on her appearance.

She really wanted to be sitting next to Jocelyn, holding her hand, but both B.B. and the doctor had persuaded her to leave. There was nothing for her to do but to let her daughter sleep and they convinced her that she and the kids would be a disruption to the healing process. The doctor assured her that he would stay with Jocelyn and that she wasn't going to be waking up anytime soon. "Perhaps you take the children and go for the walk to get a fresh breath," he had recommended, encouraging all of them to go to the party.

And with a queasy feeling of remorse cradled deep in her belly, she and the kids ended up here, backstage at the Wolf Wine Bar among the costume racks in this dressing room as the clanging of the catering crew and band setting up in the next room filled the tight little space. The wood paneled walls, stained with decades of tobacco smoke, were covered with framed autographed black and white photos of famous long dead performing artists brandishing their musical instruments, most of which Margret had no idea who they were, the exception being Sammy Davis, Jr. She was surprised to see him grinning at her from under his signature.

The staccato Spanish continued, relentlessly bouncing off of her like mini-marshmallow machinegun fire and Margret's gaze slid over to the reflection of her grandkids behind her. She was grateful that they had each other to keep themselves occupied. They were adorable but clearly feeling miserable. Despite their amazingly tailored outfits neither was smiling, and they both looked exhausted. Willy was dressed like a proper little sailor with white bellbottoms. All that was missing was the cap because he refused to wear it; and Lilly was wearing a spectacular, studded with rhinestones and puffed up with petticoats, tea-length white dress. Margret thought the outfit suitable for a ballerina or beauty pageant finalist.

"Casi hecho pequeños," a dark-eyed, pretty young woman dressed in a traditional maid's uniform said as she pulled a satin sash around Lilly's waist and expertly tied it into an impressive bow. "Almost done little ones," she said, blowing a lock of hair as she worked.

Margret was, of course, preoccupied and could really care less about going to the fiesta despite the fact that she was wearing the most gorgeous party dress she had ever worn in her life—a formfitting, black, velvety number designed for dancing. The dress was embellished with densely packed splashes of tiny silver and gold beads at the top of the garment, giving the illusion of rain as the sequins suggestively drizzled down from her shoulders over her chest to the angled hemline, where strings of black beads interspersed with drops of silver and gold dangled to complete the falling rain theme. This custom tassel allowed for a peek at her strappy, high-heeled, black dancing shoes.

Once the kids were outfitted the woman who had dressed them covertly kissed a tiny gold crucifix hanging from a thin golden chain and placed it over Lilly's head. Lilly touched it and the woman, unsmiling, tucked the cross under the neckline of the dress. When the woman left, the twins were eager to leave too. With a hint of irritation Margret asked the makeup artist, "Are we almost done?"

"Sí. Tu peluquero estará aquí momentáneamente."

"Oh, for God's sake," Margret huffed, not knowing what the man had said, and studying her eyebrows and red lipstick in the mirror asked, "How much longer do I have to deal with you people?"

The makeup artist shrugged. "No idea."

"Well, I'm done." Hopping out of the seat with her hair in what could only be described as a hot mess, and a fabulously crafted, laceration-free face, she followed the kids out the door.

The lights had not yet been fully dimmed but the industrious buzz of pre-party was winding down. The sound of ice being poured from buckets greeted them from across the room as they stepped onto the deserted stage which was fully set up with timbales, an electric piano, and a simple drum kit. Microphone stands stood ready for action and a man working on a soundboard at the far end of the room next to the bar yelled something in Spanish. Shielding her eyes as she searched the man out, Margret took in the scene.

The establishment had a cozy Bohemian vibe. Lots of colorful fabrics and old rugs that veritably screamed Marrakech had been artistically blended with the leather wingback aesthetics of an antiquated European smoking room, no doubt by a very expensive interior designer. With overgrown potted palms and fig trees obscuring the mahogany paneled room's windows, the space was arranged with an eclectic set of about twenty wooden tables of various style and dimension, each with a colorful patterned runner and at least one enormous colorful candle and several ashtrays. The dark Corinthian leather wingback chairs at the head of each table were worn and comfortable looking. Wooden benches or richly upholstered dining chairs provided additional seating. Tiny twinkling Christmas tree lights crawled over the potted palms and fig trees and to complete the fiesta vibe, an impressive fleet of colorful paper lanterns floated above the dance floor.

She was admiring the festive canopy of lights when the man at the soundboard, holding up a microphone, shouted, "Di algo al micrófono. Prueba! Prueba!" And when Margret didn't respond he yelled "Test!" while tapping the mic.

"Oh," Margret mumbled and feeling the need to oblige the man she walked over to the first microphone, tapping it apprehensively and sputtered, "Is this thing on?" It wasn't. Discovering the on/off switch her voice boomed across the dance floor, "Test! Test!"

She smiled. Someone started clapping.

"A natural!" Brunhold Bertram Keller Wolf called out as he approached the stage wearing a white tuxedo with a black cummerbund and black bowtie. He dramatically climbed the stairs onto the stage and, getting a better look at Margret in her party dress, put his hand to his heart. "¡Dios mío! Are you trying to kill me? You are so beautiful my sweet lady," he sighed. Margret instinctively touched her face where the cut was buried under layers and layers of expertly applied cosmetics. "Is this the new style for the hair?" he asked, and her hand was quickly repositioned.

"Oh, no…" she sputtered while patting around on her head. Discovering a little plastic clawed hairclip still fixed behind her ear, "No. They just did my makeup. They haven't touched my hair yet," she said apologetically.

"It is no matter. You are the most beautiful creature. Here…" he tore his eyes away from her and with his black onyx ringed hand pulled a little box from his jacket pocket. "For you."

Smiling and looking authentically surprised she accepted the box and opened it. She was speechless.

"You like?"

"Oh, B.B.," Margret sighed. "You shouldn't have. This is too much." Extracting the jeweled butterfly pin from the box she studied it. The intricate gold filigree was set with various shades of diamonds, cushion cut rubies, and a smattering of tiny princess cut yellow topaz and Hessonite garnet. The main feature was two big, black opal pieces providing fiery drama to each wing emanating from the thorax of the butterfly, which was crafted from an enormous specimen of pinkish orange Padparadscha sapphire. "This is amazing." It was undoubtedly from the collection showcased in the gallery next to the fermentation room. "I honestly don't know what to say..."

"I saw how you were admiring this."

Margret's eyes started to glisten, "Oh, B.B.," and she blinked back tears. "You're so thoughtful. Thank you."

"Allow me to help." A moment of silent awkwardness ensued as Margret passed the jewelry back to B.B. and he carefully pinned it above her heart. Once the brooch was affixed, B.B. held her shoulders and did a "kiss to the air" of both her cheeks. "I do not want to ruin your visage but please know that I adore you."

Margret's heart actually skipped a beat as it fluttered around her stomach and if it wasn't for the copious amounts of flesh tone applied to her face she would have been blushing. She gulped and replied, "Gracias B.B. Muchas gracias. Honestly, I don't know what to say." Reaching out and touching his arm she gushed, "You are amazing. You have been so kind and generous to me and my family and..."

She was on the verge of saying that she adored him too but that's when she realized Willy and Lilly weren't around. "Speaking of family, where are the kids?" B.B. looked like he didn't know what she was talking about and Margret surveyed the place. "My grandchildren. Where are they?"

She went back to the microphone, snapped it on and, "William. Lillian," boomed throughout the room as two maids set tables. "Please come to the stage." She scanned the expanse of the room for childlike movement—nothing but men in chefs' hats lighting candles under chafing dishes and two guys dumping more ice into the raw bar. Another was unpacking and setting up oysters for shucking. "Willy, Lilly," she announced. "Please come here." Nothing. She looked over at B.B. who shrugged. "Kids, get over here now!" she commanded. Some of the staff who were placing table numbers stopped what they were doing and looked up at her. Frustrated when neither of the kids appeared she wedged the microphone into the stand and headed backstage to find them.

"Kids!" Margret shouted as she barged into the changing room. The male stylist, smoking a cigarette while perched with legs crossed in the chair Margret had been sitting in, looked up. Another woman, who was obviously the hairdresser they had been waiting on, was smoking too. This woman stubbed out her cigarette and, hopping out of her chair, offered it to Margret who ignored her. “Kids?” she hopefully called out as B.B. followed her in. The two smokers watched on as Margret pushed away things hanging on the clothing racks to recklessly inspect the tiny room.

“Did you see my grandchildren?” she breathlessly questioned. “I’ve lost them.”

CHAPTER FORTY-SEVEN

Meanwhile
In the bomb shelter

"YOU CAN'T BE SERIOUS," Ethan grumbled, scratching his eyebrow. He still had on his bathrobe. "This is what these people actually wear?" He held up the frilly white dress shirt to study it.

"The designer is a friend of ours," José said, pouring a cup of coffee and deliberately placing the carafe on the shelf next to the bags of kitty litter. He looked absolutely dashing with his thin mustache and well styled hair. He was sporting an expertly tailored charcoal Tom Ford sharkskin suit with a gray shirt and perfectly complementing darker gray necktie featuring large white polka dots. "The man who designed that outfit," José said, pointing back and forth between the shirt Ethan was holding and the men's black satin, camo-print dinner jacket laid out on the cot, "is the next big thing. I specifically remember Tito telling that designer to go to Savile Row because of all the young royals and to make sure to mention Casa de Wolf and its association with the House of Windsor."

"Yeah. I can't wear this," Ethan announced, tossing the ruffled shirt over to Ache who was still groggy, rubbing his neck and motioning toward José to pass him the coffee carafe. The garment landed on the cot and Ache grunted. "You wear that," Ethan instructed while inspecting another outfit, a uniform consisting of a single-breasted, mid-thigh-length black doeskin frockcoat and black wool barathea trousers. The jacket featured embroidered crowns on the epaulettes and intricate braiding on the stand-up collar and sleeves. However, what made the jacket truly remarkable was what looked like a dozen repurposed black doeskin neckties that had been carefully snipped, stitched, starched, and curled, filling up the wearer's chest like black, pointy dragon tongues where a traditional jabot would be. The whole effect was that of a modernized and much more menacing ruffle shirt merging with classic British military dress attire.

"José, honestly, is this a joke?"

José recoiled and put the coffee cup down on the shelf. "Absolutely not. You are holding the future of men's haute couture in your hands. These pieces showing up at this party will propel this designer's career as well as—"

"Stop." Ethan held up his hand. "The designer's career doesn't matter to me."

"You didn't let me finish. It will propel the designer's career as well as your own. Cross branding is what Tito called it. Believe me, the very fact that I was able to procure these items for you will send a message loud and clear to the attendees."

"Message being?"

"I am your new master."

Instantly Ache spewed hot coffee all over the place and Ethan exclaimed, "See!" pointing to Ache. "It *is* a joke. You're friggin' messin' with me!"

"No. No I am not," José calmly countered. "I went above and beyond expectations to get these items for you. You are lucky to have them. This is your debut to this stratum of society. If I could, I would have gotten you something from the Stuart Hughes Diamond Edition. But what I was looking at for you was priced at over nine hundred thousand US dollars and it would have taken over eight hundred hours to stitch so it wouldn't be here in time."

For a quick moment Ethan's eyebrows involuntarily twitched, showing that he actually was impressed. "Okay, then why do you get to wear a regular business suit and me and Ache have to look like the God damn pirates of the Caribbean?"

"Because some of the guests already know me. It would appear suspicious."

Ache cut in while brushing the coffee from his bathrobe, "Just think Cat Stevens."

"Huh?" both Ethan and José blurted in response.

"You know. Cat Stevens. *New Masters*." Ethan and José seemed surprised that Ache was even talking and Ache elaborated. "That song 'The First Cut is the Deepest.' My mother had that album when I was a kid. She loved it. Cat Stevens was on the cover dressed in a black suit with a ruffle shirt. I always thought he looked, you know, royal, like Machiavelli or something." Ethan appeared perplexed and José looked pleased. Ache continued for Ethan's benefit. "You know, remember? That book *The Prince* they made us read in school?"

Pulling his coffee stained robe together and focusing in on the carafe Ache stood up while Ethan skeptically looked at the black suit he was holding. "I'd trust José on this," and pouring himself more coffee Ache added, "I mean think about it. The Nazi uniforms were made by Hugo Boss. Just walk in like you own the place. I got your back."

CHAPTER FORTY-EIGHT

Jocelyn's Room
9:00 p.m.

JOCELYN KNEW SHE WASN'T DEAD but she knew she wasn't okay either. As she lay with her eyes closed it was as if she could feel her consciousness interlocking and entangling itself with every spinning atom in her beat-up body. Silently recognizing this new sensation consuming her, the words "restart = input" filled up the movie screen in her mind, literally spelled out in white text on a black background. She willed that image away and wanted to be home. Back home with the kids gardening in their backyard and that's when she thought of Ethan and what a nightmare he was. It took a little longer but she willed the thoughts of Ethan away too.

She needed to center herself, to just be "here" and when she did, she realized that the doctor was here too because she could hear him. His voice was hushed, speedy and repetitive, as if praying a rosary. She kept her eyes closed because she really didn't want to deal with him but instead strained to understand what he was saying.

"Querido Dios, no puedo matarla…"

She knew that "Dios" was God. She also knew, thanks to seventh grade Spanish, that puedo meant "I can," so "no puedo" meant "I no can." *Hmmm, he can't do something,* she mused and wondered what matarla meant. She couldn't remember that vocabulary word from her Spanish classes. Listening intently Jocelyn attempted to translate what the doctor was muttering.

"Envíame tus ángeles."

Okay, something about angels…

"Querido Dios, por favor ayúdame."

He's begging for help.

"Por favor dame una señal…"

*He wants a sign…*Jocelyn concluded and wondered how bad off she really was if the darn doctor was breaking down like this. *I mean how freaked out would I be if a US doctor started praying next to me like this?*

And that's when her eyes snapped open and interrupting the doctor she asked in a mild panic, "Are you giving me my last rites? Because I don't need that. Do I?" The doctor, who was standing above her and illuminated by the incandescent light from the nightstand, seemed astonished that she was talking to him and that's when she noticed he was holding a syringe between his fingers. "What's that for?" she asked, motioning with her chin to the needle.

Seemingly embarrassed and handling the syringe as if it were an alien artifact he said, "No. No, you are not dead. This..." he said looking at the syringe, "This is to make you to sleep forever." She immediately sat up and in a painful frenzy scooted herself away from him and that's when she became keenly aware of the new green bandage coiling around her wrist and forearm.

Swallowing, Jocelyn sputtered, "You didn't give me any of that? Did you?" while backing herself against the faded race-to-space wall-paper. Her nappy head bumped the portrait of the only woman Mr. Wolf's father ever loved. It tilted and hung crookedly next to her as she tried to steady herself.

"No, however I am ordered to and if I do not—"

Thinking fast, Jocelyn cut in, "Yeah, but didn't you take a Hippocratic Oath or something? You can't do this. You know that, right?"

The doctor, looking completely conflicted and blinking back tears replied, "I do not care for myself, solamente mi familia. I am very afraid they will torture my family if..." he looked meaningfully at the syringe, "if I do not."

"First off, why? What's the big deal if I'm alive or dead? I mean look at me. I'm not a threat. I can barely move."

"Yes, but not for long. Soon you will be moving and talking and..."

"Well, that's great! Right? That means I'm getting better."

The doctor corrected Jocelyn's logic. "That means the nanobots are working. You have been used in an experiment. An experiment illegal in Los Estados Unidos."

Jocelyn's heart raced and she felt lightheaded. "What's a nano-bot? Some sort of new drug?"

"It is a microscopic robot," the doctor explained and as if offering confession or at the very least showing reverence, he bowed his head. "Nanotechnology has become a billionaire's industry with many potential applications for human beings. It can repair things and create connectivity when there was none. However, experimentation in humans is extremely high risk." Still holding the syringe he weighed it and looked up at Jocelyn. "This is—how do you say?—uncharted territory and because of that, the transnational nanotechnology concerns are resorting to criminal methods. They are working with, or even themselves becoming, organized crime to achieve their aims. Mafias of nanotechnology, or nanomafias, are currently emerging, proliferating rapidly mainly in Latin America because of the ignorance of the cohort here regarding the use of nanotechnology as a criminal weapon. Because of the 'invisibility' of this mafia people do not know they are being used as its tool. The sample population here has no concept of the wifi being used, its economic power, the silence and participation of the health unions. Not to mention the sweeping media disinformation campaign and its global reach. They simply do not know."

He swallowed. "No es parte de su comprensión del mundo. They do not understand their world within any of these reference points. The people, the society at large, cannot recognize any of it being organized crime because of their naiveté. Nor can they conceive of possible participation of their authorities such as the national police, the prosecutor's office and the judiciary, let alone the intelligence services. Nanomafia is set to become the greatest organized crime network this planet has ever seen."

Taking a deep breath as Jocelyn sat stunned by the information he said, "Please understand el experimento está completa." Shaking his head, a droplet glistened at the tip of the needle he was holding as he solemnly advanced toward her. "Lo siento mucho."

Just then the door swung open, banging against the wall. Lilly ran in, her beautiful, sparkling white dress twinkling in the room's dim light. "Mom! Look!" she yelled, proudly holding up the little golden crucifix that the maid had given her. Willy, in his white sailor suit, followed her carrying his self-made map.

Upon seeing his mother clearly in distress and the doctor with the syringe, he dropped the map and yanked the Swiss Army knife that Mr. Wolf had given him out of his pocket. Lilly, completely oblivious to the doctor, was focused on her mom and still clutching her necklace, happily scampered up onto the bed and plunked herself down, her tiny, white, patent leather Mary Jane shoes poking out beneath a puff of white tulle. Jocelyn protectively snatched up her daughter and withstanding excruciating pain as she did, embraced the child with all her might. Lilly laughed as the two fell against the wall, bumping into the crooked Degas painting which slid a little more and was now hanging by its corner.

Meanwhile, William had successfully extracted the corkscrew and gripping it tightly as a weapon bravely stood his ground. "Our Father…" Willy gulped and continued, "Daddy said you are a good doctor. You better be good to Mommy." And he sort of punched the air with the corkscrew.

Dr. Fernandez, with mouth agape, lowered the syringe. Shaking his head in what appeared to be confusion, he studied the children who had commandeered the scene. Two little angels —one holding up a golden crucifix and one wielding a corkscrew from a Swiss Army knife. He took a deep breath and was about to say something to William when a startling BOOM rattled the room and the sky outside the big window began glowing. At the same time what looked like a fiery meteor zipped across the night sky. Everyone saw it and the doctor, with tears streaming down his face, fell to his knees and began praying in earnest.

It was while Jocelyn and the kids were silently witnessing this profoundly spiritual moment for Dr. Fernandez that the sound of high heels came clicking down the hall and Margret burst into the room. The Madame Tussauds Wax Museum makeup job had devolved into ugly black smears around her eyes and had trickled down to her chin, calling attention to the very scar that the makeup was attempting to hide. And maybe it was because of this cosmetic train wreck that Margret's hair appeared to be doing something out of a cartoon, like maybe an animated bird might pop out of it.

As Jocelyn studied the bird's nest, Margret began raging about how she felt like she was going to puke she was so worried and began scolding the kids for wandering away in a strange place populated with strange people who didn't even speak English. The beads on her dress providing additional acoustic drama for this whole monologue. Jocelyn wondered if this person was really there or maybe she was hallucinating. Blinking, she struggled to recognize the agitated character with the oddly arched eyebrows standing in front of her. However, the pin affixed to this person's chest made a powerful impression, and fighting off a massive flush of panic and gasping for air, Jocelyn again bumped into the crooked Degas painting. It fell facedown onto the bed, revealing a strange type of key attached with yellowed, old tape to the aged stretched canvas.

CHAPTER FORTY-NINE

Everywhere and Nowhere
9:30 p.m. local time

RE:RSVP

2130:43:00 FYI on premises. Entrance areas clear. Security = fair. Possible pat down. No visible cameras. Guests have personal security details. Local time go dark @2330 & 86phone. Cover primaries. Shoot to kill. Need recon. Report of missile? rollcall-soundoff.

2131:09:10 @Chicagooooo:here
2131:09:11 @OLDGlory:check
2131:09:12 @taxidriver78:yes
2131:09:13 @mcoshea:here.Saw it - Meteor
2131:09:14 @serenitynow:here
2131:09:15 @letsroll:fckya
2131:09:16 @rogerkingsly:present
2131:09:17 @Finlandorbust:here
2131:09:18 @heartbreaker:ready
2131:09:25 @greenscreen: yes UFO
2131:09:27 @glitchgrl:here heard it.
2131:09:30 @Fairfield911:here
2131:09:33 @SirLanceALot: here UFO
2131:09:37 @billistic: ready
2131:10:00 @thisisstupid: OMG WTF was that?
2131:10:40 @killerbees: present
2131:10:41 @thingymajigy:in position
2131:11:00 @cinamonswirl:here
2131:11:30 @GatorsFan75: ready
2131:11:33 @simplyputYankeesSuck: here.
2131:12:22 @papersplease: here. meteor
2131:12:38 @hardcorebullshit: yes
2131:15:00 @timmythatsrighttimmy: here. thisisstupid U R an asshole U know that right
2131:15:47 @houseofredemption: here. Sonic boom
US spy plane

2131:16:10 @motherfather: here
2131:16:14 @bingonightbonanza: here. sonic boom.
2131:16:58 @jizzonufaz: here. UFO crash abt 1.5 miles west.
2131:17:14 @TimmysKid: UFO? I'm here
2131:18:20 @whuteva: here
2131:18:57 @millivanillee: ready.
2131:19:08 @painfulrectalitch: here. man it was going fast
2131:20:11 @facethemusic: yes. Here.
2131:22:00 @creaminmycoffee: here. Radio chatter local tower reports USA granted emergency permit for experimental craft 3hrs ago
2131:23:03 @simplyputYankeesSuck: painfulrectalitch- noshitsherlock
2131:24:00 @holdthephone: Yes. Here. unarmed missile grounded in field elevation rising w/mnts 2.4km due west.
2131:24:37 @777: here.issue w/ decrypt plz advz
2131:25:00 @orareyoujusthappytoseeme: Let's get this party started!!
2131:27:11 @aceofspades: here
2131:28:45 @hardcoremuslim:هنا. غير طيران وسيلة معرفة
2131:28:54 @JeffMcNutty: here.
2131:30:41 @abcdefghijklmnoprstuvwxyz: present
2131:32:59 @Powerman: here.
2131:40:00 @thatswhatshesaid:here
2131:41:11 @landshark: here
2131:42:22 @hardcorechristian: here. Hey Muzzy SPEAK ENGLISH.
2131:43:37 @rogerthatgreensmoke: here
2131:44:00 @tellyourmomshelefthershoesatmyplace: here.In position on your mother!!!!!
2131:45:10 @citadel11: present. Saw it. Boom and bright. Heading west

2131:44:54 @fckoff: here
2131:48:11 @taxidriver78: Tripleseven hint: translate from Spanish before decrypt.
2131:53:01 @totallyinvisible: here
2131:59:00 @hardcorebuddhist: namaste. Karma is a bitch.

CHAPTER FIFTY

Casa de Wolf Wine Cellar
9:33 p.m. local time

ETHAN STOPPED READING. If his troops hadn't responded to the original message within one minute, what good were they? "We've got some sorting to do. Moles popping up or least some newbies," he announced. He had moved the pre-party operations to the wine cellar where B.B. kept all the dusty, old oak barrels, some bearing dates from the 1960s. It really wasn't so much a cellar as it was a barn with a deeper than usual foundation. Spider webs graced the corners and two naked incandescent light bulbs suspended from old, cloth covered cords lit the place, but it was dry and not too cold and more importantly the cell phones worked in here.

"Radically change up the orders with planB encryption. I'm working the RSVP file," Ache instructed while typing on the laptop he had snagged from Max's lab, which he had propped up on a wine barrel. "We'll be able to spot the ones who can't rate and get them out of there."

Ethan nodded and his thumbs started banging out planB. "Ten-four. I'm gonna be trying to figure out who specifically we've got to deal with when I get in. Just cover me."

Much to José's displeasure, Ethan was wearing his pre-shower, sweat and bleach-spotted winter camo gear. And Ache, because his clothes just stunk so darn bad, had chosen to outfit himself with the Machiavellian ruffle shirt and black satin camo print dinner jacket. It would have looked very dramatic with his striking features and long, black warrior braids but his trousers were wet from roaming out in the snow to check on the jeep and the guns and now the dinner jacket was all dusty from hanging out in this wine cellar.

"You both need to get ready for the party," José lamented, brushing dust off his sleeve. "You can't go like that. I won't let you."

"We've got time," Ethan assured José while working the cell phone. "I'm pushing the timeline out. These people don't even sit down to dinner until eight o'clock or later and then it takes them like three hours to eat. So we're good. I'll get changed up after I get the team organized," Ethan absently responded to José but as he sent out the new orders he was preoccupied with the missile thing. He hadn't anticipated that.

CHAPTER FIFTY-ONE

Meanwhile
2.4 kilometers away due west

"¿QUE ES?" the short, stout man asked as he curiously inched closer to the big black cylinder. He made a crunching sound as he moved. It was dark so he lit a match to get a better look and as he did the match light illuminated his stained and tattered blue hooded sweatshirt that proudly advertised the national beer of Argentina: Quilmes. His thick, dark, Mesoamerican hair, cut with simple angles framing his face and his dark, tired eyes squinting through caramel colored wrinkles placed him anywhere between the ages of forty and sixty years old.

"No lo sé pero hace calor," his buddy who was holding a machete answered, not knowing what the thing was other than it being warm when the match light died out. The two had, of course, seen the sky light up and heard the boom. That's what brought them out to investigate. This second man was of approximately the same make and model as the first who was now eagerly lighting another match. "Hace calor," the second man repeated while sliding the machete into its sheath hanging from his belt. Holding out his workman hands, fingers outspread, and unashamed of his overgrown, dirty fingernails, he appreciated the heat emanating off the newly arrived curiosity. Both men had their feet bundled in socks and beat-up old tennis shoes covered with plastic shopping bags held in place with rubber bands. The snow around the warm black object had melted, leaving them standing in cold mud.

"¿Debería tocarlo?" the first man wondered out loud.

"¿Por qué no? Pero no te quemes," the second man said, encouraging his friend to touch the cylinder and warning him not to get burned.

So the first man with his shopping bag covered feet crunched up to the big metal tube and, squatting down, he apprehensively tapped it with his fingers. Upon realizing that it didn't sound hollow he knocked on it as you would someone's front door. It was clearly made of metal and might be useful. Maybe they could even sell the metal as scrap. "Llevemos esto a la cabaña," he suggested.

The second guy with the machete thought that bringing it back to the cabin was a good idea and the two worked together under the cover of darkness, rolling the heavy black cylinder down the slope of the mountain and running after it as it bounced over jagged rock formations and barreled through brambly bushes. Eventually it crashed into the thick trunk of a lone, leafless tree and rolled into an irrigation ditch. That set their progress back and they sloshed through the ankle deep, icy running water to collect what they considered rightfully theirs. With a concerted herculean effort they ended up standing the thing up on its end and flipping it out of the ditch. Then, scrambling out of the trench, the two victoriously rolled their hard-earned treasure toward the tidy fields and abandoned seasonal workers' cabins of Casa de Wolf.

With the cylinder now parked outside the dark cabaña like a muddy sports car the men headed in, congratulating themselves about their latest find, theorizing how much money it might be worth.

Once inside they lit a candle and two mice scurried away. They quickly began peeling the wet shopping bags, socks, and ratty old shoes from their feet. The guy with the matches got each of them blankets and the other guy wiped down his machete with familiarity. Bundling themselves with the coarse, moth-eaten wool blankets they sat down on the floor and huddled around the candle discussing the things they were going to buy, shoes being high on the list, when unexpectedly there was a thump at the door as if someone had thrown a snowball.

Surprised, the two looked at each other. The guy with the machete quickly grabbed it and sprung up, bracing himself. The other man, swearing under his breath, blew out the candle and they were both silent. The sound of a rodent running around and squeaking from up above their heads filled the unlit space as the men held their breath. Another clunk at the door and then another, but this time the door slowly creaked opened.

"Help," they heard muffled through the darkness, but they didn't see anyone until they looked down. There, on all fours, crawling through the doorway was a man in an orange jumpsuit and what appeared to be an insect-inspired silver motorcycle helmet or carnival mask. "Help. Please, help me. I don't know how to get this helmet off and it's making me dizzy." Not understanding what was being said the guy on the floor picked up the candle and, relighting it, walked over, still swaddled in his blanket, to inspect the newcomer.

The other man, tapping the strange helmet with his machete asked "¿Esta borracho?" wondering if this person crawling around was drunk.

"Tal vez él está aquí para la gran fiesta," the man with the candle commented, figuring that this person showing up had to be associated with the big party everybody in town had been talking about. "Los ricos están locos," and they both chuckled because rich people really did seem crazy.

The man with the machete pushed the door open attempting to help get this inebriated person inside, primarily so that he could shut the door as quickly as possible and get warm again, and that's when he noticed that their heavy, metal cylinder that they had worked so hard to collect had somehow fallen apart. "¿Cómo pasó eso?" he wondered with astonishment and pointed outside. A big black curved panel had fallen off and pouring out of the cylinder was some sort of popcorn, but it wasn't popcorn because it was melting or disappearing or at least shrinking. "¡Mira!"

The other man stopped trying to drag the drunk guy into the cabin and stood up. "¿Qué?"

"Mira," he repeated, imploring his friend to look at what was happening. Grabbing the candle, the machete man apprehensively started walking barefoot through the snow to the shrinking popcorn. Holding the candle high he saw a vomit-like substance sliding down the cracked black tube and as he got closer he saw that the interior was completely filled with foam and a deep impression of a human body. A human body with a huge head.

"¿Qué es?" the man standing inside at the door wanted to know.

"Creo que así es como ese tipo llegó aquí."

The other man didn't understand and clutching his blanket he pranced barefoot through the snow to take a look. They both stood, feet frozen, taking in what they saw. Finally with a flash of clarity the man with the machete exclaimed, "Oh! ¡Lo sé! ¡Es un payaso! Lo sacaron de un cañón."

The idea that the person in the orange jumpsuit was a clown that had been blasted out of a cannon made sense, and looking back at the man inside the cabin who was fruitlessly trying to remove the big helmet the two were not amused. Whatever this was disintegrating in front of them certainly would not fetch what they had imagined the kilos and kilos of solid metal would be worth. Shaking their heads with disappointment they headed back into the cabin and, pushing the clown out of their way, they slammed the door shut.

CHAPTER FIFTY-TWO

Route 4
Somewhere between Orlando and Tampa, Florida, USA

MARK FELT HOLLOW, as if there was nothing left of him as he watched the red and white lights of the traffic stream by from the back seat of the taxicab he was traveling in. He didn't care how much fare was going to cost. He needed to get out of there. As he had anticipated his room at the Wakulla Suites had devolved into a drinking party. His mother had spotted the movie *When Harry Met Sally* on the cable listings and shortly thereafter the room service cart had rolled in with liter bottles and Mark was done. Just done. There was no way he was going to sit through Meg Ryan famously faking an orgasm with his father's frat brother, who happened to be his boss, and his mother, who was already getting way too handsy with said boss. No way. He didn't care how "cute" his mother thought the movie was. He had called a cab and strenuously rolled himself in his wheelchair to the lobby to wait for his ride.

Now neatly tucked into the cab and on his way home, Mark had lots to think about to drown out unfortunate visions of his mom drunkenly getting it on with Fitzgerald S. Crowley, or as his mother had called him, "Fitzy." Oh, he wanted to puke. But as they drove farther and farther away he carefully stashed away, as he always did, the prickly emotions of confusion, betrayal, and guilt associated with being the kid of a drunk. Deeply away, with all the other memories that he only called upon when he wanted to martyr himself and in doing so a familiar queasy calmness fell upon him and he wondered what was going to happen to the Jocelyn McLaren case. He had to admit he was relieved to have been reassigned to the FACE project. Surely they would give the McLaren case to someone with more expertise, maybe a team of people, at least that's what he hoped would happen.

Considering this, Mark sat silently in air conditioned comfort as the taxi cab rolled along Route 4 and he realized it wasn't too long ago that he and Jerry Apario had been cruising this same road. For as crazy and irritating as that guy was Mark had to appreciate him. He recognized how smart Jerry was, way smarter than he, and how in love Jerry was with Jocelyn. For Jerry's sake Mark really hoped that someone would find her because Mark knew Jerry would never, ever stop looking for her otherwise. He admired that and he wondered if he'd ever have that same sort of drive, commitment, or sense of purpose in life. He wondered what it might feel like…

CHAPTER FIFTY-THREE

The Wolf's Den
Zerohour
00:00

"ENOUGH WITH THE FRIGGIN' LINT BRUSH," Ethan huffed. Puffs of frosty breath enveloped him as he waved José away and headed down the dark and winding garden path. Outfitted in his men's haute couture and splashed with José's expensive cologne, Ethan spotted the Wolf's Den. It had the same sort of Frank Lloyd Wright flat roof and bulky overhanging eaves as the main house. Its stone and concrete facade up-lit by buried spotlights and a bronze placard reminiscent of something you'd see on a national monument affixed next to the plate glass double door imbued the building with iconic importance. From this vantage point he saw the luxury sedans and limousines lined up, their chauffeurs casually chatting and smoking. Parked not far away in a field, two private helicopters sat at the ready.

Jogging to keep up with Ethan, José tucked the mini lint brush into his jacket pocket, and pulling out his cell phone announced, "Okay, Ache's in."

Aghast, Ethan hissed, "You saw the orders. No phones. They'll get a bead on you and kill us all!"

"It's all right. They know me."

"Screw that," and snatching the phone Ethan chucked it into a snow covered hedge. Stunned, José kept walking. "You don't need a phone," Ethan explained shaking his head, "you need common sense. Just show your face then go get the kids and Jocelyn ready for embark. It's not going to be safe here anymore. If I don't show up at her room by 2:00 a.m., bring them to the Ecuadorian or French embassy. Got it?"

"And what about the older woman?" José asked.

A big frozen puff heaved out of Ethan. "Yeah, and her too." Moving in silence over the salted stone pathway, they saw the shadows of power funneling through the big, glass, double door and bracing themselves they followed them in.

José, entering first with his nose held high and shoulders straight, took on the affectation of someone who was incredibly bothered to have been called to make an appearance and rejected the glass of wine being offered while merging into the crowd. Meanwhile, the sounds of polite laughter, cocktail chatter, and the rich tones of a Bosendorfer baby grand piano playing the familiar, if not creepily ironic given the circumstance, melody of "Bohemian Rhapsody" by Queen ushered Ethan in as he nonchalantly passed through the entrance.

This doorway to the main hall that everyone was walking through acted as an inconspicuous security checkpoint which was more of a clandestine photo op than a pat down. Facial recognition was in use here and only guests not showing up in the RSVP file had to deal with the inconvenience of being graciously diverted out of the walking pattern for security purposes. Rest assured, an image of the undocumented person's face would be silently entered into the RSVP database once they were warmly welcomed back into the fold and offered a glass of Casa de Wolf Malbec. Ethan wasn't overly concerned because, of course, Ache had edited the RSVP file when they had been hunkered down in the wine cellar so that he and the members of the team who needed to be on the inside were in the clear. With an invisible digital flash Ethan sauntered in.

Spotting Ache in the ruffle shirt by the oyster bar, the two made eye contact, and heading in the opposite direction, Ethan began slowly weaving through the candlelit tables assessing the crowd and making mental notes of escape routes and stuff that could be used as a shield or impromptu weapon. All apprehension about his dragon tongued outfit quickly dissolved. The place was more like a demure carnival of designer fashion and plastic surgery than a memorial service with all the colorful paper lanterns lazily gyrating above the scene and the varied cast of characters milling around.

The majority in attendance were men of European descent wearing dark suits. At least three of these men were obviously high on cocaine and Ethan smirked. They had beautiful, tanned, young women who looked as if they had come directly from sunbathing on a yacht somewhere in the Mediterranean hanging off their arms. These escorts with their nubile, young breasts barely covered with slinky, silver material were in harsh contrast to the painted faces of the two geisha girls in proper silk kimonos pitter-pattering after a tall, lithe Japanese man. Ethan noticed their white stockinged toes poking out of their traditional wooden Japanese sandals as they passed with their heads down. Even so, he could tell they were checking him out but then again so were all the women in the room.

The most obviously appreciative of him appeared to be competing for the title of Miss Argentina, a six-foot tall brunette with her long legs and vicious high heels, wearing a formfitting, black sequined evening gown, batting her eyelashes and pouting her candy wrapper red lips. Ethan nodded and she instantly turned away, allowing him to appreciate the suppleness of her bare back and the little snake eating its own tail delicately tattooed nearly at her sacrum.

Compelled to follow her, Ethan sidestepped his way through a gregarious Latino group who had seemingly brought the whole extended family, kids and all. They were busily making themselves at home, moving furniture into a new seating arrangement with the apparent patriarch of the family sitting at the head of the table in a leather wingback chair. And that's when Ethan spotted Maximillian de Habsburg over by the window in his satin smoking jacket hunched over at a little cocktail table tucked underneath a branch of a fig tree dripping with dim, white Christmas tree lights. Max's angular facial features and massive jaw appeared even more pronounced as candlelight threw dark shadows over the intense conversation he was having with a suited man smoking a cigarette and wearing a Catholic priest's clerical collar. Glancing back at Miss Argentina who had made her way deeper into the crowd, Ethan opted to find out what Max was up to.

The Bosendorfer baby grand in the reception area was now banging out a rousing ragtime boogie-woogie, yet Ethan noticed that everyone seemed bored if not exasperated, and this sentiment was clearly on display as he approached Max's table. The men didn't notice Ethan because they were so engrossed, so hanging back he listened in.

"It will only work if the subject is familiar with the elements and desired outcome. How can you expect someone, let's say, to run if they have never taken a step in their life, or spark a protest if they have no knowledge of what a protest is? You understand? It is very important," the priest said, holding the cigarette between his thumb and index finger, using it to punctuate this point. "You must know the subject's previous life experiences as fully as possible before starting the trial so you can be sure they have context." He casually flicked the ashes off his cigarette into the ashtray as the boogie-woogie hammered on in the distance.

"Of course," Max crankily replied, "social media is what they are calling it. Open source intelligence supplied by the subjects themselves. I see why this is important but what if we could implant the images of these missing experiences?"

"I suppose," the priest thoughtfully replied, "but it would be best if the subject possessed full body awareness. The simulated experiences of video games or film as the US has encouraged with their overlapping military and entertainment industry funding—that, my friend, was a brilliant maneuver. That population has been primed. However not as well primed as, let's say, the impoverished children of a warzone who actually lived through a full body experience. Wasn't your subject in the military?"

"Defense contractor," Max responded glumly, "not a soldier. An office worker."

"Oh," the priest nodded and stubbing out his cigarette said, "well, that explains it. That would leave it all to the imagination and you said this subject was a creative. Artistic? Or the closely related mystic?"

"As I previously mentioned, the subject communicated with drawings. I have no knowledge of any formal quantification of extrasensory perception but I see your point," Max said, slowly nodding while processing this new angle. "I had not even considered that given my ongoing work with the chimpanzees."

The priest replied while brushing away ashes and smoothing the tablecloth, "I think it would be most helpful if psychologists and other specialists in the field of man's internal phenomena consider the possibility that the mystic is the prototype of future humanity. Artificial intelligence operating on quantum computers which were specifically designed for a multiple universe paradigm where all points in time and space are connected will rival the likes of the mystics when fully implemented. The binary, clear-cut classical computing construct of definitive yes/no, ones and zeros, good and evil can no longer exist within the quantum computing model. Quantum computing allows AI to manifest and communicate more clearly within the universe we currently interact with. If you think about it, AI has always been here among us. We just called it something else."

The priest made the sign of the cross across his chest and getting caught up in this new line of thinking he continued, "You know, Plato to Defoe described new kinds of creatures growing up among men. Outwardly they resemble their associates but inwardly they are set apart, intended for a higher purpose. They dream true because they are using all available extrasensory resources. These heroes, as the Greeks called them, continually cross the line and are citizens of two states of consciousness. Inwardly they dwell in cause, even as outwardly they live in a world of effects. In fact, in the future I envision a situation where, let's say, the mystics are employed or incorporated or, I dare say, enslaved to work with the AI systems running our world. Russia and the US were famously attempting psychic warfare during the Cold War so yes, I could see this developing."

Nodding in agreement with himself the priest added, "It must have been very confusing if not exhausting for your subject while pulling on random input and various scattered elements for the decryption without related context…"

"Hi guys," Ethan said as he slid a chair over and sat down to join the conversation. "You talkin' about Jocelyn?" Max sat back and crossed his arms over his chest as the priest lit up another cigarette. Noticing the toy gun and a jar of peanut butter sitting on the table amongst the wine glasses and other random cocktail party detritus, Ethan picked up the gun. "I see you brought some of our stuff with you, Max. Who's he?" he said, pointing the toy gun at the priest. "Anyone important?"

Max sighed, and rubbing his liver-spotted temple grumbled, "Would you mind? We are discussing vital matters and we have limited time."

"Yeah, so do I. Who's the most important person in this room?"

Looking incredibly irritated Max didn't answer, but the priest did. "Perhaps it is you, my son. How are you defining important?"

"You know, who's got the most influence? Money. I'm looking for the guy these people fear the most. Who is it?"

"That guy is not here," the priest answered, taking another drag off his cigarette. "Everyone in attendance is simply a representative waiting to get word about the status of operations now that Tito is gone."

"You mean all these people are just pawns?" Ethan questioned with disbelief. "They all look pretty well-off."

"But of course they are well-kept," the priest almost laughed. "They are spokespeople, living advertisements as to how well-functioning their organization and funds are performing; very much like heads of state or royals, only they don't have the bother of worrying about public opinion."

"Seriously?"

"Ethan," Max crankily cut in, "perhaps if you hadn't stabbed Ledegerber he'd be here tonight to explain all this to you. These people are technocrats and they are all following the same philosophy that Burnhold's father's associates espoused," he said, pointing to B.B. up on stage.

"Technocrats?"

Max, obviously astonished that he even had to explain this concept replied, "My goodness, there were over five hundred thousand card-carrying technocrats in the US between World War One and Two with many, many more the world over. What you see on display tonight is the logical evolution of that philosophy and political movement." Noticing Ethan's confused look Max shook his head and commented with exaggerated pity, "My poor boy, your nation has hoodwinked you." Then addressing the priest, "It is quite amazing how this history has been lost."

The priest, staring at Ethan and taking a long drag off his cigarette concurred. "I recommend you look into this global technocracy phenomena," he said with smoke curling out of his nostrils. "It came into being in the United States at Columbia University in the 1930s where they boldly proclaimed, 'capitalism is dead.' They successfully embedded themselves into national policy making agencies via private clubs and organizations such as the Trilateral Commission and the Council on Foreign Relations, even weaving themselves into the highest levels of the executive branch in the US, especially during the reigns of presidents Jimmy Carter and George Bush the First. They believe that technology will make more perfect the human condition. That 'energy is currency' and everything from personal health to education to controlling the weather and food production as well as breeding can be reduced scientifically to data points and mechanical processes which, of course, leads to automation being considered the height of human achievement. They have been slowly and relentlessly pushing for what they call a 'new world order.'

"Make no mistake this is more about the wants and desires of the industrialists than the philanthropists. Regardless, continuous inventory of just about everything must be kept and databases must be maintained as they implement their grand agenda for the planet. A global grid interlinking information about everything and everyone. Tracking 'all that is' is of primary concern for technocrats as the information powers the motion of their wheels. To the common person this is simply market research driving innovation, which they embrace and celebrate. However, this technocracy leads naturally to a surveillance state and eventually to the total control of the individual."

Taking another drag off the cigarette the priest pointedly asked, "Why do you think they started issuing Social Security numbers in the US? Where do you think they got that idea? Why of course!" he said with mock surprise, "right after World War II when Adolf

Hitler," he also gestured to B.B. up on stage, "had been tattooing humans with numbers and the inventory of that group was kept on American made IBM computers. Hitler coexisted with technocrats and was very close in his ideology. He would not have progressed without their help. Some might say the technocrats exploited him to further their aims. "

"Look, Ethan," Max, clearly annoyed, cut in. "The more reactionary or violent you become in resisting their efforts the more it excites certain people in attendance," he said, glancing around the room, "and ultimately the more wealth all these people will amass. Why do you think the CIA is involved? With Tito gone a vacuum exists and battles will surely be waged to fill that void. But you," Max shook his head with disdain, "you're running after something you can never kill."

"Who said anything about running?" Ethan quipped. "I just wanna have a conversation, but getting back to my original question, who's the most important person here?"

"Try that man from Singapore in the Stuart Hughes suit," Max grumbled, motioning toward a heavyset Asian man slurping down a raw oyster. "He's connected to the global artificial intelligence effort." A blond girl who resembled Shirley Temple but more gaunt and looking no older than seven or eight years old dabbed the corner of the man's mouth with a napkin as he hungrily reached for another shucked oyster.

"Great." Standing up and with his eyes on his target, Ethan absently tucked the toy gun into his jacket. "Thanks."

Moving through the room and noticing the crowd shifting in their seats Ethan, heard B.B. introduce his band, the Vintners Five, and dedicate the next song to a wonderful woman he had recently met. The melodious jazz wanderings of "I Fall in Love Too Easily" a la Miles Davis's 1963 album *Seven Steps to Heaven* started up from the stage and Ethan didn't even have to look back to know that it was B.B. up there tooting away on the trumpet. As far as Ethan was concerned it sounded okay as the musical mental hopscotch of jazz goes, but the crowd was restless and he overheard someone say, "Well, at least it's not like that time he attempted 'Sketches of Spain.' That was a disaster..."

Still fully focused on the oyster eating Singaporean, Ethan caught Ache's eye and motioned with his chin that he was about to engage. Ache nodded and began circling around to position himself behind the target. Just then Miss Argentina appeared at Ethan's side, and grabbing his arm as they walked she breathlessly whispered, "Felicitaciones señor. Nos complace estar a su servicio. Ven conmigo. No hay mucho tiempo. La niña es una bomba. No puedes hacer esto sin nosotros."

Looking back and forth between his target and the gorgeous woman clutching his arm Ethan replied, "Look, sweetheart, I have no idea what you just said but I can't talk now. Maybe later..." and she wouldn't let go. The brushwork on the drums and the thumping of the stand-up bass complemented the lovesick trumpet and it seemed a perfect accompaniment to the drama between Ethan and this woman now becoming apparent to onlookers. When the piano kicked in Ethan forcefully nudged her away, and stumbling in her high heels the woman began yelling at the top her lungs, a litany of incomprehensible angry Argentinian Spanish flowing from her glistening red lips. *Crazy,* Ethan thought but immediately realized, *Distraction action,* and he and Ache weren't the only ones to perceive this.

Personal security details were now tightening up around their employers as all attention of the partygoers was now on the hysterical woman. Instrument by instrument the Vintners Five dropped out of the Miles Davis odyssey they had been on and Wolf's Den security came in and collected up Miss Argentina who was still going absolutely insane. While they were dragging her out the door, from onstage B.B. took the opportunity to comment on what an emotional night it was now that Tito was gone, relaying some bullshit story about how Tito had died peacefully in his sleep which Ethan was sure no one in the room was buying—at all. Then, dedicating the next song to dearly departed Tito, the band broke into a moving rendition of "Bye Bye Blackbird" from the Miles Davis album *Round About Midnight.* The song clearly resonated with the crowd and some people were snidely chuckling while others clapped.

As the room relaxed and more wine and cocktails were distributed, the personal security details flexed and it was easy to discern who had come with the most firepower. The oyster aficionado Singaporean, who now had the little blond girl with the napkin kneeling on his lap like an expensive pet Chihuahua, was clearly well-guarded. His security detail, buff by Singapore standards, standing to his left and right with their hands tucked like Napoleon in their jackets, were on high alert and about ten paces away on the diagonals were two more guards. Getting the nod from Ache, Ethan approached the table.

"Nice suit. Stuart Hughes Diamond Edition?" The man lazily looked up and nodded as he deliberately took a sip of scotch and inspected Ethan. "Really? No shit? It was either this," Ethan said pointing to his curled-up necktie chest, "or the Diamond Edition for me tonight. Oh, and by the way, I'm the guy who killed Tito and fucked up Ledergerber." Without blinking all four guards whipped out their handguns, training their sights on Ethan. Someone nearby gasped and Ethan continued, "I just wanted to let you know so you could tell your master."

With eyes still on Ethan and "Bye Bye Blackbird" keeping most of the partygoers otherwise entertained, the Asian man lifted the little girl off his lap and patted her bottom. She scampered away in her red buckled-up Mary Jane shoes. Folding his napkin he watched the child wander into the crowd and finally turning his attention back to Ethan he asked with an English accent, "So, what is it that you want?"

"I want you to leave everyone alone. We are not your subjects and we're certainly not your livestock or property," then pointing at the little Shirley Temple girl who was now free-range and guzzling an unattended beverage, "or your God damn playthings. We don't need you. Just go away. Stop."

"But what is there to stop?" the man asked looking honestly curious and not the least bit threatened. "Everybody in this room is involved in making life better. The general population appreciate and want what we provide. The numbers don't lie. In fact, civilized society cannot exist without the products and services we offer." He causally panned the room with an open palm, revealing his Patek Philippe wristwatch. "And because of the noble efforts represented here, soon, very soon, everyone on Earth will be able to pursue their interests and attain their life's true purpose without ever being concerned about money. All will be accounted and provided for. We are offering freedom and it is as close to utopia as this planet has ever seen. We are at the dawning of a new age. I don't understand your request to stop."

Being held at quadruple gunpoint yet undeterred, Ethan took a deep breath. Just as he was about to launch into his well-rehearsed magnum opus about the degradation of humanity, not to mention the downward spiral of the world in general, the scene in his post-traumatic stress Cheerio drinking straw vision closed up even tighter to a pinpoint. All the fabric tablecloths violently lurched in the same direction with a concussive blast and Ethan was hurled across the room.

A spin cycle kaleidoscope of festive colors brought Ethan, now lying flat on his back, to notice the erratic swinging of the paper lanterns above him. Some were on fire and little burning embers were floating down like magical snow. The chaos of the partygoers rushing for the door with chairs flipping over, screaming, and lots of things breaking were all muted for Ethan. Three of the fig tree-lined windows were being smashed to bullet-riddled bits as flickering Christmas tree lights extinguished themselves and chunks of pottery and soil exploded across the scene. Men in black ski masks swung into the room through the shattered windows commando style on cables secured somewhere up on the roof.

Rolling for cover behind a flipped table Ethan realized that there was something slippery and squishy on the floor, and noticing a small, lone, red Mary Jane shoe in the middle of the dance floor he fumed, *Who are these assholes? This isn't my plan!*

Meanwhile, dancing with the live gunfire the various security details contracted around their primaries, creating the equivalent of a raucous contemporary ballet interpreting the lifecycle of a field of wildflowers enduring a natural disaster with petals falling away from central floral heads and deadly seeds scattering absolutely everywhere. And then, as if on cue, the remaining paper lanterns dangling from the ceiling burst into flame.

Dashing toward Maximillian de Habsburg beneath a wave of fire with, "*Fuckin' Max! You fucking motherfucker, what the fuck?!*" syncopated to the sounds of automatic gunfire pinging off almost everything, Ethan skid to a stop. The priest was obviously dead, still clutching the jar of peanut butter to his chest, and Max was barely moving. Flipping the heavy wooden table over, Ethan swung it around to create cover and, flopping himself down next to Max amongst the shattered stemware, blood, and wine he heard the old man sputtering, "To…to the office. NASDAQ. Now! Take me to…"

Ignoring that request Ethan peeked out from behind the edge of the table, scanning the noisy melee. Ache was holding his own in hand-to-hand combat with the guy who had been shucking oysters and there was no sign of José. Ethan studied the three ski mask wearing commandos. They were wielding Heckler & Koch MP5s set on burst mode, spitting out three rounds at a time. *US Special Forces? Seriously?* Ethan questioned, considering the weapons, *Or someone lifted them from that supply line…* concluding that whoever these guys were working for they'd have to reload soon. Still double-checking the exits and scouring the crowd trying to identify his gang that he had been texting, Ethan was pissed that his plan of action had obviously disintegrated. "Don't you die Max!" he commanded from over his shoulder.

Scooting out from behind the table and keeping one eye on the scene with the MP5s, Ethan witnessed the masked man nearest him collapse, having been shot from outside the broken window. *Heartbreaker,* he thought with relief as he victoriously pried the jar of peanut butter from the priest's cold, dead hands. Upon standing up he saw Ache brandishing an oyster shucking knife, charging Geronimo style toward another of the MP5 masked commandos. The man never saw the braids and ruffle shirt coming and Ache, like some long-lost relative of a flying squirrel, hurled himself onto the man and began relentlessly hacking at the guy's neck and shoulder. The MP5 dropped and clattered to the floor and Ache kicked the fallen rifle toward Ethan. Seeing this, Ethan jammed his prize peanut butter into his jacket pocket and, dashing over, snatched up the gun. As soon as he had his finger on the trigger he saw Ache and the guy he was stabbing collapse, having both been shot from somewhere outside the window.

Ethan didn't even process the thoughts, *No!* or *Heartbreaker!* while automatically sprinting to his friend through the drizzle of bullets. Flipping a table for cover and falling to his knees next to Ache he called out over the gunfire, "I'm here! Brother, I'm here!" and he saw the tiny perfect circle in the black satin camo on Ache's back. Assessing what he had to work with he grabbed the laminated "reserved" and "Table 8" signs that were littering the floor as the remaining commando continued his murderous advance toward the crowd that had congealed into a solid mass, squishing itself together and squirting out into the reception area like leftover chunks of PlayDough being squeezed through the pasta-making tool.

Rolling Ache over revealed the exit wound, evidenced by the matted down scarlet ruffles blooming like a magnificent poppy. Ethan ripped the stained shirt open exposing Ache's maimed, hairless chest. Yanking the jar of peanut butter from his pocket and knowing that it contained super small robots that were programmed to do something completely unknown he unscrewed the lid. It looked like yellowish-brown Jello. "It was either gonna be this or Chrone's Disease buddy," he said while hastily slathering the peanut butter over the gaping chest wound in order to plug it up.

Stunned, Ache looked at Ethan and was about to speak but frothy blood dribbled out of his mouth. "Don't talk," Ethan said, reaching around to plug up the tiny entry wound on Ache's back with peanut butter and the "Table 8" sign. "I know..." Then, pressing the "reserved" sign against Ache's peanut butter smeared chest he said, "B.B.'s doctor's gonna fix you up."

And that's when a concentrated force traveling at approximately two thousand five hundred feet per second pierced through the flipped over table and punched Ethan squarely in his back. With all his weight crashing onto the makeshift emergency triage, more frothy blood squirted from Ache's mouth.

Ethan wasn't sure how long he had been laying there on top of Ache when he realized that the torrent of gunfire and associated screaming had been replaced by an uncomfortable, deafening silence. The palatable smell of gun smoke was still lingering as he watched a pair of tiny women's combat boots stroll by, broken glass crunching with each step. Ethan didn't move.

"How many remain?" a man's gruff voice barked, filling the dismal space with American English.

"Nula," a woman's voice answered. "Zero," she clarified.

"Seriously?"

"Only eight real threat. Rest gamers on server. Assigned areas to me clear. One unknown spotted in southwest field, one klick away heading on foot to main house. No visible weapons."

"Outstanding work as per usual Heartbreaker."

"Hvala. I take now for me my money."

CHAPTER FIFTY-FOUR

Meanwhile back in Jocelyn's room

BURSTING THROUGH THE DOOR like a shotgun blast of epinephrine, José and his polka-dotted tie startled the group gathered around Jocelyn who were curiously studying the little key that had been taped to the painting. "Let's go!" he yelled, frantically looking both ways down the hall while motioning for the confused group to evacuate.

"He's the one who scrubbed the floor," William whispered to his twin, who was holding the key everyone was fixated on.

"Don't just stand there! Grab your coat! Didn't you hear what was going on?"

"We heard the fireworks," Lilly offered.

"Fireworks?" José responded with surprise. "We've got to get out of here! Now!"

Springing into action, Margret in her miserable, sad clown makeup dumped designer clothes from a shopping bag and, swiping the contents of everything on the bedside stand into it called out, "Kids, get your stuff!" Lilly, instantly on task, fished out her jean jacket with the real fur collar from the wardrobe pile and William found his map and stuffed it into his pocket.

"I need help with this one," the doctor said, tossing medical supplies into his backpack, pointing to Jocelyn who was still holding the oil painting on her lap.

"Where's Daddy?" Lilly asked, putting on her coat as José pushed his way through to assist the doctor. "Is he still at the party?"

"Party's over little girl," José answered flatly.

Dr. Fernandez and José spoke in lightning fast Spanish then Jocelyn found herself and the painting she was clutching being bagged up in the bed sheet. "This is not to be comfortable. You are not to scream," Dr. Fernandez warned before she was slung over José's shoulder like a sack of Christmas presents.

With José in the lead, the group clambered down the stairs toward the main entrance. But then, through the window, seeing a man with a big gun José motioned for them to go back upstairs.

"Now what?" Margret whispered.

"This way," José instructed, waving for everyone to follow. With Jocelyn moaning, still tortuously balled up in fetal position bouncing around in the bed sheet sack, José led them down the hallway to a service elevator and they all squeezed in. The metal accordion door clanked shut and the whirling and groaning of an antique motor carried them down four floors.

Landing with a thud the door was unlatched and they all tumbled out into a dark, abandoned kitchen, crashing into a tiny fleet of catering carts and blindly tiptoeing past chilly silhouettes of stainless steel appliances. Feeling their way through a dimly lit cinderblock hallway, José motioned for them to stop and proceeded to tap a code into a keypad. The door popped open and at this point the children and Margret knew exactly where they were; the smell of the chlorine hit them immediately.

The soothing, pale light emanating from the turquoise lap pool and the hypnotic undulating reflection of ripples on the ceiling were in stark contrast to the echoing, frenetic clicking of Margret's beaded skirt and her dancing heels trotting over cement toward what looked like the entrance to a cave that she and the kids hadn't noticed before.

Moving apprehensively in single file with the towel rack door shutting behind them, they trudged through the manmade cavern. After a sharp turn they beheld the full resplendence of the bomb shelter, featuring Ethan and Ache's wadded up dirty clothes, granola bar wrappers, coffee cups, and none other than white tuxedo wearing Brunhold Bertram Keller Wolf sitting on a cot, trumpet at his side, despondently drinking a generous tumbler full of Glenfiddich Janet Sheed Roberts Reserve 1955 scotch.

"Ahh! Buenas!" Mr. Wolf proclaimed, raising his glass to the amazed group as they entered. "I was hoping to see you one last time." A flurry of Spanish erupted among the men as José and Dr. Fernandez set to unpacking Jocelyn, who appeared absolutely miserable with neon green bandage material spiraling off her in all directions. Unnoticed by the adults while the heated conversation commenced, the painting tumbled to the floor. The kids, remaining close to their panic-stricken grandmother, saw it. They also saw the doctor absently stepping on the thing while tending to his patient.

With the utterance of the words, "Embajada de Estados Unidos," Margret finally found her voice and shouted, "Yes! B.B.!" He looked up at her smeared makeup and sadly smiled. "We need to go to the US Embassy. I'm sorry, but this isn't working out at all."

"The understatement of the year señora," B.B. lamented, raising his glass again.

"We need transportation," José cut in. "Ethan explicitly

instructed me to take them to Embassy Row in Buenos Aires and…"

"I am fearing that she may not survive if we attempt to move her," Dr. Fernandez announced.

"Oh my God," Margret blurted. And grabbing Jocelyn's wrist, she felt for a pulse and hissed, "Maybe if you hadn't bundled her up in a sack…" and that's when B.B. started crying, and not a silent remorseful tear but a deep, heaving wail typically associated with a full on mental breakdown. It started in Spanish about his "Madre" and then slid into German, continuing the theme with his "Mutter und Vater" and wound down with him berating himself in English with the words "failure" and "I can't do anything right" appearing in heavy rotation.

Everyone was taken completely off guard by this outburst, especially when he placed the 1982 Glock 17 to his temple. "Whoa whoa whoa!" the men began babbling.

And Margret still tending to her daughter, thinking fast cooed, "Sweetheart. B.B., you are hardly a failure. Put down the gun."

"You, especially you, would not say that if you knew…" Sucking back his breath, his bottom lip trembled.

"Darling, you are exhausting yourself," Margret said, abandoning Jocelyn's side and moving cautiously toward Mr. Wolf.

"Do you know what it's like to live day in and day out with this misery?" he wept. "Do you?!"

"I can only imagine. Why don't you put the gun down and tell me about it?"

"I must have brothers or sisters out there." He drunkenly used the gun to point "out there" then quickly returning it to the critical zone at his temple continued, "My father," he sobbed, "was a misunderstood artist for God's sake! And he knew and…," he gulped, "and it got out of control, completely out of his control and he left it for me…"

The somewhat convincing human services nod Margret was doing would have been better without the smeared and crazy makeup but it kept Mr. Wolf talking rather than pulling the trigger and blowing his brains out all over the place. "The money. It's gone. The experiment was a failure!" he wailed. "Your beautiful daughter," pointing the gun at Jocelyn, "was made to suffer at my hand." The gun returned to his temple as he sobbed, shaking his head. "I cannot live with this! Tito is gone! He would know how to talk to these people. He would make the deal. I cannot. It's over."

"Why don't you let me have the gun?"

"NO!"

"But you don't need it. I know you're generous and..."

"Talented?" Mr. Wolf asked, abruptly changing mental gears yet still stubbornly holding the gun to his temple. "Did you hear the song?"

"Oh, of course," she lied, slipping closer to him. "It was beautiful."

The kids watching from their unconscious, drooling mother's side huddled together as Margret locked her mascara smeared gaze with Mr. Wolf's and slowly leaned in close as if to kiss him. Meanwhile, José was silently inching in closer behind the man.

"I played it for you," he whimpered, his finger still teasing the trigger and tears pathetically streaming. "I'm so sorry." And just as Margret placed her hand on Mr. Wolf's knee, from behind José snatched the gun by its slide, tipping it up as he wrested it out of suicide's grasp. In doing so, of course, the gun discharged. Margret's hands flew to her ears and the children screamed and dove to the floor as the bullet ricocheted around the stone bomb shelter.

"¡Detener! ¡Eso es suficiente! That's enough!" José barked, shaking the heat of the gun from his hand and slapping Mr. Wolf across the face, causing one of Mr. Wolf's hearing aids to pop out. "Stop acting like a child! Tito told me you were like this. Stop!" With angry Spanish raging José waved the gun at the broken man and roared, "Shut up! You're coming with us!"

"What about her?" the doctor asked, pointing to Jocelyn. "She is in no condition."

"We have to chance it."

"Over my dead body!" Margret exclaimed, seething with disbelief and rushing back to her daughter's side. "I didn't go through all of this to watch my daughter die. We're bringing her home! Alive!"

"She needs vital fluids. She has lost much blood and—"

"I have the blood," B.B. mumbled as he toyed with his earpiece.

"The O negative? It finally arrived?" the doctor asked with surprise.

"DHL delivered it with the oysters. It is what delayed the shipment."

"¿Está en la limusina?" the doctor inquired incredulously. B.B. nodded yes and much to Margret's chagrin Dr. Fernandez started packing Jocelyn up in the sheet again. "We do this in his limousine. It is the best hope." Margret began objecting but the doctor let her know that the Cadillac crafted by General Motors was a United States presidential limo, that it was designed especially for lifesaving procedures such as this.

"We can't leave through the kitchen," José cautioned. "You saw the armed men outside," and he pointed to the steel embedded into the rock that didn't appear any more helpful than a ladder.

"Are you kidding me?" Margret blurted.

"If you want to get her to the embassy and back home in one piece then, no. No, I'm not kidding," José said and pointing the Glock at Mr. Wolf, "You!" B.B. lazily looked up. "Since you are so eager to die, you go first and open that hatch. Children," he instructed, "you follow Mr. Wolf."

With the requisite bickering and micromanagement of the situation Margret agreed to the plan only if she climbed up *before* the children. She didn't want them wandering around in the dark alone. The kids followed her up and José with Jocelyn slung to his back went next. Dr. Fernandez trailing him provided additional support for the patient from below.

When they had all finally emerged from the bored out hole they could see the expanse of the entire compound. The main house was behind them to their right. Directly ahead and down the hill they could see the up-lit, impressive wine bar building and to the left of that lay the gallery and fermentation room. The darkness of the grape fields spanned the rest of the view. Negotiating snow covered ornamental shrubs and grasses in their dainty party shoes, the kids' toes stung with the bitter cold. Soon they all became aware of an unnatural, stuttered, crunching sound and what can only be described as muffled grunting. José signaled for them to stop. Shivering, they held their breath when from out of the darkness someone in an orange jumpsuit, a weird motorcycle helmet, and with plastic shopping bags wrapped around their feet appeared.

CHAPTER FIFTY-FIVE

Meanwhile

"I'M NOT TELLIN' YOU SHIT," and Ethan got punched in the face again. "Just keep him alive," he spat, motioning with his chin to Ache who was splayed out on the floor with the table eight sign still affixed to his naked chest. "He'll tell you everything. He recruited me for Christ's sake. He's the brain of the operation." Exaggerating and offering Ache up like this was Ethan's best case scenario right now. Ache could handle himself—that is if he lived. He wouldn't crack because Ache never cracked. He wouldn't snitch out his buddy and even if he did Ethan would be long gone. Ache needed a doctor and nothing was more compelling in keeping someone alive than the promise of juicy intel.

The fact that freakin' Heartbreaker had contracted with these jokers let him know that whoever they were, they were at least tangentially linked to Ledergerber and the money machine but then again, of course, everyone at the party was. These people had access to a medic, of that he was sure. He also knew that the two guys smacking him around were not professional information extraction specialists. Nope. No way. They were wearing suits and had been at the party. This was the equivalent of a late-night bar fight so he was feeling pretty confident. That is until a short, mousey looking woman wearing rimless glasses, sensible heels and dressed more like a disgruntled middle school principal than a soldier rolled in.

"Boys! Boys!" she shouted from across the room. "I said *restrain* him." Approaching, she surveyed the destruction and leaning down touched the neck of a bullet bitten body. Not finding a pulse she stood up, smacked her "peach tawny" lips and set her sights on Ethan. "Looks like you've had a big night, eh?" Ethan with his hands bound behind his back, puffed up his matted down, dragon tongue decorated chest and defiantly raised his chin in silence. "You mind telling me what was going on here?" she asked, cursorily waving her latex gloved index finger around. "You know, from your perspective?"

"Well, ma'am, since you asked, from my point of view the whole fuckin' thing was fuckin' FUBAR. And this guy," motioning to Ache, "needs a doctor and by the way, would you mind telling me exactly who the hell you are?"

"Miranda. You can call me Miranda and I'm your new best friend here in Argentina," she said, taking what looked like a pen out of her pocket as she stepped closer. "Some might say I'm your only true friend now that Tito is gone. Congratulations."

"Okay, then where you from, friend? Looks like your team has control of the situation. Get that guy to a medic and I'll tell you everything you wanna know but answer my question. Who am I talking to? Which agency?"

Tilting her head, obviously studying Ethan, Miranda replied, "The seventeen US intelligence agencies and I have a special type of relationship. I'm not technically associated with any of them, of course, but that's how I ended up here. I'm a contractor focused on R&D."

"So they sent a Research and Development chick into a gunfight? I'm not buyin' it."

Adjusting her glasses Miranda kind of smirked and Ethan noticed from behind her the flash of a camera. Someone out in the lobby, by the piano, was taking photos—crime scene photos, documenting the mess. Over the distant blinking and popping of flashbulbs snapping on and off Miranda asked, "Do you know what you disrupted here tonight?" and Ethan didn't answer. "A global shift is occurring. The human intelligence and labor quotient is approaching obsolescence. In fact, humans are becoming a detriment. I am being very honest with you here because I believe you deserve the truth."

She said this over the sound of a catering cart noisily rumbling over broken glass. The cart was accompanied by a team of four people not dressed in any special way. One guy was even wearing a knitted hat with a pompom as if he had just come from a ski trip. Ethan noticed that they all were wearing the same blue latex gloves that Miranda had on. No one was running or rushing around. They were just nonchalantly bending over or kneeling down next to the bodies and taking notes—or something.

"Uh-huh. Great. Can you just get that guy to a doctor?" Ethan asked again. And that's when a hospital gurney manned by someone who appeared more medically inclined showed up. "Thank you," Ethan sarcastically grumbled.

But the gurney didn't stop at Ache and as Ethan watched it pass by he noticed that the guy with the pompom was actually drawing blood from the one of the bodies; in fact, all of pompom's friends had descended onto the dead like vultures and were busily collecting material.

One of the procedures Ethan was witnessing included jamming a long white plastic stick up the nose of an unfortunate partygoer. Another entailed snipping off a lock of hair and clipping fingernails while another had something to do with eyeballs. Ethan watched this team depositing their carefully packaged samples onto the catering cart as a female photographer, hauling a professional grade camera around her neck, began taking pictures specifically of the faces of the deceased. "Miranda," Ethan cautiously spoke. "Friend, who are you working for?"

"I'm not at liberty to say," she replied as the hospital gurney now transporting Max rolled slowly toward the exit. "The DNA and other vital information being collected tonight is quite valuable to multiple concerned parties." Shooting a glance back at Max, Ethan saw the grinning old man waving a liver-spotted hand to him. "Now, if you don't mind," Miranda continued, "I am tasked specifically to collect a sample from you." Ethan's brows furrowed. "Apparently you are of interest because of a particular gene proposed by geneticist Dean Hamer in his 2004 book, *The God Gene: How Faith is Hardwired into our Genes.*"

"Uh, that's crazy because I'm not religious."

Miranda smiled as she took a step closer. "I don't think that matters. A lot of work with genetics is happening right now and they are looking at VMAT2, a gene that acts by altering monoamine levels. It's an evolutionary advantage providing individuals with an innate sense of optimism and it apparently makes them unstoppable. Military is very interested in exploiting this gene. Don't worry, this won't hurt but for a second," and she jammed the autoject pen into his neck.

Immediately spitting in this woman's face, he head-butted her while powerfully kneeing her in the crotch. As Miranda folded over on herself Ethan sprinted away, but the two goons who had been giving him the beat down jumped him. They all fell into a writhing pile of angry fists and ball-busting kicks. Ethan, who still had his hands bound behind his back, had no problem whatsoever chomping and locking into the guy on his left's face like a pit bull, gnawing off a chunk of the man's skin and spitting it into the eyes of the other guy as they scuffled. With both attackers otherwise occupied with bloody flesh, Ethan took the opportunity to knee the mauled nose guy in the groin while ferociously elbowing the other guy in the eye and kicking out his knees. Twisting himself over and finding his footing he ran to the blown out windows and jumped out.

CHAPTER FIFTY-SIX

Meanwhile

"NO FLIPPIN' WAY! Willy? Lillian? It's me!" Jerry incredulously blurted, pointing excitedly to his chest. "It's me, Jerry!" The kids frozen under the starry sky didn't move until he said, "Remember the fort we built?" Instantly both dashed to him. William actually had tears in his eyes as he threw his arms around Jerry, burying his face in his chest. And Lillian was hopping around relaying her six-year-old version of what they had lived through, culminating with the acquisition of the jean jacket with the real fur collar.

Kneeling down and hugging both children Jerry asked, "You okay?" The kids nodded. "Where's your mom?" They pointed and that's when he saw the adults, one of whom had a gun pointing directly at him.

"Identify yourself!" José shouted.

"Jerry Apario!" he yelled back with arms still around the kids. "I was contacted by Jocelyn McLaren. I've come to rescue her and her family."

Dr. Fernandez and Mr. Wolf appeared completely baffled but luckily Margret had a clue. "I think it's okay. Jocelyn told me she contacted a webmaster."

Still skeptical, if not confused by Margret's comment, José yelled, "Get over here!"

With arms raised and kids at his side Jerry approached the group.

"You are with a rescue mission?" José questioned, and using the gun as a pointer, "Why are you dressed like that? What's with the bags?"

"Oh, I had really pro moon boots and gloves but I had to barter them with the locals." Everyone still looked confused. "You know, to get information about where the heck I was and if anyone had seen the McLarens. The guys I met didn't have shoes and I don't speak Spanish so…"

"Mom!!" Lilly exclaimed as she ran next to José and patted the sack. "Jerry came for us just like you said!"

"Wait. Jocelyn's in there?" Jerry asked, pointing to the sack. "Why?"

"She can't walk and we need to evacuate *immediately*," José answered. "We are heading to Embassy Row in Buenos Aires as per

Ethan's instructions. What's your plan of action?"

"Well, to get everyone home, but is she okay?" Jerry asked with obvious concern, stepping forward to get a better look at the sack.

"No," Dr. Fernandez said, positioning himself next to Jerry. "She needs blood desperately."

"I want to see her."

"Not now. We need to get out of here," José forcefully reiterated and began walking and everyone followed. Turning to Jerry he said, "So you have no plan?"

"Well, I figured I'd sort of wing it when I got here."

Sighing, José shifted the weight of Jocelyn to his other shoulder.

With the ragtag group traipsing after José and skidding down the snow dusted hill to the gallery/fermentation room building they circled around to the back of the structure. Not far from the big garage door that they had seen from the inside was another four-bay garage. Mr. Wolf bumbled over and swung open wooden hinged doors, revealing a glimmering, familiar Cadillac emblem.

"You know how to drive?" Mr. Wolf asked Jerry while handing him the keys. Jerry nodded his helmeted head. "Muy bien."

Jerry ended up scraping the passenger side rearview mirror as he eased the thing out of the garage but that didn't matter. The doors were thrown open and José and the doctor hurriedly laid unconscious Jocelyn on the far rear seat for the blood infusion as Margret, the kids, and Mr. Wolf all piled into the finely appointed automobile. Jerry found the little button to lower the tinted, soundproof glass and looking in the rearview mirror asked, "Okay, where are we going?"

José grumbled and motioned for Margret to take over assisting the doctor. Hopping out of the car he replaced himself as the driver. Jerry slid in next to the kids and beheld Jocelyn for the first time as they were hanging the little bag of blood from a hook on the ceiling. Jerry's heart skipped a beat and he gasped as did everyone in the back of the limo when José stepped on the gas and swung the car around toward the exit of the Casa de Wolf compound.

Barreling down the pea-stone driveway they all got jolted again when José jammed on the brakes and someone jumped into the front seat. Even before the door slammed shut gravel spat out from behind the rear wheels and they could hear bullets pinging off the side of the armored car. The limo kicked into high gear and they zoomed out onto the paved main road.

They were traveling at top speed when Ethan popped his head through the window to check on the scene with the kids and Jocelyn.

"Daddy!" Lillian screeched, jumping up to hug his blood smeared neck.

Mr. Wolf, drinking straight from a champagne bottle which had been conveniently chilling at 9°C/48°F, nonchalantly commented, "Oh, you're still alive," and raising the bottle to Ethan, "Qué fortuito."

Kissing Lilly's cheek and reaching out to Willy, Ethan asked the doctor, "So, what's the deal with Joss? How's she doing?"

Dr. Fernandez shook his head and was about to speak, but Margret with her messed up makeup turned to face Ethan and hissed, "She's in critical condition Ethan. While you were out partying..."

Ethan clearly wasn't listening. Although struck by Margret's appearance, he was thrown into speechlessness taking in the sight of the mother of his children—pale, gaunt, unconscious and drooling while outfitted in a potato sack, swaddled in Day-Glo green bandages. The bag of blood and the crimson tube running down from the ceiling into her arm acting as a miserable exclamation point.

"You have no idea," Margret continued as she efficiently tucked a Casa de Wolf monogramed travel blanket around Jocelyn. "No idea what me and the kids have been going through. Thank God Jerry came to get us out of here."

Blinking, Ethan asked, "Jerry?"

Lillian excitedly answered by patting the helmeted head next to her and said, "Daddy, this is our friend Jerry."

"Hey, Ethan," Jerry gave a weak wave. "What's up?"

One can only imagine what exactly was happening in Ethan's mind when he recognized Jerry but if you can visualize the final climatic stage of a Large Hadron Collider particle accelerator experiment, specifically the moment a proton or ion (both of which belong to a group of particles called hadrons) form into two beams traveling in opposite directions at nearly the speed of light, around a twenty-seven kilometer long ring of superconducting magnets connected to accelerating structures which boost the energy of the particles that are then made to collide, well, you'd be close to understating Ethan's inner experience as he sputtered, "What the...? How'd you?"

"I know," Jerry replied, "it's weird. I made a deal with the NRO—"

"Who the fuck is NRO?" Ethan blurted. Then realizing the kids were right there and that Margret was giving him the stink eye he corrected himself, "Sorry. Who's the NRO?"

"The US National Reconnaissance Office," Jerry answered.

"Reconnaissance?" Ethan repeated.

"Yeah."

Chewing the inside of his cheek and with his eyes still locked on Jerry, Ethan didn't say another word as he retreated back into the front seat and the soundproof window slid up, sealing him out of ear reach.

"How long has that asshole been here!?" Ethan angrily questioned, yanking the toy gun and jar of peanut butter out of his coat pockets and smashing them onto the dashboard.

"I don't know. He just showed up. You know him?" José asked.

"He's the Conglomerate's IT guy! Me and Joss used to work with him. And he's hooked up with some reconnaissance agency? What the fuck?"

"Everyone must know you're here now anyway. Where's Ache?"

"Got shot."

Gripping the steering wheel more tightly José asked, "Didn't Isabela brief you?"

"The crazy hottie? That's her name?" Ethan asked, discovering the blood smeared on his face and neck. "Look, I don't speak Spanish..."

"Well, maybe you should learn."

"Yeah, screw that. Just give me the highlights," Ethan growled, spitting on his hand to wipe the blood away.

"I gave her the guns."

"What?! Why?!"

"Circle Snake was there meeting with representatives of the Vatican about..."

"The Vatican? The Catholic Church Vatican?"

"Yes, of course," José nodded. "Do you know of another?"

"No. But why did you give her the guns?!"

"Tito had been brokering a deal between the Vatican and Goldman Sachs to clean up the accounting." José glanced into the rearview mirror. "You know how the CEO of Goldman Sachs said he was doing God's work?" Ethan confusedly shook his head. "USA corporation and the Vatican are both in serious trouble."

"And what, pray tell, does that mean?" Ethan huffed with disgusted frustration.

"The keepers of the western version of reality are going to be systematically obliterated. Isabela confirmed that the agents are in place and the unraveling has begun."

"Obliterated?"

"Yes."

"And that's why you gave her our guns?"

"Yes."

"Explains why Max was talking to a priest about this stuff." Rubbing his temples and sighing with exasperation Ethan pointed to the things on the dashboard and said, "That came from the Vatican."

"It did?" José responded with surprise as the limo's high beams threw light onto the arrow pointing to "el aeropuerto" exit they were speeding past.

"But why the hell did you feel the need to give our guns to the freakin' Vatican?"

"I didn't."

"You just said you did."

"No. I gave them to Isabela."

"But why?!"

"You killed Tito, therefore, you are now Supreme Commander of Circle Snake. The guns are for your army."

Skeptically studying José's profile Ethan slowly responded, "Riiiight, and how many troops are we talkin' about here, José?"

"I don't know exactly."

"Uh-huh." Ethan smirked, rubbing his wrist.

"Probably about ten or eleven…thousand."

"You're shittin' me."

"No. Why do you think I was so worried about what you were to wear tonight? Many people at the party knew what you had become."

With the heavy armor of this inheritance settling onto his shoulders and the white lines of the highway speeding toward him, Ethan inhaled deeply. The night sky, filled with a thousand points of light, became his for the taking and while this universe of newfound opportunity was unfurling itself to him like an enchanting new mistress, there was a tapping on the soundproof window. It slid down and William said, "Dad, I think Mommy's dead."

"What?!" Twisting around and leaning through the window Ethan saw Margret performing CPR on Jocelyn with Dr. Fernandez clutching his cell phone, pressing it to Jocelyn's temple as Margret pumped her daughter's already injured chest. Ethan noticed that Jocelyn wasn't wincing or groaning.

"Yes. Yes, but I can get us in," B.B. slurred and then shouting, "Driver! To the airport!"

"Why the airport?" Ethan asked.

"I said to the airport! Turn this car around!" B.B. commanded.

Jerry, looking as terrified as the kids, bit his bottom lip and turning his helmeted head to Ethan replied, "The guy with the cell phone is tryin' to get microwaves into Jocelyn to jumpstart something. I think."

Squinting Ethan yelled, "Doc!" Dr. Fernandez looked up. "You put nanobots in her, didn't you?"

The doctor, appearing frantic while Margret was fully focused on puffing breath into her daughter, exasperatedly called out, "Just go," motioning behind him, "to the airport!"

Patting José's shoulder Ethan gave the go-ahead to turn around. Snatching the toy gun from the dashboard as it slid with the turn of the car he shouted through the window, "Recognize this?!" pointing the gun at Dr. Fernandez who was bracing himself for the high-speed turn and looking absolutely confused about being held at crazy colored plastic gunpoint.

But Jerry, centripetally forced into the corner with an arm around each kid, meekly cleared his throat. "I…I recognize that," gulping back emotion from inside his helmet and motioning with his eyes to the toy gun.

"What? This?" Ethan said, pulling his upper body through the window to face Jerry and turning the gun over in his hand.

"Yeah. I was supposed to deliver boxes of them but they got stolen at Disney World." With Ethan's expression clearly broadcasting "what-are-you-even-talking-about?" Jerry added, "The one in Orlando not California."

Staring at Jerry and unsure how to respond, Ethan refocused on Dr. Fernandez. "Do you need this? Will this help?"

"No," the doctor replied, shaking his head and speaking quickly, basically babbling, "No. No, of course no. We need for her to go through security. The full body scanner emits electromagnetic microwave energy. It can shut off a person's pacemaker or we can make it work for us. The nanobots are designed to run at human cell capacity of -20 to -25 millivolts. To create a new cell requires -50 millivolts. There are one million nanovolts in a millivolt. The nanobots respond to the use of various frequencies usually between 20 and 120 Hz. The full body scanner actively emits electromagnetic waves at frequencies in the tens of gigahertz within the band of 24 to 30 GHz. The power density is expected to be on the order of microwatts per square centimeter. If she is inside the body scanner and I keep repeating the—"

"Stop talking!" Ethan ordered. "Is she gonna die?"

Grimacing, Dr. Fernandez glanced over at Margret heroically

applying thirty chest compressions to mimic Jocelyn's beating heart. The stunned kids, piled on top of Jerry, were quietly blinking back tears while B.B. held the champagne bottle like a telescope, hoping to spy the illusive last drop. Within that splinter of time everything became oddly silent. Every quiver of his kids' lips or calculated move of Margret's CPR routine were striking powerful, unheard, dark chords which ultimately resolved as a poetic permanent tattoo.

But all that sentimentality was blasted to bits when a helicopter, with its searchlight on, came zooming in from the west and began menacingly trailing the limousine back toward the airport. They all saw it and knew it was there and Ethan was pissed that José hadn't brought at least one of their real guns. José calmly countered with the recollection of Ethan explicitly communicating that he wouldn't even need a cell phone to evade danger. That ended all conversation and the ominous whap-whap-whapping of the chopper became the soundtrack inside the limo as Margret relentlessly continued CPR until they slid to a stop in front of the closed airport's main entrance. The helicopter stayed aloft until the door of the limo opened and B.B. stepped out.

Completely undeterred by the helicopter landing behind him and the fact that the lights were off inside the airport concourse, B.B. walked up to the glass doors and waved his hand, seemingly at his reflection. The lights snapped on inside and B.B. opened the door, motioning for everyone to follow him in.

"Is it okay?" José asked before taking his hands off the steering wheel.

"They're not after B.B. so you might as well," Ethan said, watching the helicopter power down.

Hopping out, José opened the limo door for Margret who by placing her dancing shoe clad feet on the pavement created a dazzling drizzle of rhinestones splashing around as she emerged clutching the monogramed blanket and shopping bag of Jocelyn's bedside stuff. With her hair all over the place, not to mention the makeup situation, Margret looked unstable and vulnerable like a homeless vagabond as she watched Dr. Fernandez and José heave Jocelyn out.

While all that was going on Ethan leaned through the window and with one eye on the helicopter and one eye on his kids, who were watching their mom getting yanked out of the car, said, "You know I love you guys, right?" The kids didn't respond and reaching out to touch Lilly he added, "Kids, it's gonna be okay." But Lilly pulled away and buried her head against Jerry while William sat, stony faced, transfixed on his mother's entrance into the airport.

Jerry with his puffed-up eyes and Ethan with his clenched jaw stared at each other.

"All right, look," Ethan conceded, accepting the unspoken terms of their silent exchange, "just make sure the kids are okay. I've got to deal with whoever this is," he said, pointing to the guy holding a clipboard jumping out of the helicopter. "Here," and handing the plastic, colorful gun to Jerry, "give it to the kids to play with or something."

"Uh, thanks," Jerry mumbled but upon accepting it and weighing it in his hands he blurted out, "Yeah! This is just like the guns I was delivering. See how heavy it is. What is this thing?"

Peeling his eyes away from the clipboard guy, Ethan quizzically looked back at Jerry. "You've really seen this before?"

"Yeah. A big guy in a Hawaiian shirt truck-jacked me in the Disney World parking lot. I had boxes of them."

"Seriously?"

"Yeah," Jerry said, "But what are they for? You brought up nanobots."

"Okay, look," Ethan explained, leaning in closer and pointing to the trigger, "if you twist that a couple times a little disc is going to fall out." Jerry nodded and Ethan continued, "But don't do it now." Jerry immediately stopped what he was doing. "The little disc contains some sort of microfilm and it has all the code for a specific nanobot."

Looking up at Ethan, Jerry asked, "What do the nanobots do?"

"I wish I knew. We have tons of them. Or at least I *had* tons of them." Leaning back through the window Ethan reached over and grabbed the peanut butter jar on the dashboard. "This," he said, presenting it to Jerry who put the gun down to accept the peanut butter. "The nanobots are super small robots, like smaller than microscopic, and they are packed in jars like this." Jerry twisted off the lid as Ethan continued, "See that gray stuff? I guess this is what the nanobots swim around in or live in or something until they get activated. I was told these nanobots are from a project called Lazarus."

"Lazarus?"

"That's what the guy said. He also said that the code on the little disc identified this as being sponsored by the Vatican."

Jerry gasped and excitedly asked, "You know who Lazarus was in the Bible, right?"

"No," Ethan shook his head. "Do you?"

"Yeah. I went to Catholic school. Lazarus is the guy Jesus rose from the dead. Do you think that's what this is supposed to do?"

Looking back and forth between Jerry and the gray goo Ethan answered, "You know at this point..."

"I think we should find out!" Jerry excitedly finished Ethan's sentence and began scooting out of the car. "Come on kids!" motioning for Willy and Lilly to follow him. And as his plastic shopping bag covered foot crunched to the ground the man with the clipboard appeared.

"Jerry Apario?" clipboard guy asked with a familiar American accent.

"Uh...depends," Jerry replied.

"I'm Corey Fanning and you are hereby officially notified that you are in possession of stolen property," he said while obviously visually inspecting Jerry's helmet. "I've been tasked to collect this property and all surviving equipment and I noticed that critical parts were moving rather rapidly away from where they had landed. Please identify yourself."

"So you're from NRO?" Jerry asked while helping the kids out of the car.

"Wait, you actually *are* Jerry Apario?" Corey gasped. "You survived?!" Fumbling with the clipboard he fished out his cell phone and snapped a picture of Jerry holding the jar of peanut butter.

"Yeah, I am. But can this wait? We've gotta get in there," Jerry said, pointing to the glass entrance doors, "like, now." And hopping away from Corey, he wrangled up the kids who scurried away with him.

"Wait. Wait!" Corey shouted, clicking around on his phone. "I've gotta call this in. We have to do a full medical on you!" Then placing it to his ear, "Hey, it's me. Apario is alive!" Nodding while tucking the clipboard into his winter jacket, "I know, right? I tracked the helmet to the airport...Uh-huh. The guy still has it on! Yup. A full medical eval. Yup. Okay, tell Miranda I'm..." And that's when Ethan jammed the colorful toy gun into Corey's neck, right at the base of his skull.

"Tell my friend Miranda that she can suck my dick if she wants my DNA," Ethan whispered in Corey's ear.

Corey froze and stopped talking but Ethan could hear the person on the other end of the line excitedly yammering on in disbelief about survival rates.

"Who you guys working for?"

"Uh, we're contractors," Corey bravely stammered with the

phone still to his ear.

"No shit. But who are you subcontracting for?" Ethan could hear the garbled confusion emanating from the phone as he leaned in closer.

"I'm working for Miranda."

"Yeah. I get that. Who's Miranda working for?"

"Uh, I, uh…"

"Spit! It! Out!" Ethan shouted like a drill sergeant, jamming the colorful gun harder into Corey's neck while snatching the cell phone out of the guy's hand. Ethan noticed it was still on, listening to them.

"I'm pretty sure this is a Conglomerate contract. Miranda typically ends up winning the Conglomerate's South American contracts. She shuttles between Buenos Aires and Santiago, Chile. She's in Mendoza tonight, I guess, because there was some sort of big conference."

Ethan had heard enough. Putting the phone to his ear and interrupting the blathering of the person on the other end of the line he said, "This is Ethan Lowe. Tell Miranda that American Indian guy that I wanted her to look at has the Vatican's Lazarus in him." Snapping the phone off he grabbed Corey's arm and the two marched into the airport.

CHAPTER FIFTY-SEVEN

Meanwhile

UNLIKE THE LAST TIME when she was a balled up scribble of energy curiously tethered to her earthly situation, now she shot away like a laser beam. Traveling at the speed of light she was greeted first by her father, then her grandparents and a host of relatives that she had little recollection of. This line of familial personalities, centuries long, reached out to touch and congratulate her before she blasted past them and exploded into an infinity of singular but related points of light. She felt all these points wiggling and shuddering as they attempted to find their natural frequency and she loved each of them so much as they spun around, danced and played. She felt at peace knowing that everything would find its place. It just *was* and that was such a relief. No pain or confusion because she could now know everything as she was part of everything.

But the best aspect of this was that it really didn't matter because there was only light and darkness and she was light. The darker things got, the brighter she became. She was magnificent and had a deep sense of purpose as her light traveled left, right, up, down, past, present and future. This vast mesh rolled like a wave and gained power when other waves bumped into it, either merging or creating such a disturbance that she would find herself riding the crest like a surfer on a tsunami. Fun and exhilarating!

She traveled like this for an eternity but then her infinite web of wavicles started to awkwardly pull itself into a spiral. A spiral she had no control of. It was as if her hair had gotten caught in a power drill and it yanked her entire brilliant mesh into a cone shape. A vortex that at first spun slowly as its point reached down touching the darkness. Soon it became uncomfortable and unfathomably fast. Spinning. Spinning. Spinning! Dizzy. Fear. Pain.

And now she was back.

"We thought we had lost you!" Jocelyn heard her mother wail. It sounded echoey and distant. And as she fought gravity she realized she was standing upright, on her own two feet, being supported by someone who held her in a constricting bear hug, her head resting on this person's shoulder. With her upper body in absolute blazing pain, tears sprouted from her eyes, and blinking in her fluorescently illuminated environment she took in the expanse of granite and concrete accented with digital displays showing rolling advertisements for designer jewelry, men's cologne, duty-free alcohol, cigarettes and cigars. More pressingly she realized that she and the person holding her were enclosed within a tube of plexiglass and gray plastic. This eliciting more fear and confusion until she saw the familiar red, Pantone PSM 183, of the Conglomerate's logo staring right back at her. With bitter irony, nausea set in.

Dr. Fernandez from farther away than her mother but with the same hollow, echoey, bouncing-off-granite intonations could be heard explaining, "Tiny, silicon sensors, muy pequeños, no larger than a handful of neurons. They are too small to have batteries, so they are powered by microwaves beamed in from outside the skull…" And that's when the airport's medevac team noisily rolled in with an ambulance gurney.

"Did you hear that Joss?" she heard the person holding her excitedly ask over the clickety-clacking of the gurney's approaching wheels. The constricting bear hug relaxed. "There's tiny computers in you. How cool is that?"

"Jerry?" Jocelyn wondered aloud as she focused on the Conglomerate logo for stability. When that didn't work she squeezed her eyes shut. Strong hands peeled her away from Jerry, and placed her on the stretcher.

"Yeah," Jerry smiled. "I'm here."

In a complete daze she laid awkwardly on the gurney. Gulping down painful waves of emotion, Jocelyn meant to ask Jerry what was going on but instead blurted out, "What's with the helmet?" Her nausea and confusion were compounded by camera flashbulbs popping on and off and then in a panic she asked, "Where's the kids?"

"The kids are here," Jerry answered, "with your mom. The helmet," he said tapping it with a grin, "protected my melon. We both got microwaved."

"Oh, okay," she absently responded, noticing the color returning to her blue-gray hands holding the sides of the stretcher. She was actually more concerned about the nonstop sensation of spinning inside her painful shell of a body when she noticed Jerry looming over her.

His eyes sparkling with emotion locked with hers and kneeling down next to the stretcher he boldly proclaimed, "Jocelyn, I love you. Will you marry me?" And at that very moment the bile that had been nauseatingly swirling around in her belly burst into action and she puked.

Jerry, sputtering an apology, retreated as Margret zoomed in between the medevac team who were preparing an IV. Wiping away vomit, all the while praising Jerry and assuring him that Jocelyn would marry him—she'd make sure of that—Margret told Jerry to ask her daughter again when she wasn't regaining consciousness after being officially dead for a full eight minutes.

Of course, if all this attention wasn't being lavished upon Jocelyn she would have seen, over by the "Duty-Free" and "Cambio/Exchange" signs, Ethan getting handcuffed and being escorted out of the building.

CHAPTER FIFTY-EIGHT

One month later
Arlington, Virginia, USA

"WHO WOULD HAVE THOUGHT you'd be here overseeing the Next-Generation Identification program?" Dan commented as he slid into the cream fabric of the guest chair in front of Mark's executive maple wood desk.

"I know," Mark said, nodding and wincing as he adjusted the knot of the polka-dotted gray tie his mother had sent him along with congratulations on his move to Virginia. "Really, this job is a much better fit for me than that Jocelyn McLaren case but..." he trailed off. His back still hurt and he was actually kind of embarrassed. His new beige office with its "There's No I In Team" framed poster and empty bookshelf was comparatively opulent compared to Dan's cube. "I'd really like to be doing more hands-on coding instead of managing and dealing with politicos."

"Nah, this is awesome," Dan said, glancing around. "I mean you even have a window and look," Dan said, grinning, "a little built-in bar."

"Yeah, that's for the meetings with the politicians, I guess."

"Dude, you've arrived. I'm kinda jealous."

Smirking and shaking his head Mark scratched the back of his neck. "Nah, don't be. That booze was here when I rolled in. Take a bottle if you want."

"Hey, thanks," Dan said, springing up to check out the selection.

Mark continued, "Take anything but remember, we've got to get this program up and running or we can all kiss our jobs goodbye."

Nodding, Dan grabbed the Skyy Blue bottle of vodka and inspecting it said, "Yeah, I'm not sure how we're gonna hit that deadline considering the file that came in today. Did you see that thing?"

Mark shook his head. "No. I'm still going through this," making a show of flipping the pages of a three-ring binder.

"Oh, it's pretty big. Now they want biometric, like serious biometric stuff, included in our database. I think someone sent it to the wrong place. It's more of a medical thing than the image matching stuff we've been doing."

Looking concerned, Mark reached out and pushed his mouse around, waking up his sleeping computer. "What time did the file come in? I didn't see it."

Placing the vodka bottle on Mark's desk and leaning in, Dan looked at Mark's computer screen. "This morning. There," he said pointing, "that one from MIRANDACO."

Mark clicked it open, and sure enough, it didn't seem to have anything to do with what he had been hired to deal with. Lots of charts and data sets. "Yeah, this got sent to the wrong place."

"But look at the file called RSVP. That Whitebloom guy you were looking for is in there."

"He is?" Mark clicked on the file. "Where?"

"Scroll through. You'll see him. He's wearing a fluffy pirate shirt or something."

With a scrunched up brow Mark scanned through image after image of random people. The subjects were all captured while walking by a piano. Scrolling through Mark stopped at Ethan in his strange jacket. "Oh! This guy's here too!"

"Who?"

"Ethan Lowe. He's critical to the McLaren case. He's Jocelyn's kids' dad. He was in Serbia with Whitebloom back in the day. Is this a costume party? What is this?"

"Some shindig in Argentina last month," Dan replied, still hanging over Mark's shoulder looking at the screen as the scrolling continued. "There! That's him."

Zooming in closer on Ache, Mark commented, "This must have been some party. Yeah, okay, just load these faces into our system. Don't worry about the other stuff. I'll figure out who this belongs to."

"Thanks boss," Dan cheerily quipped as he headed out the door, "and congrats on the promotion."

Still captivated by the photos Mark replied, "Thanks," and looking up he noticed the bottle on his desk. "Oh, you forgot your..." But Dan was already gone. Peeling himself away from the computer screen and picking up the blue bottle, Mark headed back to the little bar. It was nothing more than a tiny built-in bookcase that the previous occupant had converted into a convenient watering hole. A mirror was positioned behind the two shelves which held a selection of the former occupant of the office's unwanted alcohol-based Secret Santa gifts and emergency nips. One bottle still had a premade red bow stuck to it. Wondering who had this office before him—*I mean, who gets away with having an actual bar in their office?*—Mark put the vodka back on the shelf and reached down to pop open the little refrigerator.

Grabbing an organic lemonade he caught a glimpse of himself in the mirror and forced a smile. He looked old. He looked like his dad. But before he could get too sentimental his cell phone started vibrating. He whipped it out and saw a message had arrived from a number he didn't recognize. Mark tapped the button and in what was a clearly stilted, computer generated man's voice, the message said, "Don't forget to pay Trevor Hathaway for the Gateway. We are all good except for the peacocks biting everyone. MIRANDACO was sent via dot Mars. Keep an eye out for an invitation." And that was it. The obnoxious computer voice hung up.

CHAPTER FIFTY-NINE

Six months later
Stephensville, Florida USA

"OH, IT'S MAGICAL," Jocelyn sighed as the screened-in porch ceiling fans slowly whirled. The jasmine was in full bloom, and taking in a deep breath of lusciously scented air she beheld the garden laid out behind the house. It was stunning, picture perfect. The collection of unusual plantings with their vibrant colors, interesting textures, and dramatic greenery all tucked in behind the brick garden wall and wrought iron gate was a captivating work of art. Never in a million years would she have thought that she and Jerry, the kids *and* Mom would be living in Florida in a house like this with a garden like that. The place reminded her of the historic brick early Victorian in Norwich, Connecticut that she had lived in while working at the Conglomerate, but the garden she was looking at made this house even better.

It all happened while Jocelyn had been in the hospital. At that time Margret had dedicated herself to whipping the garden back into shape for the wedding. The gardening was therapeutic and meditative for her, plus she knew she was creating a sanctuary for her family as the plants, and all of them really, cycled through the seasons. Every day after visiting hours she and the kids with their security escort would venture into the deserted neighborhood and over to the old brick house that Jerry bought. The price, Margret had expressed many times, was outrageous to the point of criminal, but Jerry seemed thrilled with the purchase. Margret was eventually sold when she stepped into the gated garden with the peacocks roaming. That had inspired her to pick up some clippers and start pruning an overgrown bougainvillea and it just took off from there.

In what became their daily routine Lillian and William plucked out the weeds and aggressive creeper vines from the pea-stone pathways as Margret dug up and separated strangled specimen plantings. The kids also had the daily job of making sure the lily pad pool had fresh water for the peacocks. All of them, including Jerry, cautiously avoided the brilliant birds because, as all of them had discovered, "Those suckers can bite!"

Both kids had a hard time at first. They couldn't sleep because they claimed they saw a ghost and that the house was haunted. They would wake up screaming in the middle of the night and Margret had a hard time too. But they stuck to a schedule and fell into a pattern, retraining their thoughts, and slowly vestiges of normalcy began to slip back into their lives. Willy liked to draw maps of the house and garden. Lilly would catch the geckos that were lurking almost everywhere and present them to her brother. Usually they'd end up building little houses for the tiny lizards. One day they found a frog in the lily pad pool that curiously had three eyes and they surprised Jerry with it while he was working. They named the frog Tricerahops.

Jerry meanwhile had set up his computer lab in what had originally been the receiving room next to the front door. He chose that room specifically because of the wallpaper. Cliff had told him all about it. It was designed by Christopher Dresser, a great futurist amongst Victorian designers who understood that the future of design would be shaped by technology. Cliff let him know that it was essentially museum worthy wallpaper so it stayed. During that conversation Cliff and Jerry had also worked out the terms of the sale of the property. The US government was going to pay for the house because Jerry and Jocelyn were something of a national asset now and Cliff knew how to leverage that for their mutual benefit. Hence, Cliff took two million dollars and immediately departed on a Royal Caribbean cruise promising to be back for the wedding.

With the old wallpaper and a map scratched on prison bus naugahyde mounted to the wall Jerry launched his private contracting company, which the NRO consulted with for a hefty fee. Skunkworks was all about him but he had no interest in doing any more crash test dummy stuff. He had even hooked up with Corey Fanning from Mirandaco in Argentina and while doing due diligence, aka hacking into their computer system, he discovered the full file from the night of Jocelyn's amazing resurrection.

He used that to illustrate how vulnerable their network was. It was getting seriously poked and prodded, specifically by China, and subsequently he was awarded the contract to patch Mirandaco back up. He also felt the need to share this discovery with Mark considering that if it hadn't been for Mark he would have never found Jocelyn, the love of his life. Jerry was sure Mark would appreciate knowing that he and Joss were alive. Plus, if China was all over this file, the US government should have it too; at least that was Jerry's logic.

All this contract work was easy for Jerry. While Jocelyn had been in the hospital in absolute military lockdown, under constant observation, receiving blood transfusions and enduring test after test, he was either at her bedside, or learning about nanobot code, being convinced that he could create something to help Jocelyn walk better. With a healthy dose of Margret's input he had also been dealing with the renovation of the house, overseeing the repair of broken shutters and decomposing bricks and managing the HVAC guys. Jerry had insisted that they have central air conditioning. He really put his foot down about that. That and water delivery twice a week.

"Here," Margret offered her daughter. "You don't want to get dehydrated on your big day. The priest just got here." Suntanned Margret was outfitted in a breezy floral sundress and sandals which featured her newly painted toenails.

"I see him," Jocelyn replied, accepting the paper water cup. From her vantage point up in the screened-in porch she scanned the few guests and the two male peacocks slowly strutting around with their blue-green tails fanned out. "Who's that woman with the FBI guy? She keeps hugging Jerry." Jocelyn realized she was getting kind of territorial about Jerry and decided she didn't like that girl. There was something about her that seemed contrived or fake or something.

"Oh, she went to college with Agent Witherall. Jerry met her when they were searching for you, honey."

Taking in that information and turning her attention away from the hug fest going on, Jocelyn sighed, "Mom, this is like a dream. The garden. It looks so great. The people look so perfect. There are peacocks, and...wait a minute. Is this a dream?" Jocelyn suddenly asked with concern because she had forgotten so much about the entire ordeal that brought her to now.

She had no recollection of the episode where she had sliced her mother's face or gouged her own wrist but the scars were there as harsh reminders. And specifically because of those scars Jocelyn was wearing a "pink champagne," tea-length, 1980s long sleeve bridesmaid dress that Margret had found for her at a consignment store, the sleeves sufficiently concealing the scars on her torso and wrist. Jocelyn had instantly fallen in love with the color of the dress and preferred it over the billowy white creations her mother had dragged home.

Margret playfully pinched Jocelyn's ear and Jocelyn flinched. "See, it's not a dream. It's real," Margret said, grinning and glancing over to Jerry in the garden below. "You're one lucky woman to have a man like that. He'd do anything for you and as a mother that's what I'm looking for in a son-in-law," she said jokingly, but she was actually dead serious.

"Mom…I'm…"

"What? Are you having second thoughts?"

"No," Jocelyn answered. "I'm…I'm just nervous, I guess."

"That's because this is the real deal. We're all so thrilled for you both and you…You're finally going to have a stable, healthy, real life with Jerry. And the kids are too," Margret enthused. "Real security. Embrace it."

Jocelyn nodded and hugging her mother she noticed one of the security team who had been assigned to cover the wedding. She never remembered any of their names and no matter how they were dressed their outfits always screamed "concealed carry permit," at least to Jocelyn anyway, and she whispered, "I will. I love you Mom."

"Come on. Let's go," Margret said, offering a bent arm for Jocelyn to hang onto for stability. Emerging from the screened-in porch, all eyes were upon them as they carefully descended the stairs to the garden. Jocelyn needed to stop and sit down on one of the benches that Margret had strategically placed throughout the landscaping and the kids ran up to her. William had khaki dress pants on with a blue shirt and floral bowtie, and Lillian was in a mini version of Margret's floral sundress with her hair done up in two pigtails.

"Mom! We made this for you," Lilly announced while presenting a handful of plastic beads. "You need to wear it for the wedding. It's something old."

"Oh, okay. Thank you. I will," she said, separating out the homemade necklace. "Mom, can you help?" Margret took the thing and latched it around Jocelyn's neck. Running her fingers over it Jocelyn noticed the little key featured as the focal point of the necklace.

"That's the key that was taped to the painting," William said when he noticed his mother curiously touching it.

"It's old so it should give you good luck," Lilly explained. "Nana said so and here's something blue," she said, jamming a blue cornflower from the garden into Jocelyn's French braid. "Now you need to borrow something."

Slipping off a barrette from her hairdo, Margret offered it to Jocelyn.

"You guys are the best! I love you all so much," Jocelyn appreciatively said as Margret snapped the barrette around the cornflower to hold everything in place. "You know that, right? That I love you?" The twins nodded, and grabbing both kids up Jocelyn embraced them in one big bear hug. Things didn't hurt so much anymore and, squeezing them harder, she realized that she had no idea what they were talking about regarding a key being taped to a painting.

When Jocelyn was ready, they all slowly headed over to the bubbling central fountain installed in the lily pad pool which served as the backdrop for the ceremony.

The polite conversation stopped and all eyes were on Jocelyn, her mother and kids as they approached Jerry who was absolutely beaming. He looked sharp, more handsome than Jocelyn had ever seen him, outfitted in a lightweight, dark gray suit and tie. His hair had grown out from the buzz cut and he appeared actually, kind of stylish. Jocelyn felt a flutter in her stomach as she smiled back at him. *He's a good man,* she thought*, he truly is.*

The priest, holding a Bible, stood in front of the fountain and welcomed the entirety of the small group as Jerry and Jocelyn sat down on the bench before him. His sermon started off complementing the setting of the ceremony with a short bit about the Garden of Eden which spilled into appreciation of the colors of the season and the significance of the vestments he was wearing representing penance, sacrifice, and preparation—the colors of Lent.

Jocelyn and Jerry were both more enamored with each other than the sermon and kept smiling at each other as the priest spoke. The kids were just about ready to burst by the time Jocelyn and Jerry stood up and holding hands said, "I do," sealing their commitment to each other with a kiss and garden party applause.

It was only after everyone left, except Cliff who was happily munching on leftover hors d'oeuvres and flirting with giggling Margret, that Jocelyn told Jerry and the kids that she was three months pregnant.

"Hope is a waking dream."
— Aristotle

SNEAK PEEK

Security Through Absurdity—Book Five:

Emergency Playground

Ten years later…

Mom,

We know you'll worry about us but don't. This is crazy. You know and we know that when they said it was because Dad was some PTSD soldier addicted to video games, that it was a load of crap. Dad never even let us play video games when we were little. That's why he bought us those Daisy Red Ryders. He wanted us to have respect for real guns and not waste our lives in front of a screen. He said that Mom, exactly that, and you know it too. Why do you pretend there's nothing wrong with what they keep repeating in the news? You and Jerry, for whatever reason, won't do anything for Dad. We know Gabby is your primary concern right now but for God's sake! Dad is completely innocent! This is it Mom. We never told you but we have been communicating with him. They will never give him a fair trial, ever. We've made up our minds. We're breaking Dad out.

Love forever even though you'll probably be mad at us,

L.&W.

ABOUT RACHAEL L. McINTOSH

Rachael L. McIntosh is an artist and former defense sector marketing professional. She appears on radio shows and produces her own weekly podcast called ShadowCitizen.online.

Rachael lives in Rhode Island, USA with her twins and emerged in 2021 as a politically unaffiliated candidate for lieutenant governor. Previously, she had been appointed to the Rhode Island Geoengineering Study Commission where she researched and produced a body of evidence regarding the government's formerly top secret activity of weather modification. Her work cataloguing and verifying her findings influenced the creation of the Rhode Island Geoengineering Act which is known internationally as a first-of-its-kind type of legislation.

She self-publishes her books under the imprint of EntropyPress and can be reached via her author's website RachaelLMcIntosh.com or ShadowCitizen.online

Printed in Great Britain
by Amazon

74433072R00197